GRASS FOR MY PILLOW

Modern Asian Literature

A PACIFIC BASIN INSTITUTE BOOK

Grass for My Pillow is the ninth volume to be published in The Library of Japan series, a selected cross-section of modern Japanese fiction and nonfiction in translation for presentation to American readers. Produced by the Pacific Basin Institute at Pomona College, as part of a plan evolved under the aegis of the Japan–United States Conference on Cultural and Educational Exchange (CULCON), this series is designed to make Americans aware of the social and cultural underpinnings of modern Japan, offering works either unavailable in English translation or difficult for most general readers to obtain.

Volumes previously published include *Silk and Insight*, by Mishima Yukio; *The Autobiography of Fukuzawa Yukichi*; *Labyrinth*, by Arishima Takeo; *Konoe Fumimaro, A Political Biography*, by Oka Yoshitake; *Kokoro and Selected Essays*, by Natsume Sōseki; *The Spirit of Japanese Capitalism*, by Yamamoto Shichihei; Ōoka Shōhei's *Taken Captive: A Prisoner of War's Diary*; and *American Stories* by Nagai Kafū. Frank Gibney and J. Thomas Rimer are the editors of the series. The editors and the publisher would like to thank the Japan Foundation for its generous support in making this publication possible.

saiichi maruya

GRASS

FOR MY

PILLOW

translated by dennis keene

Columbia University Press   New York

Columbia University Press wishes to express
its appreciation for funds given by the Pacific
Basin Institute toward the cost of publishing
this book.

Columbia University Press
Publishers Since 1893
New York   Chichester, West Sussex

Library of Congress Cataloging-in-Publication Data

Maruya, Saiichi, 1925–
[Sasamakura. English]
Grass for my pillow / Saiichi Maruya ;
translated by Dennis Keene.
p. cm. — (Modern Asian literature)
ISBN 0–231–12658–1 (cloth)
1. Keene, Dennis, 1934– II. Title. III. Series.
PL856.A66 S313 2002
895.6'35—dc21   2002017549

Columbia University Press books are printed
on permanent and durable acid-free paper.

Printed in the United States of America
Designed by Audrey Smith

c 10 9 8 7 6 5 4 3 2 1

CONTENTS

GRASS FOR MY PILLOW

translator's introduction

Sasamakura (*Grass for My Pillow*), first published in 1966, is a novel about a man who successfully evades military conscription from October 1940 until the end of the Pacific War in August 1945, and the delayed consequences of this refusal to conform as he experiences them twenty years later, in 1965.

For the Japanese the war lasted a decade and a half, from the beginning of hostilities with China in 1931 to the final surrender in 1945. Given that considerable length of time, and the number of people who go missing each year in a normal, peaceful society, obviously many young men must have been able to avoid the draft in the same way as the hero of this novel, by simply disappearing. This point was made by the critic Hajime Shinoda in his afterword to the paperback edition of 1974, praising Maruya for writing on a subject so taboo that no official figures for it are available. Shinoda assumed there must have been a model for the hero Hamada, although he admitted he had failed to get confirmation on this point. This can only mean the author was not prepared to give him any at the time, for in an interview in 1993, Maruya said he'd received a "hint" from the example of the elder brother of a close friend of his, information he could now give since the "model" was no longer alive (*Switch*, May 1993, vol. 11., no. 2; other information from this interview is used elsewhere in this introduction). Maruya's cautious refusal to name this person or say anything about him at all is an indication of how taboo the subject still remains—and of the fact that when Maruya tried to talk to this man about his experiences, he refused to say a single word. Thus reality remained concealed, and the novel is a total fiction.

The conscientious objection to military service that existed in western countries was not permitted in Japan under the Meiji constitution, and draft evasion was probably (as the novel maintains) the most serious offense that could be committed at the time. Even in countries where conscientious objection was allowed, of course, it was hardly admired; for example, I can remember in wartime London how contemptuously we children had learned to speak of the solitary "conchie" who lived in our neighborhood. One can imagine how intense such feelings would have been in a country so obsessed with ideas of obligation as Japan. During the antimilitaristic immediate postwar years, a former draft resister might have attracted some degree of admiration from certain individuals (the hero of the novel even gets two or three women into bed on the strength of his history), but hardly from society as a whole even then, since the refusal to enlist would have still been seen as a rejection of its behavioral norms.

This, indeed, is the true theme of Maruya's novel, and one that runs through all his fiction. *Grass for My Pillow* is not so much an antiwar novel (although Maruya as a young man had powerful objections to the futile war effort and the emperor worship that brought the whole insane undertaking into being) as an attempt to understand the full implications of any sustained act of rebellion against the group as a total entity. The same theme is treated in comic and therefore perhaps more complex fashion in his next novel, *Tatta hitori no hanran* (*Singular Rebellion*) published six years later, in 1972. There has been a considerable amount of war literature written in Japan, but Maruya's novel is different not only because the hero is not a soldier (the soldier's experience is given via the drunken monologue of the hero's rival for promotion in 1965) but because it goes against the normal assumption of such literature that prewar and postwar Japan are different countries: the contention of this novel is that the continuity between the two societies is their most distinctive feature. Admittedly the protagonist, now a clerk in university administration, bewails the fact that little of the Tokyo of his childhood is left: that the expressways built for the Olympic Games of 1964 and the accompanying high-rise buildings have created a landscape that looks like a cheap parody of the metropolis of the future; that there are no places where children can catch dragonflies, probably no dragonflies either; but this does not alter the fact that the society he dropped out of a quarter of a century before is the same society that finally won't let him back in again.

Although Maruya has previously had three books published in English to reasonably good notice (one even received a prize), there has been, to my knowledge, no extended or informed criticism of his work, so before going into a more detailed account of this novel I would like to give the reader some information about the writer and his work as a whole.

Saiichi Maruya was born in the town of Tsuruoka in Yamagata Prefecture on August 27, 1925, the second son of a doctor in general practice. The Japanese provinces, particularly those in the north, have always been backward (one of the pleasures of the north nowadays is that it preserves aspects of Japanese life that seem to have disappeared elsewhere years ago), and Maruya's birth in such a place is of importance for understanding his literature, since he grew up in a state of overall skepticism about the way of life he saw around him. Indeed, he has said that the dominant fact of his childhood was that he had trouble understanding why grown-ups behaved as they did; why they had such eccentric festivals, for example, where men dressed in women's underwear with towels and large hats concealing their faces and, carrying bottles of saké, accosted passersby and obliged them to drink. When he asked his father why this and other equally bizarre festivals took place, his father only mumbled incoherently, giving the young Maruya the impression he had drawn attention to something shameful, even obscene; it was only years later he realized his father had not replied because he had no reply to make.

All the experimental writers in Japan's twentieth century came from provincial backgrounds (among postwar writers, both Yumiko Kurahashi and Kenzaburo Oe are from Shikoku), and clearly an intellectual teenager in such a place would experience a more powerful contrast between the world around him and the books he was reading than someone growing up in Tokyo. Maruya relates in the same 1993 interview that he was greatly influenced in his teens by the Scottish anthropologist Sir James George Frazer, and that he experienced a sudden sense of enlightenment when he realized that the quasi-religious functions of the chieftains of primitive tribes as described by Frazer were identical with those of the Japanese emperor. This even provided a sense of comradeship, for he had always loathed emperor worship but been unable to discuss the matter with anybody, and now here was someone who encouraged him to think rationally and coherently about the question.

The next decisive event was Maruya's conscription into the army at the age of nineteen, while he was still a high school student (the old Japanese high schools were more like universities than those of the present day, and Maruya had spent a year at a cram school in Tokyo, so he did not enter high school until his nineteenth year). He was drafted into the local regiment from March to September 1945, and stationed farther north in Aomori, on the tip of Honshu, with Hokkaido just across the straits. The Americans were expected to make a landing in the Aomori region, so Maruya and his comrades were billeted in a village and set to dig holes in order to deceive the enemy into believing there were remarkable fortifications in this area that would make any landing attempt suicidal. Sometimes the digging went on all night in the pouring rain to enhance the apparent secrecy of the operation. While employed in this melancholy task, Maruya was so impressed by the lyrical beauty of the surrounding natural world that he began to feel his death must surely be near at hand. He went back to high school in September. In an interview at the age of sixty-seven, he recalled two supremely happy days in his life: one when he finished writing *Grass for My Pillow*, and the other the day the war ended.

In 1947 Maruya became a student in the English Department of Tokyo University, and English literature was to be the major influence on his development as a novelist. While an undergraduate, he began the study of Joyce that resulted some years later in the definitive Japanese translation of *Ulysses*. From his late twenties to his early forties, he also translated various contemporary, or near contemporary, writers: Graham Greene, Nathanael West, Iris Murdoch, Colin Wilson, Allan Sillitoe, Brigid Brophy; and Jerome K. Jerome's *Three Men in a Boat*, an 1880s novel little read now since its mannered humor has seriously dated it, but mentioned here because Maruya's translation is remarkable in managing to be funnier than the original, and this comic gift is an essential part of the nature of his genius. One of his earliest translations was Greene's *Brighton Rock*, and if that novel with its overall air of seediness and gloom can be seen as a counterpart to *Grass for My Pillow*, then the more comic Maruya of his later writings can be likened perhaps to what *Three Men in a Boat* could have become if Joyce had written a serious parody of it. These comparisons are obviously not meant to be precise, but to emphasize that the completion of *Grass for My Pillow* was a turning point in Maruya's literature, an achievement he would not try to repeat. He himself has said that, despite his affection for a book the writing of which finally taught him how to structure a novel in a way that satisfied his idea of what the form should be, the overall sadness of the completed work was something he wished to avoid in the future, and he is ambivalent about the fact that a number of people whose opinion he respects still consider it his finest novel.

At the age of 28 he was appointed lecturer at Kokugakuin University, after a spell as a high school teacher. Kokugakuin is an oddity among the private universities in Tokyo, being politically very conservative in character; it is unmistakably the model for the university in this novel. Since he was able to avoid the various pressures a more prestigious university might have imposed, he managed to endure the academic world until the age of forty, when he resigned to become a full-time writer. *Grass for My Pillow* was the immediate result, taking about a year to write, although he'd been trying to get started on it for the previous five years. He was chronically short of money, but lucky to be soon asked to write some casual essays by a friend who was editing a women's weekly, and such essay writing has provided him ever since with income to supplement that from his fiction writing. As a result, he has only written five novels and a few stories, producing nothing to order (with the exception of one short story), and nothing commercially serialized, making him a rarity among modern Japanese novelists in his determination to produce only fiction that seems artistically necessary.

The five novels are: *Ehoba no kao o sakete* (*Fleeing from the Face of Jehovah*), published in book form in 1960; *Sasamakura* (*Grass for My Pillow*), published in 1966; *Tatta hitori no hanran* (*Singular Rebellion*), published in 1972 (the English translation in 1986); *Uragoe de utae kimi ga yo* (*Sing the National Anthem in Falsetto*) published in 1982; and *Onnazakari* (*A Mature Woman*), published in 1993 (the English translation in 1995). Now, at the age of seventy-six, he is writing another novel.

There are two longish stories that should be mentioned: *Yokoshigure* (*Rain in the Wind*), published in 1974, and *Jueitan* (*Tree Shadows*) published in 1988. Both of these have appeared in English translation in a volume entitled *Rain in the Wind* published in 1989. The very conscious concern with literature these two stories show is something central to Maruya's writing, even if he makes sure it does not become obtrusive in his novels, for he is a highly literate author with a profound knowledge of classical and modern Japanese, as well as western, literatures that is unique among living Japanese novelists, who tend to be much less well acquainted with such things than the general reader might imagine. Maruya has no particular quarrel with classical Japanese literature, the principal background to the form his writing has taken, only with the way it has been interpreted and with what he considers misplaced emphases in the standard literary histories. Early Japanese literature he sees as dominated by the imperial poetic anthologies and thus as a corporate endeavor rather than a collection of works by individual authors, an endeavor of ritualistic functions concerned with appeasing dead spirits or living gods (in many cases the same thing) and thereby preserving the health and harmony of the social order. As the literary tradition developed, it continued to observe these main functions in more diversified forms, but literary history has tended to emphasize those forms in which the public takes little interest, such as lyric poetry and the No drama, ignoring a work like *Chushingura* (the 47 loyal retainers), which has been a national obsession ever since the event itself gave rise to its first theatrical version. This emphasis upon the purer literary forms has also, he believes, had a disastrous effect upon modern Japanese literature, with its misguided distinction between the pure and the popular novel, and has led to the dominance of the "I-novel" with its gloomy record of minimal happenings in the small world of the individual.

Maruya feels that the post-Meiji tradition in the novel came about from a misuse of foreign literatures. Writers were influenced by foreign novels, and since they wished to write in the same form decided that only the incidents and characters that appeared in such novels were suitable. In some cases this led to writers thinking of themselves in terms of a character appearing in a foreign novel, but even if a writer did not go to such extremes he would still find himself unable to write about specific Japanese realities, and this inability to put things down that are right in front of one's nose has continued to the present day. The "I-novel" was an attempt to express a more or less poetic reality, a highly selective set of events indicating a privileged state of mind of the narrator-cum-hero, the result being that most social reality was excluded. With this casting out of impurities all the pleasure of the novel went as well.

Maruya's main attempt at the comic came after *Grass for My Pillow*, partly because the natural inclination of his mind was in that direction but also because he felt that, with postwar prosperity and a new constitution, the relationship between the state and the individual had been transformed into more subtle forms of coercion, which only a comic treatment would reveal. The comic, of course, is not absent from *Grass for My Pillow*, as can be seen in the way the grim material of chapter 4 is handled, but it is not the central mode of the book as it is with some of his later literature. What the novel does share with its successors is its attempt to allow a whole society into its pages, and to grasp reality by presenting it in a closely worked out and highly complex structure. Maruya himself is most pleased with the organization of a number of disparate episodes into a coherent whole, the shifting time scale, and the dual character of the hero as Hamada and Sugiura. The movement from present to past and back again is something he claims to have learned from Conrad, whose short stories he had been teaching while attempting to start work on this novel, but the richness of social detail comes from his knowing so precisely the university world in which he spent so many years. The precision of detail bestows a sense of lived reality upon the more imagined world of the war years as Sugiura travels the length and breadth of the land.

Maruya plans his novels carefully and tends to stick to that plan in the act of writing, rejecting the spontaneity some novelists claim as they allow their characters the freedom to do as they please while the creator smiles benevolently on them. It is obviously true that any novel must have a structure or it would be unreadable, and in the case of this novel it has been imposed from the outset. The question then is how well this imposed structure works, how acceptable the reader finds it, and how well it embodies the meaning of the work. The distinguished novelist Haruki Murakami made these comments in 1997 while discussing Maruya's story "Tree Shadows" in his *Young Readers' Guide to the Short Story* (*Wakai dokusha no tame no tanpen shosetsu annai*, Bungei Shunju, 171–72):

> Since the novel is being related in the present (i.e., the mid-1960s) its time scale is inevitably (and quite intentionally) involved to an almost confusing extent, and ends with the transformation of the hero Hamada into his alter ego Sugiura. If you are acquainted with the book you will appreciate how much this ending goes against the natural order of the story it is relating. I don't think anyone would imagine such an ending while actually reading it, since the ritual whereby Hamada becomes Sugiura should naturally come much earlier on in the story, and if it did the altered reality of the fugitive Sugiura would be much easier for the reader to grasp.
>
> Obviously the writer has chosen to sacrifice that reality to his desire to hold the scene right until the last. Now, why should he want to do that? Clearly because it is the totally compelling nature of the transformation from one person to another which represents for the writer, and for the work itself, the final reality of the story, its main stress. The truth is that the novel has been essentially restrained up until that climax, proceeding in a quiet, orderly manner, its emotional tone under complete control, and it's as if these final pages represent a

sudden upsurge, a breaking free from the husk in which it had been contained. It is as if the whole work had been written in this restrained manner simply to allow such sudden emphasis to its amazing ending. This method, this device if you like, seems to me to be totally success-ful in *Sasamakura*. One reads thus far and is overwhelmed by the ending, as if the black and white screen one had been looking at were suddenly transformed into brilliant color images. For that reason *Sasamakura* is one of my favorite books.

There are details in this account of the novel with which everybody might not agree, but it is right in stressing that the essential meaning of the novel lies in the transformation of Hamada into Sugiura, and that the attempt over twenty years to reverse that process and turn Sugiura back into Hamada finally does not work. Hamada ends up a victim of the processes by which his society is run, and the final choice left to him is to drop out, as he did a quarter century before. This realization appears to be written in an affirmative tone, but the structure of the novel, with its enclosed and enclosing circular time scale, seems to negate it, as all becomes a circle out of which he cannot break, with the inevitability of ancient tragedy. That Maruya has produced this complex, resonant mean-ing via the actual form of his novel is something unique in modern Japan-ese fiction, and the intensity of the reading experience *Grass for My Pil-low* provides is the result of that achieved structure.

The novel is more than its political and social attitudes, as this empha-sis on the structure of the work has tried to make clear, since it produces by way of that structure a complexity and resonance that go beyond any message it might seem to have. Even so, this is an account of a society at two particular moments in time, and Maruya has himself so many times stressed the importance of the portrayal of social mores in the novel that clearly something needs to be said about them, and about how the author seems to want us to respond to the society he portrays.

The first thing to be noted is that the consciousness that informs the wartime years is solely that of Hamada/Sugiura. Any political discussion, for example, is either with his student friends while he is still Hamada and is simply a reflection of what he thinks about the emperor, the aggressive war, the state, the whole political set-up in Japan; or with people who express quite different views and are potential dangers to Sugiura who could cause his arrest and possible death, the statements they make, which they in no way explain or justify, merely representing the oppressive threat of the state. The result is that the ideological tone of the pages dealing with the wartime years is constant; the state is wrong and Hamada/Sugiura is right to try to escape from it; and the amount of excitement and tension generated by his situation is such that the reader is in total sympathy with him, for he is indeed a hero.

The postwar year of 1965, however, is quite different. Hamada is now more of an antihero than a hero, and this sets the reader at a certain distance from him so that our concern is objective, even cold. The forty-five-year-old registry clerk has few ideas except echoes of the thoughts of his youth, and even these he keeps to himself, for he is simply trying to keep his head above water. What experiences he has seem to occasion reactions on a neurotic or at least suspect level, as he sympathizes with the harelipped criminal who is no conscientious draft resister but someone who has committed murder while attempting an armed robbery, or the thief running away from the university with whom Hamada empathizes on aesthetic grounds, admiring his smart suit and elegant running style as contrasted with the bucolic appearance of the members of the judo club plodding heavily along in pursuit. In both cases Hamada eventually realizes he is only sympathizing with his wartime self, and this somewhat unattractive egoism is an aspect of his character that invites a reader alienation never triggered by the pages that deal with the young Sugiura. Of course, since the two versions of the same person are presented in such alternating succession as to be at times virtually simultaneous, the reader response is nothing like as contrastive as this suggests. Yet the sense of alienation is constant, for the forty-five-year-old Hamada himself is alienated from people who feel they are on his side, from the young professor of French whose attentions Hamada finds so insensitive to the student newspaper staff whose "support" he sees through so clearly. The alienation he feels with regard to his successful friend Sakai, with whom he had damned the state with such relish when they were students a quarter of a century before, provides one of those scenes that show Hamada as the total misfit, although always with the suggestion that perhaps he is right to be so.

This is, indeed, the crux of the matter. In 1965, does Hamada find out the truth about his society and realize he was right to drop out and must now do so again, or is he just a victim who made a wrong choice in 1940 that has brought about the misfortunes leading to his downfall? For a non-Japanese reading the work thirty-five years after its publication and not quite sure how to respond to this picture of Japanese society in 1965, this will remain problematic, which is not the case with the wartime sections where reader response is unequivocally conditioned by the text.

It is clear from interviews given by Maruya over the past decade that he believes Japan's economic prosperity has brought about such major changes in the Japanese way of life that many writers have been incapable of understanding, let alone writing about, what has been happening. This applies not only to observable social customs but also to the spiritual and emotional aspects of people's lives. Obviously this has affected the kind of literature he has written, but, as was stated earlier in this introduction, the main contention of this novel is that prewar and postwar are basically the same society, which rejects Hamada as twenty-five years previously he rejected it. This indicates something about the mid- 1960s in Japan that had changed by the end of that decade, when the massive student revolt of 1968–69 made everyone aware at last that society had altered in a way they had previously been unable to imagine. In Maruya's next novel, *Singular Rebellion*, published in 1972 and set in 1969, there is little mention of the war, and the society portrayed there seems a generation away from that of *Grass for My Pillow*, although in fact it is only three or four years later.

The economic miracle that started in the 1950s with the opportunities afforded by the Korean War was not yet a reality in the main consciousness of Japanese people in the early 1960s. It was still common for them to refer to Japan as only a poor country, and this was not a piece of assumed social modesty but felt to be a statement of fact. The great effort of hosting the Olympic Games of 1964, with all the upheaval they caused in Tokyo, was presented abroad as a joyful awareness of the country's reacceptance into the family of nations, whereas most people in Japan saw it as an example of overreaching, of putting a bold façade upon something not all that impressive in itself. Only after the thing became a *fait accompli* was it welcomed to any extent, the enjoyment of a festival that was still essentially a rash extravagance.

The sense that the country has recovered from the disaster of the war is very strong in this novel, and appears in any amount of detail contrasting the comparative luxury of life in 1965 with that in the immediate postwar years; Hamada's visits to Horikawa, for example, besides showing how awkward and somehow unreliable their relationship is, document that change precisely. Once any disaster has been recovered from, people will reevaluate it, and the implication of the university party at the end of chapter 2, with the mass singing of the good old wartime songs to which Hamada takes such exception, appears to be that the country has reverted to its old right-wing militaristic stance and therefore the draft resister will be appropriately punished. Hamada's remarks that he cannot endure the Japanese spirit suggest that the author feels the same, and wants to pass this message on to his readers. But nostalgia in these middle-aged men for their lost youth is probably a more important element of their drunken behavior than any political stance, and despite various critical remarks from a not particularly reliable and also drunken source about Prime Minister Sato wanting to persuade the Japanese people they need the hydrogen bomb if they are to consider themselves members of a truly advanced country, Hamada's sense of alienation from his world is more powerfully stressed than any supposedly objective valuation of the situation he is now in. During the war years the enemy is clear, and every gesture of rejection Sugiura makes is accepted by the reader as right. In 1965 the situation has become complex through twenty years of conformity on Hamada's part, so that his sense of alienation can only be vigorously roused by things that recall the wartime past. So it seems the literary function of these wartime songs is to indicate not anything about the real state of the present but only what has happened to Hamada.

There was certainly a tendency in Japanese society at that time to be more tolerant of wartime attitudes as growing economic prosperity weakened memories of the tragedy to which they had led. And some Japanese intellectuals would have felt threatened by it, at least until the student riots of 1968–69 when something much more disturbing than the innocuous, if unpleasant, nostalgia of middle-aged men made its presence felt. There can also be no question of the author's intense hatred for those attitudes and beliefs that swayed official Japanese life during the long war years. I can remember discussing with him sometime in the 1980s the changes that had come over Japanese life in half a century, and whether present prosperity compensated for what had been lost. He said it did not, but then recounted an episode from his youth, a repeated experience he had most evenings as he went on a training run that took him past the local police station. Occasionally he would hear the cries of some wretch who was being beaten up, but even if he heard nothing, he was always aware of what was going on in there. No matter what people might say about the organic society of the past, he said, with its sense of community, the pervasiveness of good taste, restraint in human behavior—all the virtues (real or illusory) that nostalgia bestows upon it—the one irreplaceable virtue in any society, whose lack makes nonsense of all the others, is a belief in the concept of human rights, and a society that is not pledged to secure those rights has nothing.

It may well be that Hamada was closer to his author at the time the novel was written than he now appears thirty-five years later, and a reader who considers him more of a mouthpiece for the writer than I do is not necessarily wrong. The great value of this novel is not only that it gives a deep analysis of the implications of any rebellion against any social entity but also that it portrays an actual society in a particularly sensitive moment of its history. Japan was to be transformed as a society during the 1970s, and this has been recorded in Maruya's later writings, but in this book we see the society before that transformation, in the one form in which it matters: the emotional and mental lives of the people who live in it. In Hamada/Sugiura is portrayed above all else a huge sense of guilt that is gradually dissipated by the passage of time, until it is summarily dismissed as this scapegoat is pushed off into the desert with all the sins of his society upon him. That is his symbolic role, and probably that is also the principal social meaning of the novel. Its artistic meaning, of course, goes beyond that and is the main reason why the novel is still read, but the sociological and historic implications are considerable and provide added reasons why the novel is of such importance.

one

How much money should he send to her funeral? That was the first thought to cross Shokichi Hamada's mind when he read the yellow postcard with its black border announcing the woman's death. In fact, it was the only thought. He'd been earnestly debating in his head the appropriate amount for another obituary gift until just a few moments before the postcard arrived, so no doubt that was only natural. Pure force of habit, as most of his life had become.

It had been a busy morning. The chief registry clerk (his immediate boss) had telephoned while in conference, wanting information on several things and giving instructions about this and that. There'd been a variety of other phone calls, and a number of visitors. The other assistant clerk was away on business, so Hamada had to do his share of the work as well. He also had to find the time during these crowded hours to concentrate his mind on the question of the exact sum of money that should be sent to the funeral of a professor emeritus who'd just died. As assistant registry clerk, he had to decide. The university president himself would no doubt be attending the funeral.

But he was unable to come to a decision. While looking up the records, he'd found that a similar professor emeritus had been valued at 10,000 yen when he'd died the year before last; but that had obviously been too little, and the cost of living had gone up enormously since then. If he raised the amount to 30,000, it would still look too small when compared with the 300,000 donated last summer to one of the directors (not an active member of the board, either); but a sum of 50,000 would probably make the chief clerk wince at such extravagance. Even if he should accept it, the executive director would hardly give his seal of approval. After all, the university was a business organization, and the idea that a part-time director was worth much more than a retired professor (perhaps even 30 times more) was the one that found favor here. It was while Hamada was still unable to make up his mind about this that the messenger girl, who'd been occupied for some time at her desk near the door, banging her rubber date stamp down on the received mail, brought him a bundle of letters, and right on the top of the pile was the yellow postcard with the black border. It recorded the death of a woman he'd been in love with long ago, someone to whom he also owed his life.

The funeral was tomorrow at one o'clock, the same day and the same time as the professor's. He wouldn't be able to do anything about it today, but he could telegraph the money tomorrow morning. He read the blurred print of the postcard again, noting how obviously it was some crude, provincial piece of work. The cause of death wasn't recorded, but he realized it must have been cancer, judging by a letter he'd received from the dead woman some three months before. He recalled the confused handwriting of the letter, its plea that he should come to see her on some pretext or other since she wanted to see him just once more; and the reply he had written, fairly short although it had taken him a week to compose, saying that he had a host of reasons why he wanted to see her too, but he had work to do he couldn't delegate to anyone else. No letters had come after that. He imagined she probably no longer had the strength to hold a pen. Still, he couldn't have managed the time; that was no mere excuse. With the academic year beginning in April, February to April is the period when all the new documentation has to be done. During those three months he'd thought about her, at least in spare moments on the tram and in conference, or at night when he couldn't sleep; thought about Akiko in Shikoku at that very moment, in Uwajima, reduced to skin and bones but still fully con-

scious, conscious of the pain. The suffering had become his, totally caught
up in his being. But he hadn't written again to her, partly because he was so
busy, partly because he couldn't endure the idea of stringing a number of
pointless, consolatory phrases together; and now that he held the news of
her death in his hand there was, he had to admit, a feeling of relief somewhere at the back of his mind, a sense of having finally been set free that
the relations of some very old person, bedridden for a dozen years, experience on the night of the vigil.

Hamada tasted this mild sense of release as he sipped the lukewarm tea
one of his subordinates had brought him, reflecting that recently he almost
never had dreams about the war period, although up to four or five years
ago he'd certainly dreamed about it once or twice a year; much more, in
fact. Hadn't he had repeated nightmares about it? There was that one with
the man on the horse, where he himself was sitting on the ground looking
up at him. . . . Well, it just showed that this was how one took leave of the
past, step by step, a gradual fading away of it, one object, then another.

There was a second phone call from his boss, this time asking him to
take his place at a conference being held at the Private Universities Hall
from one-thirty onward. It was simply a matter of putting in an appearance, as there was nothing of major importance up for discussion, or at
least there shouldn't be. He himself had to be somewhere at five o'clock,
acting as the executive director's representative, and three conferences in
one day was a bit more than he could take. Hamada kept flipping through
the documents one of the staff had just brought him, stamping the ones
that needed it and giving instructions over one or two matters of indifference, as he listened; then he finally accepted the new chore and put down
the black receiver. Since he now had to attend this conference, he really
must make his mind up about the amount of money to be sent to the professor's funeral, but before he could do so he noticed something strange
about the black-bordered postcard, which he happened to glance at again.

The postcard referred to the funeral of "my eldest daughter, Akiko," and
was signed by "Rie Yuki," who must therefore be in charge of the proceedings. The mother, not the husband, was in charge. This he found surprising,
and then he recalled that the last letter she'd sent him from the hospital had

been signed with her maiden name, not, he now realized, because she was trying to spare the feelings of her former lover, but because she was, in fact, divorced. Of course, the husband might have died instead, since he was ten years or so older than she. That was a possibility, but it seemed unlikely since a woman doesn't usually revert to her maiden name just because her husband has died. Something must have happened to make her go back to live with her mother, too. So the marriage had been a failure after all.

Akiko had been older than he. He thought of the wretchedness of this death and of the misery of the failed marriage preceding it, feeling not so much compassion as a distancing sense of pity, recalling that the last time he'd met her there had been an aura of separateness about the woman, as if she were saying farewell to someone or something. But when was that, anyway? Was it the year before last, or the one before that? Surely it couldn't have been only last year? The fact that he couldn't recall how much time had passed since he'd seen her vexed him. It was one more confirmation of the conclusion he'd already come to, that one's sense of time, or perhaps time itself, starts to go haywire once you've passed the age of forty. He looked vaguely to one side as he pondered whether it had been last year or the year before or . . . and as he was doing so his glance was misread by one of the junior clerks, who asked him if there was anything he wanted.

"No, nothing really," said Hamada. "I was just trying to recall when it was the dean of the law faculty thought he had cancer, and spent the whole evening weeping about it. Was it last year, or the year before?"

"The autumn of the year before that," said the young man, who was already grinning at the recollection. "That was hilarious. Really."

This dean was a reasonably well-known authority on mercantile law, who'd had something wrong with his stomach and decided to have a thorough medical check-up. He had arranged, on his own initiative but, naturally enough, at university expense, to hold a farewell party on the night before he was to go into the hospital, and had invited a number of professors and directors. The party turned out to be a very lively affair, with the cheerful twanging of *shamisen* and various dances performed, a certain doctor of law, who had been in a perpetual state of warfare with the dean for years, even going so far as to entertain the assembly by leaping around almost stark naked. But it all failed to amuse the dean, who spent the whole time quietly weeping. This disturbed everyone and, after the constant sympathetic murmurs from the serving maids had proved of no avail, almost a dozen men (directors, professors, even the insignificant Hamada) had gathered about him, but they were unable to think of any appropriate words of comfort and all they did was urge drink upon him. Since he didn't really need any urging, he ended up blind drunk. Naturally the responsibility for seeing him safely home fell upon Hamada, but once he'd got the dean into a taxi he had a dreadful time trying to control him, not just blubbering now but actually howling, so he had to try to appease him by suggesting they go on to Ginza or Nakano Shinbashi or some other entertainment area, and it must have been about one in the morning before he finally managed to get home.

What was then really strange was that the dean turned up a week later at the university as if nothing had happened. He told nobody what the result of his check-up had been, but simply looked very well, cheerfully resuming his perpetual confrontation with the doctor of law exactly where they had left off. When met by one of the registry staff in the corridor, he had merely laughed off all inquiries after his health, saying there had been some wild rumors flying around; and that was all.

"A wild rumor," said Hamada, forcing himself to smile, for he was thinking of the phone call he'd received from Akiko the very day after the party, and of how amazingly plump and provincial she'd seemed when they met.

"Ken," she called out to him. "Oh, I'm sorry. I've slipped back into the old habit."

"That's all right," he said, smiling. "There's no reason to call me anything else."

He was obliged to speak in a fairly loud voice since there were hordes of schoolchildren milling about. From their accents he assumed they were a group who had come all the way from Kumamoto in Kyushu to visit Tokyo Tower for some obscure educational purpose. It had been a long time since he'd heard so many people all speaking together in that dialect.

"Does your wife call you Shokichi? Or just Sho?" Akiko asked.

More than ten years, in fact more like twenty, had passed since these former lovers had met, and now they were obliged to bawl at each other like an old married couple who'd both become hard of hearing and were celebrating their golden anniversary with a tourist trip to the metropolis. But had she always spoken with so thick a provincial accent? Or had it just not bothered him at the time? But why should she change it now, anyway? It was all right as it was. Most other things had altered completely. Some things were best as they were.

"I'm not all that sure what she calls me. At least she doesn't address me like a small boy, the way you did."

"I suppose not."

The woman nodded, her pale face in the feeble light looking as if it were wrapped in semitransparent, gray plastic.

"Do you have a ten-yen coin?" she asked.

They stood there in the semidarkness created by the indirect lighting, next to a telescope that seemed enclosed in a deeper shade of dark. Hamada slipped a coin into the black slot. Akiko peered into the telescope and fiddled about with various parts of it. Hamada looked out through the glass at the night sky of Tokyo, in which rain was falling. He imagined he would probably never again look out over the city at night from so high a vantage point. They had only come here today because the woman said she wanted to. He had never been here. In the past, whenever he visited a new town or village he'd always felt that he would probably never go there again, and meeting the woman had perhaps aroused that old habit of mind.

"Can't you see anything?" he asked.

"Nothing at all. It's all dark."

"That's funny."

It was funny. At the edge of the black Tokyo night, various colored neon signs were flickering, and if he could see them with his naked eye, why couldn't she? Hamada moved the telescope up and down a few times.

"You still can't see?"

"Not a thing."

Hamada burst out laughing. At the foot of the telescope stand there was a notice saying it was out of order. Akiko bent down and read it.

"How awful. That's ten yen wasted. I suppose they won't let us have it back?"

"No point in even bothering to ask."

"What a waste. That's really annoying," she repeated, turning away from the telescope and looking about her, but there was no sign of anyone on duty, only the elevator girl standing in a brilliant shaft of light, and she seemed so busy controlling a line of customers waiting for the elevator it didn't seem right to ask her.

"You always used to be so careless about money," he said.

"And you were always so horribly mean," she replied, as if she were somehow justifying herself now. "Of course, ten yen in those days was worth a sight more than it is now."

"Much more," he said, and pointed at clusters of lights shining through the thick glass and the still falling rain.

"That's Shinjuku. That's Shibuya. That's probably Roppongi. No, wait a minute. That must be Roppongi, that blur of light nearer to us. That over there will be Ikebukuro."

He then pointed back to the right.

"That dark area straight ahead of you is Tokyo Bay."

"Those must be boats, then?"

They certainly didn't look like boats. Over the wide, black surface of the bay were scattered countless lights, but it was difficult to imagine they could be from some fleet of ships. They reminded one more of stars, of constellations: the Great Bear, Virgo, Libra.

"I was told there were lots of boats and it looked really fantastic. But it's nothing all that much, is it?"

"Perhaps there aren't many boats because of the rain," she said.

"Not very likely, is it?"

"Still, it really is cold."

"It must be out there. All right for the people who've gone ashore, but it must be pretty bad on watch."

The ones who had no money stayed behind. They were playing poker or dice for very small stakes. Some of them would be scared to go ashore in case they were caught, perhaps. Cold; and no money. A hard life. Still, they could depend upon three meals a day, and they wouldn't be cold as long as they didn't go on deck.

"I've sort of run away," Akiko suddenly said. "Well, half run away."

"Half?"

"I'll go back when I feel better. I made up my mind about that before I left."

"That's probably the best thing to do. There's no point in doing anything desperate. Did you have a quarrel?"

She remained silent.

"Did you leave a note?"

She shook her head.

"No. I shan't say anything when I go back, either. I don't suppose he'd ask me, anyway. He's like that."

He frowned. She'd probably done the same sort of thing before. Probably more than once; any number of times, perhaps. She had a natural tendency to wander off by herself. Perhaps she just liked running away, like the time when he first met her. Nearby, some of the schoolchildren had surrounded an aged American couple, producing fountain pens and notebooks and asking for their signatures. Hamada went on frowning, but the American couple and the schoolchildren were all smiling very energetically. When the wife spent days away from home without permission and the husband said nothing about it when she got back, and the two of them went on living quietly as man and wife—well, that showed a real talent for behaving as if the past no longer existed. Or perhaps it simply indicated that neither could care less about the other.

A bell rang, and above it could be heard an announcement in a woman's voice that the observation platform was about to close. The teacher in charge of the schoolchildren raised the megaphone dangling on his chest and shouted into it two or three times for them to assemble. Akiko had been staring into the black sky, and she turned around and asked him if he would take her back to the place she was staying.

He nodded. He was glad he'd sent the necessary telegram when he left his office. He could always explain that he'd spent the night playing mah jong at the house of a certain professor of international law. After all, it was a common enough happening in this world, common enough to seem almost natural: a couple who just couldn't get rid of each other.

They walked once more around the observation platform, staying as much as possible in the dim light of the glass windows. The woman's voice announcing that the platform was now closing went on sounding above their heads. Akiko smiled awkwardly at him.

"You know, it's one of those hotels. It does seem a pity it has to be a place like that."

There was nobody about anymore.

"Seems pretty appropriate to me."

Akiko stared at him in an exaggeratedly shocked manner, but the erotic glint in her eyes was unmistakable.

"You're very blunt, aren't you?"

"As soon as I heard on the phone it was Sendagaya I guessed it was bound to be a place like that. That's about the only kind of hotel they have in that area."

"It was all the taxi driver's fault. I mean, I didn't have anything of that sort in mind at all. I just got into a taxi at Tokyo Station and asked the driver to take me to a good place to stay."

"I'll take your word for it. Still, that doesn't alter what I've said. It seems a pretty appropriate . . ."

"I won't listen," she said, putting both hands over her ears and walking into a lighted area. Hamada gave a short laugh and walked after her, after the plump woman in her late forties in the light brown coat. He wondered how much she weighed now. Surely she hadn't had heavy shoulders like that before? Surely she hadn't been so squat? He called to mind how she had been then, the slender, delicate figure like a wild flower (that was the image he'd thought of); but the whole thing must have been an illusion his emotional involvement had created. Or at least it seemed so now.

They stood together at the end of the line for the elevator, which had grown quite short. The loudspeaker started to play "Auld Lang Syne." Of course, that was exactly the kind of platitudinous music one would expect to hear at a time like this; absurdly conventional and ludicrously appropriate. And tonight he would sleep with this woman he hadn't slept with for years. In bed they would talk about this and that in a desultory fashion. It was normal. It often happened. It was commonplace; a small flame conjured from burned-out embers. A commonplace incident in the life of a commonplace man.

The chief clerk arrived. The conference must have come to an end. Hamada placed the postcard announcing Akiko's death under the glass top of his desk, and glanced at it occasionally while filling in the authorization form, which included the sum of 30,000 yen for the professor's obituary donation. Once the chief clerk had stamped his approval, Hamada took it straight up to the executive directors' room on the second floor. He bypassed the registrar himself, since the post was a mere sinecure that had been tacked on to the administrative structure to give someone a job, and it had become customary to ignore him in any question of documentation. The tasteful light green carpeting and chestnut-paneled walls always impressed Hamada with their luxuriance, giving him the feeling on first entering the room that he was somewhere else than the university. But he had only to look up at the dozen or so large portraits of former presidents and chairmen of the board of trustees staring down at him from high on the walls to realize quite soon exactly where he was. Among them was a former prime minister, an ancient patriot in full traditional court dress, looking particularly ferocious; and also a viscount, impressively garbed in European-style regalia, gold braid and all, who had been Minister of Education or something of the kind, but whose major claim to fame was that his dallyings with geisha had become so extreme his wife ran off with the chauffeur.

The university had, in fact, two executive directors, and Hamada was relieved to find that the one present now in the quiet, spacious room was the man whom he could thank for being employed here in the first place, Horikawa. He was probably past seventy now. He put face downward the Go magazine he had been reading, took his ivory seal out of its deerskin case and applied it to the paper, then inclined his head to one side as if pondering the advisability of the sum of 30,000 yen; but eventually he seemed to decide it was neither too little nor too much and gave a large nod, removing his reading glasses as well. Hamada had been about to leave, but

Horikawa motioned to him to sit on a light green chair and asked him about his workload in the Registry Office. Hamada recalled the rumors going around about some projected reorganization, which would mean an increase in the number of administrative departments, and made one or two comments that the director didn't take up, choosing instead to ask him, as if it were a natural outcome of their conversation, how old he was.

"I'm exactly forty-five, sir."

"Which means you've been working here for . . . ?"

"Eighteen years. Almost nineteen."

"As long as that, is it? And it seems like just the other day you first came here. Nearly two decades. Of course, a great deal has happened since then: new university buildings, the purchase of the land for the sports ground, increased facilities, new subjects to be taught, new faculties set up, creating more high schools. . . ."

And chucking out his predecessor, a job engineered by Horikawa himself, Hamada added silently to the list, although he did this in no sort of critical spirit. The executive director who'd been disposed of had certainly been an incompetent fool, and the fact that Hamada, who was not a graduate of the university, had been promoted as far as assistant registry clerk was something he knew perfectly well could only be accredited to Horikawa's good offices. He noticed that his gray hair today had no tinge of yellow about it but looked a perfect white, which must mean he was feeling well, since it was always said by the office staff that the color of Horikawa's hair served as a barometer of the mood he was in.

"By the way, how's your wife? In good fettle, is she?" Horikawa took a filter cigarette out of his case, and Hamada produced a lighter and lit it for him.

"Yes, we're managing all right, thank you."

"Not in too fine a fettle, by any chance? Not proving a bit too much for you?"

This was a reference to the fact that Hamada's wife was much younger than he, and Horikawa made a knowing leer as he went on to crack a not very refined joke about their still having no children. Hamada merely smiled back.

"How old's Nishi?"

Horikawa was referring to the other assistant registry clerk, who was away on business.

"A year younger than me, I believe."

"So you were promoted to assistant clerk first?"

"No. Nishi was promoted before me, sir."

"Who's oldest? You or Nishi?"

"I'm one year older."

"Does he have children?"

Hamada replied that he believed he had two, which produced another pregnancy joke from Horikawa and another smile from Hamada. There was a convenient phone call at that moment, so Hamada was able to depart the light green-and-chestnut colored room. Obviously those questions were connected with the rumored administrative shake-up, with who was going to be promoted to the head of one or another of the new departments, for that would be the next rung up the ladder for Hamada. But it was precisely that kind of rise he felt he could never hope for. It seemed to be an unbreakable rule of this university that only its graduates were ever made heads of departments. There was also the fact that Nishi had been made assistant clerk before he had. They might give Hamada all the responsibility of such a post, but he couldn't hope for the office itself and the power that went with it. He was in the habit of telling himself that he didn't mind very much, since the promotion only led to a slight rise in salary and thus held little real attraction.

He went downstairs again. Most of the morning lectures seemed to have ended, and the corridor was full of students. Hamada threaded his way through them back to the Registry Office, and ate the lunch that had already arrived from the staff canteen. When he'd finished he got ready to leave in order to be on time for the conference at the Private Universities Hall at one-thirty. The chief clerk personally saw him off in enormous good humor, making it quite comically clear how pleased he was at not having to go to the conference himself. The chief clerk was, of course, a graduate of this university, who had been immediately taken on the clerical staff and had no experience at all of the wide world outside, so he had a particular dislike of conferences other than those that took place in the university. Then it also seemed likely—indisputable in fact—that the meeting he was to attend that evening would provide an occasion for drink; and he was a great one for drinking, particularly when it could be done for nothing.

As Hamada left the campus he made an excessively polite bow to a small shrine right next to the main gate. The university had a course for prospective Shinto priests, and the shrine served as a kind of practical classroom for them. On the whole the students, and those younger teachers who were not graduates of the university, tended to ignore it as they went by, but Hamada was careful not to forget to make his humble obeisance. In a university like this, where a lecture course in basic Shintoism was still compulsory for all students in the Faculty of Letters, and where the whole atmosphere was, if not necessarily reactionary yet at least very conservative, it would be asking for trouble to be seen not to comply in most matters, no matter how trivial. At least, his position being what it was, he was determined to go against no established practice whatsoever.

Once he was off university territory, he immediately noticed a Renault approaching, the driver of which waved to him. He waved back. The man with the skiing-tanned face and the flashy yellow tie was an assistant professor of French called Kuwano. As Hamada watched the amber Renault pass in through the main gate, he recalled the rumor that had circulated as to Kuwano's main reason for buying that car, and the memory made him smile. It was because he could drive past the shrine without needing to bow in its direction. Kuwano was said to have the makings of a first-rate Baudelaire scholar, although it was also rumored of him nowadays that all he thought about was skiing and bowling and he wasn't doing a stroke of work; and it was certainly true that, despite the fact he would cheerfully greet quite unimportant members of the clerical staff, he stubbornly refused even to glance in the direction of the shrine.

"There goes a professor of foreign languages, no doubt," said a man's voice behind him. Hamada looked around and saw it was Itoh, the clerk in charge of purchases. He had on a very worn leather jacket.

"Yes. It's Professor Kuwano. He's an assistant professor, in fact."

"Nice little baby car he has. One of those Yolkwagons, or whatever they're called."

"No. It's a French Renault. Because he teaches French, I suppose."

"He must be doing pretty well for himself if he can drive about in his own car."

"That's right. Why don't you get one yourself?"

"Me? On my salary? Not a hope."

Itoh went off to the bus stop, getting at the end of a line of students, but Hamada looked at his watch and found he had plenty of time, so he decided to walk instead. It was certainly pleasant walking down this gentle slope on a warm spring day with already a hint of summer in the sunlight, but he also wanted to avoid being with Itoh. Itoh had been head of the Personnel Department, with the responsible task of handling postgraduation employment, but two years ago he'd been asked to go off to Toyama Prefecture, to the town of Takaoka, where the university had a high school, to take charge of general administration there, and he'd refused. He was only allowed to remain at the university on the condition he accepted a demotion to head of purchasing. Hamada had made an attempt to cheer Itoh up when he was being particularly depressed about the business, but Itoh had promptly ignored him. Hamada found this mystifying, since Itoh had seemed happy enough to enlarge on his grievances with other people; but he had then reflected that in this university, he, Hamada, belonged to the Horikawa faction, the reigning faction at the time, and he had grinned wryly to himself at the inevitability of Itoh's response.

Since he was now taking one of his rare walks, he felt he should make proper use of this opportunity for exercise and vigorously lengthened his stride. This meant he started to pass small groups of students descending the slope ahead of him, overhearing what they were saying. First it was four or five girls.

"That psychology teacher is really awful. Apparently those who turned in blank papers got full marks."

"I was so nervous myself I just couldn't write a thing."

"Is it really true he said a blank paper was a sign of psychological health?"

Then there were three men.

"I had a hell of a time. Being in love really costs money."

"That's what you call being in love, is it?"

"You're just jealous."

"And all they had on offer was a load of old junk. . . ."

The elevator reached the ground floor, where there was a brilliant flood of light coming from an arcade of souvenir stalls. One or two had closed early and were covered in heavy, gray cloth, but the rest were a riot of tasteless ornamentation. Hamada was intent on ignoring the whole lot, but Akiko kept on stopping, taking up a packet of Tower cookies, then a Tower towel and a Tower album, and scrutinizing them with great care. She stood for some time in front of a particularly vile photograph, in a cheap gold frame, of the Tower in ghastly red and white against a vulgar blue sky streaked with what looked like aircraft exhaust. Surely she didn't intend to buy something as awful as that? Hamada edged as far away as he reasonably could from Akiko, and away from that frame, precariously balanced on a great, unstable pile of Tower bean jelly packets. He stood looking at his former sweetheart, standing there with her rear thrust out in his direction. She had turned into this appalling bumpkin (which she had always been, presumably), the awkward daughter who'd run away from home again, but now she was approaching fifty. Her face reminded him in some odd way of her mother's; of her mother as she had looked then. Of course, he himself was well past forty.

A bell started ringing in the arcade. It resounded in a false sky of hard, pure white. The number of stalls covered in gray cloth had increased and went on increasing as the bell went on ringing, while Akiko went on stopping in front of each one of those now scattered stalls that were still open. Hamada followed, but always slightly to one side, carefully maintaining the same distance from her. Tower rice cakes, Tower postcards, Tower candy, Tower ashtrays, Tower paperweights. So long as you prefixed the word "Tower," anything could become a souvenir. Perhaps this stall was selling Tower missiles, concealed there beneath its gray cloth.

The woman running the stall was recommending a couple of gold ashtrays, and Akiko stood there with one in each hand, unable to make up her mind, so finally she turned to Hamada. He briskly approached her. The choice was between one with only the Tower on it, and one with the Tower plus the Diet Building and also a low, elongated edifice that was probably Tokyo Station. He irresponsibly made an immediate choice of one of them, but she still wasn't sure. The stall woman was obviously in a hurry to get home. Hamada felt sorry for her. Her complexion was so bad he imagined she must be suffering from some liver complaint. He would have done better to take Akiko to a department store. The goods for sale were at least decent there, and one wasn't obliged to endure the feelings of wretchedness this sort of junk aroused. That time he went shopping with Yoko, while she was gazing in raptures at a Pierre Cardin dress, he had turned casually away and caught sight of his own face in a round mirror with an off-pink frame. He had looked so comic: the face of a middle-aged man married to a young wife; a face that was starting to grow old. In the hotel in Sendagaya the bedding would already have been laid out in the bedroom, and when you slid open the door there would be a huge mirror on the wall. He had never even thought of sleeping in front of a mirror with Akiko, not once. He had imagined doing it with Yoko like that, though. In front of a large mirror, sleeping with both of them, perhaps? Akiko on his right, Yoko on his left. Naturally it would be quite all right the other way around. That would really give a woman approaching fifty a thrill. But what about the one who was still only thirty? She'd be shy at first, of course. Angry probably. But then, all of a sudden, her resistance would vanish; she would be juicy and melting like an overripe pear. . . . Still, there was always the problem of whom he would enter first. Well, they'd just have to toss for it. Naturally the one who lost would gain the right to have the ejaculation inside her; that was only fair. After thirty minutes (an hour perhaps), roles could be reversed. On the third occasion (assuming he could manage it), they would have to toss again. Akiko had finally made up her mind about the ashtray. Since she'd grown as fat as this, that mole on her right thigh (or was it her left?) would be much bigger; much bigger, and lighter in color as well. The stall woman wrapped the ashtray and gave it to Akiko, then took the money. The oval-shaped mole might even have grown round; grown thick-set and plump as Akiko herself had become. The mole had hair growing on it, thick and black.

His pace suddenly slackened when he reached the light blue police box at the foot of the slope. The road widened at this point; the trams started from here and there were more cars and people, so he couldn't have maintained that vigorous pace even if he had wanted to. But the main reason he slowed down and finally stopped altogether in front of the police box was the notice stuck on its window: WANTED FOR ARMED ROBBERY AND MURDER. "The above three men are wanted for a murder committed during an armed robbery in Kita Kyushu. . . ." Hamada carefully read the details about the three wanted men, written in a crude, incompetent hand on an equally crudely printed poster: name, present domicile and permanent address, date of birth, age, occupation, height, weight, other peculiarities. Two of them had fairly similar names, but they all had aliases as well. One of them even had three, and the policeman who'd written the notice had been obliged halfway through to cramp the letters together to get them all in. All three were only in their twenties. They would each have assumed a different name now, and he was thinking about the various names that must have come into their heads before they made their final decision, wondering if they'd made a good choice or not, when he was startled by a loud shout from a group of students he'd overtaken coming down the hill.

He looked around and saw it was three men, and one girl in a red sweater. They were talking about going bowling. He watched them move away from him, then turned to the police notice again. The photographs must have been blown up a lot, and that, plus the coarse paper, gave the faces a peculiarly unhappy look. One of them had been photographed in profile, and he was wearing Japanese dress, probably a white *yukata*. Another had something like a string dangling around his neck; either a pendant or a lucky charm, it was not clear which. No doubt they must be looking even more depressed now, hungry and miserable, thinking of one more cold night to live through. They would look much more haggard than they did in these photos, faces pinched and worn, all the life drained out of them, tempted at times by the idea of giving themselves up for a bowl of hot food to restore some of the lost energy. Two of them seemed to be freckled, but that was probably the fault of the pictures. Otherwise they had almost nothing distinctive about them. But the third was different, the man in the center wearing a white vest, and the written description laid great stress upon this. He had a harelip. Plastic surgery was no doubt very advanced now, but it would be just about impossible to find a doctor who'd do it on the quiet. Of course, he wouldn't be able to afford it, anyway. He could always grow a moustache or wear a gauze mask over his mouth, but unless he could work out a good reason in either case it was arguable that they might be even more conspicuous than the harelip itself. Hamada wondered what he himself would do if he had a harelip. In fact, the answer was simple enough: he'd just have to find employment in which it was essential to have a moustache. The young man's upper lip had a vertical slit in it, like a seed pod when it ripens and partially splits open. Hamada gazed at the rich, black wound for a while, holding his breath, which echoed as a deep sigh when he finally released it. He must be on his own now. His two companions would have deserted him. Alone on the run; when he passed a police box he would lower his head, trying to conceal his mouth. Hamada's sympathy for the man was such that he found himself unconsciously performing the same gesture, and he noticed the lace of one of his shoes was untied. He bent down and retied it, then started walking again, but he didn't regain his original pace until he'd gone some distance, almost as far as the underground station.

It was nearly two o'clock before the conference started and it went on until after four, so there was no chance of getting to the university before he was due off work at four-thirty. He decided to go back, however, rather than return straight home, since there were a number of small matters he wanted to clear up, but mainly because he needed to get his post office savings book out of his locker if he was to send off the money for Akiko's funeral on his way to work the next morning. While the tedious conference had been in progress he'd been occupied not only with making precise notes on the back of the handout he'd received but also with still trying to calculate exactly how much money it should be; and just before the meeting came to an end he finally arrived at the figure of 10,000 yen, although he remained just as much in doubt about the appropriateness of this sum as he had been about the 30,000 for the professor's funeral.

He'd intended to take the underground, then the tram, but a bus that stopped near the rear entrance of the university happened to arrive just then, and he suddenly changed his mind and got on that instead. Ever since he was a boy he'd liked traveling on all kinds of public transportation, a taste that had been intensified by his wartime experiences, and it was now a cheap form of entertainment. He knew the Tokyo public transportation network practically backward, and it was mysterious he hadn't thought about using this bus on his way here. He didn't take this oversight to heart but simply got on the bus, brand new and very clean, and the scarcity of passengers and the absence of a conductor (a rarity at the time) made him feel pleasantly at ease with the world; although the view from the window of an alien landscape of ranged high-rise buildings and the meanders of the elevated expressway was, if at least not exactly like that of a foreign country, certainly very different from the Tokyo of his childhood. It was a weird city, like a metropolis of the future portrayed by some unimaginative science fiction writer. It made him feel uneasy again, as if he were being transported far into a world that was no more than an unrealizable fantasy.

Probably in reaction to this induced unrest, when he got off the bus and walked along the peaceful road over which twilight was falling, he felt comfortable again. His pace slackened to a gentle stroll as he passed by the rows of low-roofed houses, looking and not looking at them. It had been at just this time of the year, and at this same time of day, along just such winding, narrow streets as these, feeling the same slightly humid breeze upon his forehead, that he'd walked about Miyazaki, was it? Or perhaps Morioka? He wasn't quite sure which, but he felt how much he wanted to revisit both towns, towns he was fond of. Still, the truth was he recalled quite clearly now that it was autumn when he'd been in Miyazaki, and what he remembered of Morioka was that the landlord of his lodging house had been obsessed with growing morning glories, and the narrow outside sill of the window of his room had been jammed with flowerpots, the trumpet-shaped and fading blooms flowering in profusion all over it, and he had this clear image still of looking out of that window and noting a large bottle of disinfectant that had caught the rays of the setting sun; its contents had taken on the yellowish brown of urine. The morning glories meant it must have been high summer.

While he was pondering this, some sudden unusual cries brought him back from that uncertain city to the Tokyo of the present, to this place near the university where he worked. A group of young men had crossed a small bridge just in front of the rear entrance to the university and were running in this direction, apparently shouting energetic cries of encouragement at each other. Right at the front was a man wearing a suit, and he was followed at a distance of some ten yards by two or three young men in judo outfits, with another couple in the same clothes five yards or so behind them. These must be members of the judo or karate club on a training run, despite the lateness of the hour, ignoring as usual administrative memos about not doing this outside campus. It was particularly vexing to see one of the graduates of the university, dressed like a respectable member of society, encouraging this practice by running at their head.

The howls coming from the pack were as uncivilized as ever, but made worse this time by not being in unison. The road was not very wide, so he edged over to one side of it in order to get out of their way. He then noticed another group of men wearing an assortment of suits, shirts, and trousers running well behind the ones in judo clothes. He suddenly stopped walking. He had at last realized that they weren't just shouting meaningless cries at one another. They were crying out, "Stop thief, stop thief." What he'd been hearing up to now had been simply the long, drawn-out vowel of the first syllable.

Hamada stood stock still. "Stop thief! Stop thief!" The man running in front was not leading the pack but being pursued by it, then? But it didn't look like that, for he was so neatly dressed, well built, and his face (for he was now close enough for Hamada to be able to make out his features) had nothing mean or contemptible about it. The ones who seemed contemptible were rather his pursuers in their grubby judo clothes, pounding along heavily, barefoot, with their mouths hideously agape as they howled, while the man in front ran silently, with his body leaning sinuously forward. This striking contrast confused Hamada's judgment, for it seemed inconceivable that the man only a few yards away now could be a burglar who'd just been rifling some room in the university, and his initial misunderstanding of the words being shouted still persisted as a doubt that held his body so it would not move. He could hear the words clearly now, words that told him to stop this man, words that ordered and implored him to arrest this thief; and yet he did nothing. He behaved exactly as did a middle-aged woman who'd been walking toward him from the opposite direction and who stood rooted to the spot, a cabbage in one hand and a shopping basket in the other, her face grown quite pale as she gazed blankly on—as did Hamada, while the man raced straight past him, coat blowing out behind, sweat standing out on his nose and brow.

But the man did not, in fact, run straight on by. As Hamada moved his gaze a fraction to watch him, he saw a man who must have been walking just behind him. He wore a green pullover. He'd also moved to one side of the road, right back against the hedge, and was crouching down. Then he propelled himself bodily forward from the hedge and brought down the thief with a heavy tackle, his arms clasped around the other's legs, and they rolled over on the gray asphalt road like two rugby players. The man in the charcoal suit and blue tie was thrashing his legs about trying to get free and also waving his arms, but the man in the pullover held him in a vise-like grip, gradually forcing him over onto his face, and each time he raised his bloodstained face the grip was as relentless as ever. It was true he kept on beating away with his hands, but he was unable to get in any forceful blows at his captor, who remained indifferent to the weak assault on his head, his face thrust against the belly and thighs of the man he'd brought down, and refused to let go. Finally a man in a brown suit came running up, pushed his way quickly past the judo-suited students, and hurled himself astride the prostrate man, who was still putting up a vigorous resistance. He seized him by the neck with his left hand and punched him two or three times in the face with his right, shouting at the students who were now standing around them to call the police. Two of the students ran off. The man in the pullover got up and started to dust off his arms and chest. The man in the brown suit hit the thief once more in the face, although he had given up resisting now, and this made his nose bleed even more. A man in shirt and trousers approached the man in the pullover, bowed his head, and thanked him, while a student in a judo outfit brushed the dirt off his back.

But Hamada neither ran off to telephone the police nor dusted the back of the man in the pullover. He also did not raise his leg, like the man in the sports shirt immediately in front of him, threatening to kick the thief, who'd started struggling again, in the face. He just stood there, like the noodles delivery boy and the housewife and a number of small children and some other assorted observers, who'd suddenly formed a wall around the fallen thief and the man seated astride him, albeit at some distance from them. Hamada then recognized the man in the brown suit astride the victim as a young man called Sugi, a graduate of the university who'd joined the clerical staff last year, and the man in the shirt and trousers as one Hasegawa, who worked in the same Student Affairs Department, while the one in the sports shirt was somebody whose name he could not recall in Teaching Administration. If these people felt justified in treating the victim in so cavalier a fashion, then he must have been doing a job on the university.

One of the students ran back and addressed Sugi:

"They say they'll be here right away."

"Right."

"They said you were just to wait and make sure he didn't get away."

"Okay. Well done."

The thief started struggling vigorously again, so much that Sugi began wobbling on his back. The man in Teaching Administration aimed a wild kick at the thief's face, which in fact hit him on the shoulder. Since the thief was threshing about with his legs, Hasegawa of the Student Affairs Department settled himself astride them, with the result that he seemed to be embracing Sugi from behind, while Sugi himself began punching the thief in the face again. This made the man who was being punched screw up his face, and all the children burst out laughing merrily, probably because it reminded them of professional wrestling on TV. Their clear laughter echoed in the gray twilight.

Hamada decided to leave, but as he did so his eye caught Hasegawa's and he felt obliged to nod to him and say a few words of encouragement.

Hasegawa acknowledged him with no more than a curt nod, immediately transformed into a harsh stare, and then he looked sharply away, addressing his own words to the hips of Sugi.

"If you're worn out I'll take over if you like."

"No, I'm all right."

Hamada decided they must all be angry with him because he hadn't tried to stop the thief, and as he left the wall of spectators and made his way through the rear gate of the university back to the Registry Office, he began to wonder himself why he hadn't done anything but merely look on. While he was chatting idly with the remaining members of the staff, both those who had stayed behind because of the evening classes and those who had merely fabricated an excuse to remain because they wanted the overtime, and even while he was drawing up one or two simple documents, the question went on nagging at him. But he didn't mention the matter to the other people in the office. He deliberately avoided doing so, unable to answer his own doubts as to why he should have behaved as a mere onlooker. Perhaps it had been because he'd genuinely misheard what people had been shouting. Perhaps it was due to the strong prejudice he felt toward the university old boys' sports clubs, to which so many of the clerical staff belonged. But he realized that neither answer was in any way adequate to account for his actions (or rather the lack of them) over so extended a period of time. After all, it wasn't just a question of a momentary reflex. It crossed his mind that it might have been because the man looked about the same age as his brother, Shinji; but Shinji was much taller, and had a quite different kind of face. Also, he could never have run as fast as that; not now, anyway. Just after the war ended, Shinji decided to give up university and become a jazz pianist, but after a while he got something wrong with his chest and the medicine he took for it made him deaf. He now did proofreading for a publisher of music books. Hamada tried to recall when he had last seen his younger brother run, and was surprised to find it must have been at least ten or fifteen years before. In fact, he hadn't seen him at all recently. Presumably he was all right.

He took his post office savings book out of his locker and got ready to go home, saying good night to the people in his office and making his way to the staff toilet. For some reason he went into the ladies' room by mistake, but after two or three paces inside he noticed that the wall seemed peculiarly empty and finally realized he was in the wrong place. This produced a wry smile, which persisted after he had pushed open the door to the men's room. The simple blunder seemed to take a weight off his mind, and he ceased to feel troubled by the question of why he had behaved as he did about the thief. He just seemed to have lost his grip today. That was the trouble. That was all it was. He needed to get hold of himself.

But he was only allowed a momentary respite. He washed his hands, and while he was drying them with his handkerchief, he heard voices through the half-open window, and his brief peace of mind was lost again. Just below that window on the outside wall was a row of taps, and a little while before there would have been the sound of sportsmen washing their faces and hands and changing out of their gear. At this time it was normally quiet, as it had been when he first entered the toilet, but suddenly the silence was broken by a quick burst of laughter and a number of voices raised together.

"That was a tremendous tackle."

"All over in a flash."

"Not many of the first team could do that. And he's only in the reserves."

"He must keep himself in pretty good shape, anyway."

"Bit different from me. I'm a total wreck. Just ran a bit and I was completely . . ."

"Of course, the fellow did run very fast . . ."

"Being in the karate club would have helped as well."

"Karate as well, is he?"

"You mean Arai is . . ."

"If you'll just let me get a word in edgewise. At the time I . . ."

"Sorry, old man."

". . . suggested a trip to the first aid room."

"What on earth for?"

"Should have thought a glass of beer was what the doctor ordered."

The conversation coming in from outside had all the conviviality of a foursome celebrating at the nineteenth hole and the animation of people who'd spent the day hunting. This side of the window, Hamada turned his back on those voices and ceased wiping his hands. He was afraid, trembling with a sudden impulse of fear whose presence he could not explain. Another burst of laughter made him glance automatically toward the door. The best way to escape would be through that door into the corridor. But how could he be sure they wouldn't catch him in the corridor? Certainly it wasn't far to the entrance hall, and then to the main gate (but perhaps the rear gate would be safer?); and yet it felt to him at that moment like the longest and most dangerous journey in the world. There seemed to be fewer people now outside the window. He took his eyes away from the door and caught sight of himself in a small mirror just in front of him. He stared at his own face. Held there in that rectangular space, it seemed to remind him of something, but he couldn't work out what it was. The men outside all seemed to have gone away, and the fear slowly receded from his stomach, finally going far off too. He could feel the sweat on his forehead; cold sweat probably. He went to wipe it with his handkerchief, but it was no longer in his hand. It had fallen into the basin at some time and now, soaked by the still flowing thin drizzle of water, it was stuck flat to the bottom. He wrung it out vigorously, then washed his face and wiped it with the damp handkerchief. The whole thing felt like a nightmare, but as he pushed open the door he decided he must make himself forget about it, and he walked down the corridor with his eyes fixed upon a far-off group of night school students, then turned a corner into the entrance hall.

As he passed out of the main door he met Professor Sakurai of the English Department, who must have come out of the block of classrooms on the right. Sakurai had started teaching here after he'd reached retirement at a national university, and he gave an impression of relaxed fatigue that one associates with someone energetically enjoying his old age.

"Oh, is that you, Hamada? Sorry, I didn't recognize you at first."

"How are you, Professor? As fit as ever?"

"Kind of you to ask. Well, I suppose I'm as well as can be expected. You know, one gets so busy at the end of the academic year it only really seems to be over when the new one starts."

They walked together toward the main gate, and Hamada said with a smile,

"We feel just the same way in administration. Nothing's really over until the new academic year starts. Still, it's not a bad feeling, is it? The feeling that it's all over."

"Yes, not bad at all. It's over. Everything is finally over," the professor mumbled, and now they were passing the shrine, and he readjusted the dark bundle, presumably of books, he had in his right hand, clasping it to his breast with both hands as he bowed deeply in that direction. Hamada followed suit. Crowds of night school students were passing in through the main gate. It was late twilight now, with only a faint blue remaining in the sky, and as they were engulfed in the flood of students, Professor Sakurai turned to him and said,

"Any idea which god this shrine is dedicated to, Hamada?"

"I'm afraid I don't."

"Just like everybody else, even those who've been here ages. Even old Oda failed the test," said Sakurai, referring to a very ancient professor of English who was in charge of the whole Foreign Languages Faculty. "Make sure you remember. The director told me so it must be true."

"You mean Dr. Horikawa?"

"No."

"Then it must have been Dr. Kobayakawa."

"That's right. Kobayakawa told me, so one can be quite sure. This shrine is dedicated to and celebrates . . . all the gods that exist in heaven and on earth."

Hamada wasn't sure if the professor was being serious or making some kind of jest, so he only murmured vaguely in reply and decided to change the subject.

"Still, sir, not everything has come to an end. Baseball has only just started."

"That's the trouble. All one does is waste hours watching it on television. And I'd always thought I'd have so much time to read once I'd retired."

They walked together as far as the underground station, and then parted. Neither on the underground nor again on the suburban commuter train did that nightmarish sensation reappear which he had experienced standing before the mirror, straining his ears to listen for something that carried so intolerable a feeling of threat; it had, indeed, vanished completely from his mind.

The apartment where he lived was at the end of a long cul-de-sac, and just before turning into it he dropped in at the corner tobacconist. As he left he was greeted by a man in a leather jacket who was just coming out of the supermarket next door, carrying a large bundle in his arms. At first he did not recognize him, but then he realized it was a businessman who had moved into their apartment block about a year ago, a man, in fact, whom he hardly knew. As they walked home together the man began to thank him profusely for the gift he had recently received. Hamada had no idea what this gift was or what it was celebrating, and as the man went on expressing his gratification at the splendor of the gift his good lady had bestowed upon them on the birth of their child, clearly the look of mystification on Hamada's face only deepened, for the other suddenly stopped short and said,

"It is Mr. Hamada, isn't it?"

Since there clearly had been no mistake, Hamada now offered his own congratulations, inquiring if it was a boy or a girl and also after the mother's health, and while this obvious conversation was in process they arrived at the apartment grounds.

"I'm afraid we're having a few people from the office over this evening to play mah jong—as a kind of welcoming party, you see—but I will do my best to make sure they're as quiet as . . ."

"An excellent idea. No doubt the child will grow up to be a remarkable player."

The leather-jacketed man showed a fine array of white teeth as he smiled cheerfully in reply, and went up a different staircase to the one Hamada took.

Naturally that was the very first thing he talked to his wife about. She said she'd given them a baby dress and booties she'd bought cheap at a bargain sale, since although they didn't know them very well it was, after all, their first child, and she'd already bought the things because she thought they might have come in useful for themselves next spring, perhaps. Hamada listened to this as he was changing, nodding and grunting his acknowledgment. He remembered how his dead mother had done the same, cleverly buying up things on the cheap because they might "come in useful sometime," and using them as returns for gifts unexpectedly received. At home this habit had been referred to as "storing up," although around the time of the "China Incident" in 1937 it became a tabooed word, being a bit too reminiscent of the act normally condemned as "hoarding" in the world at large. Hamada thus nostalgically recalled that period of his adolescence, a quarter of a century ago now.

When he sat at the table in the combined dining room and kitchen he was surprised to find among his mail the same postcard as he had received at the university announcing Akiko's death. He went through the motions of reading it and placed it at the bottom of the pile, then picked up another postcard, this from a man who'd formerly been employed at the university and was now working for a trading company informing him of a change of address, and as he again pretended to be reading he pondered why the same black-bordered postcard should have been sent to his home as well as to the university. Was it just a mistake, or was Akiko's mother deliberately being malicious? Akiko had not been happy during the final years of her life; probably not during the whole of it. Akiko's mother, at least, would certainly be of that opinion. It would look abnormal to her, not the kind of life she had expected for her daughter. Of course, if one considered her life objectively, those abnormal aspects were surely commonplace enough, nothing in the least to be surprised at or bitter about. But it was that kind of objectivity the mother lacked; she saw it at close quarters, with none of that redeeming sense of distance Akiko's former lover had, and no doubt she saw him as the man who had ruined her daughter's life and hated him accordingly. He tried to imagine the hateful expression on her face, but she must have aged a great deal by now, to a degree he was finally unable to conceive, and no image arose in his mind.

Yoko placed a small pot on the table and looked him in the face with evident self-satisfaction on hers. It was a dish of miso soup with seasoned vegetables that was a particular favorite of his, but she normally disliked cooking because of the way it made her carefully manicured hands smell. This day, however, she had done so, and she urged the soup upon him, since she'd even added some of the beer she had been drinking; but the fact was she didn't prepare the bean-paste stock (which needs to be stirred every day if it is not to lose its flavor) properly, and it had a very indifferent taste. She had done her best, however, and Hamada accepted this as one of the consequences of living with a young wife, as inevitable as having to take his meals uncomfortably seated on a wooden chair at a cramped kitchen dining table, instead of in the comfort of a living room, seated on a cushion on tatami. The fact that he had also not realized until now that his wife invariably produced this dish when relations between them had grown comparatively distant only emphasized the difference of age between himself and her.

The second bowl he decided to take with some pickles, and he finished the last piece (which even a generous person would have found difficult to say tasted nice). His wife was still eating her boiled fish, and she glanced at the two postcards on the table.

"Has some friend of yours died?"

"Yes. Someone who did me a favor years ago. It seems to have been cancer."

"I wonder if they'll ever find a cure for it?"

"Probably have something ready in time for you. Too late for me, I suppose."

"I do wish you wouldn't say things like that."

"Well, you never know. I suppose I might be lucky, but . . ."

He realized there was no point in saying something gratuitously unpleasant, so he discontinued the sentence. Yoko, however, apparently had other things on her mind.

"How many years ago?"

"During the war."

"Was she pretty?"

"Now, look, don't go getting the wrong idea. She's an old granny. As you ought to know, I have no interest in the mature woman."

Yoko smiled happily, apparently assured that the woman had meant nothing to him, and poured the tea. Of course, he had told her nothing about any of his relationships with other women. While their marriage was being arranged he had first requested his go-between, Horikawa, to tell her everything about his wartime behavior, and Horikawa had assured him that he'd done so, but he had no idea what he had told her, or even if he had mentioned the matter in any more than a casual way. He himself had never once talked about it, either to her parents or to Yoko, and she seemed to have realized that he didn't want to discuss what had happened during the war and never raised the subject herself. Whenever for some reason he happened to mention some of the various places he'd visited, she asked him in a perfectly innocent way how he'd managed to do so much traveling, and he gathered from the way she spoke and the expression on her face that the executive director had probably told her nothing. So he told her that he'd had a great passion for traveling when he was young, and the answer was, in fact, not untrue.

They ate half each of a cheap apple, and while his wife was doing the washing up he went into the small living room and switched on the TV. He didn't watch it, however; he just wanted to listen. He lay on his stomach smoking a cigarette, ignoring the woman with the long face like a horse's (the screen was badly adjusted anyway, and reception poor) and listening instead to the "chansons" she was singing; or perhaps it would be truer to say that he was just taking in the sound. The set was of a kind readily available on the market, but he'd transformed the sound by adding stereo loudspeakers he'd made himself, which were perched on the long shelf on the wall. It had been like that for about a year now.

Hamada had always liked music and tended to be fussy about the tone quality, and when Yoko had finally managed to persuade him to buy a television set he was astounded by the poorness of the sound; but since she soon lost interest and hardly switched it on at all, he'd not been all that bothered. Then, just two years ago, she'd become pregnant and almost immediately had a miscarriage and, for that reason or perhaps because the age of the cinema had come to an end about that time and television took over, she started to spend nearly all her time watching it, and he found the sheer awfulness of the sound more than he could endure. So he finally did what he'd meant to do when he first bought the set but had kept putting off. Hamada had graduated from the radio engineering department of one of the old National Technical Colleges, and while at college he'd submitted, on the advice of his professor, articles to a magazine for radio enthusiasts, even if only of a fairly elementary kind. He was, of course, perfectly well aware that the education he'd received was mostly irrelevant to the present-day world of electronics, and that his interest in it was only a form of amusement, in the same category as Horikawa's concern with *go*. One of his articles of faith (to use an exaggerated expression) was that he was a mere weekend engineer, although his very insistence on so obvious a fact was in itself a little peculiar perhaps. With the progress of the electronics industry after the war, most of his college contemporaries had done well for themselves as top-class technicians; in particular, his closest friend, a man called Sakai, had become vice president of a radio company that was said to be one of the great success stories of the postwar economy. The fact that Hamada himself, a clerk in university administration, still went on writing the occasional short piece for that radio enthusiasts' magazine probably indicated some basic dissatisfaction in himself at the way things had turned out.

Ten years before, at a time when Sakai's company was just starting to become well known, he'd received an unexpected telephone call from him at the university, and they'd had dinner together. There'd been no contact at all between them since the war, but Sakai had seen something Hamada had written in that magazine and found out where he was by inquiring at the editorial office. Compared with how he'd been while at college, Sakai seemed to have become peculiarly astute and quick-witted, giving Hamada a very powerful impression not so much of the dignity of middle age but of a positive, fearless attitude toward life that he'd acquired and Hamada had not; although he was certainly just as big and fat as ever, with the same gluttonous appetite that disposed of every dish almost as fast as it appeared. Sakai urged Hamada to join his company, work he would have enjoyed doing and that would have meant an increase in salary as well, but after thinking about it for a couple of days, he'd declined the offer. The two had hardly met since then, and when they did, Sakai never raised the subject, although once, about the time he'd bought his TV set, they'd met quite by chance in Ginza, and while they were drinking coffee together Hamada had said he wondered why nobody ever seemed to bring up the subject of the quality of sound on TV, since he thought they ought to try to get that right before becoming involved with color, for eventually viewers were bound to start asking why they got such bad sound when the same frequency modulation was being used as on radio. Sakai listened with obvious interest to what he was saying, although he made no suggestions of his own, giving the impression he was deliberately holding back, and Hamada started to feel sorry for him since he was clearly struggling with the prohibition on divulging company secrets to outsiders. So he changed the subject.

Hamada had the habit of clicking his tongue when he listened to TV, and he was doing so now as he listened to the chansons, which eventually changed into mood music—accompanied on the screen by three ballerinas dancing out of step with each other, although naturally Hamada didn't see this since he wasn't looking—while he still went on clicking his tongue. In fact, it had become more like a tut-tutting of annoyance, for although he'd gone to all the trouble of giving the set stereo sound, the actual tone quality had not improved in the least. Obviously the idea of a console television set didn't make any sense at all. It was an open secret among specialists that the wavebands used on TV were slightly narrower than the ones for radio, and that the setting of the microphones was slipshod so that the sound being sent out was only of poor quality; when that was combined with a lousy receiver, obviously you couldn't expect very much, so all an improved receiver gave was a precise version of what was basically only an indifferent sound. Still, surely there must be something that could be done about it. Probably there was, but he was only an amateur and he'd done all that he personally could. He wondered why Sakai's company hadn't produced a set with a decent sound. Were they still working on it? Hadn't the breakthrough occurred yet? It was a question he thought about sometime every day, but as he reached this point Yoko had finished the washing up, lit the gas for the bath, and come into the living room.

"You don't mind, do you?"

"No."

She changed the channel, and giggled merrily at a comedian who was just coming to the end of his act, a laughter somehow full of both invitation and dissatisfaction, like a glass jar jammed tight with a complex mixture of powder, implying that not only were they to watch TV together instead of just listening to it but also there were various other services she expected her husband to provide. An American television film was about to begin, and he sat up and started to watch it with her. There was that postcard announcing Akiko's death, for one thing, and he felt he was obliged to pay court to her in some way or other. This itself aroused his indignation again, whether at the spitefulness of Akiko's mother or at the incompetence of some other person he was not sure; but the great thing, he told himself, was that it was all over now, and he was free to enjoy the almost unbelievable and still, in fact, illusory feeling of being at peace with the world that not the program itself but the act of watching it with his wife bestowed upon him.

At first he watched the film because he felt obliged to do so, but suddenly he found himself absorbed in it. The opening sequence of a young woman talking to an old man was over, and now it was a young man, soaked in the cold rain, hiding in a gas station. Hamada felt himself quite caught up in the sequence as the young man, on the run, managed to remain concealed not only from the men working at the gas station but also from the police and even the police dog. The lingering suspense aroused by whether the hero would be caught or not was painfully obvious and contrived with a skill that was almost unpleasantly obtrusive, but Hamada succumbed to it. As the young man walked off shivering in the rain, and the cold rain came on heavily, falling in long, thick, white, slanting needles across the screen, beating into his face, as his situation became more and more desperate, Hamada found his hand reaching out and switching it off. The road wet in the rain and the young man suddenly dwindled to a point, and then went out.

"What did you do that for?"

He was unable to reply to her shrill question. He merely sat and looked at his right index finger that had just pushed the button as if it belonged to someone else. His wife repeated her question, but this time in a positive wail, and then added:

"There must be something wrong with you. Just at the most exciting point too."

"I'm feeling tired. I thought we might have an early night."

This reply immediately cheered her up, and she replied in a very gentle voice this time.

"I was thinking the same thing myself. If you know what I mean?"

He indicated that he did and, the next moment, that he had heard something funny.

"Is that bath water all right?"

The noise was of it bubbling furiously away. Yoko stood up with theatrical howls of dismay and disappeared into the next room to turn the gas off.

He lay waiting for her, reading the evening paper by the light of the bedside lamp. When she came into the bedroom wearing only a towel wrapped around her, he put down the newspaper. She didn't even glance at her own bedding but came straight into his, casting the towel aside as if she were throwing it away. The large blue towel lay sprawled over her bedding as she came naked to his side. Hamada was not naked. He was wearing a *yukata*. Yoko had once bought him some pajamas and tried to make him wear them, but he preferred the old-fashioned style of nightwear. He felt the warmth of his wife's nakedness through the thin cloth on his left arm and shoulder and directly upon his thigh and leg, and did as that warmth demanded and turned toward her on his side, noting as he made the movement that the sheets couldn't have been changed for some time. No doubt she'd put on fresh sheets tomorrow. She always did. She'd once even proudly explained how it was such a waste to spoil nice clean sheets. He tried to recall Akiko's habits, thinking that her policy about changing the sheets had probably been exactly the opposite of his wife's, searching in the half light of his memory, but finding nothing except the realization that it was over now, all over, and that once he'd telegraphed the money tomorrow morning it really would have all come to its final end.

"What are you thinking about?"

He didn't reply at first, but she asked him again in a sweet, wheedling voice like a cat, and suddenly he told her about what had happened that day.

"It somehow felt it was not me but them who'd got things wrong. I was just walking along, just having a pleasant walk. It was a nice, quiet road, like the way Tokyo used to be before. Of course it wasn't really a bit like the old Tokyo. There's nothing left of that. That was just how it felt, though. And then straight ahead of me, from the university, I started to hear these shouts, these voices shouting 'Heh, heh'—no, more like 'Hoh, hoh'—no, not like that either; more like a lot of wild animals howling. You see, they weren't just shouting at each other the way they do when they're running. They were chasing someone, a young man. Not young, really; about thirty, I think. Could have been a good bit older than that. Well dressed, well-built physically, moving beautifully. A complete contrast with the mob plodding after him. Shinji would have run like that when he was young. If he hadn't had that thing about being a jazz pianist he would-n't have got TB probably . . . run just like that, moving really sweetly."

"Not yet. I won't be able to listen to what you're saying."

"Yuh."

But he didn't remove his hand. As he went on with his story he slowly fondled the nipple of her breast with the wrinkled tip of his thumb, mas-saging the halo of it with the smooth inside of the same.

"I realized it was a thief they were all running after. That really shook me. I mean, I just didn't seem to be able to take it in, that the man running out there in front was a thief. And while I was still wondering what to do he ran past me. Now I've done it, I thought, but there was a man just behind me who went for him with this terrific tackle. Then all the others came running up, and there was this man sitting astride him who kept on hitting him, and all these kids laughing each time he got hit, all those inno-cent voices, pure and clear like music rising into the deep purple dusk. I just couldn't stand it. He was well built, you know; pretty good-looking too. Why did a man like that have to do something like petty sneak-thieving? Still, they were really vicious to him. Like what they do in a fox hunt. At least I suppose it is, because I've never seen one. Downright cruelty. They didn't have to go that far. . . ."

He'd finished his story, but she stayed quiet with her eyes closed. There was something funny about the expression on her face. He removed his hand from her breast and moved it down her body. He'd been erect for some time, but now it was his turn to ask her if there was something wrong.

She didn't answer. He moved the four fingers of his hand over her thigh and asked her what she was thinking about.

"You really are peculiar, aren't you," she murmured.

"Why?"

He slowly moved his fingers upward, following the soft warmth of the inside of her thighs.

"Feeling sorry for a thief, for heaven's sake."

Her lips were close to his ear as she whispered this, her lips barely moving as she did so, but he felt the shock to the depth of his being. At last he had understood the meaning of all the apparently disparate things that had happened to him that day. His fingers remained where they were, but they were quite listless and inert, all the strength drained out of them. His body was still turned toward her, but his head now rested back again upon the pillow, his eyes staring upward into space. He heaved a deep sigh. He'd spent his day involved in the lives of the pursued, the whole day feeling sorry for men on the run simply because they were running away, and he hadn't been in the least aware of what he was doing or why. There was that grubby poster stuck on the police box, the three armed murderers. The man in the suit who'd robbed the university. The young American in the film on TV. But it wasn't really them he'd been feeling sorry for. It was himself, his past self. That was the real object he had empathized with. The others were only shadows of himself, and today, through them, he had been watching himself, the young Hamada who'd spent the war years as what had then been called a draft resister, fleeing desperately through the whole length and breadth of the land. It was like one of those pornographic photos where the face of a well-known film star is stuck atop the body of a whore, as if quite unconsciously he'd imposed his own face, his own twenty-year-old face, upon that of the thief who'd just been robbing the university.

From the autumn of 1940 to the autumn of 1945 Hamada had been a draft resister. He'd managed to maintain that refusal for five whole years. It was 1940 when the Triple Alliance with Germany and Italy was signed and the puppet regime was set up in China. The Pacific War began at the end of 1941 and came to an end in August 1945. National conscription was the basic thing that sustained the militarist prewar Japanese government, and naturally anyone who rejected conscription faced either the prospect of death at the hands of a firing squad or being sent to one of the most dangerous sectors of the front line, where death was just as inevitable by the guns of the enemy. Resistance meant death, and he had spent five years, the first five years of his twenties, perpetually on the run, constantly living with that desperate possibility. What he saw most often in his darkest dreams was the faces of the military police, but it wasn't only the police, either military or civil, before whom he'd had to play his constant game of deception; rather, it was the total entity known as the country of Japan, its stations, its ports, its towns, since all were the enemies of him alone. But he had gone on running, gone on escaping, and he had won. He'd maintained his refusal right to the end. He was unable to conceive how he'd been able to achieve what could only be considered a miracle, and nor, presumably, could anyone else. Then the war came to an end, the Japanese army was disbanded, and that hostile power, the power of the state, crumbled away as well. Now he was living in peace, a clerk in university administration. Nobody pursued him now; only in his past was he pursued, a past that still forced its way into his present with its constant reproach, a past he tried so hard to forget but that still lived on as it did this day, come back again although he'd thought he was about to dispose of it forever.

His wife's thighs moved a little, and he found his fingers were wet. He wiped his fingertips on the inside of her leg, and this had the same effect as an intentional embrace, for she groaned in pleasure, although Hamada did not notice this misunderstanding, as he was still thinking of other things. Why had he stopped in front of that police box today when he always walked past it without taking the least notice? The poster that had drawn his attention looked as if it had been there for some time, so why today? The answer was simple enough. Today he had received that postcard with the black border. The announcement of her death had sent him back in time, back to the war, back twenty years to the time of his youth; returned to him all the sensations of that time, of fear and hunger, that dreadful, painful longing for something he could never lay his hands upon: his freedom. In the men's room he had been a young man again, slim and frail again, trembling, bathed in cold sweat at the voices outside the window. The face he had seen in the small mirror there had looked like that of a man wanted by the police; sullied by the fading light, it had looked like one of the blurred, spoiled images of the badly printed police poster.

The girl from the pawnbroker's shop in Shikoku had been on the run with him. Now she was dead. During the whole of that last year she had taken complete care of him. She had fed him, lodged him, clothed him. If it hadn't been for her, he would most likely have given himself up. Or simply starved to death. There was no doubt about that. It was called malnutrition at the time, but it was the same thing. He used to complain that they didn't have enough to eat because of her, that lodging would have been much cheaper if he didn't have a woman with him, but when they just had to get hold of railway tickets it was Akiko who went to the station master and pleaded and wept until they got them. Of course, it was always just an act she was putting on. She was good at making the tears come. And she went on getting thinner and thinner, just as he did, and so there was nothing left but to go to her mother's in Shikoku. Why had they done a thing as rash as that? In his own case it was because once he'd committed himself to something he was unable to go back. But in her case? He just didn't know. Was it love? Probably. It was certainly passion. They'd both had that: a passion dedicated to opposing the whole power of the state in his case, and he'd made use of her different passion to keep himself alive. Once he'd succeeded in that, he neatly disposed of her, although it was certainly true that she was the one who'd suggested they should part. But was it because he'd always somehow managed to imply that, once the war was over, their own relationship would inevitably come to an end as well? He wasn't sure. At least he couldn't say that there hadn't always been some implication of that kind. She had always loved talking about Tokyo, about Ginza and Asakusa and getting completely lost and ending up in Nabeya Yokocho, but when the war ended on the fifteenth of August all such talk immediately came to an end. What followed for her was an arranged marriage, as an older man's second wife; divorce; death by cancer. If he was responsible in some way for her death, then he was even more involved in the death of his mother, because she'd committed suicide while he was absent resisting the draft, and the fact was that as the daughter of a military man she must have taken his . . .

"Oh, come on, can't you?"

Yoko made a huge grimace of displeasure, moving her face so close to his left ear that her lips were touching it. He muttered something in reply and she placed her hand upon him, feeling that he was no longer hard or warm. Now he realized it himself, and also that all the persuasion of his wife's hand would have no effect. He wouldn't be able to do it tonight, not like this. Her tongue had made his earlobe damp. It was an unpleasant feeling. The dampness inside the ear itself was even more obnoxious. He certainly wouldn't be able to do it tonight. If she hadn't said that about him feeling sorry for the thief, he wouldn't have noticed anything. It was her fault. She'd sent him back twenty years in time. And his ear still felt unpleasantly damp.

Probably his liberal father had been ashamed of his own feelings, or he might have made his contempt for the military quite clear, but being a local doctor and his own father only in trade, perhaps he felt . . . and anyway he was probably trying to spare Mother's feelings and hide his real opinions, although it would have been clear enough even to a child at the time of the young officers' rebellion what he thought of Mother belonging to the Patriotic Women's League, trying in all sorts of roundabout ways to make her stop because he just didn't like it, although she didn't listen or perhaps didn't understand what he was trying to tell her, since she wasn't all that bright. Father ought to have told her more plainly what he thought, there was no need to make all those obscure hints; and her family paid his school fees, it was true, so perhaps she had to take that into consideration, but he really hated that red sash she wore, with the color fading in places on it and . . .

Yoko was trying to coax his wilted object back into life with her fingers and tongue, but that was no use either. Occasionally he felt her teeth upon it. He didn't like that. He didn't like it being made all wet like that either, and he particularly disliked her hair brushing against his belly. The regular spurts of breath coming out of her nostrils he found positively comic. Then she turned to him like a diver who has just broken the surface of the water, her face emerging next to his.

"What's gone wrong with you?"

"Not sure. It just suddenly. . . . Let's make it tomorrow. Tomorrow evening. There's a party tomorrow. After that."

"I suppose you are getting a bit past it."

She went back to her own place.

"God, these sheets are cold."

He said nothing. She had her back firmly turned toward him, so he turned his on her. He switched off the bedside light, and the hard click echoed back from the white plaster of the ceiling. Better do something about it tomorrow morning, he supposed, and she could make as much fun as she liked about him being past it, but after all there was an age difference between them, and she ought to be prepared for things like that—particularly when the past suddenly came back, much more real than the present ever was. He heard her breath suddenly quickening in the dark, and now she was making little suppressed cries. She was getting her own back on him, just like she had that time before when he'd come back drunk late at night and she'd been waiting up for him, and they hadn't done anything for ten days but there was nothing he could do about it in that state. He wondered if she made those sounds when she was doing it with him, low, weird sounds, almost gruesome, a persistent rhythm that broke upon him in one slow wave after another. That time she had kept the light switched on so that he could see her doing it, deliberately shaming him into knowing this kind of woman sometimes had to do things like that, and what he was thinking at the time was that he already knew and he'd just been pretending not to hear before. Mother had died and Akiko was dead. When Akiko's mother died there would be another black-bordered postcard, and he'd be pushed back into the past for another day or two, perhaps longer, into a worse depression than he felt now. Her voice had reminded him that time before somehow of when he'd been on a boat in the Inland Sea and he'd seen a great swarm of jellyfish in the clear, bright water; two or three hundred of them there must have been at least, perhaps even as many as a thousand, all lined up close to each other. It had been like looking down at the cramped houses in Ginza from a high building; they were like round, soft, white umbrellas, and on each tiny umbrella there were four pink spots making a perfect rectangle, and the spots trembled and swayed on the backs of the brilliant shining jellyfish, trembling and swaying. . . . He had gone on listening to her until it was over and she had gone off to sleep, while he didn't feel like sleep at all because the drunkenness had worn off gradually and it had been so cold, being winter, but he would be able to fall off in a while, and while he'd been thinking so an unpleasant hole seemed to open up somewhere in his mind and he'd been drawn down into it. . . .

It was still going on. Taking a hell of a time over it, the two fingers of the right hand kneading and threading, lighly beating out that pointless, continual rhythm, over and over, can't wait till the morning, waiting for it for how many days and nights now, and swarms of jellyfish with neat, pink marks upon them, not being up to it, being too old for it, and he'd kept quiet about it but it was her fault, her fault, just those few words of hers and suddenly it was all impossible. But he regretted nothing. If he started regretting anything, it would mean that he thought he'd been wrong. But he hadn't been wrong. He'd done the right thing. There hadn't been anything else he could have done. The only thing he could have done was to run away, to refuse to become a soldier. He'd been right. He still felt he'd been right. The only thing was that he hadn't foreseen all that would happen afterward, all that would follow from that moment of refusal, all the totally unexpected things that had come about because of it. If he had known, would he still have done it? Would he have changed his mind, or just not cared? He'd known it was bound to look bad for his mother and father, but he'd imagined they'd be able to live with it. His mother's being in the Patriotic Women's League was only a form of socializing, anyway. That was what he'd thought. He had just hoped for the best. In fact, he hadn't worked things out seriously when he'd made that decision. If he'd not thought like that he'd never have been able to do it. All his mother seemed to be serious about was her singing lessons and her craze for the theater, so did she really feel so bad about what he'd done that she'd deliberately taken an overdose of sleeping pills, or had she simply made a mistake? Perhaps she'd just been feeling lonely and depressed. But had he been a part of that loneliness, a major cause of that depression? After all, it wasn't just that he wasn't there, but why he wasn't there. But how could one die in a meaningless war? How could one go about killing people for no reason? Regret was useless. Regret was a bottomless swamp, a quicksand in which if once you set your foot. . . . A refusal to cause death to some led to the deaths of others. There was Shinji. Certainly he liked playing the piano, but he became a pianist too because that was a way of making money. At the time Hamada couldn't get a job and was just killing time all day. If he hadn't refused to be called up (and assuming he hadn't got himself killed at the front), his mother wouldn't have committed suicide, perhaps, and his father wouldn't have gone to pieces like that so early, perhaps, and Shinji wouldn't have got TB, perhaps. Then what about Akiko? Well, maybe she would. . . . But what could he possibly imagine about her?

She seemed to have finished. Would she go to the bathroom now, or just go quietly off to sleep in that state? She was young, of course. You soon drop off to sleep when you're young. Probably hear her quiet breathing quite soon. He couldn't seem to sleep himself, but he knew he'd be asleep in a while. When he'd seen that postcard that morning, he'd thought it was all over at last, but nothing is ever over; the past is always clinging to you, never letting go, and then suddenly when you don't feel it is close at all it is there right next to you, all in a moment, threatening, bearing down upon you, just like being in a taxi and hardly noticing the radio is switched on until it suddenly turns a corner and the reception becomes true again, the song blaring forth in a great clatter of sound, in its inexorable presence.

two

The next morning Hamada got up much later than usual. Yoko was in a very good mood, cheerfully preparing breakfast and waiting upon him, also eating very heartily herself. Hamada, however, did not feel all that hungry and only managed one slice of bread, although the raw vegetables and hot tea felt pleasant in his parched throat. Finally he left the house at nine o'clock. It was a bright, clear morning, and he stopped at the corner tobacconist to telephone to the university that he would be in rather late. His normal office hours were from eight to four-thirty.

When he got off the train, he started to walk in the opposite direction of his place of work. He was going to the post office to send off the money for the funeral. Up until he'd left the house he'd been constantly thinking what he would reply when Yoko asked him how much he was going to send to Shikoku, but his wife had been satisfied that morning and had apparently forgotten all about the postcard. There was practically nobody in the gray post office. Most of the windows were closed, and at the one that was open the clerk was idly puffing a cigarette. Hamada purchased a money order, and also received a message form. He noticed there were a number of set messages of condolence he could choose from, but they were too stereotyped to convey anything of what he felt, although the message he finally managed to concoct, after ruminating quite a while with the post office pencil, secured by a piece of string, in his hand, was only as conventional and hackneyed as they:

Painfully grieved by sad news Akiko's death: Shokichi Hamada.

He handed over the message form, requesting that it should be delivered in a special envelope, and the young post office clerk nodded while reading through what Hamada had written. He read it through two or three times before apologetically asking Hamada if he would mind reading it out loud to him, and Hamada obliged, upon which the young man's attitude changed abruptly, all apologetic concern vanishing as, tutting ostentatiously, he picked up his red pen and ruthlessly rewrote, in the proper, modern way, all the old-fashioned characters Hamada had used. He didn't even look at Hamada as he asked for the money, merely shaking his head over the message form. Hamada paid up and left.

He walked toward the bus stop in front of the station, overwhelmed by a feeling of how horribly old he was. He was still only an hour or so later than usual, yet the rush-hour bustle he normally experienced had almost completely abated, so he presumed that must have induced in him the sensation of being some old man in retirement who no longer had to go to work. But this explanation was quite unreal, as he was aware as soon as it occurred to him. It was simply the fact of having his old-fashioned characters rewritten that had made him feel suddenly out of date, unwanted by the new age. Naturally enough, documents at the university had to be written in the new style, and he had never found any difficulty in complying, but when he was at home and had to write a letter or postcard he always seemed to find himself reverting automatically to the old script. His relationship to the writing of his own language, then, was that he wrote new style when wearing a European suit and shoes, but old style when he had changed out of them back into Japanese dress; and the fact that he had accidentally used the old script when dressed in the new way had come as a shock to him: this confusion of the neat compartments into which his life had been fashioned aroused all the melancholy a man of still comparatively few years must feel when he has been forcibly retired, realizing that he has no longer any proper role to play in society.

"The mere remnant of a man": the phrase suddenly crossed his mind, a phrase he'd read somewhere, but where or when he couldn't remember. That was exactly what he was now, he thought, suffering the illusion that somehow he'd been in tune with society as it had existed before the war.

He got on the end of the line, but two or three buses must have just left one after the other and the next was a long time coming. He remembered the way the post office clerk had clicked his tongue in annoyance, and this aroused genuine anger at the thought that a man who could still write in the old style ought properly to be an object of respect, yet it was something for which he'd been despised. There was something really odd about a world in which things like that could happen; yet, of course, the world had changed a lot, he had to admit. It was like the view from that bus only yesterday: things had changed completely. As he consoled himself with the idea, he began thinking about places that had been victims of this violent change. There was that temple in Aoyama, for example, where he used to play as a child, the grounds of which were now only a third of their original size. Of course, things that were big when you were small looked small when you were grown up, but that place genuinely *had* grown smaller and so now looked positively minute. First of all the Olympic highway had taken one chunk, then an apartment block had been built, and now the inner gate displayed itself to view between two large billboards advertising restaurants (one Western and one Japanese-style). The priest must have made a pile out of it, but what about the children who had no place to play? There'd be no more catching dragonflies as they perched on the gravestones, no hunting cicadas on the thick trunks of the pines. Still, there weren't any dragonflies or cicadas in Tokyo anymore; no butterflies, either. Probably there weren't any insects left in the whole country, for that matter.

Among the confused voices of this morning in late spring, in front of the station, Hamada felt a deep longing for the natural sounds of his child-hood, for the high-pitched whirr of the cicada, noting that other kinds of song had disappeared as well. You no longer heard people crying their wares in the street, and some of the tradesmen themselves, the pipe mender, for example, had vanished completely. The goldfish seller merely made his rounds in silence now; the baked sweet potato seller used a microphone, and the sound was of particularly appalling quality. He smiled to himself. He was remembering a time last summer when the cry of the bamboo pole seller, which he didn't seem to have heard for ages, so surprised him he stuck his head out the window of his flat, although he hadn't the least intention of buying anything, and was further astounded to see that the old man selling the poles was dressed in a crepe shirt and blue jeans. Obviously he wouldn't be smoking the old-style long pipe, but filter cigarettes instead.

The line had grown much longer, and Hamada realized he was at the head of it. He turned around and saw one or two faces he knew, and bowed in their direction. They belonged to an assistant professor of economics and a professor of Shinto, as well as someone he was not quite sure about but thought was a part-time lecturer, a professor or assistant professor at some other university. He noticed that none of them was wearing a hat; nor was he wearing one himself, for that matter. It was the greatest difference in men's dress between now and before the war. Certainly some of the older generation still wore hats, but that was normally for some particular reason, such as to conceal his gray hair in the case of Horikawa or his baldness in the case of Kobayakawa. Then everyday greetings had grown so abrupt since the war, one blunt word seeming to cover almost everything, while the quite commonplace words of thanks, of saying hello on the phone, of saying good-bye, had taken on the antique air of the outmoded past. Hamada muttered the word "good-bye" to himself, and it reminded him that Akiko had died. There was always something mysterious about the death of someone close to you; it remained unreal unless you had witnessed it with your own eyes. Perhaps that was why people dropped everything and dashed off when they heard someone was dying, so they would be able to see it themselves and really know. He still did not truly believe that she was dead. If she were to ring him up that afternoon, asking him to take her to the Olympic stadium or the sky lounge of some hotel, or any of the tourist spots of the new Tokyo, he would not think it in the least strange. What seemed truly incredible was that he should have been able to send off that telegram of condolence to Akiko's mother (or perhaps to Akiko herself?). Then he remembered the summer of the last year of the war, a sunny afternoon twenty years ago, when he'd suddenly realized he couldn't hear the sound of a single cicada, and he'd asked Akiko if they had them in Shikoku. They'd been standing in a terraced field, and she'd been putting tomatoes in a basket while he'd been working with the hoe. And she'd laughed, telling him not to be so scornful of "us poor country folk."

Two buses arrived together, and the line began to move.

He clocked in and went immediately to the Registry Office, where he apologized to the chief registry clerk and to the other assistant registry clerk, Nishi, for being late. Naturally neither of them had any words of reproach. Nishi was talking about the tremendous welcome he'd been given at the high school in Takaoka where he'd just been on business. He spoke in his normal, grossly exaggerated style and produced his customary loud bellow of laughter, his mouth wide open yet still achieving an oddly guttural effect. Hamada found neither to his liking. When Nishi's relation of his travels came to a momentary halt, Hamada was able to give the chief an account of yesterday's conference and then get on with his own work.

They were fully staffed today, with both the chief and Nishi at their desks, but there were far fewer visitors and phone calls than yesterday, and Hamada found he had time on his hands. In fact, the only phone calls were about the party being given that evening for the various department heads and their main assistants, and it appeared that the person who was to ensure the smooth running of the proceedings was to be not Hamada but Nishi. Around eleven o'clock, Hamada was going through some documents related to the library and noticed there were two or three matters that needed to be discussed. He thought about doing this over the phone, but decided if he went in person there was a better chance of his getting his own way, and he left the registry, vaguely noting that Nishi didn't seem to be around, and telling one of the staff where he was going.

He passed through a bright reading room, then along an equally well-lit corridor before turning into another that was conspicuously dark, at the end of which was the library administration office. He made a formal knock on the door and walked straight in. The room was full of library staff working, most of whom were girls since few men worked there, and the first thing he noticed as he was about to enter the large, bright room was the sudden grimace that appeared on the face of the girl seated immediately before him. She looked extremely perplexed, but it was a perplexity she obviously could do nothing about, for her face turned quite pale. He automatically hesitated, stopping awkwardly in the doorway, with the result he was able to overhear two people making insulting remarks about him. They were both concealed behind a bookcase, but it was clear from their voices that it was Nishi and an assistant librarian called Hanamura.

"It's only natural that a squirt who was scared of Roosevelt and Chiang Kai-shek should have been afraid of a burglar."

That was Nishi talking.

"Not so much scared, you know. He just let him go, being a fellow member of the criminal fraternity."

That was Hanamura's voice.

"Criminal fraternity. Mmm, not bad. A criminal; of course. You know, after they shot a draft dodger they used to wrap the box in a cloth made out of his prison uniform. Just to make the point absolutely clear, I suppose. Hah, hah, hah."

Another voice, obviously Hamamura's, joined in laughing with Nishi, and at that moment the whole room had gone deathly quiet, as if to allow Hamada an uninterrupted audience of the jeering laughter aimed at him. He stepped back into the hallway.

He walked along the dark corridor, then the bright one, then along the passageway that led from the library to the main building, sometimes acknowledging members of faculty and staff who passed him and sometimes not. Did all of them know about what had happened yesterday, about the burglary and . . . ? When he was back at his desk in the registry he rang up the library and gave the librarian, Watanabe, as businesslike an account of the matters he'd gone to discuss as he could. Both the voice of the girl who answered the phone and that of Watanabe sounded highly embarrassed. The business was easily settled, however, and he put down the receiver and tried to get down to the work on his desk again, the desk with the black-bordered postcard still there under its glass top. But he found it impossible to concentrate on his papers for any length of time. Had he done the right thing just now? He wasn't at all sure, although he did feel certain that in the past he wouldn't have just walked away like that, at least, not without some kind of struggle inside. But what else could he have done, and how?

The twenty-six-year-old Hamada was sitting in a shabby easy chair in Horikawa's house. He was wearing one of his father's suits that had been sent off into the country for storage with a number of other possessions to escape the bombing, and so it stank of mothballs. The easy chair Horikawa was sitting in looked particularly worn, and the white cover it had on had clearly been made some years ago out of something originally designed for some other purpose. It was like everything else, like padded cloth air raid helmets made out of quilts, like Sunday-best breeches made out of *haori* jackets of the finest Oshima material, everything transformed into something practical; and in the summer of 1946 there was still no way of replacing the quilts or the Oshima haori jackets or Horikawa's chair covers.

On the mantelpiece were two framed photographs leaning against the wall, both in sepia, one of a heavily moustached man and the other of a woman with her hair done up in the old-style chignon. Hamada guessed they must be Horikawa's parents. Since it was June, naturally no fire had been lit, but no doubt that would have been the same if he had come six months before. The fact that there was cube sugar to put in the tea struck him as a tremendous sign of opulence.

Horikawa finished reading the letter he'd been given and said,

"I see. It's a pity Shinjo didn't let me know about this a bit earlier. June is rather a bad time, you see. The decision isn't mine to make, you know, so I can't be sure how it will turn out. There are some pretty funny types on the board. Still, if we act with prudence . . ."

"I should be most grateful for anything you could do."

Hamada bowed his head in great reverence, but Horikawa seemed irritated by this heavy formality, and changed the subject.

"Shinjo was always very close to your father, I believe? He seems particularly worried about you, for a number of reasons apparently. Is your father very ill?"

"He's confined to bed at the moment."

"Oh, that's too bad. It's just not good to get paralysis in your fifties; not good at all. Overworked during the war, I suppose. There were no young doctors around, so the old ones had to do their share of the work as well. I remember what a martinet he was when we were together in the varsity eight. He really used to put us younger ones through our paces."

Hamada had arrived home from Shikoku in November of the previous year, and one night only two months later he was playing cards with his younger brother Shinji and Hiroko, the sole remaining nurse, when his father came back from making a house call. He looked no different than usual, but when he was in the room next door changing his clothes, he suddenly seemed to lean with a great thud against the partition door and then collapsed. Hiroko immediately ran screaming into that room, and the two brothers followed.

As his father was bedridden, Hamada had to find work, and he had to find it quickly. Rebuilding the house that had been burned down during the war had cost a great deal of money, and except for this house in Aoyama and its adjoining land, they now had no possessions or financial resources to speak of. For the first time Hamada understood that being a local doctor was the same hand-to-mouth existence as running the local bathhouse, both occupations depending entirely on the earnings of that day for the food to be eaten that evening. Shinji started earning something by playing the piano, and Hamada began to get really anxious about his own prospects. He tried enough places, but there were very few jobs in electrical engineering at the time, and his record as a draft resister didn't seem to be doing him much good. While he was wondering what he could possibly do, an old friend of his father's called Shinjo paid a visit to see how he was, and he said he would make inquiries about work for him to Horikawa.

When he'd left the house, Hamada had been thinking that Shinjo would have certainly worked out what the relationship between his father and the nurse Hiroko was, and relayed the information to Horikawa as well.

Once Mother died, Father had established a liaison with her. In fact, if one was to take Father's word for it, the whole thing had started before that, so perhaps Mother had been given one more reason to kill herself. As Hamada drank his tea and looked at Horikawa, he felt a number of times almost positive that the old man must know.

"I'll need to have a copy of your curriculum vitae."

"Yes, of course," said Hamada, and produced the envelope he had brought with him. The other looked at it for a while, then gave a quick little yelp of surprise. They both remained silent for a few moments, until Horikawa said,

"Look, there really is no need for you to record your military service."

After listing his educational career and employment record, Hamada had written the following:

Military Service: Refused conscription from October 1940.
Traveled all around country, returning to Tokyo November 1945.
Rewards & Punishments: None.

"All right," said Hamada.

"You must understand that it is simply not customary to record military service on a c.v. form. That's all I'm saying."

Hamada lowered his head apologetically as the form was returned to him. Horikawa said he was going to the university and would see him to the station. Then he opened the door and howled at some unseen person, presumably as an indication that she was to attend to his needs.

When what was required had apparently been satisfactorily performed, Hamada swung his bag (one made out of the stiff padding for a woman's sash sometime during the war) over his shoulder and walked with Horikawa along a road between allotment fields, broken here and there by holes made for sheltering from air raids that had still not been filled in. As they were passing a hospital, Horikawa decided to mention a subject quite unrelated to what they were then talking about.

"From what Shinjo told me, I gather you have a rather beautiful nurse still in your service."

"We've only got the one nurse. I wouldn't say she's all that good looking, but, well, she's certainly very sweet natured."

"That is the main thing, of course."

Horikawa seemed to have been reassured by that and went back to their
original subject.

The telephone rang. Hamada picked up the receiver and listened to a tiny,
barely intelligible voice that informed him:

"About that matter we were discussing just now. Well, that's really
Nishi's province, isn't it? I believe he's in the library at the moment, so
why don't you try him there?"

He pretended to be reading through some documents, but he was
instead recalling that at the time, Horikawa hadn't actually promised to say
nothing to anyone about it. Quite obviously he had talked too. But even if
he had, it could hardly be considered the divulging of some top secret, and
it might well be that Horikawa had been obliged on some occasion to give
the real facts to someone. Anyway, Hamada didn't feel he was in any position to make an issue of the matter. Still, even if quite a lot of people might
know about his past, the kind of humiliating experience he'd just encoun-
tered had never happened before, nor anything like it. As he listened to the
clicking of the abacus, to the noises of people at work and of the visitors
who came and went, to the ringing of the telephone and all the normal bustle of the Registry Office, he recalled the sound of Nishi's laughter and the
great hush that had suddenly fallen over the library administration office,
and the very weirdness of the contrast made him ponder the rightness of
what those two had said about him. Was he really a criminal? Certainly up
to August 15, 1945, draft resistance had been a more serious crime than
robbery and murder. In fact, there had been no more serious crime. But
even if it was true that after they'd executed a draft resister they wrapped
the box containing his remains in red cloth used for prison uniforms, that
still proved nothing; it still didn't mean that draft resistance was the act of
a criminal, certainly not since August 15, at least.

Yet he could not forget the sound of Nishi's laughter piercing the frozen
silence of that room. It would not go away but stayed to torment him. He

imagined himself as he had been twenty years before, when he'd written down the truth about himself in public form for anyone to see. If he'd still felt as he had then, he could imagine what he would have done. And he imagined it. He imagined himself walking right on into that room, and the words he would have addressed to Nishi and Hamamura.

"Look, don't get me wrong. I didn't refuse to join the army because I was scared of Chiang Kai-shek or Roosevelt. I wasn't afraid of being killed. I just didn't like the idea of killing people. And I've always hated war and armies as long as I can remember. I was just born like that. For a start, I was bound to've been put in the Signal Corps because I went to radio engineering college, and the chances of being killed in an outfit like that were almost nothing. So I didn't resist the draft because I was scared of getting killed. Anyone can see that. Look, you can say anything you like about me. That's up to you. But there's one thing I want you to be quite clear about. I still think what I did was right. I don't feel one bit ashamed of it. If you want proof, just have a look at my c.v. I wrote myself. It's all down there in black and white. Draft resister. Go on—take a look. You'll find it in the files in the registry, the second cabinet on the right. . . ."

When he'd gotten this far, Hamada glanced at the cabinet in question, a large brown cupboard with a list of the main events of the university year stuck on its door (together with the menu of the local noodles delivery shop), and called an immediate halt to this fantasy hectoring. The curriculum vitae lodged in there was the revised version. There was nothing on it about his military service. What was immediately recorded after his employment record was the section entitled "Rewards & Punishments." It was still "None." Nobody had punished him.

That form was misleading in other ways as well. In his employment record, all that was written down was the period of less than six months he'd spent working for a small radio company immediately after he left college. He hadn't described all the things he'd done during the five years he'd spent wandering the length and breadth of the land, just to keep himself alive. He'd started off as a radio repairman and ended up as a parasite at Akiko's house, although a blunter (and truer) description would be not "parasite" but "fancy man."

He became aware that Nishi had come back, sensing his presence as he entered the room. Nishi sat down noisily at his own desk, which was next to Hamada's. Then he swiveled his chair in Hamada's direction. His complexion was quite normal, pale and smooth, but his eyes had a tenseness about them Hamada had never seen before. Nishi said in a low voice,

"Sorry about that just now. I gather you must have overheard some stupid joke I made. Only a joke, you know. There's no need for you to take it to heart."

Hamada said nothing in reply, simply making a slight nod of the head. After a very slight pause, Nishi turned back to face his own desk. It seemed that nobody else in the office had noticed this exchange between the two, certainly not the chief clerk; but Hamada felt that the way he had responded, his silence, his slight nod, his inability to respond verbally to the overture from the other, was a mistake on his part, the first really serious mistake he'd made since entering university employment. In fact, he had tried to say something, but the words wouldn't come. It was just like his inability to stand in the path of that man yesterday. And now this other man had been put in a position where he'd had to apologize, and his apology had been turned down. He certainly wouldn't forget that in a hurry. It hadn't been much of an apology, it was true. Hardly an apology at all. But Hamada had made an error, and he knew it. And after all the trouble he'd taken all these years to avoid upsetting anybody, to get through the days without anything going wrong. There really had been something funny with him since yesterday morning.

People came in delivering lunches from the canteen and two of the local noodle shops. It was the midday break, and there was a lot of coming and going in the corridor. Everyone in the office started to stand up and carry plates and bowls about. The messenger girl was going around pouring tea. The delivery boy from the eel restaurant arrived, bringing something fairly expensive looking, but Hamada made do with the cheap lunch provided by the staff canteen. He noted with amusement that all the married men had only very plain food, while it was the bachelors, almost to a man, who indulged in comparative luxuries. He pointed this out to Nishi, seated next to him eating exactly the same lunch, but Nishi didn't seem to find the observation amusing at all. He did not even smile as he replied,

"No, it just means they haven't had any breakfast, that's all."

Obviously Hamada was perfectly well aware of that, but it seemed ridiculous to point out he'd been making a joke about the wretchedness of the married state. Also, he couldn't be sure if Nishi's response had been deliberately ill tempered or merely an indication of genuine obtuseness in understanding a casual jest. Nishi left half of his lunch. Hamada felt like leaving some of his, but forced himself to eat it all up since he didn't like to waste food, a habit that must have been established by those five years during the war.

Some of the younger staff invited a few of the girls to go outside and play volleyball, and out they all trooped with the ball. Hamada thought about joining them, but hesitated. Almost certainly girls from the library would be playing as well, and his presence would only embarrass them. While he was wondering about this, suddenly the idea of playing volleyball aroused a sense of distaste at the thought of going outside into the bright sunshine. He thought of leaping to strike the ball and how the sun would dazzle his eyes at that moment, a sun as unreal and repugnant as a globe of luminous vermillion in the light of day. So he leaned back in his chair and sipped his tea, while Nishi and a staff member called Murakami started playing *shogi* in a corner of the room. There was an unwritten rule that board games like *go* and *shogi* could only be played during the lunch hour or while on night school duty. Nishi and Murakami had always been on friendly terms, but they looked particularly so today. Nishi had originally been under the wing of the executive director Horikawa had managed to throw out, and after that he attached himself to Kobayakawa; Murakami had gotten his university post through Kobayakawa's recommendation. Hamada glanced occasionally at the two of them while flipping through the pages of a magazine that had arrived in today's mail, and he decided Murakami was making increased efforts to butter up Nishi because he'd decided Nishi was going to be the next chief registry clerk.

The magazine Hamada was reading was a slim, privately published affair called *Totality*. The editor, also the sole contributor, who not only wrote everything but did the publishing and distribution as well, was the second son of a Shinto priest and a graduate of the university, who'd previously had a job on a trade paper that he appeared to have lost. His name was Inuzuka, and his magazine consisted of some brief, inoffensive "essays" sandwiched between various bits of gossip, either of a flattering, time-serving kind or exposing some supposed scandal, or even just outbursts of plain malevolence. Inevitably the magazine's editorial position tended way over to the right. He was always turning up at the university, even coming into the Registry Office to pester people into buying his rag, and eventually Hamada had paid up and become a subscriber, and each time a new number arrived he wondered how anybody could make a living doing this, although there were, in fact, another two graduates producing virtually the same thing, with the result that Hamada subscribed to three different magazines.

He managed to reach the end of a dreary account of how butterbur blossoms make all the difference in the flavor of miso soup, reflecting that this dull piece could surely only have been put in to fill up the page in order to get the magazine out on time and deciding he'd had enough. As he turned over the page, however, he noticed there was a lengthy denunciation of the young professor of economics he'd seen in the bus line that morning, although it was hard to work out if the attack was on the professor himself, or the dean of the economics faculty, or perhaps just the university authorities in general.

Having thus considered the ten volumes that appear to be essential to Professor Nomoto's economic research, what do we find? We find, to our unrelieved disgust, that two are by Karl Marx, of all people. It is a complete outrage, a blatant contradiction of the whole spirit upon which our university is founded. I may only be a lowly graduate of this university, but I am certainly not prepared to have the red flag fluttering from the rooftop of our newly rebuilt alma mater.

Hamada was about to deposit *Totality* into the wastepaper basket at his feet but changed his mind. If, by the slightest chance, Inuzuka should come to hear of it, the consequences might be bad. One couldn't be too careful, he thought, and he was in the habit of disposing of magazines of that kind, as well as anything the university itself published, by taking them all home and burning them in the incinerator there. He stood up and went to the corner where the two were playing *shogi*, reaching past them to take down the newspaper file. They only took one paper at home, and sometimes he liked to see what the other papers had to say, a feeling particularly strong at this moment, as he wanted to get rid of the taste of what he'd just been reading.

Unsurprisingly, that was not what happened. The recital of suicides, murders, traffic accidents, and especially a long article about war (not written in quite the same appalling style as *Totality*, but not all that different) could hardly be expected to have any soothing function. But Hamada did not stop immediately, probably because he felt vaguely that news about incidents he'd already come across in his own paper at home was bound to be uninteresting, and he turned to the features page. Here there was a large photograph of a landscape at the northern tip of Hokkaido, and this and the accompanying paragraphs both gave him pleasure. Spring had at last arrived at those distant shores, and the sunlight fell gently upon the sea and the land, quiet and soft (probably an effect deliberately aimed at by the photographer), with none of the harsh brilliance of the south. There was a small map of Hokkaido just below the picture, and he recalled how he'd spent the summer of 1942 there, starting from Hakodate and traveling over a great portion of the island, but never as far north as Wakkanai, which he regretted now. He remembered the Moriya Department Store in Hakodate, a tall building painted a surprising green, and a line of poplar trees before a long row of low houses facing a wide road in Sapporo, the leaves as white as paper, and when they fluttered in the wind, that was like the sound of rustling paper. He'd gone as far north as Asahikawa, so why not to Wakkanai? Then he remembered. He'd been in Asahikawa in August, and so exhausted by the heat he'd been foolish enough to allow the local paper, which was very short of material, to take a photo of him. Luckily the picture that appeared was very blurred, as was normal in regional newspapers at the time, but he'd still felt he ought to be prudent, and he left the island and went south again. Even the heat of Asahikawa felt pleasant to him in memory.

But this pleasant mingling of the present and the past didn't go on for long. After noisily turning over another two pages, he came across a short lead article that made him frown. The article appeared to be suggesting that since Japan had become so powerful a country, it should now behave like a major power and acquire the hydrogen bomb, thereby increasing the pride the Japanese people would be able to take in their own land; this was expressed in so slovenly a way, either because the writer had produced a rush job or perhaps because that was his natural style, that Hamada could not be quite sure what precisely he was getting at, but a second reading suggested that his first interpretation had been right.

He was not particularly shocked by the point of view itself. He had, in fact, heard it bawled out by drunkards a number of times already. What surprised him was that this farcical view of things should be expressed, apparently seriously and with no trepidation, in a respectable newspaper. The wind of change had turned, and he hadn't realized it until now. The deep sense of unease this aroused led to another realization: the fact that he'd felt able to write down his wartime record on his c.v. then was because he'd been perfectly well aware that the general mood of society immediately after the war was one that permitted antiwar sentiments. To recognize that he'd been willing to write down something like that because he'd known, at least unconsciously, he'd be able to get away with it did not please him, and even if it hadn't been the main impetus behind his action, he certainly couldn't deny that it must have been present somewhere. And could it also be that the reason he hadn't confronted Nishi in the library and argued the rightness of his wartime behavior was that he already knew somewhere at the back of his mind that the times had changed? Changed they certainly had. This was a different society now. Hamada looked around him, sensing the existence outside and enclosing this Registry Office of the university, and beyond that Tokyo, and farther beyond the whole country itself, becoming at last aware that not only had society been changing in a way that at some stage had become disadvantageous to himself but its enmity was now aimed at him personally as he sat there in that room. The strength of this awareness transformed it into a feeling of self-pity, a sense of complete solitude like that of a dog abandoned in an arctic waste, and then into a trembling of real fear; but that also changed into a rejection of this new, small, terrified self he'd become, for since when had he been the kind of man who had to depend so meekly upon the various currents of the outside world? He could get by without worrying himself about them; hadn't he spent five years in the past going exactly contrary to the ideas by which everyone else was living?

The boy came from the eel restaurant to collect the empties. An assistant from one of the departments came to get some ink and tea. Hamada put back the newspaper file and returned to his desk. Due to the placement of the overhead strip lighting, he could see his own face reflected in the desk's glass top, and in that poor mirror he observed the face of a fat, forty-five-year-old middle-aged man, with the eyes of a slim youth of twenty-one. Then the other people in the office who'd been playing volleyball came back, first the one with the ball, then the other young men and women, all with gleaming faces, cheerfully chatting to each other as they drank tea. He smelled the odor of sweat drifting from their bodies. He stood up to pour himself another cup of tea and felt himself drawn into their talk, his depression gradually lifting as the lunchtime break came to an end.

Then for a while he was fully occupied with his work, reading through documents, writing in alterations, stamping them, and when he stopped for a while he realized Akiko's funeral would be in progress now, for the lunch hour ended at one o'clock. He looked at the clock and saw it was nearly two; he wondered if it was already over or just about to be. In the provinces they normally had a funeral procession from the house to the temple. There was nothing on the postcard saying this wouldn't be done. Things had hardly changed at all in the country; their customs were pretty much the same as ever.

Old Koyama of the local neighborhood association office got hurriedly to his feet and went out in front of the shop, turning his back on Hamada and holding himself erect and straight. Hamada had no idea why the old man had come here in the first place, but while he'd been mending the clock Koyama had sat with him discussing what should be done to finish off Chiang Kai-shek, and so he felt impelled to go outside and join him, slipping on the *geta* that belonged to the owner of the clockmaker's shop. Two swallows flew over their heads, then another, cutting their way incisively through the air. Down the road strewn with hard-baked horse dung came a funeral procession. At the head of the procession walked a man wearing a people's uniform and carrying the flag of some other neighborhood association. Hamada seemed to know the man's face, but he had only come to live in Yokote a month before, so he did not immediately recognize him as the local barber. Two people followed after him, both bearing white banners, then a man wearing the uniform of the Youth League. The banners had large letters written on them, looking as if they'd been soaked in rain. Hamada read as far as IN MEMORY OF PRIVATE . . . , and was glad that he'd come out to watch, for it was deemed patriotic to do so. But this joy soon turned into more confused, perplexed feelings, as the sense that this young man had died in his stead filled his mind to overflowing. It was the same experience he'd had a number of times before on encountering a procession of this kind, in Miyazaki, in Kagoshima, and once already since he'd come to Akita Prefecture. When he saw relatives holding the box containing the ashes of some dead soldier, on trains or at a station, the momentary feeling that he himself was still alive was immediately followed, or even preceded, by this intolerable sense that he should have died and not the other. As he now watched the long procession passing by, first in two columns, then in three, he did his best to pour derision on his sense of guilt. Nobody had died for him; it was as foolish as the belief of the lamas that when a living buddha died he was immediately reborn as some man child whom they instantly went forth to seek. In fact it was even more absurd than that, since the idea of someone dying in one's place made less sense than that of being reborn as somebody else. There was no basis for any such assumption, any more than there was for believing that one of the three swallows that had flown overhead was a reincarnation of the man who had died.

Two men, both dressed in black, came carrying poles with white paper lanterns hanging from them, then two more men, dressed in *happi* coats with cloth caps, bearing artificial flowers. Two girls holding small bunches of live flowers were dressed in the navy blue uniform of the local girls' school, while two more girls carrying large wreaths wore black, to which a small, white cloth was attached. He was not sure what the white cloth signified; mourning, probably. Four men came after them, two in suits carrying large candles with a flower pattern on them, and two in people's uniforms with even larger candles. At that point the two columns became three, with finally a boy in his mid-teens carrying a box covered in white cloth before him, suspended by a white cloth around his neck, two men in black bearing cylindrical paper lanterns walking on either side of him. He also wore a piece of white cloth, attached to his sleeve by a safety pin. He had a thin neck and over-red cheeks. An old man walked immediately behind him, the same white mark of presumably mourning stuck to the shoulder of his black, formal dress, a sprig of green bamboo in his hand, trying very hard to hold himself stiff and upright. As the remains of the dead man were carried by them, old Koyama lowered his head reverentially, as did Hamada. The old man must be the grandfather. No father, it seemed. He'd not caught sight of anyone who looked like the mother, either. The old man must have planned to have his grandson marry early, settle down, and take over the household. Now he had died in the war. Poor old man; the war had ruined all his plans for the future. Hamada raised his head again. He died in my place. But that was insane; nobody had died for him. Lamaists might believe he had, of course. Yet even if the dead man had not taken his place, somebody most surely had, the young man called up to fill the place he had deserted. Did that man have a younger brother with a thin neck?

When the funeral procession had gone, the two went back into the shop. Hamada commented on the magnificence of the funeral, and Koyama said that was because it was for the young master of the one timber merchant in Yokote, and the way he spoke suggested some pride in his native place for having a splendid merchant of that kind. Hamada had learned to understand the Akita dialect reasonably well. Koyama thanked him for mending the neighborhood association office radio, commenting on the excellence of the reception they now got, and begging "Sugiura" to have a look at the one he had at home, since it really made him feel bad to think he might have to miss the program that night, one of those tearjerker ballad recitals.

Hamada/Sugiura hadn't accepted anything for the previous repair job, and clearly the old man had had difficulty finding the words for this second request; as he went on repairing the clock, he experienced a sense of relief at realizing why Koyama had been sitting around for so long. He'd been plucking up courage to ask him to mend his radio, nothing more. Rice was about to come under rationing, and he'd been worried Koyama might have come to plague him about his registration papers, saying they were urgently needed. He'd done this twice already, and both times Hamada had said he'd had to write off to Nobeoka for them, and it might take quite a while. In July of the previous year Hamada had duly had his name entered in the provisional register in Tokyo entitling him to rations, but the name he'd used had been his real one, Shokichi Hamada, not his present assumed name, Kenji Sugiura. The live-in assistant at the clockmaker's in the town of Yokote was on no register, provisional or otherwise, for Kenji Sugiura had not existed a year ago.

Koyama stuffed some powdery tobacco into the tiny bowl of his long, thin pipe, then puffed cheerfully away as he announced that he was going to Sendai at the end of next month and was very much looking forward to seeing his grandchildren. The vagabond clock repairman Hamada was aware of what a tremendous journey it meant for people in this small town to go to somewhere as relatively nearby as Sendai, and he found it hard to believe anyone would think of getting in touch with a town as far away as Nobeoka, in the south of Kyushu, to investigate the genuineness of his claim to be a resident there. In fact, the address he had given was perfectly real, since he'd been living there before he came here, but he was neither a native of that area nor on any family register in that part of the world. The draft resister had first gone to Miyazaki, saying he'd come from Tokyo for reasons of health, stayed there a month and then gone on to the town of Nobeoka in the same prefecture, announcing he'd come from Miyazaki in order to convalesce.

The reason he'd left Kyushu and come up north was that rationing of basic commodities had started in the six major cities of the country in April, and it was fairly obvious the practice must gradually spread to the regions, and he decided a rice-growing area like this shouldn't suffer from any real shortage of food. There was also the aim of getting as far away as possible from the place he'd decided to make his fake permanent domicile; also, he'd been living in the warm south for almost six months and he felt an intense, even irresponsible longing to see snow. That must have had some slight effect at least on his decision to leave. So after moving around Kagoshima Prefecture for a short while, he traveled to the town of Masuda in Akita Prefecture, staying at a lodging house and then walking through small towns where traces of snow still remained, trying to make a living as a radio repairman. He'd believed while he was still in Tokyo that the only trade he'd be able to follow would be repairing radios, but here in Akita, just as in Kagoshima, he was depressed to find it just couldn't provide him with any sort of livelihood. There were very few orders, for a start; the amount he could charge for any job was extremely small; and if he was to do the work properly it meant humping about a considerable amount of luggage, which made it hard to keep on the move. The train fare to the town of Akita, where he had to go occasionally to get spare parts, was no joke either.

Then one day the landlady of his lodging house in Masuda said she'd heard the electric bell of the primary school needed mending, and she'd been asked to approach him about it. This bell had been installed some years ago as a considerable novelty by the headmaster, who had a passion for the latest gadgets and was most put out when it broke down. Up to now someone had always come from Tokyo each autumn to service it, but no doubt they were short of staff and it didn't look as if anybody would ever turn up. So Hamada went off to the school on the hill where the snowbreak fences made of logs and thatch were still in place, and where the intervals between lessons were indicated by the joyful cries of the children and the old caretaker doing the rounds shaking a handbell, and spent half a day tinkering with the machine and more or less fixing it. The headmaster was so pleased he bestowed upon him a dozen tough, salted flatfish and the sum of two yen fifty.

A couple of days after that he went to the nearby town of Asamai, well known locally for its cherry trees. They were just coming into blossom, but, probably because he was able to get almost no work, he returned to his lodgings thinking how very melancholy a flower the cherry was, only to be greeted by his landlord with the information that the clockmaker in Yokote was looking for an apprentice worker to live on the premises, and wouldn't that be just right for him? Hamada/Sugiura agreed that it would be, for if he took the job he could expect to qualify for the rice ration, and for some time at least he could stop worrying about food and accommodations; although the principal reason was that he could get hold of the trade of clock repairing in around six months, and this and radio repairing would give him two strings to his bow, and he might even be able to live on just clock and watch repairs alone. Also, clock repairing didn't have the implication of being aimed at a somehow westernized, intellectual market that radio repairing seemed to. What most occupied the twenty-year-old young man was that he should not arouse suspicions of any kind, and radio repairing had gradually come to seem to him a slightly suspect trade. His very youth itself was, of course, suspect as well, but fortunately he looked older than his years, and when asked his age he always replied that he was twenty-eight. That was what he had written on the form applying for residence permission he'd submitted to the Yokote town hall.

What the owner of the shop, a man approaching sixty, really had in mind was not so much an apprentice worker as a servant to look after himself, and his wife who had a bad chest. The young man who'd been there before had apparently left at the end of last year saying he was going to work in a munitions factory in Yokohama or Kawasaki. So Hamada was kept busy chopping firewood and doing other household chores, as well as spending quite a few hours in the fairly extensive field at the back of the shop, and had very little time to learn about clock repairing. But a natural deftness with his hands meant he still managed to pick up quite a lot, and he felt it probably wouldn't require as much as six months to learn all this man could teach him.

The old man from the neighborhood association said he was thinking he'd go for certain to see Matsushima. Hamada had visited the well-known beauty spot on a school outing, and as he went on bending over his work he gave an edited account of his visit there, trying to remove all the schoolboyish details. Koyama asked him what sort of souvenirs you could buy there, and Hamada said it was the local bean jelly, Matsushima *yokan*, although he hadn't bought any himself since it would have been awkward with the amount of things he already had to carry. In fact he had bought some, but everyone at home had said how awful it tasted; in particular, his sister Mitsu had been quite insulting about it, and he had a feeling they'd finally thrown it all away. Koyama was, however, sufficiently impressed by Hamada's account of this delicacy as to be worried that they might have stopped making things like that now because of the shortage of sugar.

Hamada stopped working for a while and, still with his head bowed, wondered why his boss hadn't mentioned that it was for someone who'd died on active service when he left for the funeral. Of course it was stupid of him to worry about things like that, since obviously the man couldn't possibly have any idea that Hamada might be someone who was evading conscription; yet his worries on this score weren't entirely groundless. Just two nights ago, he'd been giving possible reasons why his ration card still hadn't arrived from Nobeoka (it was hardly likely to, of course), and he'd said the only person there was his grandmother and when he'd left he'd tried to impress on her that the one thing she really mustn't forget to notify him of if they turned up was his call-up papers. She could ignore everything else, but she must immediately send him a telegram when they came.

"Looks like she followed your advice all right about ignoring every-thing else, anyway," said the clockmaker with a smile. "But do you mean to tell me, Sugiura, that while you're wandering all over the place like this mending radios, you have to keep on writing home telling them each time you change your address?"

"That's right," he replied, nodding. "But since I'm graded C2 I reckon I'm probably safe."

The other thought about this for a while, and then muttered that he had a special reason for it so he didn't suppose he'd get into trouble if he did have to report late. At least they'd hardly knock him about for not turning up on time, would they? Yet he spoke the words rather anxiously and had a worried look on his face; but as Hamada recalled this, he told himself once more that he really should not waste his time in futile worrying about such things. There was just no cause for anxiety, for all that had appeared in the man's words and on his face was merely the pity someone of fixed abode feels for the wanderer, a pity mingled with satisfaction at his own, more fortunate lot; and that was all he'd had in his mind. For a clockmaker in a town where the last serious crime had been the murder of a pack driver six years ago, the idea that he was harboring a real criminal, a draft resister, in the tiny, dark back room upstairs would be inconceivable, because draft resistance was now a more dreadful crime than robbery, even than murder, and so the less likely to be committed.

The old man was now stretching out his right hand with the strikingly long nail on its little finger, picking up some incense, which he added to that already burning, and he assumed a very solemn expression as he began muttering the invocation for the souls of the dead, although this didn't put an end to the nervous twitching that was a constant habit of his. Perhaps it was that he'd just been waiting for the right moment to make this offering, Hamada thought as he restarted work on the clock, inserting occasional grunts and comments on the other's remarks about the difference in sweetness between sugar and saccharine. Yet why should the old fool go on dithering here for so long?

Finally Koyama reminded him about the repair of his radio, explained how to get to his house, and took his leave with a courteous bow. But he came back almost immediately, muttering to himself and taking something from the inside of his kimono, which he placed on the shelf, and went away for good this time. Hamada had been too preoccupied fiddling with the clock to do more than say a brief farewell, but after a while he happened to glance at the shelf and hastily stood up, running over to look at the thin register book that had been left there. It was the register of those entitled to rations of principal foodstuffs, and when Hamada turned over the coarse paper cover he found himself right there on the first page, in the third column: *Sugiura, Kenji, Male, 11 September 1914, 28.**

---

* This is the old-style age reckoning, whereby a baby is considered one year old at birth and everybody becomes a year older on January 1, regardless of their actual birth date. This is the spring of 1941, so Sugiura is one year old in 1914, 2 years old from January 1, 1915, and thus 28 years old in 1941 (from January 1 onward).

A veteran assistant professor in education telephoned and said with a suppressed snigger that he was about to bring two of the younger assistant professors to discuss something with him. Hamada guessed it was probably to do with the purchase of office fixtures of some kind, and said he would visit him in the Education Department. One of his set practices was to avoid as much as possible the presence of third parties when discussing questions of funding with members of staff, both academic and clerical. As he walked along the gloomy corridor to the Education Department office, he began thinking about that old man in the neighborhood association in Yokote, whose name he just could not recall, and wondered if he was dead. He could only wonder, since he was hardly likely to have any information on the subject, but he assumed he probably was. If he was still alive he'd perhaps have stopped smoking because he'd be worried about cancer. Did he go to Matsushima? Did he buy any of that awful *yokan*? Hamada didn't even know that much, because less than one month had elapsed before he decided he'd just about got the basics of clock repairing, and he left Yokote, equipped, of course, with an officially stamped declaration of intent to change address, in the name of Kenji Sugiura.

When he arrived at the Education Department office door, it occurred to him he'd have done better to have them come to the Registry Office instead. He knew there was no chance of meeting here the same kind of experience he'd had in the library, but the fear of that happening again was something he couldn't avoid feeling. Rumors about yesterday would be all around the university by now, so why shouldn't they have reached here? But he shook himself free from the desire to remain there, forever hiding in the darkness of the passageway, and knocked on the door.

The three assistant professors were sitting in the bright fluorescent light drinking beer out of teacups. Hamada was invited to join them, but he declined. A professor came out from behind the bookshelves and joined in the conversation, but also declined the offer of beer as he said he still had a lecture to give, which made one of the assistant professors awkwardly scratch his head. They wanted two, if possible three, new bookshelves, and when that had been discussed the veteran assistant professor took up a more relaxed posture, and said,

"You seem to have been extremely active yesterday."

Hamada gazed back at him with a bewildered expression on his face, but the other went on cheerfully,

"Chasing after a burglar, bringing him down, beating him up . . ."

"No, that wasn't me. I was just watching."

"That's right. Hamada's a pacifist, you know," the professor put in, at which they all laughed, and even Hamada smiled, although he could feel how strained his smile must look. Rumors of what had happened yesterday had obviously spread throughout the campus, and as they passed from mouth to mouth the account of the incident would have been embroidered upon and the names of the participants become interchangeable. Since the professor had used the word "pacifist," it was fairly clear he knew about Hamada's having been a draft resister, and from the way two of the other three had laughed, they must know as well. Still, in this room it was just as obvious that "pacifist" was not a dirty word.

Hamada withdrew at an appropriate moment. They all knew about it now, all the people he passed in the corridor, those he greeted and those he didn't; and that was all he could think about, and all he thought about once he was back at his desk. He found it particularly hard whenever he happened to stop work for a moment and look up and catch someone's eye, whether it were that of Murakami or of the messenger girl; and the brilliance of the light also was painful, light flooding in through the windows and yet they still had the overhead lighting on, a veritable avalanche of light falling on him, brilliant, dazzling, and he loathed this office in which there was so much light, even wanting dark glasses to protect his eyes against it. Would it look very bad if he cut the party that evening? It would mean ignoring a specific invitation from the directors, and it would look particularly strange after what had happened yesterday. In the past he'd often thought about becoming a coal miner, walking in the north, in Hokuriku, still trying to live by repairing radios and clocks, and stopping at a small bridge with the inflated name of "Bridge of Meditation on the Three Provinces," eating a bean-jam bun there that didn't taste sweet at all; and then he went on to Kanazawa, a quiet town between two rivers, low-roofed, ancient houses, rows of them going on and on. . . . Of course the main reason he'd thought about being a coal miner was that the radio and clock repairing weren't bringing in much money, but probably there had been a much more basic reason, the desire to run away into the dark, to escape into a place where no one could find him. That's what must have been working in the deeper layers of his mind, in his unconscious, perhaps. The fact that criminals often end up working in mines is probably connected with some profound need of that kind. Hamada screwed up his eyes to keep out the excessive light, and in his mind's eye appeared a small man with a bent back, wearing a black suit, who started talking to him, urging him into the dark, into the dark places.

There was a powerful stench of dried rushes in the waste land by the primary school, so strong it made his head ache a little. But it was midsummer, and it would be the same anywhere in a town of earthen walls like Kurashiki, and Hamada thought he might just as well set up shop here. In fact, it turned out to be a good place to have chosen, for children went on gathering about the sand artist with the bushy beard, and he was kept so busy he didn't take a break for lunch. That was just as well too, since he was running out of meal vouchers, and the less he ate the better. So he made up his mind he'd have no lunch, and went on drawing his sand pictures, laughing and joking with the children. When he thought about the coming evening, he could put up with his empty stomach. He hadn't imagined a separation of only a month would feel so long.

As evening approached the children suddenly went away. Normally at this point he would shut up shop, but there was one grown-up still there, a small man with a bent back wearing a black suit and a field service cap, and glasses with lenses in them that looked like the bottoms of beer bottles, and he'd been passionately watching proceedings for some time. He didn't look as if he were going to buy anything, but Hamada always maintained the practice of continuing with his painting so long as even one potential customer was present. "If we go on with our drawing as if we're enjoying it, Sugi, then they might always get in the mood to buy," was what the bald sand artist had told him in Niigata, and Hamada had taken the advice to heart. He was also swayed a little by the thought that this man, who looked about forty, might well be a schoolteacher, for it was always best to be in with the teachers if your principal customers were schoolchildren. By the way he had gone on standing there so long in silence, Hamada thought he might well be a teacher of drawing.

Hamada wiped his forehead and beard with the towel dangling from his waist, then took up a piece of thick white paper, square in shape yet not too large to be held in the left hand, and began talking to his one remaining customer who was squatting in front of him.

"This paper is leftovers from the mill, cheap and just right for the job, but you can use almost any kind, ordinary drawing paper if you like, although you do need something with a bit of spine in it that won't bend."

The man in the black suit nodded. Hamada took up the painting brush in his right hand, and dipped the tip of it into an old ink bottle that now contained a thinly diluted paste.

"As I was telling the children just now, you can use anything as an adhesive: glue, calamus, aseptic. I use gum arabic myself. Even the dextrine they use for clogs or pure soya is all right. So long as it doesn't turn white but keeps the original yellow, and really sticks, of course. Still—and this is something I don't in fact tell the children—the real trick is to dilute the paste as thin as possible."

"Why not?"

"Why don't I tell them? Well, I don't have any personal objection myself, you know, but the gentleman who taught me all I know said the worst thing that could happen would be if the mark learned to draw better pictures than us making them. In our business we refer to the customers as 'the mark.' "

The man laughed out loud, and Hamada smiled. He didn't add that the reason was when the paste was thick it used up too much sand. He stopped smiling and drew a number of wet, colorless, vertical lines in the right-hand corner of the paper with his brush, picked up some pinkish sand with the fingertips of his left hand, and sprinkled it on the dampened portion. This created a number of dark pink lines, and on top of these he made some thick, horizontal strokes with the paste, on which he sprinkled some dark green sand. He had created a conventional image of a grove of pine trees.

He explained that he used powdered marble for the sand, colored by a cosmetic dye, but he couldn't get a good blue-green for the sea, and the view of Mount Fuji from the pine groves at Miho needed the sea if it was to look right; and his listener sympathetically agreed with him, saying what a shame it was he couldn't do the sea.

Hamada then drew Fuji with snow on its peak, clouds drifting about it, and the sun rising. The knack here was to wait a bit before adding the red powder to give the sun on the clouds and the mountain. The man said he saw what he meant but he couldn't imagine kids being able to do it. He praised the painting, however, handing over the sum of forty sen, for which he received a sand artist set consisting of six colored sands wrapped in waxed paper with a thick paper label stuck on each small bag, the name and address of the Japan Educational Sand Artists Association stamped on it. Hamada also threw in this view of Fuji from the pine groves at Miho, and another one he'd already made of a bush warbler perched on the flowering branch of a plum tree.

"Have you finished for the day, then?" the man asked.

"Yes."

"In that case, I wonder if you could perhaps spare me a little of your time?"

"I'm afraid I wouldn't be very interesting company."

"It's just a small matter I'd like to discuss with you."

"I see."

"Well, then, shall we go to wherever you're staying?"

Hamada decided he had to be very careful. This thrusting oneself upon somebody without even bothering to inquire about the other's convenience was the way detectives and people of that sort behaved. This was clearly no primary schoolteacher, no drawing instructor either. Still, if he was some kind of plainclothes policeman, what was he suspecting Hamada of having done? The odds were he'd mistaken him for someone else, and yet he hadn't heard of any crimes committed recently in this part of the world, either gossiped about in Hiroshima or from the lips of the maid in the boarding house here. So there was always the faint possibility this man had somehow sensed what kind of person Hamada was, his real identity.

In order to put off the moment of truth as long as possible, he packed up his gear very slowly, while the man in the black suit mooned vaguely about, finally producing a packet of cigarettes from his pocket. The scent of Turkish tobacco mingled with the stench of dried rushes. They were Cherry cigarettes, an expensive brand, not the cheaper kind one associated with a plainclothes policeman. Did that mean he wasn't one? A member of the military police would normally smoke army-issue cigarettes, not Cherry.

Hamada put on his cap, swung his sand artist gear and the goods he hadn't managed to sell onto his back, and set off walking while the man followed a little way behind. Probably making sure he didn't try to run away. But just as he'd finally realized that a military policeman would hardly be as small and myopic as this, and with such bad posture, the man started talking and caught up with him.

"That stench like new tatami isn't as bad now as it was during the day, is it?"

"So you don't come from Kurashiki yourself, either?"

"Um."

Hamada had assumed he'd give no details about himself; also that he'd not ask him directly where he came from. Instead he asked if he'd been to the local art museum, and Hamada replied he hadn't, although he knew about it by reputation. In fact he had not been to see it, although he was very eager to see the Ohara collection, with its originals by Gauguin, Van Gogh, and Renoir, but he'd restrained this desire since he wanted at all costs to avoid doing anything that might draw suspicion upon him. He had noticed as he walked by the building something that seemed to be Rodin's *Citizens of Calais* in the entrance hall, but he hadn't even slackened his pace.

"I should have thought it'd be particularly interesting for an artist like yourself. You might even pick up a few ideas for your own paintings."

"I suppose I might. I'm idle, you see; just can't be bothered."

"You've been to Kawanishi, then, have you?"

Kawanishi was the red-light district of Kurashiki.

"No. Not yet, anyway."

"Believe in keeping your money tight, don't you?" the man replied and grinned.

They walked on together through what was more twilight than dusk, and Hamada said,

"It's dead easy to get lost in the streets of this town."

"Just like a maze."

"Yes."

"Pity there aren't more of those white-walled houses the place is supposed to be famous for."

"Yes."

They reached the boarding house in front of the station, and Hamada showed him upstairs to his small room, through a peculiar odor made up of smells from the kitchen and the lavatory.

"You've got a room all to yourself?" said the man in the black suit, apparently very surprised by the fact.

"Um." Hamada didn't add that he'd been sharing up to now, and had only moved into this room today. Then he asked the man what the business was he had to discuss with him.

"Well, nothing in particular, you know. Just this and that."

Having said this he produced his card, which gave no information about him except his name, Keiichi Asahina, and an address in Fukuoka. Hamada apologized for not having a card himself, writing his name, Kenji Sugiura, on a piece of the thick white paper he used for painting. Asahina leaned back against the windowsill, scrutinizing the name written on the paper, and then asked a few things about sand painting, but as if he had little interest in what he was saying, until finally he asked what seemed to Hamada a more pertinent question, although still in a quite unconcerned way.

"I'd have thought you'd sell more if you painted airplanes and battleships, the sort of things kids are interested in nowadays."

Hamada felt himself go tense but did his best to hide it. He moved the saucer with the mosquito coil on it around in front of him and wondered if his hand would shake as he struck the match to light it. It would look bad if it did. But perhaps the man really was only trying to be helpful when he suggested he paint airplanes and battleships, although it could always be he was trying to find out something by a leading question of that kind. The end of the thick whirlpool of green turned red, and Hamada replied:

"I did once think I could make something out of parachutists coming down, and worked on it a bit, but it wasn't any good. I'm just lazy, you see; can't do anything else, like I said, but go on with the bird in the plum tree and things like that."

Asahina nodded, and after they'd talked a bit about doing a fireworks scene, although white paper would be no good so it'd have to be colored, like the one they used to have each year at the river carnival in Ryogoku, in Tokyo, he said,

"You must have been born in Tokyo, I think, Mr. Sugiura, gathering from your accent."

"That's right. I grew up there."

"What part?"

"Tabata."

"Really? And where are you now, if I may ask? Sorry, this is starting to sound like I'm investigating you."

When he replied that it was Nobeoka in Miyazaki, Asahina asked whereabouts in Nobeoka, and Hamada proceeded to give him a halting description of the geography of the area in which he'd lived. So Asahina followed this up with the most hackneyed of ploys.

"I have an acquaintance in Nobeoka who must be about the same age as you. I wonder if you know him? Name of Sasaki."

"Sasaki? I don't seem to recall anyone of that name."

The idea of returning the question by asking in which part of Nobeoka this Sasaki lived and what his father did for a living didn't occur to him. In fact, he was in no state at all to manage that kind of counterattack. All he could do was get ready for the next question, which he was pretty sure would be about his age.

"Perhaps you're of different ages? How old are you, in fact?"

This time he was able to reply promptly enough.

"I'm thirty."

"Meaning you were born in the year of the Dragon?"

"No, 1914 was the Tiger."

This reply was also very prompt, but Asahina didn't seem in the least discouraged, and went on:

"Ah. Born in 1914. A bit after Sasaki. That beard of yours makes you look older than your years. I don't want to sound too inquisitive, but isn't it a bit unusual nowadays to grow a beard at your age?"

This was an easy one. All he had to do was give the reply he always made. He smiled rather sheepishly, and said,

"Well, it certainly doesn't feel too good in the summer heat, I'll admit. And it gets soaked in sweat. But you've just got to have some sort of trade-mark like this if you're trying to sell things to children. It gives them something to call you: 'uncle with the beard.' "

They both laughed together at this, but Hamada sensed the other's eyes focused sharply upon him behind his thick lenses. Did it mean the prelim-inary investigation was now over and they were going to get down to real business? It wouldn't be long now before he knew who this man really was, or so he thought, but all that happened was Asahina smoked his Cherry cigarette, talking a bit more about sand painting and asking him how much a day he made by it, before suddenly changing the subject to how much a coal miner earned, around two hundred a month, and urging Hamada to become one. On realizing that the man was nothing more than an employment agent for the coal mines, Hamada experienced not so much a sense of relief as almost one of letdown, and he declined the offer. Asahina vigorously stubbed out a still only half-smoked cigarette in the saucer stained black by the ash from the mosquito coil, and began to explain at great length that all outdoor trades were about to become strictly controlled by the issuing of permits and licences, and that although it was true if he were sent off to the pits in Hokkaido he'd be treated just like a Korean, down in the Kyushu mines Japanese and Koreans were com-pletely segregated, and the food given the Japanese miners was really good, and on top of that the pay in Kyushu was miles better than in Hokkaido.

Since Hamada still made no response, Asahina went on to say that if he was worried he might not be up to the physical side of the work he could forget about that, since he could assure him a job on the clerical side would easily be found, as he was obviously a well-educated man and wrote a very good hand. Hamada protested that he'd never had a proper education, not even managing to graduate from the commercial middle school he'd had to leave halfway through, and he'd never be up to such difficult work; although as he was saying this he told himself he might have been better off not insisting on that point so much but just casually letting it go.

"The fact is, I just want to keep on with my own job of sand painting. I feel I can best serve the country in this way, by doing something for the children. I just like children, you see."

"We're not living in times like that anymore. Look, Sugiura, if things go on like this the country is finished. It'll be the same story here as in Italy. Mussolini was bad enough, but Badoglio is worse.* Do you know what's going to happen to your view of the peak of Fuji, your pine groves of Miho?"

He picked up the sand painting Hamada had made and stabbed his finger at the blue sky and the white sand.

"They'll have the Stars and Stripes fluttering from there; the Red Flag too, I shouldn't wonder. Let's face it, the probability of that happening is very high, and we've got to stop it before things get any worse. I don't care what happens to Tojo and his cabinet, and probably you don't either; but I'm not going to stand by and see this country destroyed, and if you feel about your own country as I do, then you won't either. If you've got a jot of patriotism in you, you'll go down the mines."

Some sort of right-wing fanatic who'd got a job working for the mining companies. Probably been a card-carrying Communist Party member at some time. When they were converted they often went way over to the right. Hamada stayed silent, listening to the hum of the mosquitoes. Asahina added nothing more to what he'd said. Outside in the corridor someone was joking with a servant girl. She laughed and said something back. Finally, just when Hamada was wondering if this pregnant silence meant Asahina had run out of steam or if the tense clenching of his jaws meant he was seriously weighing the meaning of what he would next have to say, the man poured forth another string of words.

* Pietro Badoglio was made Italian premier after the fall of Mussolini in July 1943.

"We've had murderers come to us, thieves, all sorts of men on the run. They reckon they're safe once they're inside the mines. And they're right. They didn't need any movement permits. Some of them could never have gotten one. But in the mines they get as much as they want to eat. We get lots of extra rations, you see; lots of special perks. There's quite a number of draft resisters as well."

On hearing the term Hamada was surprised to find how little he was flustered by it, and he managed to produce the question he'd always meant to use in such a situation.

"What's this draft resister?"

Asahina remained quite expressionless, explaining what it was in some detail. Hamada listened steadfastly, nodding in places. Had the man seen through him? Could be. Had he been trying to entice a confession out of him? It certainly looked as if he might have been, but then it might be quite simply that. . . . Anyway, he'd just have to bluff it out to the end. That was all he could do.

"You mean the mining companies are sheltering people like that?"

"They're making them of service, putting them to work for their country. It also helps them to feel they're making up in some way for the crimes they've committed. Hand them over to the military police, and what good would they be to anybody?"

"And people like that are getting better treatment than Koreans?"

"That's right," said Asahina. "After all, they are genuine members of our people."

"Well, I don't know," muttered Hamada in a slightly aggrieved tone of voice. "I don't think I can really accept the idea of working with a crowd you wouldn't normally let associate with ordinary, decent people. After all, I'm just what I seem to be, a respectable member of society running a small business. I haven't done anything wrong; I haven't swindled anybody."

"I understand how you feel," said Asahina in a terribly cool and businesslike tone of voice, to which Hamada responded by feigning a weariness with the subject that made it tiresome to make this statement of the obvious.

"Look, friend, I'm telling you. I've got a ration book as good as anyone else's, just like any honest member of the public. Three rations a day I'm entitled to, three square meals. Not the best quality white rice, I'll admit, but it's still something even if it's only foreign imported stuff, and as long as it doesn't go on raining for days on end, then I don't have to go short of something to eat. Believe you me, I hardly ever need to go hungry."

"All right, Sugiura—if that's really what your name is—all right. I'm with you. But now what I really want to know is how you're going to respond to this next little proposition of mine."

Asahina's whole attitude had changed, as he leaned toward Hamada, rising slightly on his hips, and staring him full in the face. But as he was about to start making his proposition, he was interrupted by an exotic, cheerful voice from outside.

"Are you there? Can I come in?"

"Sure," said Hamada, and the door opened and in came Akiko, wearing a jacket of ordinary *meisen* silk, which looked like the top half of a kimono, and the standard wartime breeches of splashed-pattern cotton. She had a net over her hair, a rucksack on her back, and cloth bundles in both hands. The awkward, stilted atmosphere that had existed in the room vanished in a flash, as Akiko knelt down in a decorously formal way and bowed low to Asahina, whom she dealt with as if he were a person of some importance in Hamada's life, thanking him for all the favors he had bestowed upon him, thus establishing the closeness of her own relationship to Sugiura, so that Asahina automatically readjusted himself to the formal kneeling position and bowed back.

"You won't have had your supper yet, I hope, because I've brought something really nice," she said, looking at Hamada, who didn't in fact reply to this, but asked her if she'd been able to get a seat on the train.

Asahina could only gape on in surprise at this exchange between the two, and the stern, suspicious atmosphere that had seemed to envelop him until just now had totally disappeared as well.

"I didn't realize you had company with you," he said to Hamada, almost as if he were complaining of the fact.

"Yes. I don't like being alone."

"Got your own little love nest here. No wonder you don't need to go to Kawanishi."

Akiko was fanning herself about the throat, and smiled cheerfully at this remark. Asahina stood up and took his leave, although he made one parting remark as he went out of the room.

"If you do ever feel like it, just let me know. All it needs is a postcard."

Akiko listened to his footsteps going down the stairs and asked Hamada who he was, but he only placed his left index finger lightly against his lips, a finger stained yellow and pink with cosmetic dyes, so she just shrugged her shoulders and giggled. But quite mysteriously, at that same moment Hamada could feel within him a slight yet distinct urge to run after Asahina, to call out and stop him, to ask him to let him have that job in the mines, feeling how easy life would become if he only did that, as he took Akiko by the hand. He was weary of this struggle with the military police, this battle with the State, sick to death of this life of vagrancy. He often asked himself how long it was going to go on, and always he could only give himself the same answer: that it was for forever, for eternity, or at least until he died. He didn't really trust any of the promises that Asahina had made, that he would always have plenty to eat, that he would be treated differently from the Koreans, but it was the images of such a life that so deeply attracted him: to flee into the bowels of the earth, to walk the dark galleries, to move slowly, pushing forward a trolley, or even to die in an accident as the roof caved in. While he'd been talking to Asahina he'd entirely forgotten that Akiko was due to arrive on the late afternoon train, and that was probably not so much due to any feelings of fear and tension but to a strong, latent desire to find a place of rest in the darkness.

There was a phone call for the chief clerk, and it was clear from the way he responded that it must be from some important personage. He bowed his head as he lowered the receiver, and then glanced at his two assistants with a look intended to catch the eyes of both of them at the same time.

"That was Dr. Horikawa. He said he wants both you, Hamada, and you, Nishi, as well as myself, to accompany him in the car to the venue for tonight's gathering."

While Hamada inwardly lamented there was now no way whatsoever of getting out of tonight's party, he also wondered why the man had put his name in front of Nishi's, despite the fact that Nishi had been promoted before him. He wished he hadn't; he even felt quite peeved about it. Probably he was just repeating the order in which Horikawa had said the names, but it wasn't him or Horikawa against whom Nishi would feel a grudge because of this, but Hamada himself; and as he thought about this he had the premonition something unpleasant was probably going to happen that evening, although he'd no idea what form it might take.

As if he just couldn't wait for the workday to come to an end, at half past four the chief clerk went off to the Alumni Club to play *shogi*, and a few moments later Nishi said he was going to the same place and went out as well. Hamada knew that the best thing for him to do would be to go to one of the other offices to while away the time before the party, but he remained sitting at his desk with the clerks who were working overtime and those who were on night duty. One reason was that it was his job to call the chief clerk and Nishi when the car arrived, but he could always have delegated that to one of the juniors. What he was really afraid of was that he might meet with the same experience he'd had in the library if he made a call on some other department.

He tried to cheer himself up with assurances that it was basically a drinks party, no formal supper, and he could sit unobtrusively in a corner until it came to an end, and that there'd be no need to go off with the others someplace afterward; but this kind of reasoning had no effect. Finally he told himself that he'd had more than enough problems in his life so far, and they'd all worked themselves out somehow, so there was no point in worrying about the kind of thing he might encounter in the future: this party tonight, for example. Look at the way he'd managed to get employed at this university. He could hardly have chosen a worse time to apply, and yet Horikawa had managed to fit him in. Then there was his marriage: how had he been able to acquire a woman as young, good-looking, and docile as that? In fact, he'd often thought there must be some reason for it he didn't know about. She'd been a virgin, though, so it wasn't that. Probably all it meant was that he was just naturally lucky. Some people were lucky; some were unlucky. He was lucky, just born that way. Look how he'd managed to get hold of that flat at the very first try. It was true he'd had to put down a pretty big deposit, but the rest of the installments were spread out over fifty years, and it had two rooms and a dining room–kitchen. Then look how easily he'd gotten into high school. Certainly he'd wanted originally to get into one of the classy ones, but the entrance exams were really hard before the war and he'd made a mess of it; but he'd found entry into technical school dead easy. Then he'd managed to get away with draft resistance for all those years too. It was an absolutely mystery why; yet now here he was, leading a perfectly straightforward life as an ordinary member of society. He'd thought he'd be an outsider for much longer than that; he'd been prepared to endure the hardness of that life for the rest of his days.

After three months in Yokote he'd set out again on his travels, having learned enough about clocks to be able to mend them and radios as well; but it was just as bad as when he'd only been mending radios, maybe worse, in fact, and those times when there was no money coming in at all he'd felt like giving the whole thing up as a bad job. No matter how far he walked each day trying to get work, all he really gained was the understanding that radios and clocks were genuinely treasured by their owners, in many cases were probably the most valuable possession they had, and they weren't prepared to entrust these precious objects to a homeless vagrant, a stranger they knew nothing about. He was always telling himself he ought to try his hand at something else, but he'd no idea what that might be, so he just went on reluctantly, trying to find clocks and radios to repair. Of course, the smart thing would have been to buy up broken goods cheap, mend them, and sell them dear; but he always seemed to end up selling them cheap as well. This didn't mean he got no income at all, but his outlay was high and he kept on eating into his capital. So he had left Akita and gone south, as far as Fukui Prefecture almost in the Kansai region, then moved north and east again, to Ishikawa Prefecture, then made a longer push to Niigata, always staying on the northern, Japan Sea side of the country.

He'd had the feeling that his luck might change, but business went badly here too, and when he had to break his last hundred-yen note in a boarding house in the city of Niigata he regretted all he had done, and roundly cursed himself for not having done better. It wasn't merely that he'd failed to see what resisting the draft was bound to mean, but the fact that he hadn't left home with more money, that he'd been reluctant to touch money that wasn't legally in his name, which filled him with anger at the naiveté of his ideas, his ignorance of what life was really like. And the reason he'd had to break into his last hundred yen was that the laborer he'd shared a room with had pinched two radios he'd been repairing and run off with them, and he'd been obliged to fork over compensation. Still, even then things had worked out right for him, by accident it was true, but still leading right out of that misfortune.

The sun-faded partition door, crudely patterned in plain squares of various sizes, slid open, and a balding man in his fifties came in. He put down his baggage in a corner of the room, stared intently at Hamada's face with his hands clenched together and, still in a posture intermediate between standing and squatting, addressed him at great speed in a very peculiar voice.

"I beg your pardon, but might you be one of the lads, by any chance?"

Hamada could only stare blankly back at him, still holding in his hand the newspaper he'd borrowed from downstairs, the *Niigata Daily*, which had an article in it about the resignation of the third Konoe cabinet* he'd just been reading. The man had a toothbrush moustache that was going gray in patches that, either because of the poor light from the low-powered bulb or because they were stained by nicotine, looked as if they had been dyed a crude brown. The man noticed how surprised Hamada looked, so he waved his hand frantically about as a gesture that the question had been withdrawn. He then knelt down properly, bowed his head a number of times, giving a good display of his bald patch, and spoke again in his extraordinary, high-pitched voice.

"Now I've put my foot in it again. My fault. Entirely my fault. You will forgive me, won't you? You won't be upset, will you? I'm always jumping to conclusions like that. I can't think how I came to mistake a gentleman like yourself for one of us."

* October 16, 1941.

Hamada remained sitting cross-legged, his left hand resting on the paper spread out on the tatami, and he shook and roared with laughter until the tears came into his eyes. He found it comic that he should be mistaken for a traveling street vendor, but the real source of his pleasure was a feeling of intense relief that he'd been given direct proof he no longer looked in any way to a third party like the son of a Tokyo doctor who was running away from conscription. It was probably the first experience of carefree delight he'd had since he left Tokyo.

The man with the tiny moustache started smiling too, constantly scratching his head in embarrassment. He introduced himself as a maker of sand paintings, name of Inaba, from Tokyo. Hamada (who had naturally introduced himself as Sugiura) said he'd often seen sand paintings at shrines and temples on fête days when he was a boy, sometimes even bought one; and from that point they started talking about Tokyo, then comparing notes on the places they'd been in their travels. They took their bath and dined together. Despite the fact that the pickled cabbage was very bitter, Inaba insisted on pouring soy sauce all over his, and as he ate this eccentric delicacy he began to give his opinions on the current world situation, angrily condemning the trade embargo the Americans and their friends had imposed on Japan as a dastardly act, and pointing out that the places where goods were most easily available nowadays were first of all Taiwan and then Korea, regretting that he hadn't so far managed to get to Taiwan, but he had been to Korea. And now in October, if you went into the Korean countryside, on all the roofs of the farmhouses you saw masses of red peppers put there to dry, all the roofs covered with them like a red cloth, like the cloth used in Japan for the dolls' festival, exactly the same color; he spoke as if he really looked forward to going there again.

When he'd finished his dinner he enjoyed an Asahi cigarette, then got down immediately to work on his sand paintings before Hamada started on his radio repairs, quickly doing Fuji and the pine grove at Miho, a bush warbler amid plum blossoms, a red-crested white crane perched on a very gnarled and twisted pine tree, etc. The previous night Hamada had found it almost impossible to get on with his work properly because the light was so poor, but when he asked the landlady if he could put in a larger bulb he'd brought with him she refused, and he felt what a good trade it must be if one could do it so easily even in light as bad as this. When he commented that it must be quite a job carting all that equipment about, Inaba said the wholesale merchant (or the "connection," as he called him) in Tokyo sent him anything he wanted on the receipt of a money order, so there were no problems in that direction.

He moved around a lot because he got tired of being in any one place for too long, but in fact it was good for business to go to new places or ones you hadn't been to for some time, and you'd be surprised at the "packet" you could make at "markets" (fête days) if you were able to get a good "pitch." While he kept up this cheerful, optimistic chatter, Inaba still went on working away with his brush, scattering on the variously colored sand, occasionally flipping the nail of his right thumb against the edge of the white paper to remove the surplus. Hamada certainly felt envious of this man but didn't think of becoming a sand artist himself, probably because as a doctor's son he didn't much fancy the idea of descending so low as to follow a profession that meant squatting by the side of the road, but also because he was basically wary of becoming a street trader, which would expose him much more to public view than he was at present.

Inaba said he was off to a "market" in Niitsu the next day, and he'd have to get there early if he wanted a good "pitch," and he went to bed at nine. Hamada decided to follow suit, since the dim light was getting on his nerves anyway. But the next day Inaba didn't go off to his market, only just managing to crawl out of bed, and not looking at all well. He said his heart hadn't been so good recently, and it was feeling really bad today and he was going to take the day off. Hamada spent the day trying for orders in the neighborhood, and when he got back late that afternoon he found the man with the small moustache working away at his pictures, but only very slowly and lethargically, occasionally pressing the back of his head with his hand, mumbling to himself that it made it feel much better. When Hamada offered to press it for him he was overjoyed, constantly thanking him as he did so. Hamada also got his bedding out for him, and insisted that Inaba would have to do without a bath that evening, although he said he wanted one.

During the night Hamada was awakened by a tremendous thud. He switched on the light, and there was the balding man fallen on the ground, his body half in and half out of the room, looking for all the world like a huge beetle, and groaning as he lay there. Apparently he had been on his way back from the lavatory. Hamada dragged him into his bedding and tucked him in, but the sick man complained he felt terrible, repeating over and over again in a thin, feeble voice that he thought he was going to die. He had no temperature, but his pulse was fast and his face a deathly, ashen color; even the brown parts of his moustache seeming to have faded. So Hamada went downstairs and woke up the landlord, saying they must call a doctor immediately, but he just paid a token visit upstairs, sitting by the patient's pillow and refusing to budge from there. As he obviously wasn't going to do anything, Hamada tried phoning a number of doctors in the neighborhood, but they all refused to come, so finally all he could do was go back to the room. But the patient's condition was still poor, and he decided that if he actually went to some doctor's house the man wouldn't be able to refuse to come back with him.

He walked the midnight streets of Niigata, by the stagnant waters of the fosse, then up a long slope that went on and on, until the third doctor he tried agreed to look at the patient. The doctor was an old man who wore an Inverness cape, and as they walked together he kept on complaining about the gasoline rationing, which prevented him from using his car, although he also added that now the national policy was to extend south, the Dutch oil fields would soon be ours and we could all have as much gasoline as we wanted. This reminded Hamada of the way his father would berate the military whenever there was some new shortage, and yet occasionally make the same kind of optimistic statement about the way things were going. Perhaps his own father was also out making a house call at this very moment.

The fact that he'd been seen by a doctor cheered Inaba up a lot, and the next day he was able to get up for a while, although the doctor's diagnosis that there seemed to be something a bit wrong with the patient's heart struck Hamada as a peculiarly evasive way of putting things. That evening, as he was again pressing the back of Inaba's head, he remembered an anatomical chart he used to pore over with great interest at school, and he began to think that perhaps the real trouble was with the semicircular canals of his ears, since that would produce the same kind of pain and also affect his sense of balance, and he urged him to go to the university hospital. Inaba didn't seem to like the idea at all, but when Hamada asked him if it was because he couldn't afford it he said that he could just about manage, so it was agreed they'd go together the next day, early in the morning. After being sent from one department to another, they were told what his illness had been diagnosed as, and Hamada turned out to be quite right, for although the heart condition was not good, his real problem was with the semicircular canals.

While they were in the hospital itself, and then on the bus back, one of the famous Niigata buses that ran on natural gas, the sand artist, dressed in jacket, golf pants, and cap, kept on thanking the clock and radio repairman in polo shirt, khaki trousers, and cap, with a persistence that got on Hamada's nerves. Inaba said Sugiura was a saint, just right for a traveling salesman or any kind of confidence work since he had the sort of character you could really trust, like a holy man with the healing touch; whereas naturally the young man replied modestly that he'd just happened to be around and his diagnosis had been a lucky guess. Still, when they got off the bus and were walking along an avenue of sparse willow trees that looked peculiarly gloomy in the low light of the declining sun, and perhaps because his effusions of gratitude had been too vigorous and prolonged, Inaba was obliged to hold on to Hamada's shoulder as he dragged slowly along, and he didn't look in the least well or happy. The two walked in silence, like a father with his son, while along the road on the other side of the fosse a boy was running along selling a special edition of the evening paper, clanging a bell as he ran. When they got back to their boarding house they learned it was because the Tojo cabinet had been formed.

Inaba had to go to the university hospital twice a week. So twice a week Hamada had to give up his work and go with him. On those occasions he didn't feel he was acting out of kindness or even obligation, but more from a resigned feeling that this was just the way things had worked out. On the third time, as they were sitting on a bench in the hospital corridor, the sand artist, who'd become fairly emaciated by now since he was on a vegetarian diet because of his heart, turned to Hamada and said,

"You know, Sugi, I don't think your game's much of a winner, is it?"

Hamada's first response to this suggestion that his trade didn't bring in much money was, despite the slight shock at having his name abbreviated to "Sugi" for the first time by this man, to reply quite frankly that he wasn't making much at the moment; although he went on to protest, partly in order not to draw suspicion onto himself and partly out of sheer vanity, that he'd been doing well enough in other parts of the country. But Inaba simply leaned back on the bench and, looking up at Hamada, explained in explicit detail why his game just couldn't be a winner, and Hamada was amazed at how accurate his analysis of the problem was. Inaba noted this obvious admiration, then asked him in a slightly shamefaced way if he wouldn't like to try his hand at sand painting, and Hamada's automatic response was to leap at the idea, wondering why he'd never thought of it before. He bowed his head and asked Inaba to teach him, and the old man nodded in reply and said,

"Sand painting will take you far, Sugi. As far as the brothels in ward thirteen, anyway. Won't give you access to the geisha in the old district, though."

The bald-headed sick man sat by the hospital window in the light of the October sun, smiling feebly as he talked about the pleasure quarters of the town.

Then every day, for thirty minutes or at the most an hour, in order not to tire out the sick man, Hamada learned the art of sand painting. He'd belonged to the art circle at school and knew enough to be able to produce conventional pictures; in fact, it had been a piece of good fortune for him that he'd rejected the more realistic methods his art teacher, a man of advanced views, had tried to teach him. First of all, you didn't need to be all that skilled at drawing, since what really mattered was getting the paste to the right consistency, and also having the knack of holding the paper so it was facing somewhat away from you and the "mark" could watch what you were doing. There was no need for a lot of patter, either. They didn't want explanations; what they wanted was to see you were really putting your heart and soul into it. That was what attracted people. Inaba's final piece of advice was that he should grow a beard, since there was no way he could make himself bald. Hamada took the advice seriously and started only shaving his upper lip, much to the amusement of the serving girl, who poked a great deal of fun at him about it. The result was that, before a week was out, he'd just about got the hang of it, and off he went with the borrowed equipment to a spot near a primary school in the center of town suggested to him by Inaba, and made a considerable amount of money. Twenty percent of that was "source" money, being what the materials had cost, but the rest (sixteen sen out of every twenty) was straight profit; but when he tried to give half of it to Inaba the old man just smiled and refused. The sand artist lay face downward on his thin mattress, and as he rubbed his toothbrush moustache against the hard pillow he said he'd write a postcard of introduction for him to the "connection" (the wholesale dealer who provided the materials) called Mr. Sugawara in Tokyo.

Hamada went off with the others and got into the car, which was as highly polished as the show apples in a greengrocer's. In the back sat Horikawa with the chief clerk and the head of administration, while Nishi and Hamada were in front; yet there was still plenty of space. The subject of conversation in the car was the purchase of some land in the suburbs that had finally been brought off, apparently at a ridiculously low price, and was a great cause for celebration. If that's all they're going to talk about tonight, thought Hamada, everything should go fine. The Bentley slid smoothly forward, a pleasure to ride in, and the chauffeur sitting next to him, whom he recognized as formerly the driver of the school bus, was obviously taking great pleasure in handling this expensive piece of merchandise very different from what he'd been used to, for it showed in the remarkably benign expression on his face. Hamada spent the drive either slipping in an occasional remark to the conversation going on in the back or talking to the chauffeur about the cost of second-hand cars, a discussion in which Nishi occasionally joined. There really was nothing to worry about. He'd managed to get through all sorts of trials and tribulations up to now, any number of them. Something or somebody always turned up, totally by accident, always just when most needed. It had been the case with Akiko, with old Inaba. One stroke of luck after another. Of course, if you were going to take on the whole might of that massive system called the State, take it on all by yourself, then you needed a lot of luck in order to succeed. There was no other way you could do it.

The director questioned Hamada about his negotiations with the Ministry of Education, and Hamada replied. The director then asked Nishi about what was happening with the high schools, and Nishi replied. Hamada noticed that his gray hair was looking very glossy today. A bit different from Inaba's moustache. Now that was really weird. It was still just as grubby even after he'd given up smoking. His own beard had taken quite a long time to grow, and people had laughed at it, but there was no doubt it attracted the children. Part of the know-how of the business, that was.

Hamada got back to the boarding house fairly late that night. Inaba was lying in bed reading an old number of the magazine *King*, waiting up for him.

"How'd it go, Sugi?"

"A winner."

The two smiled at each other, and Hamada gave an account of what had happened that day, the first time he'd done the "game" at a "market," making liberal use of street traders' argot. He'd gone, at Inaba's suggestion, to the fête day or "market" at Hakusan shrine.

"Your not having a proper family name didn't bother anyone?"*

"No. The man in charge was very nice about it, very helpful. Admittedly, he did suggest I'd do better if I had one."

"He's right, of course. I'd let you have mine, Sugi, you know, but there's something about you, I don't know what it is, like you're holding back on me about things."

"I'm not holding back on anything. Not as far as I know, anyway."

"Well, it doesn't matter much. You can get by without a family name. So long as you don't get too queer a pitch."

A "queer pitch" was when you'd set up shop and found you were in the

---

*In many fields of traditional Japanese life the apprentice learner will eventually receive a name that has been handed down for generations.

worst kind of place for the trade, and Inaba gave detailed accounts of what this sort of place was. But even then, he went on, a traveling singer can get a crowd together anywhere, and that makes the stalls lively, and before you know where you are the mark have gathered. That's why they used to call traveling singers "angels of mercy" when he was young, and he started on a series of recollections of his youth.

When these had come to an end, Hamada pointed out they were low on materials and would have to order some more from the connection. It was true he could get no more business in town, and he'd already worked the nearby areas, but there were plenty of villages within a day's return journey he had his eye on where trade should be brisk enough. But Inaba's reply to this was something completely unexpected. He was going to take him to Tokyo as soon as he could get hold of the rail tickets.

"Come off it. You can't do that. You still mustn't move for at least another fortnight."

The idea seemed to have occurred to Inaba during the last couple of days when he'd been getting up occasionally and generally mooching around; all he could think about now was this plan of taking Sugi to Tokyo. The doctor at the university hospital had told him he was much better (Inaba seemed to be ignoring the fact that Hamada still had to take him there), and although he admitted he'd said that just a postcard would be enough, in fact it was much better to meet their connection, Mr. Sugawara, in person, at least just once, because that was the custom in the street traders' world; and Sugi himself must surely enjoy going back to the town where he'd grown up, and although they said you had to stand in line every time you wanted to buy anything in Tokyo, Tokyo was still Tokyo, a bit different from Niigata, lots of really tasty things to eat, and the women were good looking and he didn't imagine you had to line up in the pleasure quarters of Yoshiwara and Tamano'i. Inaba gave any amount of information and cheerful suppositions in a wholehearted effort to make Hamada agree to the idea.

Hamada himself was, in fact, genuinely worried about Inaba's health, but mostly worried because he was prepared to go anywhere except Tokyo, for he was certain he'd be arrested by the military police if he went there.

It was the dread of the consequences that made him refuse, but Inaba wouldn't listen. Here was a man who'd been a model patient for three weeks, always doing exactly what he was told, and now, as if determined to make up in one evening for that long period of self-restraint, he behaved like a petulant small child.

Since he could only lose any argument centered on the state of his health, Inaba maintained, sitting up on his mattress with the eiderdown wrapped around him, that it was all just a lot of talk anyway, and Sugi knew it, and the main thing was that he, Inaba, wanted to go, it being a question of human feelings, and he couldn't see any reason why Sugi shouldn't see him as far as Tokyo, and he would pay for the tickets, and if Sugi still wouldn't have anything to do with it then there must be something wrong with him, he must be just plain unfeeling, that was all he could say.

Hamada tried to explain, calmly and logically, that he'd got it all wrong, but realized as he was doing so he was simply making Inaba more and more sulky, so he stopped and just sat there with his mouth shut tight. This produced an immediate change in Inaba's face, transforming him into a totally different person, a nasty, vulgar person with a face to match. His eyes had narrowed, and he looked up at Hamada from beneath lowered eyelids with a revolting smirk, and spoke in a loathesomely insinuating voice such as he had never used at all before.

"Here, Sugi, are you scared to go to Tokyo?"

Hamada told himself he'd got to look this man straight in the eyes and did his best to do so; but Inaba's eyes were moving all over the place and it was almost impossible to meet them with his own. Then, sometimes with eyes lowered dejectedly and sometimes glancing up with a sullen leer into Hamada's face, Inaba went on:

"Spot on, wasn't I? You're scared someone's going to nab you as soon as you get off the train at Ueno. Huh, looking like butter wouldn't melt in his mouth, and got a record as long as my arm, I'll bet."

Hamada felt instant relief at this, and said,

"I don't have any record. I'm just worried about your health, that's all."

"Huh. The local fuzz don't bother him, but the Metropolitans are a bit dicey, are they? Got him nearly wetting his pants, have they?"

"I couldn't give a hoot about any of them. What am I supposed to be bothered about? I can't think what's got into you. I'm just trying . . ."

Inaba had been sitting looking glumly at the floor, saying nothing, when suddenly he burst out crying, explaining between loud howls of grief that he'd written any number of times to his wife and never got a word out of her in reply, and he knew she must be carrying on with someone, probably that bloke working on the buildings, or the flash one who played the guitar, or some damn copper on the beat. . . .

Hamada could only find this ludicrous, no doubt out of a certain sense of relief that Inaba hadn't seen through him at all, but perhaps mostly because he was still a virgin who'd never been in love with a woman himself. Thus he found this sight of a balding, toothbrush-moustached man of fifty making such a tremendous racket over the supposed infidelities of his wife preposterously comic. He managed to keep this feeling of absurdity to himself, however, attempting to comfort the man in a variety of clumsy ways, but this only made Inaba feel even more sorry for himself, till he finally indulged in a completely unrestrained outburst of sobbing. It struck Hamada that this was a real man's problem (although he was past twenty, he still had the peculiar habit of sometimes thinking of himself as a small child), which needed a proper grown-up in attendance, so he went downstairs and asked the landlord (who was listening to the Miyamoto Musashi serial on the radio) to come upstairs because Inaba seemed to be having some sort of attack.

But this only made matters worse too. Inaba had always disliked the landlord because he didn't show any proper consideration for the sick, and he was also feeling very sensitive about having disclosed a shameful aspect of his personal life to someone as close to him as Sugi; so this calling of the hated landlord into so delicate a situation appeared to him like a straightforward act of betrayal. Thus when Hamada came back with the landlord, Inaba had immersed himself in his bedding and was feigning sleep, his back turned resolutely upon them, and refusing to answer no matter what the landlord said. Since there was nothing to be done, Hamada decided to go to bed as well, and the two of them lay there in the dark, saying not a single word to each other.

The following morning, as soon as breakfast was over, the sand artist
changed out of his padded kimono into the golf pants and jacket he'd not
worn for some time, and began packing all his belongings. While doing this
he was acutely aware of Hamada's presence, clearly hoping he would stop
him, or at least offer to go with him. But Hamada was sitting in the light of
the window, doing something he hadn't done for a long time either, namely
repairing a watch, and said nothing, although he knew perfectly well what
Inaba was waiting to hear. When Inaba did at last put on his sweat-stained
cap, shoulder his burden, and shakily slide open the door, Hamada finally
looked up from the delicate piece of machinery he was repairing and said,

"Don't be a fool, Inaba. You'll never make it to Tokyo in that state."

Those were not really the right words for the situation. What he should
have done was plead with him not to go, apologize for what had happened,
and then Inaba would have apologized even more fulsomely and things
would have worked themselves out. Unfortunately the young Hamada had
found Inaba's behavior of the night before more than he could take, and he
wasn't in the right mood to be so considerate of the other's feelings. So Inaba
didn't even look at him but went out without saying a word, the slamming
of the door being his only response to what Hamada had said. Hamada listened to the sound of him going shakily downstairs, his hand obviously
gripping the banister desperately, and finally heard his voice at the bottom
of the stairs talking to the landlord, arguing about the bill and this, that, and
the other; and as Hamada listened to the dialogue in chirpy downtown slang
and bumbling Niigata drawl, he went back to his watch repairing. Even when
the landlord came upstairs and said he thought something ought to be done
about it, he paid no attention to him. But when, after a while, the landlady
came up and pleaded with him to stop him, her voice breaking tearfully as
she said she just couldn't bear to watch as he went off looking all broken like
that, he finally stood up. It was pure stupidity having a battle of wills with a
sick man, he told himself, as he had told himself a dozen times already.

He slipped on his geta and made his way to the bus stop, past the fosse
with its black surface covered in dust and scattered bits of straw refuse,
through the avenue of willows upon which not a single leaf remained. A
small line was waiting for the bus, and there, a little apart from it, was

Inaba seated on a black dustbin, resting with his cap in his hand. As he walked toward him Hamada thought he looked much better, at least sideways on, than he'd expected him to; but the bus arrived and he had to run to catch him.

When Hamada called out his name Inaba turned, and his flabby face suddenly creased all over with that pleased embarrassment a hospital patient displays on receiving an unexpected visitor. But the line began to move and, as if enticed by that motion, Inaba put on his cap and stood up. Hamada tried to say something, but the bus conductor was shouting out at them all to hurry along, so he took hold of Inaba by both arms. There must have been something wrong with the way he gripped him, for Inaba merely allowed himself passively to be held, neither resisting nor responding, but just glared at him and said,

"Are you really that damn desperate to work the sand game?"

Hamada withdrew his hands, and Inaba got on the bus while the conductor rebuked him for taking so long over it.

Hamada went back to the boarding house and spent the rest of the day thinking about what he was going to do, repairing an alarm clock and a watch, and wondering if he might not be better off traveling around mending electric bells in schools and places like that. Perhaps it might be a good idea to have a card made with "The Imperial Bell Repairs Division" on it. Up north in Akita he'd got two yen fifty and all that dried fish for mending the bell in a primary school, which wasn't bad wages at all. It ought to pay a bit more now, and he wouldn't have to spend anything like as much time over a job of that kind as he had then. The point was, however, just how many schools had an electric bell system installed in them, and the more he thought of the probable answer to that question, the less likely this plan of his appeared to be.

Still, he had to do something. He'd simply starve to death if he went on like this. Winter was coming, and he needed to move to a warmer place; Izu, for example, although that might be a bit dangerous, being too near Tokyo, so perhaps someplace he'd never been, like the Kii peninsular. He drew up a draft of his new card, Kenji Sugiura of the Imperial Bell Repairs Division, making up an address for it at 10–53 Yarai, Ushigome, Tokyo, giving a great shout when he'd finished to cheer himself up, and getting energetically to his feet. As he was leaving the boarding house, a newspaper was hurled in, and he picked it up, glanced at the front-page headline, KEHI-MARU DISASTER: SINKS AFTER STRIKING SOVIET MINE, and handed this evening edition of the *Niigata Daily* to the landlord, who was seated behind his tiny desk. Then he went to the nearby name-card shop to get his new card printed, noticing with some interest that more than half of the cards set out on display under the glass top of the table were those of geisha, each with an alluring photograph, although what provided a much more powerful stimulus was the aroma of frying tempura coming from the back room of the shop. He tried to recall when he'd last eaten it as he ordered a box of Kenji Sugiura cards, and all the way back to the boarding house he was thinking about the same thing, a reverie interrupted by the landlord who'd been waiting for him, and who pointed to a small article among the news snippets: FIFTY-YEAR-OLD MAN DIES IN TRAFFIC ACCIDENT OUTSIDE STATION.

It seemed almost certain that this must be Inaba. The time fitted exactly, as did the brief account of his appearance and the accident itself, falling in front of a bus "as if he had been dragged under it," the kind of thing one might expect to happen to a man who had something wrong with organs that affected his sense of balance. The landlord and Hamada went to the police station, which Hamada found himself entering without any trepidation, much to his own surprise, and from there to the university hospital, where they learned their supposition had been quite correct, and where a member of the medical staff, on hearing the details of Inaba's trouble with his semicircular canals, was delighted and said his case history was one of remarkable academic interest.

The next day the police contacted the address Inaba had written in the boarding house register, but it seemed his only close relative, his wife, was not well enough to travel to Niigata, so the postmortem was held immediately and the body cremated the same day. While Hamada was waiting in the reception room for close relatives of the deceased at the crematorium, being the only person to attend the funeral, he spent the time occasionally looking at the house of the cremator, which had giant radishes hanging from its eaves to dry, and also composing a long letter. The letter was written to a Mr. Sugawara at the address in Tokyo stamped on the sand artist kits he had sold, but he didn't know his full name since he'd only heard the surname, and he apologized profoundly for this breach of etiquette in his letter, explaining that Inaba had promised to introduce him to his connection but had suddenly died in an accident, and although he himself was a person of no reputation and with no family name, he most sincerely hoped that Mr. Sugawara would provide him with materials from now on, and would he please send him the following items forthwith. He found it a particularly difficult letter to write, since he had to appear extremely courteous and semi-illiterate at the same time.

Hamada got hold of a shallow wooden box and divided it into latticelike partitions, imitating the one Inaba used to have. He then inserted paper boxes (Inaba had used foil) into these partitions and filled them with colored sand. Inaba's own equipment, one metal and one wooden box, had been totally mashed up by the bus, and all the dead sand artist with the toothbrush moustache had left to the living one with the beard was a *Complete Guide to Shrine and Temple Fête Days*, which Hamada appropriated with the landlady's permission. It was a fairly small book, with a ragged cover, published in 1931, but presumably there would have been no great changes in ten years. The landlady also insisted he take Inaba's grubby notebook, since no doubt she wished to dispose of everything pertaining to the old nuisance, and he even speculated a moment that she could be of a mind to thrust the ashes of the deceased upon him as well.

That did not happen, but the letter he'd sent to Sugawara came back with RECIPIENT'S ADDRESS UNKNOWN stamped on the envelope. Things were now looking quite hopeless, and for the first time since he'd left Tokyo he drank alcohol, a bottle of ration beer. As he drank this beer, he came to the conclusion there were but two courses open to him. Either he'd have to make his own materials—buy powdered marble, color it himself with cosmetic dye, and put it into little waxed-paper bags—or he could try mending electric bells. Neither course seemed to open any cheerful prospects. The twenty-year-old youth, probably because of the desperate state of mind he was in, managed to get drunk on this one bottle of beer,

woke up in the middle of the night with a parched throat and an empty
stomach, then drank glass after glass of water in an attempt to appease his
hunger; then he remembered Inaba's notebook and had the idea that there
might be something in there. His mouth and his jaw still dripping with
water, he flipped excitedly through its pages until, toward the end of the
book, he found "Ryukichi Sugawara: 2–93 Shinjuku, Yotsuya-ku, Tokyo,"
a quite different address than the one he'd written to. Presumably Sugawara had his own reasons for giving the office of the Japan Educational
Sand Artists' Association a false address, thought Hamada as he read-
dressed the returned envelope in very large letters.

The party began with an address by Hirokawa, and after an hour or so,
during an interval in the songs and dances performed by the serving maids,
he and the other executive director left. This meant the party became even
noisier. The head of administration sang a crude traditional song in an
uncouth dialect; the chief registry clerk performed a sword dance, everybody applauding wildly; and Hamada sat in a corner drinking whisky and
water. These days Hamada had quite a good head for drink, being able to
put away half a bottle of whisky without serious effect, provided he didn't
mix it with anything else. The assistant clerk from Teaching Administration was just about to pour saké into his glass but stopped short.
    "Oh, you were drinking whisky and water, weren't you, Hamada?"
    "That's right."
    The chief accountant, in a voice that suggested he'd already had a bit too
much, said,
    "How about some beer instead?"
    "It always blows me up."
    "Japanese food and whisky don't mix, don't mix at all."
    The chief accountant delivered these words in a peeved, vulgar bellow,
and the assistant clerk in Teaching Admin. felt some mediation was
needed.
    "Well, everyone to his own taste is what I always say."
    "Yes. It's a European affectation of mine. Unfortunately this isn't
imported whisky, though," said Hamada with a smile, speculating, as he

ate a leg of fried chicken, if this cuisine could properly be called Japanese and wondering why beer should be allowed to mix with it while whisky did not. He'd still only drunk about a quarter of a bottle, or so he thought.

The dean of students gave an imitation of Frank Nagai, the sentimental pop singer, and then one of his underlings gave a rendition of a more traditional song, "Though My Blade May Rust, My Honor Shines Bright," although severely declining the offer of *shamisen* accompaniment, for he said it only confused him. While this was in progress Nishi approached with a flask of saké, and Hamada hurriedly gulped down his whisky, placing his hand over the glass to indicate he was refusing it.

"Japanese spirits don't agree with this man. Just like the Japanese spirit," said the chief accountant with his usual sparkling wit, and Nishi laughed out loud and went on laughing while the mediatory assistant clerk went off somewhere to replenish Hamada's whisky and water. Hamada thought it looked a bit strong, but downed it in one go.

The maid with the *shamisen* was going around perpetually asking people to sing, but because no one would, at last in desperation she struck up the cheerful chords of "The Army Song." One or two voices took up the words:

> If we but now relied
> On sword strapped to the side

Then everybody, except Hamada, joined in:

> 'Twould be so easy, dear,
> To take you everywhere;

Finally the serving maids joined their voices to the swelling chorus.

> To take you with me, that
> Would be so easy, but

> There's rides for girls no more
> In the old Tank Corps.

But the chief accountant had sung out his own emended version in a great bellow:

There's rides for girls galore
On my old small bore.

Everybody thought this was great, and there was a massive burst of mas-culine laughter, thick with the gurgle of booze and saliva, enlivened by thin, gay threads of women's voices: "Oh dear, what a thing to say," "Well I never," "Isn't he rude?"; and one of them, presumably from bitter expe-rience, said they'd all be a bit too heavy for her. But Hamada really had gone to war accompanied by a woman, and if this lot knew that they'd hate him even more, a mixture of jealousy and rage; and the slobs all knew what he did in the war, and they could still sing a song like that. Not the women, of course; they didn't know. They would, though, if he caused any trouble. Some bastard would explain after he'd gone. Like that Nishi, when they arrived at this place tonight. "Cherry red the flashes on my collar." How the hell could they expect him to join in that? Just go on leaning against the wall with lowered eyes. "In Yoshino a storm of petals blown." Just lis-ten to them: a song aimed at him, everyone in the whole country, every man and woman jeering at him. "Wert'st thou not born a son of Yamato?" They were bellowing at him now, at the draft dodger. God knows he'd thought about it enough; thought enough before he did it, while he was doing it, and when it was all over as well. "Scattered like blossoms, down the soldiers fall." Had he been a coward? Had he been afraid? Was he still afraid, even now it was over? No, nothing was ever over.

He had classified his reasons for refusing conscription into four. He liked neat divisions. He'd never shaken off the mental habits of the stu-dent, and he was even more like that when he was young. Four reasons. Like dividing the world into five continents and seven seas. Like writing a schoolboy's essay, he worked out the bases for his act. One: opposition to war in general. Two: opposition to this particular war. Three. What was the third reason? Couldn't remember. It would have come tripping off his tongue then. Always thinking about it; all day, every day. The third reason was . . . ? Remembered it. Three: opposition to armies in general. Four: opposition to this particular army.

Number one is absolute pacificism. If you take that position, then you aren't allowed to defend a permanently neutral country when its borders are invaded. Number two is about an actual war, not a theoretically possible one. It's a matter of whether you think fighting in a particular war is right for yourself or not. It's difficult because all sorts of questions about what kind of war it could turn into, of how it is possible to calculate all its effects, get mixed up in it. Look at the China Incident, the war with China under that fake name. What a mess. Did anyone ever bother to work out if there was a chance of winning it? Look at Kanji Ishihara, the man who started the Manchurian Incident just about single-handedly, and yet even he was opposed to extending the war to China itself. Then what were they thinking about when they took on the Americans? Nothing. Just trying to prove something to themselves; just being pig-headed. Or just letting things slide, was probably more like it. Can't be helped, boys, so let's get on with it. Some people defend the Pacific War (or the Greater East Asian War, as they call it) on the grounds it led to the independence of many countries in Asia and Africa. Pure accident. It's an ill wind that blows nobody any good, that's all. Might as well say we fought the Americans in order to establish Korean independence. In fact, that makes a bit more sense than the other bullshit. Number three is just a rejection of the system; any system. An anarchistic idea. Human Liberty. Christ, why can't they shut up? Are they going to sing the whole damn anthology of old army songs? What's happened in postwar Japan is that people have been given independence, and now they're longing for a period when they didn't have it; i.e., wartime Japan. But old Hamada was independent then, my boys. Putting aside the question of Akiko. The bloody row they're making sounds just like those cheerful buggers yesterday after they'd finished with their fox hunting. That was all aimed in his direction too; aimed at the Hamada they couldn't see (he was hiding in the toilet, boys). Hamada was in the toilet and he was independent of the lot of you. As he still is now, in this room. He's not singing, he's not clapping his hands, he's not tapping his plate with his chopsticks, boys. He's all by himself.

Pretending he was drunk, and now he really is. He really is drunk. But to get back to number three. What was wrong with this was that anyone could counterattack by asking why you didn't accept the army if you said you accepted the social system as such. He'd never got his ideas about the State properly worked out, never, and the day had come and he'd gone ahead with it, and he'd felt ashamed of himself, ashamed for not having any proper ideas or theory about the State. He was only twenty, so he really didn't need to feel ashamed of not knowing what the State was, and yet he did. He was ashamed. Then number four: here one accepted the idea of armed forces in general, but objected to this particular army, loathed the Japanese army for its barbarity, its gross and evil vulgarity, and its overall appallingly low standards (so well expressed in these vile military songs being sung at the moment). Of course, it was basically the army; not that he had a particularly high opinion of the navy, either. As he thought about each of these four reasons, they all seemed to explain to some extent the nature of his act, but even this simple attempt to discriminate didn't allow him to pick one reason and say that was it. Not surprising, of course. People don't choose a course of action on one reason alone. But at the age of twenty he'd wanted a reason, one clear reason, and bitterly regretted not having one. His youth had started with too large a confrontation, a question much too big for him to handle, and it had led to a renewal of the state of mind of his boyhood, dominated by enormous feelings of shame, self-inflicted, self-tormenting.

Self-tormenting. For example, how many times had he asked himself if it wasn't perhaps true that he really didn't give a damn about three of them, because it was a hatred of the Japanese army alone that turned him into a draft resister? (He still went on asking himself, for that matter.) Wasn't it really all that slapping about the face—the Japanese army's noted method of imposing unofficial punishment—that he objected to? Wasn't it the front- and backhanded slap, the running of the gauntlet, the "Private Hamada requests corporal's permission to untie corporal's puttees, sir"? No, it wasn't very likely. At least, it couldn't only have been that. Then he'd asked himself an even crueler question. He'd asked himself if he didn't dislike the army because the people in it looked so smart, were so beautifully elegant. Ridiculous. Ridiculous what you do when you're young, screwing your guts up to punish yourself, never prepared to forgive yourself anything. Just the opposite of the way a man in his forties behaves. And he sometimes accused himself of standing by while other people died for that reason, because he was reacting somehow against some aesthetic he knew was completely superficial anyway. Not all the time, though. Nothing like it. But when the feeling came it was violent enough. Standing by while others suffered. Just looking on; an onlooker. Looking on as they carried the boxes with the remains of the dead inside them. Then on that night train, with those Korean boys who'd been brought to this country to do forced labor. Poor devils; press-ganged as they were walking around their villages, brought over here whether they liked it or not. When their two-year contract was up, made to sign a new one, made to sign a plea they be allowed to go on working here. They signed; the specials came in, screamed at them, and beat them if they didn't. On the night train one boy burst into tears as he talked about it. Being sent to a military farm unit in Shinshu, into the cold mountains. Pale, sick face; unattractive; couldn't pronounce the Japanese voiced consonants.

He soon worked out who'd started singing the next song. It was the head of Teaching Administration, and his voice was unmistakable. "The young blood of our pilot lads." That poor kid. A mere child, that's all he was. The *shamisen* made a hectic effort to catch up with the singing voice, clacking out the accompaniment to "The Song of the Trainee Pilot." Then they all started singing—the chief accountant, Nishi, the chief registry clerk, the chief of student affairs, the serving maids—beating on saucers and trays with chopsticks, or just clapping their hands if there were no chopsticks nearby.

> The anchor and the cherry
> Are the signs we proudly show
> Emblazoned on our buttons
> Seven in a row.

And he just felt sorry for him, just looking at him and saying nothing. But then, what else could he have done? Was there anything else he could have done?

Ardent dreams and deep desires
And our nation's hopes are ours
Flying to the farthest shires
Rising with the clouds.

As the song came to an end he heard a woman's voice, and soft fingers nudged his knee.

"What you need is a good drink, and plenty of it. You look like you're sinking really fast."

He opened his eyes.

"Here you are. I'll hold it for you."

The woman closed his hand around a large cup full of saké.

"Make it whisky and water, if you don't mind," he said. "I'm afraid the Japanese Spirit just doesn't agree with me."

three

Two weeks after the executive directors' party, one Saturday morning, Hamada was sitting at his desk when the phone rang. It was a woman's voice on the line.

"Guess who?"

"I've guessed."

"Could I have a few words with you? I've got some good news. How about a stroll on the roof at lunchtime?"

"Fine," said Hamada, and put down the phone.

He'd ordered a lunch of pork cutlet and rice from a shop called Hare at ten o'clock, but it still hadn't arrived at noon. Nishi said cheerfully he'd had enough experience of their curry noodles, so he'd not ordered anything today, and went off to the staff canteen. The chief clerk was nibbling a bun and drinking some milk. Hamada left the Registry Office, repeating the joke about the tortoise really being faster than the hare, which must have been made hundreds, perhaps thousands of times in this room.

As it was Saturday there was almost nobody about, although as he went through the door onto the roof he overtook two male students wearing suits. They were talking about Trotsky.

"Of course, Stalin had a better grasp of reality. . . . All sorts of things wrong with what he did."

"People admire Trotsky because he was a failure like Minamoto Yoshit-sune."

The two students stopped talking when they noticed one of the staff nearby. On the wide expanse of the roof itself, right in the center, were six women students, jumping around with a skipping rope. He wondered why the girls here always managed to achieve such appalling combinations of colors in their dress. Perhaps because they came straight from the provinces? On the far side there were about twenty men in black student uniforms, buttons glittering, making a cheerful racket among themselves. Members of some supporters club about to start a cheerleader practice session. There was also someone sitting on a bench, smoking a cigarette and reading a sports paper, and another leaning against the railing. Hamada leaned on the railing as well. He looked toward Tokyo Tower in the distance, appearing even more unreal than in the picture postcards, white and red against the blue sky, then down at the graveyard of a temple next to the university campus, waiting for a woman whom he'd once promised to marry.

"Have you been waiting long?"

Masako soon turned up, speaking in her usual purring manner. She'd always prided herself on how well she looked in Japanese dress, and recently this had reached the point where she even came to work at the university dressed in a kimono.

"No, I've only just arrived. In the past I always . . ."

". . . used to keep me waiting. Yes?" she said, and went on smiling.

He said nothing and smiled back. He'd only met her a dozen times or so before he'd asked her to marry him, perhaps fewer than that, but it certainly hadn't been because he was head over heels in love with her. It was the spring of his fourth year at the university when a young girl just out of high school, big and tall, with large eyes and a rather dark complexion, had come to work in the Personnel Department. She was the youngest sister of a lecturer in archaeology called Aochi. Her brother didn't believe that a woman should go to university unless she had a particular devotion to scholarship, so she'd given up the idea, but she got so bored after only a month at home she decided to go out to work instead. The professor in charge of the Archaeology Department was well known as a boon drinking companion of the executive director whom Horikawa would kick out just six months later, and her career prospects were clearly involved in that camp, looking bright enough when she was first appointed. Despite her physical size, there was a peculiar innocence about her, as if one could still catch the whiff of her mother's milk, and this, combined with the fact that she was the sister of a member of the academic staff, meant she gave the impression she felt she was different, whether she meant to or not. For a long time Hamada was completely unaware that she was interested in him, just feeling occasionally that the new girl in personnel certainly looked at him sometimes in a rather fresh way, mistaking the coquetry of a grown woman for the naiveté of a child.

The misunderstanding was put right at the end-of-year party. This was a joint affair for both academic and clerical staff, which the academics usually cut to a man while the clerical staff always turned up in force, and that year it was no different. When it had ended, a dozen of the younger clerks, including three women, went on a tour of the stand bars, led by a man called Akasaka in Teaching Administration who, like Hamada, was not a graduate of the university. Among the three women was Masako, who'd just been taken onto the permanent staff. Whichever bar they went to, she made a point of sticking close to Hamada, even imitating his drinking habits by having whisky and water instead of the ladylike gin fizz. While the others made fun of her for this, Hamada was obliged to read it as a clear declaration of love. At the last bar Masako was the only remaining girl (although she'd given up drinking alcohol by this time), and there were only three men, Hamada, Akasaka, and someone else, so inevitably it became Hamada's task to see her home. When they got off the train and were walking along a dark road by the railway track, Hamada tried to link his arm with hers, but she insisted on holding hands, putting her right hand and his left hand inside the pocket of his coat to keep them warm, and talking about the dog they had at home. Hamada grew so weary of this recital of facts about something of which he was totally ignorant that, in order to put an end to it, he invited her to go to the cinema with him on the following day. She made only an ambiguous reply to this so Hamada, probably because he was fairly drunk, asked her to pay him a visit at home instead, since there'd be nobody around to bother them. As they passed beneath the yellow light of a street lamp, the girl nodded in acceptance.

The following day he had a hangover but thought he'd better get up and make himself decent because Masako was coming, although he still felt he had to lie down again in the afternoon. By about three o'clock, however, his headache seemed to have gone and he was beginning to feel hungry, so he got up, decided she wasn't coming after all, and went off to a local restaurant, locking the door behind him. His father had died the year before, the nurse Hiroko had gone back to her hometown (and also hired a lawyer to sue him over the distribution of his father's estate), and his brother Shinji had tuberculosis and was in a sanatorium. For the past six months, Hamada had been renting half the house to a married couple, while the thirty-year-old clerk himself was living alone, using the former examination room as a bedroom and living in the waiting room, sometimes cooking his own food but mostly eating out. The married couple seemed to have gone out around lunchtime, presumably to buy provisions for the New Year holiday.

He finished his meal, did the shopping for his dinner, and also bought a bottle of whisky on the assumption it might do something for his hangover. As he returned home holding the shopping parcels in both arms, he saw Masako standing by the front door, next to some insignificant azaleas that had been planted to replace the trees burned down in the air raid, playing with a neighborhood mongrel. The dog was very quiet, allowing itself to be stroked about the neck, its fur horribly matted much like a sand painting brush the day after he'd forgotten to wash it. He was astonished by this sight on two counts; first because she really had come to visit him, and second because a dog that did nothing but bark whenever it saw him should be acting so tame with her. In fact, the dog did burst out barking as soon as it saw him, but Masako instantly made it be quiet. When he asked her how she'd managed to get so friendly with the dog, she said (to the dog):

"That's because you really love my homemade cookies, don't you?"

The dog obligingly licked its chops, and the two humans laughed.

They went into what had been the waiting room and ate up her cookies, washing them down with cheap whisky and tap water, since there was no ice. The resulting intoxication, plus the fact that this sweet, coquettish young thing seemed to be there for the taking, proved too much, and after the first kiss he carried her into the next-door bedroom. She put up very little resistance. He was also surprised to find a girl who looked so large should have such a slim waist.

They were awakened from their trance by the harsh sound of the dog scratching on the glass of the long window. They talked, and she said her brother respected him enormously for doing something he'd wanted but never had the courage to do, and for succeeding in the most wonderful way. He said her brother must be just being sarcastic, but she insisted that he really did admire him. Hamada guessed that what had made this girl interested in him was his wartime record, but it didn't in the least surprise him. Gathering from past experiences, it was perfectly conceivable. It had already happened twice, first with a young widowed student and then with a nurse in the infirmary; both short affairs, and in both cases they'd been attracted to him by an interest in his past. It was as if a draft resister appealed to some women in the same way as a film star or a famous sportsman; and, in much the same way a really handsome man ceases to be surprised that women should fall for his good looks, so he got used to the idea that women could love him for the past he possessed.

What had shocked him was that Masako was a virgin. Of course the widowed student had not been, nor had the nurse or Akiko, so none of the three women he'd known before Masako had been virgins. On first sleeping with a virgin, therefore, he'd been overtaken by a flustered excitement, like a hunter suddenly confronted by some rare animal species. In the former exam room with its high, white ceiling, as he saw the dark stain on the sheet even darker than the surrounding twilight air, or even before that, when he'd caught the raw odor of blood coming from the fingertips of his right hand, he'd felt himself caught up in an onerous emotion combined of a harsh, naked excitement plus a dull sense of responsibility. Naturally the feeling of responsibility was intensified by the fact that the girl was a sister of a member of the academic staff, and he promised the face lying there in the growing dark that he would marry her.

When he went to Horikawa's house to offer the traditional New Year greetings, he told him about Masako as he sat there in front of a blazing fire on a chair that had been given new covers some time ago, long enough for the colors to have started to fade, and asked him to approach the girl's family on his behalf. The director agreed, but about two weeks later Hamada was called into his room and informed that he'd talked to Mr. Aochi, who didn't seem very enthusiastic about the idea, and so he'd be wise to forget about it. Hamada had heard a few days before from Masako that her family was opposed to the marriage, and—in contrast to the extraordinary circumlocutions of Horikawa's account, so involved one could hardly catch even the gist of it except by paying very close attention indeed—she had been quite blunt about the reason, repeating a number of times with tears in her eyes her brother's words that he could accept an academic member of the staff, but not someone on the clerical side. As far as she was concerned, her brother's word was law, and Hamada had no intention of asking the director to intervene again. The two of them met a number of times after that, but the brother got to know of it and gave her a severe telling off, and that was the end of their love affair.

Before two months had elapsed she became involved with an assistant professor of civil law, but he left the university to take up a post in a legal office in Kansai. Then she had a love affair with a very young man, almost a boy, in the accounts section of the library, followed by one with a lecturer in German that went on for two years (by this time Aochi had become an assistant professor and also ceased interfering in his sister's life), until she became friendly with Professor Uno of the Japanese Department. This had been going on until the present day and had virtually been given official sanction, although marriage remained out of the question since the professor had a wife who had long been in the care of a mental institution. Since their affair had ended, Hamada and Masako had been on very distant terms, although it would be hard to say whose fault that was. When they met on campus they would address each other in a friendly way, friendly enough to make people nearby prick up their ears, but it meant nothing and their actual relationship was quite cold. He had always felt something in her attitude (and obviously in her brother's as well) that suggested a powerful grudge against him as the man who had started her off on the road to misfortune, so when he'd heard her voice on the phone that morning, speaking in terms even more intimate than when they'd been lovers, he'd been surprised at how quickly he'd recognized this quite unexpected caller; now that he was meeting her on the rooftop he was overjoyed that the reserve, the ill feeling in fact, that had existed between them for so long had apparently quite disappeared.

"You've got news for me?"

"Yes. In the reshuffle, you're going to be made chief registry clerk. I don't imagine you've heard anything about it yet?"

"You must mean Nishi, surely?"

"No. Don't worry, this is for real. Nishi's being made assistant in the new Welfare Department they're setting up."

"In that case . . . ?"

"Right. The present chief registry clerk's being made head of the Welfare Department."

"Who'd you hear this from?" asked Hamada, who was still finding it hard to believe.

"My brother phoned me last night. He told me to please tell you."

Masako explained that it was something Kobayakawa had let slip to the dean of the law faculty, who in turn had divulged it to a professor of natural science on the general education faculty, and he had whispered it into Aochi's ear; and this meant it must be completely trustworthy information. A low-flying airplane zoomed by, its grating, metallic reverberations piercing and filling the whole sky for a moment, and the woman in her thirties now working in the Editorial Section moved her lips energetically, trying to conterbalance this disturbing sound, adding that the official announcement should be made sometime the week after next.

"Thanks for taking the trouble to let me know. Frankly, I'm astonished, as astonished as I was when I heard your voice on the phone."

"No doubt our conversation was overheard," she said, shrugging her shoulders. "Although I did make sure to use the phone when there was no one else in the room."

It was well known that the operators on the switchboard were in the habit of listening in on conversations, both as a form of diversion and because they were instructed to do so in certain cases by the directors and heads of departments. If the really veteran switchboard operator had been on duty when Masako rang him up, she would most certainly have listened in.

"I wonder if anyone's come to spy on us?" said Hamada, looking about him, but there was no likely suspect around. The girl students were still skipping. The cheerleaders were being drilled by their commander. The two students in suits, now sitting on a bench, were presumably still talking about Stalin and Trotsky, or perhaps Yoritomo and Yoshitsune.

"I was a bit worried they might put me through to Nishi's desk by mistake," she said.

"That wouldn't particularly bother you, surely?"

She looked intently at his face for a while, then said,

"Didn't you know?"

"Know what?"

"Nishi really pestered me at one time. Just before he got married."

"What, Nishi had a crush on you? It's the first time I've heard of it. So that's why he got married in such a hurry, because you'd given him the push?"

She nodded.

"He still tries it sometimes, even now. Asked me to go with him to some comic theater, the kind where they have all those dirty jokes. I refused, of course."

"Certainly seems to plan his campaign," said Hamada, and laughed.

"Makes me sick," said Masako, frowning histrionically.

At last the cheerleaders burst into full cry.

"Let's go," said Masako.

"Let's get out of here," said Hamada at the same time.

He recalled reading somewhere, probably in some weekly magazine, that when two people think the same thought in the same moment it is evidence they are falling in love with each other, but he decided not to mention this to her. They smiled faintly at each other, a slightly formal yet also a slightly intimate smile.

"I'll go down after you."

"All right then. Good-bye."

"Thanks again for everything. And thank your brother for me, will you?"

He watched the woman in her kimono of Toyoda pongee as she went away, and leaned on the railing, smoking a cigarette. In the graveyard below a middle-aged man was standing vacantly in front of a newly erected wooden grave tablet. He was accompanied by a small boy who was running energetically about along the paths between the graves. In the bright, cheerful light of a fine day in early summer, the sadness of those two didn't look all that terrible, he thought, feeling pleased that in some way his own happiness was being shared with that bereaved father and child in the form of the perfect weather.

Hamada was happy, and he allowed himself to rejoice, explaining to himself that it wasn't so much because he'd been promoted (he was already thinking in the past tense) to head of the office, but because he was glad the bad relationship between himself and Masako and her brother had come to an end. He'd often felt guilty about her probably feeling that he was responsible for the unhappy life she'd led, and sensed she and her brother must hold a deep resentment against him for that reason. He was glad about that; surely he was. But, of course, the totally unexpected promotion gave him tremendous pleasure, particularly the thought that he'd managed to overtake Nishi; and the news that Nishi had been rejected by Masako was the icing on the cake. Also, the fact that Masako and her brother should have brought him the news seemed a good indication of the importance of the position he would have in the university from now on. He hadn't felt as happy as this for a long time, and even when he'd been lucky in the draw first time and got the flat and when he'd passed the exam for technical college, they had both seemed infinitely more likely to happen than this. He went down the stairs, passing through bars of light and shadow, from the roof to the fourth floor, then to the third. Even the war coming to an end on August 15, 1945, astounding as it had been, had not been as totally unexpected. And the sense of joy had been much slower in coming.

The eleven o'clock bus to Uwajima was surprisingly empty; almost all the passengers were able to get seats, closing their eyes as soon as they sat down and falling asleep. The constant air raids meant that nobody was getting enough sleep. Sugiura took off his jacket and draped it over the rucksack he'd placed on the floor in front of him, closing his eyes too. The rucksack was full of rice he'd managed to get hold of, and he could feel the hard swelling of it against his putteed legs. The bus ran no longer on gas but on charcoal, and it took a long time to get the engine started. He also happened to be sitting on the rear seat, right above the charcoal boiler, and this made the midday heat of August even worse, while the occasional breeze that blew in through the window brought little relief, only the bitter charcoal smoke and specks of soot. When the bus at last got going, however, things became just about bearable, and Sugiura took off his field service cap, placed it on his lap, and dozed off.

He'd been that morning to the small town of Yoshida, quite near to Uwajima, with a horse and cart carrying Akiko's household valuables there for safekeeping, and was now on his way back. Since the beginning of summer Uwajima had suffered a number of air raids, and two thirds of the town had been burned to the ground. Akiko's home—the Yuki Pawnbroker's—was still intact, mostly thanks to the strenuous efforts of Sugiura, and they were even giving refuge to two families who'd been burned out of their houses. But, like huge black fountain pens, the incendiaries would still go on raining down at intervals of a week or even less, and the remaining third of the town was bound to go the same way. The town's main buildings were all gone, so why shouldn't the Yuki pawnshop meet the same fate? Akiko, Akiko's mother, and Sugiura agreed that their clothing and what was of value among their other possessions should be sent to the house of a distant relation (although all the items on pawn would be left in the shop as they were). They were amazed to find that what they'd believed to be a fantastically exaggerated rumor was indeed true: the horse and cart required for evacuating their possessions did cost 100 yen.

He was in Uwajima because the encounter with the black-suited employment agent in Kurashiki had frightened Akiko. Naturally enough she knew all about Hamada's secret, and they left the town early the following day, spending two months wandering from Okayama to Ako to Himeji to Akashi, while the sand artist with the wife plied his trade. At

Akashi he did well at the big festival, making what would have been enough to enable him to take it easy for a while if he'd been traveling alone, but then decided it wouldn't be safe to go to Kobe since there were too many military police there, crossing over to Awajishima instead. During those two months Akiko had insisted every day, in fact almost anytime they were quite alone together, that they'd be much better off going to her home in Shikoku and lying low there. One reason was her fear of other men in black with high military collars turning up and being suspicious of him. Another was that they were extremely short of money and often didn't know where the next meal was coming from, for it was quite clear that two of them couldn't live on the earnings of a sand artist, and the money Akiko had brought with her was disappearing fast. Things were particularly bad after they'd crossed over to the island of Awajishima. It seemed another sand artist had been there just before them, going all around the island, and the children were no longer interested. But Sugiura didn't at all like the idea of hiding away in the pawnshop at Uwajima, feeling it would be shameful to him as a man. Then he also had no guarantee that the mother would welcome him, despite all Akiko's talk about being an only child and her mother doing exactly what she told her to do, which made him feel even less inclined. But he also didn't want to leave Akiko and go off alone, since he gravely doubted he'd have been able to get even this far if he'd been traveling by himself. The upshot of all this confusion and hesitation was that he finally agreed to do as she said, and they took a small boat from Fukura to Miya, from one obscure fishing village to another. On board he picked up a piece of newspaper that had probably been used to wrap some food, which had a headline in very large type announcing that the commanding officer of the garrison on Attu* had been posthumously promoted three grades to lieutenant-general.

This did not mean he spent the whole of the two years from September 1943 until August 1945 in Uwajima. The mother certainly spoiled her

*The westernmost of the Aleutian Islands. It was occupied by the Japanese in 1942; U.S forces reinvaded in May 1943 and recaptured it after three weeks of fierce fighting. The Japanese garrison all died in a "death rather than surrender" suicide charge at the end.

daughter, but she was not prepared to give the same soft treatment to this man she'd picked up somewhere, even though she knew perfectly well that Akiko had been involved with at least one other man before. In fact, she was openly disgruntled about it at first, but finally she neither welcomed nor dealt harshly with him, merely accepting him and treating him halfway between a guest and a servant, letting him sleep in the guest room upstairs and also having him spend the day working in the small terraced fields on the rise at the back of the house, chopping firewood, or being sent off to buy rice and fish. Yet the main thorn in his side was not Akiko's mother but the man in charge of the shop, who lived out but came in every day, called Inoue. A scrawny man of about forty, he seemed to be worried he might lose his job to this intruder, and when Akiko and her mother weren't around he would give minor displays of spitefulness, being peculiarly inquisitive in the question of military service, apparently determined to get to the root of why Sugiura wasn't in the army. Although certainly well used to answering questions on this subject, Hamada was faced with a very persistent character this time, one whom he had to see day in and day out, and the situation was very different from those in the past, when he'd normally only had to deal with such inquiries once or twice from the same person and had always been able to evade quite easily the more awkward of them. Also, when he decided to shave off his beard as unbecoming to his new role of parasite and shop assistant, he found he felt weirdly naked to the world, as if he had just removed a very effective mask. So one evening in early September, around the time when the Italian armed forces surrendered, he was alone with Akiko and asked her if Inoue might not be in love with her and thus fiendishly jealous of him; but she only laughed the idea to scorn, which made him feel even more worried, although he wasn't particularly annoyed by the fact she hadn't taken him seriously. She maintained, saying the same thing a number of times, that he had nothing to worry about, because you could hardly imagine anyone living in a sleepy place like this with the wit to conceive that such a monstrous thing as a draft resister had appeared before their very eyes; and he tried to believe what she said.

Toward the end of October there appeared in the *Ehime News* (a newly amalgamated newspaper formed in keeping with the policy of just one newspaper to each prefecture) a small article that claimed the rumor, which had even reached this town, that Diet Member Seijo Nakano* had not committed suicide but been murdered by Tojo was totally without foundation. This seemed to Sugiura an example of provincial obtuseness in these matters that was much like Akiko's insensitivity toward his own genuine anxieties. He came to realize that all the neurosis and terror she'd demonstrated during the two months they spent traveling from Kurashiki to Awajishima was no sensitive concern with the safety of her lover but rather the fear a young girl, a young provincial girl, feels when she has left her hometown and is journeying in unknown territory. That was why, he suspected, she was able to react in this nonchalant, carefree fashion: she was back on home ground again. Finally he even came to think that, rather than trying to put up with this constant state of anxiety she would never try to understand, he'd be better off on the road again, the solitary, vagabond sand artist.

This vague sense that all was not well was transformed into a feeling that something was quite definitely wrong one night in the middle of November. It was early evening still, and Sugiura was sweeping the floor, occasionally glancing out of the corner of his eye at Inoue, who was working away with his abacus, while Akiko was cooking dinner. They'd just received their oil ration, and it seemed that night there was going to be tempura as a rare treat, for he could smell the aroma drifting into the shop. The mother had gone to some memorial service for one of her relatives, and she was due back shortly. She was always saying how much she loved tempura, so he could hardly imagine her failing to be in time for dinner.

Then the door slid open and a plainclothes detective came in. He hardly bothered to reply to the greetings Sugiura and Inoue made, immediately inquiring of Inoue, at great speed although quite good-humoredly, why he'd declined the fifteen kimono the maid from the inn had been asked to

---

* October 1943. This suicide remains dubious, and it has been claimed that one of the MPs stationed in Nakano's house to "guard" him later boasted of his murder. He was one of a group opposed to the Tojo government who was arrested, released without being charged, then allegedly committed ritual suicide on the evening of the day he was released.

bring here. Inoue narrowed his eyes as he searched through his memory until he finally remembered, but still chose to return the question by asking the detective if they had turned out to be stolen goods. The detective nodded, resting his buttocks on the step up into the main shop area, while Inoue courteously urged him nearer the porcelain pot that provided the sole, meager source of heat in the room, then explained at tedious length how much he'd been attracted by those particular items, all the goods of finest quality, but somehow he'd just not felt right within himself, felt there was something fishy about the whole thing. The detective grinned back at him, telling him not to be shy but let him know how he'd caught on to the fact they'd been stolen. So Inoue went on again about how good the kimono were, both the men's and the women's, and it was a very fair price being asked for them, he couldn't deny that, and the maid who'd brought them and was acting on someone else's behalf was a most trustworthy person, working at a very respectable place too, but he'd still felt there was something fishy about it. It was a difficult business to lay his finger on it, but first of all it was a bit funny that the men's and women's kimono hadn't been separated but were all jumbled up together, which he didn't like the look of at all; and then one of the kimono had been folded in a quite different way from all the rest, and that had seemed a bit queer too.

The detective gave a sigh of admiration, saying you always ought to go to the specialist, the real professional, turning to Sugiura, who'd been listening in, and asking for his agreement; and he gave a large nod of assent. Sugiura knew this policeman well, and was on good terms with him as he'd once mended his alarm clock for nothing. But Inoue modestly declined this estimate of his abilities, wisely praising the owner of the shop instead, saying that the madam here wouldn't have hesitated the way he had but known what they were at a glance. The detective had a cursory look through the accounts book, and Sugiura went on with his sweeping, although he did not miss the opportunity to say a few more words of praise concerning the sharpness of Inoue's judgment to the detective as he left. He'd been feeling for some time that the only thing to do was to try to get Inoue on his side, which now resulted in this open piece of flattery. But Inoue did not smile in response at all, only looking at him coldly and saying, in an ominous way, that in this business we have to be able to size up not just objects but people as well. This prompted Sugiura to wonder if the reason Akiko had been able to work out that Kenji Sugiura wasn't his real name had nothing to do with her womanly intuition, but was that she had a pawnbroker's blood in her veins. He pondered this idea all evening.

Late that night he talked to Akiko about Inoue, saying the man really scared him, but she only laughed and said Inoue was like an old woman so he had a good understanding of kimono, refusing to discuss it with him any further; so he told her he'd finally made up his mind about what he had to do, having come to this decision after Inoue had gone home and he'd been left alone looking after the shop. She listened and didn't object, but didn't say she would go with him. The next morning he sent off a telegram to the connection in Shinjuku, asking him to send five hundred sand painting kits to Sugiura, care of Kochi Station. Provided he stayed in Shikoku, particularly in the south of the island, he shouldn't have anything to worry about, and should be all right until the hair on his face had grown again. In fact, he was thinking this time of growing a toothbrush moustache, something he'd previously desisted from in deference to old Inaba, growing a beard instead. That kind of moustache would make him look even older. Speculation over the various ways he could let the hair grow on his face was about the only pleasure he had in life now.

But the travels of the toothbrush-moustached sand artist lasted for less than six months, and he was back in Uwajima in April 1944, just a short while before the news was announced that the Grand Commander of the Combined Fleets had died heroically at his post. He was feeling even worse about coming here than he had the time before, returning in a state of virtual fear and trembling. But in fact there was little for him to worry about, for Inoue had been given a job with the gas company where they were short of staff, and since this meant the current labor shortage was directly affecting the Yuki Pawnbroker's, Akiko's mother was delighted to see him, not only as help in the shop but because his skill as a clock repairer would be invaluable. New clocks and watches were no longer appearing on the market, so timepieces of all kinds were about the best-selling line in the pawnshop business. In fact, foreign models, provided they weren't in too bad a state of repair, were fetching the same kind of prices as genuine antiques or works of art.

So he had stayed there this time, looking after the shop, repairing clocks and watches, doing the various chores of a servant, right up to this very day; remained from April 1944 until August 15, 1945. The abundance of provisions in Uwajima, plus the general confusion of the period leading up to the end of the war, had both helped him to survive. One other thing that made life easier was that Inoue, whom he occasionally saw in town and sometimes talked to and sometimes not, was rumored to have been killed during an air raid in mid-July that took place during a remarkably heavy rainstorm, and that put his mind at rest a good deal. Although he was not particularly aware of it himself, he was in fact leading a life of ease, a life of libidinous ease, for, in the intervals between the air raid warning and the all-clear, he would invariably indulge in the delights a woman's body affords, stimulated by the obvious needs of a twenty-five-year-old man and intensified by the fact that Akiko herself was overjoyed to partner him in these acts.

Certainly there were sights that would cast a damper over such pleasures and recall him to the world outside. There were the air force cadets running along the road outside his window every morning, for example, and in particular a sight he observed on two occasions, that of a boy who had fouled himself as he ran yet went on running, running away from him with his white cotton trousers stained yellow about his buttocks. Each time these unwanted stimulants assailed him he remembered that his real name was Shokichi Hamada, and that all this was no nightmare but the real way things were. Yet he drifted on in his world of sloth, refusing to permit himself any hopes for the future, although he'd heard on the radio the night before, the night of August 14, that there was to be a special broadcast of grave importance at noon on the following day, and it had occurred to him this could well mean Japan had at last accepted defeat; but he immediately rejected the assumption, telling himself he shouldn't indulge in idle dreams, for the Japanese military would hardly have the sense to do anything as wise as that, and at lunchtime tomorrow there would be an address from Prime Minister Suzuki urging them all to fight on to the bitter end. To think pessimistically was perhaps the only method available to him of imposing some kind of harsh discipline upon his soul.

The atomic bombs had already been dropped on Hiroshima and Nagasaki, but Akiko's mother said it was rumored the Americans only had two of these "new-type" bombs; Sugiura's opinion was that this was wishful thinking and they probably had another hundred or two all lined up. He had enough scientific knowledge to work out that the "new-type" bomb must, in fact, be an atomic bomb, but his loathing and contempt for the Japanese military were such that he grossly overestimated the scientific potential of the United States. For this reason, when he heard that the next one was not going to be dropped on any of the three major cities of Shikoku, Matsuyama, Takamatsu, or Tokushima, but on Niigata up there in the north, he did not so much think of that particular place—of the Shinano River, of Bandai Bridge, of the willows by the fosse, or of the view of an island he had seen with old Inaba, standing on the dunes and looking across the sea to that violet shadow far off—but more of scenes from the whole country he had observed in his travels, of bridges, of rich houses, of memorial stones in the corners of parks, images that assailed him confusedly and unceasingly; he thought that the atomic bombs would fall on Niigata and Okayama and Osaka and Tokyo, and on Uwajima as well, of course. He'd heard dreadful stories of the plight of the victims, some of whom had fled to Uno, from any number of people, but he experienced very little fear, feeling rather the melancholy expectation that he too would see the blinding flash and the mushroom cloud and the black rain, as this town also would be reduced to ruins, and his own long flight brought to an end. At the age of twenty-five he had grown used to living without hope.

As soon as he got off the bus he was stopped by a policeman. At first he thought he was going to have his rucksack searched, but he felt a certain relief on seeing this was a man he knew, for he had sometimes come to the shop investigating something or other. The policeman took half a towel out of his pocket and used it instead of a handkerchief to wipe the sweat off his face, and said, in the thick dialect of the region,

"Now we're really in for it, aren't we?"

These words made Sugiura feel even more relieved, the words of a man who seemed to have doffed his uniform, or had it removed for him, and was voicing the same kind of complaint as an ordinary citizen. The policeman went on talking about something very much in the tones of a man moaning about the increasing amount of soya being mixed in with the rice ration, but Sugiura wasn't at all clear what he was going on about, and when the policeman finally noticed the mystified expression on his face, his own took on the happy look of a man who is blessed with real news to tell.

"Well, Mr. Sugiura, it's just that His Imperial Highness has read us a rescript saying we've lost the war. You didn't know, did you? Some people are saying that what it really said was that we weren't just dealing with the Americans and the British anymore, but we'd have to take on the Russians as well; but they've got it quite wrong, it seems."

So his prediction had been proved amazingly right. He'd been dead right! And yet he felt not one iota of joy.

He left the policeman and went back to Akiko's house, dumping his heavy load. Akiko had gone out with both the wives of the two families lodging with them to buy some fish. Akiko's mother was looking after the shop, playing cat's cradle with two little girls who belonged to one or the other of the families, or perhaps to both. She looked up at his face with eyes like those of a dead fish and told him Japan had lost, looking at him very intently in a way she had never looked at him before; and he gathered from the expression on her face that she must have known all about his secret for some time now.

He went out into the garden and spent quite a long time weeding it, and when he'd reached a natural stopping point he went to the outdoor bathroom and carefully bathed himself. Then he wound his puttees back on, put on his field service cap, and said he was going for a little walk. Just as he was going out of the shop, a shop with no sign above it but only a small plaque by the side of the door, the woman stopped playing cat's cradle and said it was quite certain the war had been lost because she'd heard it on the radio he'd very kindly mended for them, and although a lot of the language was very hard, it wasn't only her but Akiko and the two other ladies who'd heard it, and they'd heard the same thing so that made it positive; and she looked at him exactly as she'd done before, a look he felt was telling him it was because of draft dodgers like himself that Japan had been defeated.

He went to the local office of the *Ehime News*, which was still intact, and opened the door. In the large room there was only one man, sitting down, wearing gray trousers but naked to the waist. He had his back to the door, facing a grubby bamboo blind, with his head lowered. Hamada addressed his naked back.

"Excuse me, do you mind if I ask you something?"

"All right."

The man replied without turning toward him or even raising his face. Perhaps he was bewailing the fate of the nation? Weeping, perhaps? Hamada did not wish to intrude on his grief but felt he had to know, so he walked over the dirty wooden floorboards toward him. As he approached he realized that the thin, middle-aged journalist was in fact leaning over a *shogi* board, absorbed in some problem.

"Is it true that the war's been lost?" he asked.

"Yes, it's true. It's quite true. The end of the war was . . ."

Sugiura found it a bit difficult to follow his mumble at this point, but then the voice picked up again.

"They're having a dreadful time in Tokyo, it seems."

"In what way?"

"Well, probably not all that bad," he said, in flat contradiction of what he'd just said, and then readjusted a move he'd made on the board.

He thanked him and left. He still felt no joy at all. He climbed up Castle Hill to look out over the town, or rather at the blackened area where it had been, then looked at the bright blue of the sea. Because the intervening houses had vanished, the sea looked much nearer than it used to. There were three burned and blackened frames of trainer airplanes on a field with several holes in it, namely the airfield. The mountains, the streets, the sea had all become silent again. The war was over. The Japanese army had ceased to exist, and he no longer had any opponent to fight. This meant he had won. But he felt hollow inside, deprived, the empty achievement of a young wrestler who gains a formal victory over an unbeatable Grand

Champion because his mighty opponent has been forced to concede the contest through injury. He'd always known that if he were to defeat the Japanese army, his victory could only come in this form, and now that it had actually happened he understood he'd never really believed he had any chance of living to see this day.

But what was he to do now? He sat on a stone bench in the shade of a tree and gazed at a far-off bamboo grove. The bamboo grass, moved by the passing breezes, displayed a variety of fine shades of different colors but always returned to its original one. He unwound his puttees, reflecting that there would be no more air raids, but did not throw them away, holding them in his hand as he went down the hill. What was he going to do? It would be fine if he could go on living under these same conditions, with no war and no Shokichi Hamada. He was slightly afraid of reassuming his real name. He'd thought enough times about the war ending, but never about what he'd do when it ended. Perhaps he could go on working in the pawn-shop?

Then he felt the first sensation of true joy, felt it in his legs, a queer sensation like smoke enwrapping them. Since he'd taken off his puttees, his trousers flapped and wound about his legs, making it quite difficult to walk, and this was a remarkably new sensation, a pure apprehension of release, perhaps, although when he recalled the ease with which he'd walked up this hill he began to have doubts, wondering if it wouldn't be better to put the puttees back on again; but the feeling of being unrestricted, of the bottoms of his trousers flapping, was so pleasant, and the sense of pleasure grew stronger and stronger, so when he arrived at the bottom of the slope he was thinking that the best thing would be to celebrate by doing something he really wanted to do. But what did he want to do, now, at this moment? Play *shogi*? Cat's cradle? Go hunting for food? Then he smiled. That's it: the bowl. It was a bowl he'd seen in the local antique shop a month ago, and although he'd wanted it he'd decided it would be extravagant to buy it. Now he'd decided to buy it. There was no need to worry about five yen anymore. He smiled again as he thought how Akiko, who was always accusing him of being so tight about money, would be surprised at this cheerful piece of extravagance, and wondered what she'd say.

So he would make this a memorable day, as it would be for the children and the journalist, but with a quite different consciousness of the day from theirs. But what consciousness of the day did Akiko's mother have as she played cat's cradle with the children? What was she feeling? What were any of them feeling?

From the third floor to the second, from the second floor to the first, through bars of shadow and light, Hamada descended. For years he'd had this oppressive feeling that she really hated him, Masako hated him for being the cause of the way she had to live, and that her brother hated him for the same reason; and now it was gone, completely vanished. It was more than likely that Assistant Professor Aochi was thinking of making use of Hamada in his future influential post, and had gone to all this trouble to let him hear the news so quickly in order to get on good terms with him again. In the first-floor corridor a professor of international law called out to him,

"Hello, Hama, how's it going these days?"

The professor made it clear by his gesture that he was talking about mah jong. The lawyer, with his hair parted chronically close to the side of his head and spectacles with silver frames, was no great intimate of his but had this jovial way of addressing people as if he felt he really belonged to the world of entertainment.

"Not getting in enough practice these days, I'm afraid."

"That won't do. We'll have to have a session soon."

"An excellent idea."

"Just had a letter from old Shiba in the library, who's over in the States at the moment. He says our gang over there mostly go at the rate of fifty. What do you reckon that means? Fifty cents a thousand?"

"I suppose so. It could hardly be fifty dollars."

"Guess not. Then it's two hundred yen. Well, see you around."

He waved his right hand vaguely and moved briskly away. Hamada went into the lavatory, where Hasegawa, one of the messengers, was washing his hands.

"Hello."

"Hello there yourself, Mr. Hamada; and may I offer my congratulations?"

"What about?"

"Now it's no use your trying to pull the wool over the eyes of a young lad like me who's always got his big ear close to the ground."

The young man dried his hands by flapping them about, while he thrust one of his ears in front of Hamada's face. It was indeed almost grotesquely large, and also peculiarly dark in color, in striking contrast to the pallor of his face, and somehow seemed inappropriate to the honest expression he wore. Hasegawa went out and Hamada had a long, enjoyable leak, thinking it could very well be that the professor had invited him to play mah jong because he'd already heard about his promotion.

The food from the Hare restaurant had arrived, typically well before the time at which he wanted to eat it, and it had been placed on his desk, where it was getting cold. He was just finishing eating the thin, hard cutlet and the meager helping of hard, cold rice when Nishi came bustling in.

"Enjoyed his date, did he . . ." he said perkily.

Hamada wasn't particularly taken aback by this, since it wasn't in the least strange that he should have tamed one or two of the switchboard girls. Yet it could also be that someone had been watching them, perhaps. What he did find so astonishing, however, that he mistrusted his own ears was the way Nishi completed the sentence, after a slight pause.

". . . the new boss?"

Hamada merely looked at Nishi's face in silence and put down his chopsticks, trying to look as if he had not quite caught Nishi's words or did not fully understand what they meant. Nishi sat in a corner and started reading a newspaper. Hamada got up, smoking a cigarette, and went over to a round table that had a teapot and a Thermos on it, wondering if the man really knew anything and why he'd made what looked like an effort to unnerve, even intimidate him. Hamada was aware of a deep contradiction within his own emotional responses to all this. In the case of the professor, he'd found himself happy to believe the seeming proof the rumor was spreading, and yet with Nishi he found he was trying hard not to believe it could have spread so far. The fact was, of course, that he was afraid of

Nishi. He just couldn't be sure what he might say or do. He stood by the table with his back to Nishi, smoking, sipping tea, and thinking. Would Nishi look right in a black suit with a high military collar? Or would a people's uniform suit him better?

In April it was still cold in Shinshu, the mountain region west of Tokyo, and although Sugiura preferred to eat soba in the summer fashion, served on a wicker basket and dipped in cold sauce, he ordered it in a bowl of hot soup, since he needed the warmth to avoid catching a cold. He'd put his sand painting materials on the table before him, sitting with his overcoat still on. As he read the menu on the wall, he noted you could get a variety of soba served in miso soup and garnished with duck and onion, and he was sorely tempted to try it but decided not to. He'd put up with the food he'd decided on, a double portion of it. Business wasn't going too well nowadays, and he couldn't afford any luxuries. Also there was the question whether a dish as fancy as that could possibly be available, considering present-day shortages. It seemed very unlikely. There wouldn't be any duck, for a start. Chicken instead? Pork? There wouldn't be any of those, either. An old woman with bloodshot eyes appeared and took his order, repeating it to make sure she'd got it right. *Kakesoba*, double portion. He nodded, and then noticed there was another customer in the shop, up on the raised tatami area to the back. He thought of going there himself, but it had a slightly exclusive air about it, and he was worried something extra might go on the bill if he did. He could just hear what Akiko would have said: "Ken, you really are tight-fisted, aren't you?"

Still, it was a great thing to be eating soba at all, particularly when you had no meal vouchers. It was almost miraculous. You couldn't get soba in most towns in this country; not to eat like this. The noodles were mostly cut up fine and mixed with rice, distributed that way as part of the rice ration, being the most edible of all the various rice substitutes.

It was April 1944. The war was being lost, and the common people were leading lives of extreme poverty. He'd heard on the train from Kofu to Matsumoto that old tea leaves were being mixed into the rice given out in Tokyo. One of the passengers squatting in the crowded corridor had whispered that, and the old man next to him vouched for the truth of it, saying it was no rumor but the plain truth since he'd eaten some of it himself, then eating a delicious-looking ball of pure white rice. Sugiura found himself staring at that ball of rice, and thought how long it was since he'd eaten rice as unadulterated as that. When he'd left Akiko's house in Uwajima in November 1943, she'd made him rice balls exactly the same as the one the old man was eating, pure white; and that was the last time. He'd been on the road now for still less than six months, and yet it seemed a fantastically long time.

A little girl with a grubby face came out of the back room of the shop, kicking off her tiny rubber boots in order to climb up onto the tatami area and switch on the radio, which was right next to the other customer. The radio took some time to warm up, and finally it was someone singing a song addressed, presumably, to a child, assuring the child that when it grew up big and strong Japan would have grown big and strong as well. Then it was the news. The announcer described the Imperial Army's assault upon Imphal* in the vaguest possible terms, giving no information whatsoever with a remarkable fluency. The old woman brought his food on a tray. Just as all Japanese people had started to do recently, perhaps because they had at last begun to suspect it was no longer the truth, Sugiura simply ignored the news as he got down to his meal. The soup was too bitter, but the soba was nice and hot.

When he was starting on the second bowl, the old woman began talking to the other customer, telling him, in exactly the same tone of voice she had just used to scold the little girl, that if he should fall off to sleep like that he'd catch his death of cold. This customer was dressed in a people's uniform, half sprawled on the tatami but with his back propped against a wooden pillar, and he took no notice of the old woman's warning and looked as if he were about to drop off any moment. She then suggested he at least cover himself with his overcoat, but he only made an irritated grunt in reply, and the woman was not sufficiently concerned to step up there and do it for him. Sugiura glanced in the direction of the man as he

* Scene of a decisive defeat for the Japanese army in the Burma campaign.

sipped his soup, looking neither at him in particular nor at the little girl quietly playing dibs by his side, not paying attention so much to the fact that he did seem now to have dozed right off but to what was on the small table beside him. It was this bottle of alcohol placed next to his spectacles that surprised Sugiura, since it was clear from its chunky shape and the old-fashioned lettering on the label that it was Old Parr. His father had been very fond of whisky, but only quite exceptional patients or their families ever sent him a gift of that quality, and when such a bottle had been received his mother would not have dreamed of dispatching it elsewhere, as she did with most presents, unless it were for some very special occasion indeed. Old Parr just never had been easy to get hold of (or at least not during that period when the young Hamada had been aware of its existence), so what on earth should this precious object be doing in a dirty little noodles shop on the outskirts of a town like Matsumoto at a time when everything was in chronically short supply? It was obvious he could only have brought the bottle with him, and Sugiura looked at the open bag from which he must have extracted it, feeling he was looking at something that possessed genuinely magical qualities.

As he went on eating he naturally began to pay attention to the possessor of that magic bag, and this time he truly was astounded, with a surprise that could hardly be compared to the mild sensation he'd experienced just a few moments before. The man who wore what looked like a brand-new, still brightish yellow people's uniform, and who lay in a drunken stupor before him, was the very same man he'd met in Kurashiki who'd talked to him about coal mining, although he'd been wearing a black suit with a high military collar then. Keiichi Asahina was certainly much plumper than he'd been when they met in Kurashiki, but the reason Sugiura hadn't recognized him though he was only a few feet away was that he'd taken off his glasses. Sugiura told himself he had to get out of this place, and quick, but even while he was delivering this message to himself and acknowledging its aptness, he still went on sitting there finishing his meal, although he'd completely lost any appetite he'd had. But this calmness was only an index of the state of fear he was in, for he was anxious that any sudden change in his behavior might possibly cause the sleeping man to open his eyes, so he went on eating the noodles and sipping the soup. His hand was shaking as it held the bowl. It didn't cross his mind that now that he'd exchanged his beard for the kind of moustache Asahina himself had, he must look very different from what he'd been in Kurashiki.

The night before he'd left Uwajima he'd been tidying up his sand painting materials when he'd come across Asahina's stained and mottled card at the bottom of an empty cream jar he used for diluting his paste. Sugiura tore it up into very small pieces, then took the pieces into the kitchen and threw them on the fire. Akiko laughed and said he surely didn't need to hate him that much, but this was no outburst of hatred on his part. It was more a fear that during his coming journey he might eventually become weary of heart, choosing the easy way out, escape into the mines, and so try to get in touch with Asahina. What was on his mind at this moment was not only a sense of fear but also the knowledge that he had only to call out to the man in front of him and then he could find "rest," certain rest, in the darkness under the northern Kyushu earth, or even perhaps under the sea's bed.

A comic recitation program began on the radio, and the old woman came out of the kitchen to sit on the step up into the raised portion of the shop and listen, entranced, to a well-known comedian's account of various ways of drinking. Sugiura finished drinking his soup. The little girl came to the old woman's side and begged her to play dibs with her, for which she was promptly scolded again; and perhaps it was this voice, or a sudden rise in that of the comedian on the radio, that made the sleeping man open his eyes and Sugiura hastily lower his. But when he looked up again the employment agent—if that was what he still was, since the Old Parr suggested he'd lost his original indifference and joined the Tojo faction—had fallen asleep again with his elbows propped on the table. Sugiura signaled with his eyes to the old woman, now playing dibs with the little girl, and placed some money on the table, and as she approached to pick it up finally drank what remained in his bowl. It was a muddy white, lukewarm liquid that greeted his lips, and after this gesture he quietly shouldered his sand artist gear and left the shop.

As he walked hastily through Matsumoto, almost running rather than walking, the trembling in his body failed to stop. Asahina might have grown plump, removed his glasses, and gotten drunk, but Sugiura was still scared of him. In fact, he found him terrifying now in a way he never had those nine months ago in Kurashiki, when he'd hardly feared him at all but had been quite calm and collected during the time he'd spent with him. It was that one remark of his, "Sugiura—if that's your real name," that had taken on a variety of inflated implications as he'd turned it over and over in his head. Then all the way from Kurashiki to Fukura, Akiko had gone on and on about the man in the black suit, saying they must get across to Shikoku, for then they'd be safe from him, and presumably this must have had a powerful effect upon him as well. He went straight back to his lodgings in front of the station, got back the ration card he'd only handed over the day before, paid his account, and after waiting in line for three hours, fearful all the time that Asahina might suddenly turn up by complete accident, he finally managed to get hold of a ticket for Nagoya.

According to the *Complete Guide to Shrine and Temple Fête Days* that Inaba had left him, there were a number of "markets" in the Nagoya area in mid-April, all of which were marked "average" for attendance; besides which, it was just the right time for cherry blossom viewing. What he planned to do was make enough money in a few days to buy his ticket back to Shikoku. Back to Shikoku, back to the terraced fields of Uwajima as soon as possible. Sugiura didn't know that the dreaded Inoue was already employed by the gas company, but he did keep on assuring himself that even that man, with his ability "to size up objects, and people," would be infinitely easier to handle than someone like Asahina. He'd often wondered why he'd managed to get so upset about someone as insignificant as that but failed to reach any answer, except perhaps that Akiko had been right and he'd just become neurotic about him, as she had insisted any number of times. From Shikoku to Kumano, then to Ise, then along the Tokaido, on to Kofu and now to Matsumoto, and all the time that he'd been traveling away from Uwajima and his former life, his feelings about it had gradually grown deeper. One reason was that life itself had become harder all over the country, as food shortages had grown a stage more acute than they'd been on his previous travels, and so each day became more tiring. Also, since practically everybody was being called up these days, very few people asked him why he wasn't a soldier, assuming he had some obvious physical disability, but they did inquire how he'd been clever enough to get away without being drafted to work in some factory or other, and he found that for some reason much harder to take. But the main reason he wanted to go back, which hardly needs saying, was that he wanted Akiko. He was still only twenty-four, alone physically and mentally, and he needed his older mistress, needed her both body and soul.

The forty-five-year-old Hamada put his cup down on the small, round table. Nishi wasn't wearing a black suit with a high collar or a people's uniform. He was wearing a brown suit with a dark reddish hand-woven tie, and the only things made of black material that he normally wore, the wristbands to protect his shirt cuffs, he didn't have on at the moment. He was nothing to be afraid of. And then, even if some totally inconceivable miracle were to occur and he should turn around and find himself facing not Nishi but Asahina, the one who'd be utterly confused by this encounter would be not himself but the other man, the old man now, with the stooping shoulders. The war had ended years ago; times had changed completely, and he was the victor, not the defeated. He'd just make a few cheerful jokes, always being considerate enough not to wound the other's feelings. "Well, Asahina, it's a pity the coal mines haven't been doing all that well lately; the slump in business must have hit you pretty hard. By the way, was that genuine Old Parr? I started drinking whisky after the war, but I have to admit I haven't managed to get around to drinking Old Parr yet."

While he was holding this imaginary conversation with the employment agent, the chief clerk came into the office with a very fierce expression on his face. Hamada made a slight bow in salutation, but he didn't seem to notice. This didn't give Hamada any particular cause for concern, and he went back to his imaginary conversation. "No, there's not much money to be made working in a university office. Hardly likely to be. Do you mean it was actually you who was responsible for the fall of the Tojo cabinet? You know, when I saw that bottle of Old Parr I'm afraid I jumped to the conclusion you'd gone over to the Tojo faction. Really sorry about that." The employment agent, the patriot, had looked extremely embarrassed, even guilty, at the beginning, but he gradually regained his composure, until at the end he was smiling happily all over his wrinkled face. At this point the confrontation delayed some twenty years came to an abrupt end, like a film breaking down, because his attention had been seized by the whispered conversation between the chief clerk and Nishi.

Certainly he couldn't grasp the actual content of what they were saying, for he only caught occasional fragments of their talk, but the secretive and vital nature of it was clear enough from the way they were behaving, even if it was all going on behind his back. He also didn't enjoy the fact that two people should be having this furtive conversation while the only other person in the room was being ostentatiously kept out of it. If only somebody else would come in, then he could chatter away with that man or that woman, thereby somehow putting a brave face on things; but all the young staff members had gone outside, probably to play volleyball, so all he could do was swallow his mild annoyance and leave in as casual a way as possible. But once he was in the corridor he remembered he'd left his cigarettes on his desk, so he went back to get them, and overheard the chief clerk's voice through the opening of the door that had been left ajar.

"It's a question of how relevant people will finally decide it is."

"Put it like this, then. We, the undersigned, maintain primarily that the question of draft resistance must properly be considered pertinent to the matter at issue."

That was Nishi's voice. Hamada's face turned dark as he retraced his steps and then headed for the main entrance. They'd heard rumors about the proposed reshuffle and were giving vent to their respective dissatisfactions, for the chief clerk would object to being made head of a new department as being effectively a demotion, which it was, and Nishi wouldn't at all like the idea of being overtaken by Hamada. Not only was this undoubtedly what was going on, but also it seemed perfectly natural to him that they should respond like that. He certainly didn't think they were just having a friendly chat with each other because they were going to be buddies again in the new Welfare Department. He'd always assumed that the chief clerk must think more of him than he did of Nishi, and although he was quite prepared for any ill will Nishi might be disposed to display, he found he was more or less defenseless against this obvious enmity on the part of the chief clerk. Of course, they might both just be having a little game with him, mocking the way the draft resister had risen in the world in the form of a parody of some Imperial Rescript to the Armed Forces, which was what Nishi's bureaucratic style had reminded him of; but that didn't seem very likely, and its effect upon him had been too potent for him to be prepared to laugh.

He headed for the entrance, exchanging greetings with the chief librarian and an ancient professor of civil law who passed him on the way, and then he was outside in the bright daylight. The young clerks were playing volleyball. A group of students, about a dozen girls and a dozen boys, were washing denim trousers. He wondered what club they belonged to. He wanted to get the bad taste out of his mouth, so he took a few deep breaths and set out toward the main gate, bowing to the shrine on his way and then leaving the campus, intending to take a turn about the neighborhood. But he was soon stopped in his tracks. Professor Kuwano had his Renault parked on the pavement in front of the university, and he rolled down the window, waved his hand out of it, and bawled at him in that notoriously loud voice of his. Hamada said to the suntanned face,

"Are you just going home?"

"Yes. I've been stuck with Saturdays this year. No one wants to teach on Saturday. All morning classes, and I hate getting up early."

Hamada stuck his head in through the car window and said,

"This car certainly seems to give you a good view of the road."

"Yes. That and the steering are its two redeeming features."

"This is the gear lever?"

"That's right. I didn't know you knew how to drive."

With his face still stuck in through the window, he explained they'd had a car at home before the war and he'd just picked it up. He'd gotten his license when he was a student, and a year or two ago he'd taken the new driving examination and passed it quite easily, although he didn't have a car himself.

Probably because he was pleased that Hamada approved so much of his car, Kuwano opened the door, slid over to the passenger seat, and let Hamada sit in front of the steering wheel.

"Could I drive it a little? It would mean driving illegally while not in actual possession of a driving license, since I don't have mine on me."

"Sure. Have a go. I'm afraid the clutch is a bit weak . . . one of the things that's wrong with the Renault . . . so please try not to use it only half out."

He drove the Renault once around the university, praising the car while Kuwano admired his driving, and then parked it again in the same place. They both stayed seated inside the car, talking about the prices of second-hand vehicles. Kuwano said he'd gotten this from a friend who'd bought it while on sabbatical in France. He'd paid 400,000 for it, but imagined you could probably buy a fairly similar Renault for about half the price. Then he offered Hamada a cigarette, and they both sat there smoking Peace cigarettes. Hamada said how good the first intake of a Peace tasted, and Kuwano said it was the same with the first mouthful of beer, and from that point they got onto the war and the period just after, when it had been so difficult to get hold of cigarettes.

"That's right, of course, but I didn't smoke during the war. Didn't drink, either."

"So you're postwar generation in terms of tobacco and alcohol?"

This reply itself wasn't particularly brilliant; in fact it was boringly obvious; but the way in which Kuwano said it was in complete contrast to the words themselves, sounding strangely emotional. Hamada politely laughed at what was, in formal terms, a witticism, realizing at the same time that not only did this assistant professor of French know all about his war experiences, but also he'd guessed correctly that Hamada hadn't smoked or drunk during that period because of restraints he felt obliged to impose upon himself, both economic and moral.

Then Kuwano started abruptly to talk about the persecution he'd suffered when he was a soldier. In the school cadet corps he'd been struck during drill by the officer instructor, and this had so annoyed him he got sick at all drill sessions afterward, with the result he had "unsuited for any position of responsibility or command" written in his record book. For that reason, despite the fact he was due to go to the university, he was not given military deferment and was called up in the winter of 1944–45 and sent to the division barracks at Utsunomiya. Although the other new recruits only started to get knocked about on their second day, and only with the flat of the hand as well, he alone caught it from the very first day, with a slipper made out of an old army boot with plenty of studs sticking out of it. He was told this would make a decent soldier out of him, but it didn't, and he'd had no intention of becoming one in the first place. The result of the three months of basic training was that everybody was promoted to private first class except himself, who remained second class, as when he had begun. They were formed into a company and sent off to a different place, but he went on being beaten up just as he had at division barracks.

"It's not true that the one pleasure unhappy people have is the prospect of sleep. I didn't have even that small amount of joy. When lights out sounded, all I could think of was that this would all start again tomorrow. You know that song: 'A soldier's life is really sad, Each night he weeps himself to bed.' Whoever wrote those lyrics—if lyrics they can be called—was some sort of genius. If he were alive now he'd be making a fortune writing TV commercials."

Hamada smiled, but only out of politeness. It gave him no pleasure to hear this recital of the misfortunes of the soldier's life. He knew this man was well disposed toward him, and could only wonder that he'd chosen a subject that seemed almost like a personal affront. Kuwano went on about his military experiences, however, while Hamada became progressively bored, even disgusted by them, although he also reflected that someone professing to teach foreign literature presumably needed this ability to go on and on about a subject regardless of whether anyone listening was interested or not.

Kuwano nearly got himself killed on the great day of August 15, 1945. He was still only a private second class. The whole company had been ordered to assemble in the garden of the house of the village councilor, in orderly ranks, to listen to the Imperial Message, but the radio reception was so poor, the Emperor read so badly, nobody seemed to have realized that the style of the Imperial Rescripts was not suited to oral communication, and the whole thing was so littered with bits of literary Chinese that no one in the whole company had been able to work out what it meant. No one except Kuwano, that is. When the broadcast ended, the company commander bluffed his way out of it by saying they had been ordered to redouble their efforts, to strive with might and main for the Empire, which made no one any the wiser. But that afternoon private second class Kuwano, in response to inquiries from the privates first class in his section, interpreted the Imperial Rescript's basic meaning as being that the war had been lost. An NCO turned up to ask the same question, then people from other sections and platoons, but they found his interpretation hard to accept, so eventually he wrote large with a stick on the earth the more pertinent of the broken phrases he could remember, then gave a lecture indicating the kind of meaning these must imply if they were taken all together. But all remained only half convinced and half skeptical.

Those few hours from lunch to dinnertime were the one period of glory in his whole military career. In fact, it went on a little longer, for after dinner a number of soldiers tended to gather about him, and he gave the same lecture (or rather the same *explication* of an inadequate text suffering from numerous missing pages) over again. His section was billeted in a fairly large wooden barn, with the section corporal's bed separated from the others behind a curtain. The corporal was, at the time, lying on his bed drinking saké from a canteen. Kuwano knew he was there and was choosing his words very carefully, but still the result was that people finally came to believe what he was saying. First of all one private soldier became convinced of the truth of it, making the major discovery that this must mean the entire Japanese army would henceforth cease to exist. This announcement gave hope to a number of soldiers, and one of them was so overjoyed he mentioned the name of a corporal in charge of another section, saying he was such a social misfit he'd never be able to get any job in civilian life, and cheerfully wondering what would happen to people like that.

"Our corporal was absolutely furious, and came rushing out from behind his curtain and started laying into me, first with the slipper, then with the belt, and finally both together. He kept it up until daybreak. I still sometimes get pains in my cheekbones . . . on cold days. The man was a complete moron, of course. Volunteer NCO. He couldn't stand the idea there'd be no Japanese army and no employment for him anymore, that the whole enterprise was bankrupt, so it drove him half crazy. God knows how I lived through it. I should by rights have died. The unkillable Kuwa. The only time in my life I've ever been passionately involved in the teaching process, and I get beaten for my pains. Ridiculous. *Absurde.* I'm still not able to work out if that event was a symbolic representation of the final fling of wartime repression of freedom of speech, or whether it wasn't rather an indication of what was to come later, a nominal freedom imposed upon what remains an essential lack of it. It could have been either."

Kuwano continued talking in the same casual manner, and Hamada smiled as politely as ever, although he was finding all this progressively intolerable and he thought of glancing at his watch and saying he was due back at the office; only Kuwano was so obviously enjoying himself and just as obviously relating his martial exploits with no evil intention at all, that Hamada hesitated to do so. As he went on listening, he began to suspect that the man perhaps was ignorant of his past, and finally came to the conclusion that he must be.

Kuwano got onto the subject of the awful treatment he still went on receiving even after the war had ended. All the others, from the company commander downward, were raised one rank and given the relevant six months' salary when they were demobilized on September 15; but he remained a one-star private second class and was ordered back to division. Naturally this made him angry, but his feelings of despair were stronger than his rage. The one sensation of pleasure he felt, mild though it was, was that he managed to get his own back to some extent on the section corporal. The corporal had to escort Kuwano back to the barracks at Utsonomiya, and kept on complaining all the time that he'd lost out on a good deal because of it. They seemed to have stopped beating people up at Utsunomiya, so he was unscathed in that respect, but he was kept working a long time as an office clerk and didn't get out until almost the end of the year, on December 20. What he received as a parting gift (the bundle of blankets, overcoat, uniform, and army shirts) he hurled into an open drain right in front of the barracks.

"You seem to have had a really bad time," Hamada put in at a break in the recital. Kuwano's response to this remark did genuinely shake him. With not a trace of irony in his voice, he said,

"You must have had the gift of foresight to avoid places like that."

Hamada made only a vague reply, realizing that this scholar of French literature had intended to indicate feelings of respect, even of kinship, by giving this account of his army experiences, and he was amazed not so much by the man's innocence as by his obtuseness. It must never have even crossed his mind that his listener might be made to feel acutely uncomfortable by that sort of thing, and right up to the end he hadn't noticed that Hamada wasn't enjoying the experience in the least. If a teacher of French, a student of a culture reputed to be remarkable for the delicate sensitivity of its grasp of human affairs, was able to do this, then how unbelievably obtuse must be those members of the academic staff who specialized in English and German!

"Things just turned out that way," Hamada offered as a vague conclusion, hoping to put an end to the subject, and Kuwano repeated the words in agreement. Then, looking for something else to talk about, he noticed two books on the seat between them, one in French and the other in Japanese, and he pointed to the Japanese book and asked him what it was. Kuwano picked up the slim, red cloth-covered volume and handed it to him. It had been borrowed from the university library and its title was *Collected Poems of Lord Shunzei's Daughter: Revised Edition.*

"Ah, you read this sort of thing?"

"Yes. It doesn't actually mean I've gone off European literature, but the kind of Japanese one finds in newspapers and magazines nowadays is so awful I prefer to read things like this. It cheers me up; gets the bad taste out of the mouth, like drinking first-rate tea after a dish of instant noodles."

Kuwano offered him another cigarette, lit both Hamada's and his own, and said,

"I like the poetry of this period, anyway."

"What period don't you like?"

"The Manyoshu. Perhaps just a reaction to the fact it was so popular during the war. The folk songs are all right, although I still prefer the later ones in the Kokinshu."

"This poet is later, then? Kamakura era?"

"Yes. Shinkokinshu period. Adopted daughter of Lord Fujiwara Shunzei. Also known as the nun Kashibe. Active from the twelfth into the thirteenth century," said the Baudelaire specialist as if he were quoting from a literary dictionary.

Hamada turned over the pages, and read aloud one poem that caught his attention:

> Again this fitful
> slumber   bamboo
> grass for my pillow
> one night of dreams
> alone to bind us.

"Pretty difficult stuff, isn't it?"

Kuwano glanced over his arm at the page, and said: "Not all that difficult, you know. There's a certain amount of word play that perhaps requires elucidation, the bamboo associations, for example . . ." But he paused, looking slightly embarrassed. "I mustn't lecture you, though. If you want a contemporary parallel, then imagine, say, a woman instructor from some school of fashion design traveling abroad and writing something like it in a hotel room in Rome. . . ."

"What does 'bamboo grass for my pillow' mean?"

"Well, I'm not absolutely sure, but I suppose it's much like the conventional pillow of grass on which the traveler always laid his homeless head, and is thus the same symbol of transience, etc. What's going on in this case is, presumably, a shared pillow; one night of love while traveling around, over as soon as begun. Like the woman I mentioned, spending the night with a persuasive Italian. It is perhaps conceivable that, in the Manyoshu period, people really did sleep while they were traveling in places where there was lots of bamboo grass. After all, it's a very tenacious weed. Luxuriates all over the country. Still, it couldn't have been very comfortable, prickly stuff like that. Hardly the sort of thing for a pillow."

Hamada interrupted the flow of professorial talk:

"That rustling it makes wouldn't let you sleep very well. Almost unbearable, with no place to rest your head. A restless journey."

Kuwano went suddenly silent, looking intensely at Hamada's face. The association he'd made between the sound of bamboo grass and restless journeying had obviously been read as a direct reference to Hamada's wartime experiences as a draft resister, and Hamada immediately regretted his own words since he didn't want to get back onto that subject again. Kumano went on looking at him, and Hamada went on being looked at, for the phrase "bamboo grass for my pillow" had certainly meant something to him, but he couldn't think what. Could it be the sprigs of bamboo grass used for the Festival of the Weaver in July? No, surely not that.

The town of Wakayama was full of soldiers, and Sugiura, the sand artist, lived with an oppressive awareness of them, feeling a peculiar shock one morning when he saw a group of them, who'd spent the night in the same lodging house as himself, going off to join their division. There were ten of them, skinny-looking midgets of a kind who'd never have been called up only a short while ago, and they walked off wearily down the road, showing a form of energy only in the way they puffed what they presumably thought were going to be their last cigarettes for some time. In their overcoats and raincoats they all looked so uniformly feeble it was almost impossible to connect them with active service, or to imagine the grayish yellow army-issue wallet for personal belongings that must be wrapped up somewhere inside the cloth bundle each held in his hand. Also, the sight of tired-looking old people and women, off to see their kin no doubt, going from the station toward the barracks, holding square packages containing boxes of food, made his face grow dark. Still, he told himself there was bound to be a barracks in any large town in Japan now, and he'd been in Wakayama for about a month, since mid-December 1942. He liked the boarding house he'd come across on the outskirts of town, and even the tiny upstairs back room itself, if he ignored the dreadful howl the wind made whenever it blew with any force. Then, since he'd quit Hokkaido in August and gradually been making his way south, this was one of the best places he'd found as far as money was concerned. He'd done pretty well over the two days of the New Year, and again on the ninth and tenth with the Ebisu festival, which involves blessings upon business and most other money-making activities, so it attracted huge crowds and his own trade was so brisk he had to write off in a hurry to Tokyo for fresh supplies, and went to a box factory to get in a new load of leftover paper. Things were going so well he was thinking of staying on for the Old New Year in a month's time, which would provide a six-week delayed version (according to his *Complete Guide*) of the same profitable "markets."

Yet on this particular day nothing had gone right. He'd set up shop in an unpaved side street near a primary school, but although the weather was bright enough it was still very cold, and probably for that reason few children gathered around him. There'd been two or three looking on around eleven, but by twelve there wasn't even one, although normally at that time the lower-grade students would be going home, lots of them hanging around and making a cheerful racket. He'd let them touch his beard, offering a strand of it as an extra if they'd buy. Perhaps it was just that the pitch was queer, or maybe there was an epidemic of colds at school. He went on painting his red-crested crane, his view of Fuji from the pine groves of Miho, his warbler amid the plum blossoms. He'd been working at this trade for more than a year now, and felt himself he'd grown quite accomplished at it, even devising a few more pictures, including an elaborate bunch of roses and the shrine gate in the sea at Miyajima, although he had to admit that the ones taught him by old Inaba were not only much less trouble to do but also unfortunately much more popular with the children than his own newly contrived exercises.

He'd just finished drawing the paste outline of the body of the crane when he heard the sound of a horse's hooves approaching, but he took no notice, merely scattering on some white sand and tapping the paper with his thumb to remove the surplus sand, which he allowed to fall neatly into a small paper bag. He was startled suddenly by the whinnying of a horse now near at hand. The sand artist-cum-draft resister looked up and saw, first of all the brown, dusty shape of a powerful-looking horse, then the man in yellow uniform astride it, and finally the white armband with red lettering. He couldn't read the letters, but he didn't need to since it was obvious what they were: MILITARY POLICE.

The military policeman was gazing down at him, reminding him of a bronze statue, perhaps because he was unconsciously recalling that of the medieval hero, Kusonoki Masashige, he'd seen in the Imperial Plaza in Tokyo.

Sugiura was sitting cross-legged on a cushion placed on top of a small piece of plank, and from this lowly position he looked up at the horse's belly and the thick neck of the young military policeman, looking down automatically as soon as their eyes met. The horse's hooves disturbed the gravel, producing a harsh, grating sound. He wondered if he'd looked down too quickly, but he went on with his work, holding the paper tilted away from him, taking up his paste brush with his right hand, dipping it into the diluted solution in the cream jar, squeezing the excess paste out on the rim of the jar, and making the marks on the paper that stood for the red crest. But as he was doing so, both his right hand and his left hand went on trembling as, his shoulders stiff with tension, he found himself taking long, deep breaths.

"What's wrong, sand artist? Why are you trembling?"

Sugiura did not look up, but he managed a series of quite impromptu evasive replies with a fluency he could only marvel at himself.

"I can't stand horses, ever since I was a kid. Must be allergic."

"What, a big grown man like you? With a big beard too, just like my lance corporal," the man said with a smile, telling him to get on with his drawing.

Sugiura nodded in reply. He was able to complete the bird without trembling this time. But when he put it to one side the soldier still showed no signs of moving. So he picked up another piece of paper and took hold of his brush, still not looking up as he asked,

"That horse of yours won't piss all over me, will it?"

"Don't worry."

"You'll pay for all the kits he messes up if he does, will you?"

"I told you to stop worrying like an old woman," said the soldier, this time in an obviously bad-tempered voice.

Sugiura started drawing his picture of the shrine gate at Miyajima.

"Come on then, boy. Up."

The military policeman went. The sand artist forgot to sprinkle on the red sand, listening for the sound of hooves among the various noises of the town at noon. The damp, semitransparent outline of the shrine gate dried out, then vanished.

If that had been all, he probably wouldn't have spent a very disturbed night, but there was one more incident on the same day when, mysteriously not very long after the military policeman had disappeared, a large number of children turned up and kept on coming. He was surprised that so many of the older children should be interested in his pictures while the young ones were mostly indifferent, but he went on painting and selling his sand artist kits, having very little banter with the boys, who simply said loudly they'd buy one and handed over the money. They at last started to disappear, however, until there was only one left, a small boy who'd been too shy to buy anything while the big boys had been around. He had on a brownish kimono that was a glossy white about the cuffs of the sleeves, probably from the habit of wiping his nose on them.

While Sugiura was working on a view of Fuji from the pine groves for this boy, a tall man wearing a black, tapering gauze mask over his mouth and nose happened to be passing by, who glanced casually at what was going on, then stopped in his tracks. He observed Sugiura's face from a variety of angles, looking as if he were waiting for an opportunity to talk to him. While Sugiura was suspiciously wondering what the man had on his mind, his own attention was distracted from his work, with the result that he made a botched job of the mountain. He handed the painting over to the boy, and then the man said something to him, but his voice was so muffled by the medical mask it was no more than an unintelligible groan. So the man removed the string from around one ear, revealing his face, which Sugiura felt he might have seen somewhere before, coughed, and said,

"It is Hamada, isn't it? Shokichi Hamada?"

Sugiura wondered if his face had taken on the expression in that moment of a man who has just heard his name called. He didn't know, but he did know the man's voice, and it brought back recollections the face alone had not, memories of his school days. The man was much thinner than he'd been then, almost shrunken in appearance, probably because he was consumptive now, but it was certainly Iwamoto, who'd been one year his senior. He'd been a renowned bully of the younger boys (Hamada had been punched by him on two or three occasions), a big, rowdy person, and now he was this feeble-looking, long streak of nothing, speaking as if he was really pleased to meet an old chum.

"Hamada, isn't it? Shokichi Hamada. It's Iwamoto. You remember . . ."

Iwamoto gave the nicknames by which they'd been known at school in an attempt to jog the sand artist's memory. The partly removed black mask hung from one ear, dangling against his pallid cheek and swaying as he talked.

Whether it was because he himself had recognized Iwamoto by his voice rather than his face, or because that peculiar groaning he'd heard from behind the mask had given him some sort of hint, Sugiura felt he must make no verbal reply to the long streak and immediately feigned the behavior of a deaf-mute, producing a low gurgle from his throat and waving his hand frantically about in a gesture of dismissal; keeping a watch out of the corner of his eye on the astonished small boy, who must have thought "uncle with the beard" had suddenly taken leave of his senses. Iwamoto leaned his head to one side in perplexity, put his mask back on, walked away, stopped after a few paces and looked back, then did not look back anymore. Sugiura sold a sand artist's kit to the small boy and hurriedly shut up shop.

Up to quite late that evening, he didn't take either incident all that seriously. Because of the fuel shortage, there was no hot bath available in the boarding house that day, so he went to the local public bath. The water was beautifully clean, and he seemed to be the first in it, and also just the right temperature, so he spent a long time happily soaking, after which he washed his hair and beard. He then got back in the hot water again for another long session, smiling as he recalled how smartly he'd fooled the military policeman and Iwamoto, pleased with the speed with which he'd worked out the correct response in both cases.

But as he lay wrapped in his meager quilt that night, all sorts of anxieties began to assail him. First of all there was the slightly ludicrous worry that it might have been unwise of him to go to a public bath where he could be seen naked by so many people. He found this comic himself, reflecting that he'd been to public baths a number of times since coming to Wakayama, but the more he thought about it the less absurd the worry started to become. After all, clothes are to the body what a beard is to the face. If he could be recognized with his disguise on (as had been the case with his face), how much more easily would he be seen through when he was stark naked (assuming there was somebody around in Wakayama who knew him—and that had shown itself to be no baseless assumption that very day). As he lay in the dark, he began thinking of any physical peculiarities he might have. There was the scar from his appendix operation, a mole on his left breast. What else? Then he tried recalling one by one the faces of the other men in the bath, trying to work out if one of them might have belonged to some former Tokyo acquaintance. When he at last grew weary of this labor, he began to laugh at himself for what he was doing, wondering if counting faces might be as good a method of getting off to sleep as counting sheep. But then another, quite unexpected idea crossed his mind. Might not that military policeman and Iwamoto conceivably be acquaintances? Was it totally inconceivable? In such a small town as this? The idea became truly disconcerting if thought about. First of all, he began to feel he'd been unwise to close up shop as soon as Iwamoto had disappeared. If he'd retraced his steps, as he could well have done, he would surely have thought it odd that the sand artist was no longer there. Wouldn't he, indeed, assume it to be proof that it had really been Hamada? He started to imagine all sorts of possibilities, even arriving at the idea that the military policeman had in fact been Iwamoto in disguise. He'd been an absolute fool not to get out of Wakayama that evening. Why had he been so stupid as to remain here just asking for trouble? Still, it was all very well to say that, but what about his ration register? That had to be taken into account. Then there was all the stuff he'd ordered to be sent here, although he could always tell the people at the station to send it on somewhere else; that was quite true. Still, if someone had become suspicious they'd be lying in wait to arrest him as soon as he went to pick it up, whether it was at Wakayama Station or at Kumamoto Station. He would run away like an animal, enwrapped in the foul stench from behind the station lavatories, and they'd come after him, be all around him suddenly, and down he'd go on a great heap of coal dust like he remembered at Usuki Station. Or perhaps. . . . Perhaps they were already looking for him, now Iwamoto had told them all about him, going through every boarding house with a fine-toothed comb. That military policeman with the thick neck would be, at least, even if he were all on his own. Iwamoto had told the policeman all about him, and now he'd been seen through completely. His disguise had been ripped off. His imagination began to run away with him (but was this only imagination? And was it really running away? Wasn't it rather just a series of reasonable suppositions?), and in his efforts to suppress it he suddenly found all these pains he was taking about nothing laughable. He decided to laugh, to laugh himself to sleep. But when he'd finished laughing out loud, he was aware of himself listening for the sound of horses' hooves in the silence of the night. The night deepened, and a strong wind arose, sounding through the bamboo grass on the hill behind the house, then on the farther mountains, covering the sound of those hooves, whether real or imagined, with that constant rustling sound: dry, brittle, melancholy.

Assistant Professor Kuwano averted his eyes, lit up another cigarette (not offering one to Hamada this time), and remained looking away from him. It appeared he was now suffering severe pangs of remorse at having intruded on Hamada's past, and this made Hamada wonder how a man who'd displayed such insensitivity to what he might be feeling about his war experience could now overreact in this delicate manner, amazed that someone should be so obtuse and so oversensitive at almost one and the same time, and feeling there must be something odd, almost neurotic about him. So the man who was shortly to be promoted to chief registry clerk told the assistant professor (who was still looking away from him) that he had to get back to the office, and Kuwano's dark face reddened slightly as he apologized for keeping him. Hamada assured him it was quite all right since it was Saturday, saying how much he'd enjoyed their long and varied conversation. Kuwano responded so diffidently to this Hamada realized he must be really worried that he'd said all the wrong things, so he tried to cheer him up a little by talking about something else.

"You never used to park here before, did you, Professor?"

This did cheer up Kuwano, for it allowed him to return to his earlier flippant manner, and he replied in his normal boisterous tones,

"Well, I bought the Renault mainly because I thought if I parked on campus I'd be able to get away with my failure to salute—to use the military term—our noble shrine. But then, after rigorous self-questioning, I came to the conclusion that my behavior was a cowardly evasion of the central question at issue—if you will permit this switch from military terminology to the phraseology of the Party. How exhausting it is to belong to our confused generation. However, this means that, starting this week, I leave my car, walk in, walk past that shrine, and ignore it. Do you bow to it yourself?"

"I do."

"Meaning you believe in all those gods in there, all the deities in heaven and on this earth?"

Hamada picked up the reference to old Professor Sakurai's way of speaking, and produced a reasonable parody of how he would maintain that "surely all we Japanese do." Kuwano laughed with pleasure and praised the skill of the imitation, adding,

"I shall still fail to salute. I'm a bona fide, card-carrying member of the academic staff, and it needs the approval of a majority of faculty to get me kicked out."

"That's where you academics are lucky."

"Then you ought to form a staff union."

"Even if we had a union it wouldn't do me any good, since I'm about to join the bosses."

Hamada replied quite casually to Kuwano's suggestion, and didn't notice that he'd said something ill-advised.

He got out of the car, went through the main gate, bowed to the shrine, and, as he raised his head, reflected once more on the peculiar mixture of dullness and sensitivity Kuwano showed toward things, deciding that the assistant professor was not really interested in life as it was lived, but only in making interpretations of it, as though it were a difficult text that needed careful reading, not a situation in which one was nakedly involved. He grinned wryly to himself at the thought of all the odd people there were in the world, and saw Horikawa come out of the main entrance, just about to get into the black Bentley. Horikawa noticed Hamada, and raised his hand in salute and called out to him—something he almost never did normally.

"How are you? Is your wife all right?"

"Very well, thank you, sir."

"Good. That's good."

The executive director got into the car, and Hamada, together with the member of the university president's staff who'd come down for that purpose, bowed and saw him off, confident now that if Horikawa actually went out of his way to greet him deliberately in public, then the rumor of his promotion must be true.

Yet strangely, two weeks passed, then three, and there was still no official pronouncement giving Hamada a place among the bosses. He started to feel suspicious and thought about getting in touch with Masako just to make sure, but it seemed a rather petty thing to do so he desisted, reflecting that he'd probably hear tomorrow or the next day. So he passed his days, and outside the registry window the pomegranate tree with deep vermillion. . . .

four

So that's the way a wife addresses her husband, is it? Better watch yourself, I'm telling you. Need a bit more respect than that. At moments like this it's kindness that's required, understanding: "a certain inward softness"—that's what that bogus twit—forgotten his name for the moment—said. Can't say I've ever experienced much of it. Perhaps he was trying to be a bit racy? No, as far as smut goes he's about as racy as those articles in that lousy mag of his. Way off target. Can't believe a word he says; or writes, either. Now look at her, and when hubby's come home all mellow too, in just the right mood for it.

Hello, is this all we've got left? Have it cold? Warm it up? Have to go steady. Musn't knock it back quick, must we? Got to make it last. Sip it down, sip it down, drop by lovely drop. Like a gentleman, right? A gentleman remains one even in his cups—in hic cups, hah, hah. What a game, warming the stuff myself. Rushing about. Busy, that's what I am. Nishi is busy: Nishi ish bishy. Rhymes. Nearly.

Still, can't really be true, can it? Them making that bastard chief clerk. Just a rumor. When the boss heard it, he came and told me, looking like he was having a blue fit. The trouble was, I knew already, but I still had to look like I was having a blue fit too. Not easy. Not with someone like me who's a simple, honest character at heart. So I should've made a mess of it, by rights. Didn't, though. I've got acting ability, that's what it must be. Looked like I wasn't just having a blue fit, but a red one as well. Do they have red fits? Pretty good acting, anyway. Not quite up to the movies, maybe, but all right for TV.

Making his debut in JTV's Saturday night show, *The Three Undertakers*, is an interesting face new to the screen, that of Masao Nishi, who works as principal advisor in the registry of a certain Tokyo university. He was spotted in the spring of this year by the director of the program, on a visit to the said university to arrange, by underhanded means, his eldest daughter's entry into that prestigious institution. The station is plugging his suave, mature good looks as absolutely right for the teenage market. The man in question said he'd been warmly exhorted by the university president to get in there and give it his best, and he was confident he would act in such a way as to astound us all.

Still, that messenger boy really does seem to have his ear close to the ground. I mean, you expect the switchboard operators to get news early. That's only natural. But, Christmas, making that creep chief registry clerk! It's plain crazy. The boss thinks it's funny. Of course, he thinks it's even funnier he's being moved to head of Welfare. He thinks that's much funnier than me being made assistant to him. Thinks he's got more to complain about than I do. That's a real laugh. If you ask me, the way I'm being treated is a sight worse. Fifty thousand times. A hundred thousand. After all, what is he? It's a miracle he ever got made chief clerk in the first place. Even more amazing he's managed to hold on to it so long. All he's any good for is knocking back the drink and singing songs.

> I'll tell you the tale of the bold chief clerk
> Who wived and made three babes in the dark,
> But the father of these three promising boys
> Was a seeker after furtive joys.

If it's free it's mine, was ever his cry;
Just give me a drink and I'll spit in your eye.
But for Horikawa, our Di—rec—tor,
'Twas a sight that made him sigh full sore.

So he ups and hies to meet his lackey,
The bold chief clerk, and says: Now, chappy,
Though meek and mild I appear, I know,
I don't wear bifocals just for show.

Of your furtive imbibings I have full ken.
You're too old for that game, so don't do it again.
Better dandle a grandchild on your knees,
And teach it about the birds and bees.

Now, if they were to make me chief clerk, that really would make sense. But what happens? They've set it up for that bugger, let him overtake me. Bit queer, isn't it? What I want to know is, what's their reason? Give me a reason, that's all I ask. Let's have a thorough investigation of the matter, then we can all go home happy. After all, I am his superior. I arrived before he did; was promoted before he was. I'll admit he's older than me—only by a year, though. Then I do just happen to be a graduate of the university. Graduates first, that's always been our motto. If that bastard Hamada wants to push me out of the way and get promoted that damn quick, then why doesn't he go back to his alma mater and try it there?

Why? Because he can't, that's why. And why can't he? Because he's one of them draft dodgers. When he was discharged (bit funny for a draft dodger, but let it stand), he wagged his tail at old Horikawa and got taken up by him. And he just doesn't understand the basics of our place; he's got no clue about what we stand for, because it's damn all to do with him, isn't it? Can't grasp the spirit of the university. THIS INSTITUTION IS DEDICATED TO INQUIRY INTO THE NATURE OF THE NATIONAL POLITY is what it says. Of course, the reds in law and economics say there's a problem about what the national polity is, going on about it being quite different under the New Constitution from what it was under the Old. But that's just a lot of theory. Lot of old hogwash, if you ask me. I mean, I'm a realist. I believe in looking facts in the face; not like one of your commies.

Shake it all about, but not a drop comes out. Looks like the end of the road, pal. Reckon we'll just have to. . . . Wait a minute. There should be a bottle of whisky around here somewhere. Just one little bottle of Suntory, more's the pity, but better than nothing. Ah, here it is. Christ, it's half empty too.

Never mind. As I was saying, I never could stand that creep right from the start. I mean, when I'd just put out a few gentlemanly feelers, then nobly resigned myself to my fate, the bugger's right in there snuggling up with Masako Aochi. There'd been talk about goings on in that direction some years ago too. Doesn't he ever give up? Disgraceful behavior, that's all I can say. MEMBERS OF STAFF MUST BE STRICTLY CONCERNED WITH THE PROPRIETY OF THEIR BEHAVIOR AT ALL TIMES. Quite right, too. Of course, I'm not saying there's anything wrong about asking a young lady to accompany one to some artistic performance. Nothing wrong with that.

Still, I mean, it is pretty damn incredible. Doing that. A draft resister. Actually doing it. I mean, just like anyone else, I'd've liked to've done it. Who wouldn't've? I didn't want to become a soldier, I'll admit. Still, I didn't have the gall to go through with it. Wonder how he managed for a living? Down the mines with the Koreans, digging away at the coal? Could be. He always seems to have a soft spot for Koreans. Perhaps he went over to Korea? Might even have been Taiwan. They say Taiwan was a good place to be during the war. As much food as you could eat, was what someone told me. Probably exaggerating. Still, would have been all right only if it were half true. . . . He had the time of his life, I expect. Still does, I suppose. Now it's naked ladies, before it was his gut full of silvery rice. Taiwan food must be basically Chinese. . . . Makes you sick—and there was I down south eating frogs and crayfish. Some people have all the luck.

Could have stayed in this country, of course. Sometimes lets on he's been around a lot. We were in a coffee shop and there was this baseball player being interviewed on TV, and he starts going on about how he must come from Akita because he can tell by the accent, looking as if he thinks he knows all the answers. Lot of nonsense, if you ask me. I can't tell the difference between the way any of them talk.

And I was promoted assistant before he was too. I'm not going to let some draft dodger do me down. I'm not standing for that. I may be a quiet sort of guy, but when I get my back up it stays up. That's just the way I am. I mean, when I saw him having his little date on the roof, and when I heard what that messenger told me, well, I wouldn't be a man if I took that lying down, would I? After all, our Hama was fixed up with a nice bit of stuff by old Hori; young, a good looker. If he's got that at home, what the hell does he mean by carrying on with her, nearly forty if she's a day?

They say it's darkest near the lighthouse, so maybe the crafty sod didn't go anywhere but just hung around Tokyo, going underground like some high-ranking commie. Pretty smart thinking. Get inside one of the slums in Shinjuku or Ueno and even the big boys in the M.P.s wouldn't be able to get at you. Or perhaps he was all nice and snug in some enormous building, renting a little cubbyhole right up there under the roof. How much would it cost to rent a place like that? No idea. Still. Then his relations would bring him meals three times a day, on the quiet, of course. No. That wouldn't be any good. They'd soon find out. The M.P.s would be watching the family. Traveling around on foot's not a bad idea. Keeping on the move, covering up your traces all the time.

The M.P.s surround the hideaway, pistols in hand. The game's over, Shokichi Hamada, come on out with your hands up. All the roads round about packed with cops, shoulder to shoulder. The M.P.s kick down the door and rush in. The nest is empty! The bird has flown! All the M.P.s grind their teeth in sore frustration. But their chief approaches the bed. He stretches out his hand. Ah! Still warm! The M.P.s rush to the window. And there he is, that mastermind of crime, cat burgling Shokichi of Hamada, brushing contemptuously aside the wild howls of "Arrest that man!," nimbly leaping from building to building as he makes good his escape.

Just my luck. Whisky's run out at a really good point in the story. Well, off to the kitchen again and see what we can find. Must have some goodies somewhere. Let's have a look in here. No. What about here? No. Never know what to do when the wife goes off to bed like that. I suppose she does it so I'll appreciate her more. Does it on purpose, as far as I can see. Keeps everything in the funniest places, just to mess me up. Keeps on changing the places she puts things in as well. That's where women are clever, of course. Make you depend on them. Could always wake her up and ask, but she sulks like mad if I do. Not that I'm scared of her in any way. Scared of my own wife? Huh, certainly not. It's just that I don't much like the look of her when she's sulking. Puts me off. I feel my love for her diminishing, all draining away. That's what worries me—as her husband. Ah, here's something to go with it. Nothing like stone-cold soup. No, I'm serious. Tastes fine. What about some saké then? Here's some. For cooking purposes only. Ah well, it'll do. Quite a lot of it, anyway. When you're as far gone as I am you can't tell the difference. Almost can't.

That bugger only drinks whisky. I wonder what that's all about? Must mean something. Sometimes goes on as if he's pretty well up on food, what the goulash tastes like at some little place he knows, where you can get decent soba, and all that jazz. Doesn't take me in, though. Look at the way he knocks back that muck they dish up in the canteen and the Hare. Here, this soup tastes terrific. The potatoes are really great.

Still, it does look like he's living off his "culinary experiences" when he was one of "the gilded youth at college," don't you know. That's why I don't swallow it. After all, what do you know about things like that when you're a student? Experience is what counts so far as proper discrimination goes—in food and in women. Really lived it up when he was young, I suppose, being a doctor's son and all that. Make medicine, make money: that's what they say. Naturally they're talking about doctors and the big medical companies, not some poor sod slaving away at the corner drugstore. Come to think of it, I first heard that remark at a drugstore. Perhaps you can't put much store by it, then? Still, Dad makes a bundle out of medicine, and sonny boy uses it to dodge the draft. That's how he did it. Dad had some jewels or what have you stashed away, and sonny boy went off with them, selling off the odd one occasionally. He wouldn't go short if he was traveling around like that. Be living in the lap of luxury. That's it. In human life you've always got to get down to the economic base of the problem. Still, be a bit difficult selling jewelry. Easy to carry, hard to sell. That's the trouble. Went off with a wad of money, then? Fifty thousand? He'd've needed ten thousand, at least. He'd never've had the nerve to do it otherwise. If I'd had ten thousand I'd've done it too. You bet I would. Then off on the Grand Tour, around every famous fucking whorehouse in the land.

If you can't get it up, then don't you come in here,
Is what they say in Yoshiwara each day of the year.

So far off to the South, and looking o'er the sea,
You feel your courage rising as the breeze blows free.

Edoichi, Ageya, Susaki, Magane,
Abekawamachi where the girls come out to play.

Farewell with fond regret to the roly-poly waves,
To the whores of Okazaki, your servants and your slaves,

To dyspepsia at dawn, to the grinning yellow sun
That wakes you in the morning when your money's all done.

For Gion's too expensive, and if you go elsewhere
You'll hear the air raid warning well before the last all clear.

So fly away to Tobita, my fine feathered friend,
And hide yourself away inside, and start it all again.

Great stuff. And what did I get, for Chrissake, stuck on that island in the South Pacific? Well, at first we got it once a month, with a Korean whore, that's all. Died after a while, so that was that. She died, of course. Not me. So it meant that an experienced stalwart like myself didn't get any oats at all after that. Ridiculous. Had some at the beginning, as I said, but it was-n't much. Like I said, she was a Korean; didn't have any hair thereabouts. Probably kept the ones with hair for the officers? As it turned out, it did-n't matter much one way or the other. And there was the draft dodger get-ting it all the time. Honestly, it makes my blood boil, while good men and true have to carry the can, as per always. They say the three things most hidden in darkness in this world are stars, ships' anchors, and the human face;* but I reckon that last one ought to be draft dodgers.

That island. How I remember that island. We were with the division in North China, and I'd just been made orderly lance corporal, when there was a rumor we were going to the South Pacific. Rumors being rumors, there are sometimes false ones in the army, but mostly they turn out to be true. Like rumors in a university. Just like rumors in a university. The boat made a brief stop at Manila; then we were landed at an island in the Moluc-cas called Olave. It's not a name I'm likely to forget. That was in December 1943. At first it was all talk about us being the invincible Northern Chinese Army and we'd soon take care of the Americans, but it was just hopeless. You can't win a war in that state. For a start, we didn't have anything to eat. Couldn't even fight, let alone win. But the American field rations were ter-rific, and I spent my fighting career just trying to get hold of them. Instead of going to be a soldier, I'd gone to be a thief. Of course, something like that was happening all over the place, even with H.Q. platoon. Always fiddling with the numbers (the army's crazy about numbers) so as to get more than your fair share, and that's just a kind of thieving.

It was pretty bad even before the Americans landed. There wasn't any rice; had to make do with bananas and yams. They used to fill empty gaso-line drums half full of rice, then chuck them into the sea from the trans-port ship, but the damn things just floated out there and hardly ever washed ashore. At night we'd go down to the beach meaning to swim out and get them, but they were always a long way away, and there were sharks in the sea. Quite a few died that way; died in active service against sharks. A glorious death, naturally. Made the gods weep. Then the Yanks

---

* A reference to the motifs on the insignia of the army, navy, and air force.

knew those drums had rice in them, so they'd pump them full of holes with their machine guns. That really used to get me. I didn't see why they had to be that bloody nasty. We were having a bad enough time as it was. Then the transport stopped coming, and finally the Yanks landed.

Scared stiff, I was. I can still remember the feeling. Still feel mystified at times that I'm still alive. Mysterious. Can't think why I didn't die, with the Yanks and their damn automatic rifles *ping ping ping*ing all over the place. Fate, that's what it was, fate. My number wasn't up. Then the machine guns—*pom, pom, pom, pom.* No, that's not right: *rat tat tat tat tat?* Not really. *Dah, dah, dah, dah, dah?* That's a bit more like it, but still not quite right. Anyway, they didn't get me either. Then those damn great bombs thudding down, just like an earthquake, great roar and everything shaking. Terrible sound, like they'd gotten all the temple bells from all over the country in one place and were banging the whole lot together. Booming? Banging? Bonging? No.

> Ringing out the old, and ringing in the new,
> The *bong* of the atomic bomb says Happy New Year too.
>
> Its gentle breezes blow away all sense of sin,
> Softly swaying heaven and earth to welcome the year in.
>
> We've had our share of dreams, we've had our troubles too,
> We've got a lot to think about: Happy New Year to you.
>
> Time passes, days go by, weeks, months, and then the year,
> And as we take our last farewell let's drop a tender tear.

For dear comrades, dearly beloved brethren, let us all recall at this sad hour of parting, not only the impermanence of our brief lives here upon this earth, but also how all of us, at this solemn moment, have different little thoughts, different little worries, different little concerns, and so let us accept them in one another. Think also, here on the Isle of Olave in the Moluccas, of all those innocent natives in our pastoral care who assembled here in this place, splendid fellows every man, woman, and child of them, and of how gracefully they fell, and of how their black skins were washed by the purity of the rain, the long white needles of the black rain, falling forever and ever, world without end, amen. *Flashbangroooaaarcraasshshsh.*

That great blast like an earthquake blew the dugout in, and all my squad were buried alive, except for me and a lance corporal, who weren't in it because we'd been sent crawling forward to a little knoll and told to put their flamethrower out of action. Scared out of my wits, I was, and the hand grenades we threw didn't seem to hit anything. But if it hadn't been for that flamethrower, I wouldn't be alive today.

The flamethrower seemed to have gone somewhere else, and we were just starting to feel relieved about that when a machine gun got us. The lance corporal bought it straight away, stone dead, and I seemed to have been hit too and went down with him. When I came to I noticed I'd just gotten a graze on my left wrist. Still, I'd been hit. Pissed and shat myself as well. I was that scared, I suppose. Afterward I found a dent in my helmet made by a bullet.

Now we really have run out. Damn nuisance when you run out of drink at a time like this. Have to get in fresh supplies. I hereby declare that Corporal Nishi with a detail of four men will advance in the general direction of the kitchen. Your mission is to search out and capture any bottles of drink located in that vicinity. Is that understood? Very well, proceed; and the best of luck. Found any? Doesn't look like it. What about here? No. What's this? Cooking Wine Sherry Type. Well, your sherry is a very noble kind of drink. Proper alcohol, anyway. Tastes damn sweet, doesn't it?

Coconut juice tastes all right. Sharp, really refreshing. A bit like lemonade. Gin and coconut would make a pretty good cocktail, I should think. Trouble is you'd have to think of some fancy name for it. That's the problem. Hell of a job climbing up and knocking them down. Hopeless if you didn't have a head for heights. Never make it. Funny business being a soldier. All the stupid things you have to learn how to do. Fiddling with the numbers, doing the sergeant's washing. That didn't cause all that much trouble, since you could always filch new stuff out of the stores instead in a pinch. Never went that far myself, though. What next? I was being pushed around a bit too much at H.Q. platoon, so got myself posted into the field. Now, in the field, the great thing is digging holes, so you start off as a laborer. Digging's bad enough, but it's lugging the dirt about in baskets on your back that's real murder. There's a knack to swinging the stuff up, and if you can't manage it you just can't get going. It's all in the hip movement. Then you need the butcher's art. Got to learn how to carve things up right. I mean, you've just found your peacefully grazing cow and shot it, and it would be an awful waste if you didn't know how to skin it properly. Like that time with the monkey.

> Once upon a time in a far-off land there was a little boy called Masao, and he was having a nice walk in the hills. Then a bad man came in an airplane and chased after Masao, so Masao ran away and hid under a nice big bush by the river. But the bad man dropped a big bomb on Masao. Happily it did not hit Masao, and for a little while he kept perfectly still under the big bush, and then a monkey, which had just died, came rolling down the river, rolling rolling down the river.

That monkey tasted really good. Just melted in the mouth. I couldn't have had meat for months. I reckon you could make a fortune if you started a monkey meat restaurant in Tokyo.

> "Darling, how did you manage to find a wonderful place like this?" If you want to hear those magical words from your lady companion, then why not try Nishi's in West Ginza Six? This is the only place in the whole country specializing in monkey cuisine. The charcoal-grilled monkey steak is excellent, but the *pièce de resistance* most heartily recommended is the monkey brains *potage*. The flavor has real body.

Got it. I shall call my cocktail, gin base with cold coconut juice lightly shaken, Farewell, brothers-in-arms. Maybe it wouldn't go down too well

nowadays. People might not get it. I got it all right, though. The whole platoon was wiped out. We were cut off from the others so there wasn't anything I could do except try to get back somehow. Set off walking using the
platoon officer's sword as a stick. I meant to hand it over to his relatives.
My pants were all sticky with crap. Felt disgusting. Only at times, though,
only at times. Most of the time I was too preoccupied with other things to
notice. After a while I got this terrible parched throat. Didn't have a drop
in my water bottle, because a bullet had gone right through it and spilled
it all. But I found a coconut tree, climbed up, and knocked a couple down.
Couldn't manage any more, because I was completely flaked out. But that
coconut juice tasted marvelous. I wished I'd been able to give them their
last drink before they'd died. All of them. That's what I was thinking at the
time. Farewell. Farewell, brothers-in-arms.

> Masao Nishi. I, the above named, lost one of my nine lives in the
> conflict on Olave Island in the Moluccas. I desire reunion with any of
> the heroic spirits of the second squad of No. 2 platoon of A Company
> of the 3rd Battalion of the 109th Division, hoping to talk over again
> the events of that time. I should be grateful to be informed at your
> earliest possible convenience of the most appropriate methods for
> such conference, whether by planchette, medium, sorceress, or any
> other suggestion you might have to make. (University Admin.)

After I'd quenched my thirst I went on walking until it got dark, then
lay down to sleep, woke up, walked a bit more, slept again, and the next
time I opened my eyes there was another Japanese soldier close by. He was
from a different company. Name of Naganuma. Absolute dimwit. He
asked me to take him along with me. I asked the nit if he had any food,
and he said he didn't but he had some salt in his canteen. "Hand it over
and you can come along," I said, and he hesitated, but then he put it in my
pack. I tried a good bit of it, a piece about the size of my thumb. Tasted
super. I don't know. I reckon young women nowadays just can't follow a
story like this. Doesn't make any sense to them. Ought to do something
about it.

That Good Old Wartime Mood.

Shinjuku Kabukicho's Military Cabaret "12–8"* now has a new manager, Masao Nishi, and he is giving the club a complete overhaul, not just the furnishings but the whole spirit of the place. What he's doing is creating the genuine wartime atmosphere among his luscious lovelies. Don't worry, fellas, that doesn't mean they're a crowd of golden oldies, but as young as they come. Only they're being educated. He's set up a reading corner in their dressing room with the right magazines, anthologies of wartime literature, and military histories. This means they should at last be able to join in conversations with club members over forty. We welcome this promising idea, and look forward to a visit sometime.

I walked three whole days with that creep Naganuma. His dad was some innkeeper in Odawara, and he said the one thing he could do was cook. Nothing to cook, though, so that wasn't much use. There's nothing worse than wandering around a lot of hills with your stomach empty and getting emptier. One hill after another. All made of rocks. I thought enough times of going back to that place where the coconut trees were but couldn't remember the way, and I was scared to go too. We met a few Japanese soldiers on the way, but they were all dead or dying; hard to tell the difference. Couldn't do anything for them. Hopeless. One or two asked for hand grenades. Wanted to put themselves out of their misery. Didn't give them mine; never know when you might want to use it yourself. Naganuma's leg wound had been getting bad, though it had hardly been anything when we started out, and I reckoned I'd probably need two grenades, one for him and one for me, if worse came to worst. Naganuma was skinny, and getting thinner and thinner, all skin and bones. Face started to look like a Korean's. What my face looked like, I don't know. Anyway, we kept on moving east, and on the third day at last we got down out of the hills. At least I think it

---

* 12–8 = December 8, date of attack on Pearl Harbor by Japanese time; December 7 by Hawaii and Washington time.

was the third day. Can't be sure. Probably was. And I felt really pleased we'd managed to get that far. Also thought there might be something to eat now. But there wasn't, not a thing. Well, just couldn't move on anymore. Flaked out. There was some flower I'd never seen before, and I ate that, very gingerly, then the leaves. Then Naganuma discovered some frogs. We went crazy trying to catch them. Got nine in all. It's one hell of a job catching nine frogs. Naganuma asked if he should barbecue them or make soup, and I said soup. There's less waste that way.

The soup started boiling in the canteen, and Naganuma asked me for some salt, so I gave him a bit. Wasn't enough, and he didn't seem all that happy about it, but he put it in the soup, then poured half the soup into the other canteen so we'd have half each. Four and a half frogs each. I had a great gulp of frog soup, and it struck me it needed a bit more salt to help the taste along. So I reached inside my pack, took out a pinch of salt, which was all mixed up with the dirt and fluff in there, and put it in my own canteen. It tasted just right this time, and I started drinking again. I'd forgotten all about Naganuma and his soup needing it just as much as mine.

So Naganuma watches me putting the salt in my soup, and he says,

"Corporal, let me have some of my salt."

"My salt," he calls it. That riled me, that really did. Perhaps I tend to be a bit tight about things, wanting everything for myself? No. What pissed me off was that silly way of talking. "My salt." Wouldn't have minded if he'd said "the salt" or "our salt." That's all it was. I'm not mean. Never have been. I just didn't like the way he'd put it.

"What's all this about 'my salt'?" I said, but that illiterate twit from the sticks didn't catch on, just said,

" 'My salt' is my salt, corporal."

Well, I wasn't going to give him a grammar lesson on the proper use of pronouns, because he was too thick to follow things like that, so I didn't say anything but went on drinking my soup. Drank it all up too. It wasn't at all bad, either, and I was just thinking that maybe the frogs the French eat might be of this variety, when that fool Naganuma moves over, stretches out his hand, and takes my salt out of my pack.

"Stop that!" I cried, exerting my authority as his NCO. Absolutely in accordance with the drill book too. "A person in command shall pay particular attention to his military bearing at all times, being correctly dressed and a model of vigorous precision in the various forms of his behavior, thereby exemplifying and encouraging a proper martial spirit in the men under his command and exerting the most powerful influence upon them."

Well, that did exert the most powerful influence upon thickheaded Naganuma, although in a pretty funny sort of way since he appeared to take great exception to my shouting at him, and turned on me. I was taken right aback, responded a bit hastily, and pushed him away. So over he went, and stayed down, unfortunately kicking over all his frog soup as he did, the bloody fool. What a waste of a lovely dish of frog soup. I've never been there myself, but I'd be surprised if they could produce a bowl of frog soup like that even in Paris.

Just at that moment I spotted a couple of enemy planes coming in our direction. All planes were enemy planes. You didn't have to waste any time identifying them.

"Naganuma! Enemy aircraft! Take cover!" I shouted, and made a beeline for the nearby forest, only about a hundred, maybe two hundred yards away. Naturally I didn't forget my rifle; nor that sword. I got in among the trees and took cover, but when I looked back, there was old slowpoke Naganuma dawdling along with his canteen in his hand.

"Look out!" I shouted. "Get down!" But he didn't.

So what happened was bound to happen. It was bound to happen. When he still had about thirty yards to go, the Yank plane got him with its machine gun. *Rat tat tat tat tat tat tat tat.* No, not quite like that. *Dot tot tot tot tot tot tot tot tot tot tot* is more like it.

When the planes had moved off I raced out to him, but he was gone. Stone dead. Had been hit in the chest and the head. There was a bullet hole right through his helmet.

So I dragged his body into the trees and dug a hole and buried him in it. There was a sapling right next to the grave. I don't know its name. It's a tree with big leaves and a thick trunk. The forests are full of them, the most common tree there. Anyway, a branch from the sapling was sticking out above Naganuma's grave. I had his helmet in my hand, just sort of holding it. My finger happened to feel the top of the helmet where the Yank bullet had gone through. Big hole it was. Perhaps two bullets had done it. A big, jagged hole, the size of my finger. So I got the idea of sticking that branch through the hole. Two or three small, fat yellow leaves got squashed flat, then opened again to the size they were before.

Twenty years ago. I wonder what's happened to Naganuma's grave? That sapling must have grown big by now. They do in the tropics. Plenty of rain; and it's hot too. It was only up to my chest then, that tree. About as tall as my boy. It'll be taller than me now, as thick as my thigh. Thick with leaves. But that branch will still only be as thick as my finger, at that point where it comes out from the trunk. Maybe it has gotten thick, though; making the hole wider, splitting open the helmet. And I don't know its name.

Watch over his grave, tree. Watch over the grave of my brother-in-arms. Don't let his helmet fall. That's all there is to mark it. That brown painted steel helmet was the only medal he ever got.

Twenty years gone by.

And if that idle slowpoke were alive now he'd be past forty. A man in his forties. He'd be running that inn in Odawara, slicing up food in the kitchen; trying the maids and they keep on running away from him; worrying about his son getting into high school.

Instead he's become a tree on Olave Island. A slowpoke tree. The tree goes on living, and it goes on wearing his helmet. Every year the helmet grows higher, gets nearer the sky, gets nearer the clear, sharp, sad light of the Southern Cross. Gets nearer the dazzling sun. Growing all the time, but with no blood flowing through his body, only green sap. When the wind is really bad branches are split, leaves scattered. Then the sap gleams on the broken wound, but the wound heals over, then the scar, and the limb is healthy again. Then the branch breaks in another big wind.

Still, it survives. It lives. Go on living, Naganuma. Look after yourself, slowpoke tree.

Perhaps he's better off that way. It's no good being a slowpoke if you're a man; hopeless if you're a soldier, or if you're running an inn. . . . All right if he got hold of a good woman to do it for him. But that kind of wife gets really full of herself. Whereas if you're a tree . . . all trees are slowpokes, that's the only way they know how to live, even the best of them. Just standing there unmoving. Birds and insects visit them. Frogs too, probably. Just stand there, looking at things, doing nothing, blown by the wind. When you can't sleep at night you can talk to some bird who can't sleep either. The bird hoots, and in the silver-gray light of the moon the slowpoke tree moves its leaves in reply. Sometimes, according to the wind, the thick leaves brush against the steel helmet.

Death.

Christ, they all died, and only I was left. And I don't know what to say to them, don't know how to tell them that I'm sorry, that I'm rotten with this lousy guilt because I lived on and they all died. And that's why I hate the filthy war.

Still. I didn't dodge the draft. I wanted to. Yes, I wanted to all right. But I joined up, and all sorts of things happened to me, slapped on the face, beaten with the belt. Do you think I enjoyed it? I hated every minute of it. But I joined up: I went for a soldier. Active service too. Fighting in the field, and the whole platoon got wiped out, except for me. Yes, I got taken prisoner, but I didn't give myself up. I fell asleep, that's all. Couldn't help it. And when I woke up they had me all tied up. I didn't go with my hands up, like some cheeky guys with white flags.

So you just listen to me, Shokichi Hamada. Listen, and don't you forget. I didn't want to do it, but I did. And you didn't. Just don't forget that, because we're different, you see. Got the difference, have you?

So what I'm going to do I'm not doing for myself. When I fix you, you bastard, it won't be for me. It'll be for them. It'll be for him.

So come on out, Hamada. Come on out and fight. Fight like a man. I was pretty good with the bayonet, though, so you won't stand a chance. And if you won't fight? Then we'll have to think of something else, won't we?

How about throwing a wrench in the works of your promotion? I can't say I've thought of anything special at the moment, but I will. I will.

Didn't handle that business with the burglar the other day all that well, I'll admit. Lost a good chance there. But the draft dodger affair, that's a different matter. That's a really good idea. That should fix him. But exactly how, that's the problem. Let's give it a good think. Now, there's not much I can do directly. The chief clerk's hopeless because all he can do is drink. Could ask some other head, I suppose. Wouldn't do much good, though. Old Kobayakawa's a complete loss these days. Horikawa's the one in control.

Looks like the end of the sherry. Never say die, though. Go on searching and you're bound to find something in the end. The long road back, as Douglas MacArthur said. The long road back to the kitchen. Hello, what's this? Bottle of soy sauce. This looks like sauce of some kind as well. Something written on it. Plum wine. Well, plum wine ought to do. After all, it's wine. Wine is wine.

Don't taste all that good.

That's right. The twit's name is Inuzuka, it's come back at last. Runs that magazine. What's it called? *Teetotaler*? No, *Totality*. How about making use of the gutter press this time?

five

. . . So he passed the days, and outside the registry window the pomegranate tree with deep vermillion flowers bloomed, and it was now the season when Yoko would start nagging him about taking her away for a holiday this summer, and still he'd heard nothing. He started to rebuke himself for his foolishness in so easily believing a mere rumor, and began to forget the rumor itself. Then one morning, just two weeks before the summer vacation was due to begin, he had a phone call from Nishi asking him to meet him in the staff canteen, as there was something he urgently wanted to talk to him about. He told the chief clerk where he was going, who scowled because it was not customary for both assistants to be absent from the room at the same time, then made a large nod of assent; and Hamada went to the canteen. It was still not lunchtime and there were few people about, except some students arranging their notes or looking something up in them, and in the area partitioned off by screens for members of staff only, Nishi was sitting. When he saw Hamada he half stood up, waved his hand, and smiled.

A waitress came to their table, and Hamada ordered Coca-cola. Then the two talked about the coming summer, wondering if it was going to be hotter than usual or not, until Nishi lowered his voice and indicated he was going to get down to business, taking a slim magazine, the latest issue of

Totality, out of his inside pocket, laying it in front of Hamada, and looking him straight in the eyes as he said,

"I was wondering if you've read the latest number of this maniac's magazine. It's only just arrived today."

"No. Not yet. Not this number."

It had in fact arrived by that morning's mail, but he hadn't looked at it yet, and didn't feel all that much inclined to, either.

"It's the article on page three."

Hamada picked up *Totality* and read the article, which had a typically labored title: PRESUMPTUOUS ATTEMPT TO INFLUENCE STAFFING POLICY REFLECTS GRAVE CONCERN OVER SAD DEMISE OF FOUNDER SPIRIT. The article itself, although not actually mentioning Hamada by name, pointed out that there was a man working as assistant clerk in this university (not a *graduate*—underlined) who had cravenly evaded conscription during the Greater Asian War, and it was now rumored that this cowardly draft resister was shortly to be appointed head of a clerical department, which only indicated most regrettably how far the university lately had departed from the spirit of its founder, and how tainted red it had become.

When Nishi saw that Hamada had finished reading, he opened his mouth to give a spiel about Hamada probably feeling a bit put out by it, though there was no need at all to take any notice of what that maniac said; and although most people thought Nishi was Hamada's rival, in fact it was only a friendly, constructive rivalry arising from the fact that they stimulated each other since they had fruitful differences of opinion, but he didn't see how this scoundrel had any right to criticize Hamada in this way, and it was quite preposterous to say he was a red; and although he'd mentioned Hamada's past when in the library office, that was, of course, only a piece of fooling around, and it was impermissible that this outsider should be allowed to interfere with university internal affairs, and finally, it did appear that the rumor the idiot had overheard probably had no basis in reality anyway.

Hamada listened to this in silence, recalling the coarse envelope with *Totality* stamped in large letters on it he'd received from the messenger girl and placed casually upon his desk, marveling he'd been able to sit indifferently for an hour and a half with this bombshell next to him. Nishi went on to say he thought Hamada ought to have a word with Horikawa about it and see what could be done, and Hamada again just listened, holding his glass of Coca-cola in his hand but never once drinking from it. His hand shook slightly, and the lumps of ice floating on top of the brown liquid knocked against each other, producing a small clink. It was as if he were holding a device in his hand precisely made to measure the perturbations going on somewhere in his mind.

"I thought you ought to know about this as soon as possible, and hope you don't think I've been a bit presumptuous . . ." said Nishi. Hamada assured him he didn't, thanked him, drank his Coca-cola, and said he was a subscriber to the magazine himself, but if he'd known this kind of thing was going to happen he'd never have given the man a penny, and now sorely regretted that he had. This game attempt to laugh the business off was taken up by Nishi, who roared in his usual boisterous way, and while Hamada was listening to this he reflected that the thing he'd always been afraid might happen ever since he'd been first employed at the university had finally taken place, after twenty years. It was like a bomb dropped during an air raid being found now, unexploded, on a building site.

"Nomoto in economics," said Nishi, mentioning the professor who'd been labeled a leftist in *Totality* because he recommended Marx's writings to his students, "said the same sort of thing, only the other way around."

"The same sort of thing . . . only the other way around?"

"Yes. He said his only consolation was that he'd been pestered any number of times to subscribe but had always refused."

A crowd of students came into the canteen, and it became noisy.

"Professor Kuwano's French class has been canceled," shouted a girl student who was standing quite close to the partition.

"Shall we go?" said Nishi, rising from his seat.

"Yes. The chief may be having problems all on his own," said Hamada, and stood up, once more expressing his thanks; and they walked off with Nishi leading the way.

"I thought the best thing to do would be to let you know as quickly as possible. I noticed it almost as soon as the post arrived, but wasn't quite sure if I ought to tell you, so I came here to think about it."

When Hamada got back from the canteen he opened the gray envelope and read *Totality*, the article in question, and looked through the whole of it to see if he wasn't being pilloried somewhere else; and he must have read the PRESUMPTUOUS ATTEMPT at least a dozen times in the interval between then and eight-thirty that evening, when he was finally free to go home, since he was on night school duty that day. Night school duty was mainly a matter of being in attendance, and there was little real work to do, so he had time to read. When he had first read that article in the light of day he'd been more or less in agreement with Nishi that it was the work of a maniac and could be ignored, since nobody would take it seriously. To be more precise, that is what he tried to think. But eventually he began to be of the opinion that there could well be some connection between this article and the fact that a temporary halt seemed to have been called to the administrative shake-up, and even that the article should be considered an expression of a change in the whole atmosphere that seemed to have come about. Wasn't it perhaps that this man Inuzuka had speedily grasped that there was an anti-Hamada mood in the university, vaguely engendered by the thief incident and the rumor of his coming promotion? If that was so, then the real problem was not the article itself but this general anti-Hamada feeling, even if it probably only existed at this moment among the clerical staff. Then, might it not be that someone had gotten Inuzuka to write the article? And if someone had, who was it? The most obvious candidates for the role of instigator were the chief clerk and Nishi, and they were the two who constantly came to mind; but as he was wandering the wide, vacant Registry Office, empty except for himself and the clerk in charge of night school documentation, with the crude strumming of a guitar coming from one direction and the voices of two members of some other department (he was unable to work out which) barking farewells at each other from another, he noticed among the untidy heap of documents on the chief clerk's desk a number of envelopes containing copies of *Totality*, and all of them were unopened. Clearly he had no interest in the magazine at all, and so Hamada removed him from his imaginary list, deciding to cross out Nishi's name at the same time, with the result that there was now no one on it. Hamada always considered the two in collusion with each other, and he was satisfied he had no reason to mistrust the behavior of either of them as far as this matter was concerned.

At about nine o'clock he left the university, walking along the dark road with the students. Yoko was in bed with a cold, so he had to get his own bath. He was at last able to relax only when he had gotten in it. This diminution in his chances of promotion was annoying, but he'd never had much hope that it would ever take place, and there seemed no real reason to get all that upset about it. He arrived at this state of mind while he was washing himself, pleased with the cool, objective way he was regarding the situation.

During the lunch break of the following day a student wearing a sports shirt under a dark suit and spectacles turned up, approached Hamada, and asked him for an interview.

"An interview?"

"Yes."

The student presented him with a card that proclaimed he was a reporter on the student newspaper.

"I think you'd be better off with the chief clerk," he said, and was just about to call him when the student whispered,

"No. It's not that kind of thing. Not a university matter, but something of personal concern to yourself."

Hamada expressed bemusement, and the student asked him if he wouldn't mind coming to the editorial office.

The student spoke not only politely but persuasively. So Hamada allowed himself to be led to a grubby room in the basement of the student union building. There was one other student there, in shirtsleeves, clumsily making calculations with an abacus. The student in glasses tidied up a large desk that had a newspaper file opened on it and offered Hamada a chair. He then sat down beside him. The rest of the contents of the room consisted of a dictionary with a torn cover, an ashtray, a dozen scrapbooks, a blackboard, two battered baseball gloves, and a poster for some art cinema.

Hamada had already guessed what the matter "of personal concern" must be, but while walking along the corridor he was surprised to notice the student was not carrying a copy of *Totality*; nor did he see one anywhere in this room, and he began to think he might have guessed wrongly and it was some other business they were interested in. But just as he'd arrived at this conclusion, the student reporter produced, as if by some mystifying sleight of hand, the latest copy of *Totality* from under the file of newspapers.

"Have you read this? On page three."

Hamada nodded silently in reply, noting that the click of the abacus had come to an end, and the student went on,

"You are the one being criticized, aren't you?"

When Hamada nodded again, the student went silent. Perhaps the idea had crossed his mind that he might be intruding in a matter that was no concern of his. So this time Hamada spoke first.

"I assume there is nobody else in the university who resisted the draft, and so it must be me. Still, what about it? What do you want to ask?"

"What is your reaction to this article?"

"Why do you want to know that?"

"As part of an article."

"What sort of article?"

The student suddenly started speaking at great speed.

"The editorial aim is, firstly, to make it absolutely clear that we support your antiwar stand and see it as something young people nowadays would do well to imitate. Secondly, we wish to eliminate all interference in internal university affairs by external rightist reactionary influences. . . ."

At that moment a student with several days' growth of beard and wearing a brown corduroy cap came in. The bespectacled student motioned to him with his eyes, and he sat down on the opposite side of the desk from Hamada, removing his cap.

"What's happened to Marko?" said the one in glasses.

"She's gone to get some bread," said the student with the abacus, who appeared to be working on the accounts.

"Look," said Hamada. "You're putting me in a pretty awkward position. I really don't want to give this interview."

"You mean it's not okay?" said the one in glasses, and when Hamada nodded he asked why not.

"It would make my position in the university very difficult. I'd find it hard to go on working here."

"There's no need to mention you by name."

Hamada thought there most certainly would be a need to mention him by name if the article was to be written, but he only replied,

"It would still make things very hard for me. All I want is a quiet life. I just want to let this thing blow over. I don't want trouble. I don't want anything stirred up."

The unshaved student then broke in, speaking with a northern accent that Hamada placed as from either Morioka or Aomori.

"Mr. Hamada, the situation is this. We've got two aims in mind for this article. We want to stamp out this parasite who represents the very worst elements among the graduates of this university, and his rightist, gutter journalism. Then we also want to express our sympathy with the draft refusal movement that's spreading all over America in opposition to the Vietnam War, and make our own protest against American imperialism as it exists on both sides of the Pacific. There's lots going on now. They're even distributing pamphlets on how to avoid the draft. We're thinking along the same lines. The young people in this country have no interest whatsoever in the question of conscription, and we think this is a really good opportunity to shake up the apathy of the great mass of readers here by making use of a question much nearer home, and we feel it should have a considerable effect."

"That's just what I don't want. What someone in university administration always wants is to avoid being conspicuous in any way. Colorful ties aren't allowed. You shouldn't have your own car. I'm sorry you feel so strongly about this, but I just can't . . ."

"Are you opposed to our aims themselves?" said the one in glasses.

"Well, I'm not actually opposed . . ." Hamada mumbled, feeling rather guilty he'd never given any thought at all to the young Americans who were resisting the draft in opposition to the Vietnam War, reflecting that he was as apathetic about it as the young people in Japan who'd just been criticized. The two students said nothing, and the sound of the abacus started up again. Hamada began to wonder why he was so afraid to read newspaper articles about war, always avoiding them as much as possible. But then it was just the same with news about whole families committing suicide, or women past middle age who did away with themselves. Then the idea of taking what he'd done and writing a pamphlet about it seemed to him ridiculous, for it had no connection with what these young Americans were doing. At least he felt it had none, a conviction that came to him in a flash of dazzling insight. It just hadn't been like that. What had it been like, then? Like those young criminals on the wanted poster. Like them. The one with the harelip might well be standing trial now, perhaps at this very moment.

A girl student wearing a black shirt-style blouse and a checkered skirt came in, putting a paper bag and some milk on the table. Judging by the oily stains, the paper bag must have fried bread in it. She lowered the leather case dangling from her shoulder, then pointed a camera at Hamada. The lens looked like the muzzle of a rifle.

"Are you going to photograph me?"

"Yes."

Hamada looked down and covered his face.

"Oh, don't you like being photographed?"

"Please stop all this, if you don't mind," he shouted; and the cry, muffled behind his hands, echoed emptily in the room.

"Isn't it allowed, or something?" said the student with the northern accent.

Hamada, his face still covered with his hands, pleaded with them to drop the whole thing.

"Then we won't be able to fill the front page," the girl's voice said.

The four students went into a huddle in a corner of the room, talking in lowered voices. Hamada raised his head and withdrew the dark palms of his hands from his face. Marko and the one in spectacles were eating as they talked. Hamada lit a cigarette and looked at the poster on the wall, then thought it was ridiculous to go on sitting here. He called out to the students that he was going, stubbed out his cigarette in the ashtray, and walked toward the door. The north country student came sliding nimbly toward him.

"This is what we've decided to do. Your name won't be mentioned. There'll be no use of initials, either. We'll just refer to you as a certain person. Naturally there'll be no photograph. We'll just say that you declined to be interviewed. Is that all right?"

Hamada nodded and left, but the whole afternoon he wondered about the wisdom of giving his assent to that. Still, as anyone in the university knew, it was much harder to suppress an article in the student newspaper than one in something like *Totality*. The student paper was protected by a group of people now working on the large dailies who'd been on its staff when students, and under their guidance it took a relatively objective stand about most things, criticizing the university administration and also various student activities, including the union, and its right to freedom of expression was fairly highly guaranteed. If he was going to do anything about the situation, it could only be through those older journalists, but he knew from his experience of two or three of these graduates that they were remarkably like the sort of journalists one saw on TV drama: there was nothing they liked more than some kind of rumpus, and they would hardly turn upon their own kind. They would be about as likely to want to put an end to this as the chief clerk himself. All he could do was try to treat it as something of little importance and just ignore it. After all, there really was nothing else he could do.

At half past four most of the staff were getting ready to go home. While he was watching this, Hamada recalled there was something he had to buy and searched in the pocket of his shirt, finding a small piece of paper. It was a shopping reminder, written in Yoko's hand. Because of her cold she couldn't go to the department store and had asked him to get something for her. During the last couple of years he'd gotten into the habit of forgetting to buy things when she asked him to, hence the slip of paper. He hurriedly got ready to leave.

He completed his shopping in the basement food section, to the urgent accompaniment of the closing bell, and as he was going upstairs he heard someone screeching out his name. He turned around and saw it was his sister, Mitsu. She was forty-nine years old now. She was carrying two large paper shopping bags in her arms, with her handbag dangling from her wrist. Without saying a word, she handed the two bags over to her stationary younger brother, then said with an enormous sigh,

"Let's have a cup of tea somewhere. I'm absolutely starving."

She spoke exactly as if they'd made some previous arrangement to meet at this place. They went into a crowded shop near the store and ordered coffee and meat pies, and listened to the waitress crudely howling out their order so as to make it heard above the cries of the other waitresses and the general hubbub.

His sister appeared to be genuinely hungry, since she finished half of her meat pie in no time, and then talked cheerfully away as she drank her coffee. She started with reminiscences of her life in China, about the German lady who'd taught her how to make meat pies in Dairen, and what the color of the sky in Harbin would be at this time of the year. Then she went on to the subject of the son of one of her company directors and how much it had cost to get him into college, wondering what the market price would be at Hamada's place, although he evaded the question, and then about her husband's having to retire next year, and her daughter having gotten married only six months ago and how lost she felt without her. When she'd reached this point he felt, just as he was about to put a piece of meat pie into his mouth, a profound desire that she should not go on, having a sudden, if only mild intuition that the conversation was leading in the wrong direction. But she went on.

"I at last begin to feel I understand what Mother went through," she said briskly, glancing at her brother from just above the rim of her raised cup. "She was just lonely because I wasn't around anymore. I really feel ashamed now that I blamed it on you at the time. I don't think that could have been the reason at all."

"Still, she was the daughter of a military man."

"Yes, but she was much more the wife of the local doctor. That's what she'd become. After all, the military officer and his wife had died ages before."

"Um."

"If your grandfather had still been alive, he would probably have fixed things so you'd have been classified grade C."

"I hardly think so."

"She'd so lost connection with that world she didn't have any influence in it at all. It was quite dead to her."

"Even so . . ."

But he wasn't able to express what he wanted to say. What he wanted to say was that his leaving home had been worse for his mother than hers, and so the responsibility for her death still lay more with him. Then there was the responsibility that lay with his father and Shinji, who'd both been at home and should have been a comfort to her. But had the business with Hiroko started before or after her death? He didn't know, and there was no way of knowing. In fact, there was no way of knowing anything about any of it. His sister's insistence that her leaving home had been more important to their mother than his seemed to imply some sort of rivalry with him about the places they held in their mother's affections. Then it was also strange that she could talk in this cheerful way about the reasons somebody should want to commit suicide. Surely that implied she could have no real understanding of such reasons? Also, why should she now be concerned enough to make this attempt to wrest the affection of her mother from him, twenty years and more after she'd died? It certainly was true, however, that Mother's suicide had taken place precisely six months after she'd left home to get married. It wasn't at all unlikely that a mother would be more affected by the loss of a daughter than of a son.

A nearby waitress howled out the same order of coffee and meat pies, but three of each this time.

Tokyo Station was black with grime, virtually in ruins, and horrifyingly full of people. Although he hadn't thought it strange to see mobs of people squatting on platforms in stations in the provinces, he found the sight unnerving here in the capital. He pushed his way through the station crowds, with his overcoat over his arm and the large rucksack he'd used for carrying rice in Uwajima on his back. Now it was full of rice, mandarin oranges, a few clothes, and the bowl he'd bought on August 15 carefully wrapped in his raincoat. The trains and streetcars were all crowded, and as he was being shoved here and there he worried about the oranges and the china bowl. He was twenty-five, a young man with neither beard nor toothbrush moustache (although his hair was long enough), and he thought alternately about the contents of his rucksack and the death of his mother.

His father had said in his letter that she'd died in March 1941, but he hadn't given the cause of her death. Hamada had assumed this was because he'd written with the brevity normal in a male parent, and had decided, with feelings halfway between certitude and surmise, that she'd probably, almost certainly, died of some illness. When he looked at the shambles Tokyo had become—a Tokyo he'd not seen for five years—with its dugout shanties, its allotment fields in place of gardens, its burned shells of buildings, and the rows of low, low roofs between those buildings, it seemed to him perfectly natural she should have died, either through illness or some accident, in an environment like this. He'd forgotten at that moment that this destruction Tokyo had undergone had almost all happened during the last year or so.

Their home was in the same place, but now transformed into a small, cramped house. That did not surprise him much, for what shocked him was that all the trees and vegetation in the garden (which had been one of the most splendid in the neighborhood) had been burned to the ground. There was a new placard, in his father's hand, announcing the HAMADA CLINIC, suggesting that the stone pillars of the gate on which the name had originally been carved had been destroyed by the flames as well. He rang the bell, and the nurse Hiroko opened the door, very grown up now and not at all like the slim girl of five years ago, fresh out of nursing school.

"Oh, it's Shokichi," she said.

He made the normal greeting, took off his rucksack, and asked where his father was.

"He's in the examination room with a patient."

"Right, I'll come in, then."

"Please do. I'm afraid everything's all rather untidy."

This conversation was very much like that between the lady of the house and some visitor. He glanced at the waiting room and noticed it was empty of patients, then traversed a narrow space, a combination of corridor and kitchen, and entered a small living room some ten feet by ten in size. Its furnishings consisted of a low table, a tea cabinet, and a porcelain bowl or *hibachi* for heating purposes. There was no one there, "no one" meaning to him the absence of his mother rather than no one in particular. Hiroko took a cushion out of the built-in cupboard, placed it on the tatami, and motioned politely to him to sit on it. Then she set about making tea.

"It's all right, Hiroko. You get back to the exam room."

"No, really, I'll do it. Dr. Hamada tends to work alone these days."

While he was failing to work out what those words implied, he heard his father's voice dismissing the patient. His voice was no different from five years ago, but when he finally came into the room, his face and overall physical appearance had aged considerably.

"Ah, back at last, are you?" said his father, still standing.

Hamada adjusted himself to the formal kneeling position and bowed his head. No words of greeting would issue from his mouth. His father went on standing in silence while Hiroko helped him take off his white coat, and Hamada looked up and was astonished to see he was wearing Japanese dress under it. He'd only ever seen his father wearing western dress in the examination room before, a shirt and waistcoat under his white coat, and he knew that he had despised doctors who wore Japanese clothes on such occasions as being slovenly. Perhaps he'd lost his suits in the air raid? Or perhaps he just found it more comfortable like this, being old enough to want to feel casual and relaxed even when examining his patients. Father and son faced each other across the table, and drank tea. The son talked about how crowded the trains were, and the father gave his recollections of a trip he'd made to Shikoku for a Medical Association conference, and then of all the problems he'd had rebuilding the house. He still had the same habit of sticking his stubbed-out cigarette ends in line in the ash of the porcelain *hibachi*, but the pot itself was a wretched substitute for the splendid one they'd had before, and the cigarettes he smoked were no longer the expensive Shikishima brand (he'd refused to smoke anything else) but hand-rolled with tobacco he probably got on the black market. Hamada made the occasional interjection and nod as his father talked, noting how completely gray his hair had become.

When Hiroko got up and went off to light the wood fire for the bath, this allowed the father to talk about the real question of importance.

"Look. You mustn't take the business too much to heart, you know. Yae just took an overdose of sleeping tablets by mistake."

Yae was the name of his mother, but before Hamada had even had time enough to be surprised by this statement, his father went on,

"Hiroko's looking after me now. Shinji seems to object, but you're a grown-up so you'll understand."

"I just thought it must have been some illness."

"She wasn't sleeping all that well. I was careless. I blame myself."

So she'd committed suicide, thought Hamada, and blamed himself too. To think that someone leading such an active social life, always dressing up and going out somewhere, should have had such patriotic feelings hidden away inside her. Or could it be someone who prized the social round so much was obsessed with what people might say, and had been filled with shame about things that were not really shameful? Or was it that it had been . . . ? Since the doubt had occurred to him, he felt obliged to state it.

"She killed herself because of me?"

"Of course she didn't," said his father. "Anyway, it's all over and done with now. You shouldn't worry too much about it. At least that's what I've decided to do myself."

Hamada realized that the issue his father was really concerned about was not Yae's death so much as the fact that Hiroko was no longer a nurse but his common-law wife. So he asked in as unconcerned a voice as he could manage,

"What should I call her now? I called her plain Hiroko just a moment ago."

"That should be all right," said his father.

An expression of satisfaction at having been able to deal with an awkward subject without having to be too forthright about it slowly appeared on his father's face. He was able to switch the subject to that of being worried about having received no word from Mitsu and her husband, who were in Manchuria, and then talked about Shinji's university.

Hiroko came back and said she would like him to wait a little longer before taking his bath. She appeared to understand from the attitudes of both of them that the question of her own position had been discussed and satisfactorily concluded. Or perhaps she had in fact been eavesdropping? Whichever it was, she said, looking as if she were about to burst into tears at any moment,

"If only your mother could have been alive to see this day."

Hamada noted that she did not refer to her as Mrs. Hamada or Madam, which she would have done in the past when she'd been a servant.

"I've always said we ought to have a Buddha shelf so that we can announce things like this. But the doctor . . ."

His father said nothing, and Hamada, in order to retrieve an awkward situation, said he would go and visit the grave tomorrow or the day after. He felt he had no right to blame anybody for the way things had turned out, and he opened his rucksack and produced the rice and oranges. Then he gave the bowl to his father, who was very pleased with it.

"I'm sorry this is all I've been able to bring back, after all the trouble I've . . ."

"That's all right. There's nothing to apologize about. The only trouble I had occurred just once a year. The rest of the time it didn't matter."

"Once a year?"

"When I had to go to the military section in the ward office and report you hadn't come back yet. I hated doing that."

Hamada bowed his head once more. This time too he had no idea what to say.

"There's this as well, although it's probably no use."

He produced from the inside of his coat a piece of paper, a certificate of change of address issued by the Uwajima Town Hall to "Sugiura, Kenji, Male, Born 11 Sept. 1914, 32 years old." In the section headed "Reasons for Transfer" the words "Return to Home Domicile" had been written.

"Would you like mine?" said his sister, indicating the half of her meat pie she hadn't eaten, but Hamada declined the offer. She then called out to the waitress for some water. At that moment he suddenly felt he had to ask her at last, after all these years.

"Did it cause you any trouble? My behaving like that?"

"Trouble?"

The waitress brought a glass of water and she drank it in one gulp.

"No. None at all."

"I thought in a place like Manchuria it might have gone down badly."

"It was a surprisingly carefree sort of place. Besides, I didn't tell anyone about it. Mother wrote to me about you in one of her letters, but I didn't even tell Takahashi."

"You didn't tell your husband?"

"Not until we were on the boat coming back. Then I did. He said he was astonished that someone who always let her tongue run away with her should have been able to be quiet about it for so long. He meant to praise me, I suppose. Quite sure he did. So there was no harm done, as far as I was concerned."

Hamada had been smiling, but he felt something was being implied by that last remark.

"You mean there was harm done to somebody else?"

"Harm done?"

"Yes, harm done. Somebody suffered."

A tense expression came over her face, and she didn't reply.

"Who did I harm? Tell me."

After a little while she said,

"I suppose I really do let my tongue run away with me. Well, I've said it now, so there's nothing else for it. You won't be upset, will you? Promise you won't be upset."

Hamada nodded.

"It was Shinji. He had a really bad time because of it. Well, perhaps it really wasn't all that bad, but still. The M.P.s were always watching him. Then the officer at school used to beat him up. He got a perforated eardrum. Just the one ear. Didn't you know?"

Hamada shook his head. He hadn't known. Mitsu looked awkwardly at her watch and stood up in a great hurry, saying she'd have to rush home or else she'd be in trouble with her husband. He wasn't to worry about it because there was no connection between the eardrum and the kind of deafness Shinji suffered from, and it was silly to bother himself about things that were over and done with twenty years ago. When Hamada asked her if she'd heard all this directly from Shinji, she was only very vague in her reply, taking the two straw-colored paper bags from him suddenly as if she was snatching them away, and leaving him standing there on the corner in the blue light of dusk.

On the train, and after he'd gotten home, he tried to remember if Shinji had had anything wrong with his ears before the illness that made him deaf, but there was nothing he still retained any memory of. On that evening in November when he'd met his university student brother for the first time for more than five years, and after that right up until the time Shinji became ill, he felt he had never once thought that his brother had something wrong with his ears. Or perhaps he had? If he hadn't, it could well be Hamada had wrongly assumed he couldn't be hard of hearing because he played the piano so well, confusing his excellent ear for music with the question of whether his ears were actually good at hearing things or not. Certainly Shinji had never mentioned any trouble with one of his eardrums, but might not that have been because he wanted to earn money playing the piano and was worried he might be stopped if the fact were known? He could only find out the truth by calling the music publisher where he worked, sometime in the near future, and asking him, and then he would apologize if it was true; but he immediately rejected the idea and blamed himself for having thought it. It would be much too cruel to Shinji to raise the question again, just to satisfy his own conscience.

Each day the summer deepened, and day by day the summer vacation approached. It was noticeable how sparse the numbers of students on campus had become, and how many classes were announced canceled on the notice boards. And it was in this atmosphere, of growing heat, of laxity, of doors and windows left wide open, that Hamada, one day with sleeves rolled up, the next in open-necked shirt, went on with his work of stamping documents, writing memos, and telephoning.

Late on the afternoon of the day after he'd refused the student paper interview, the assistant head of Administration stopped him in the corridor and said there'd been an inquiry from the student newspaper about what the Staff Association thought of the matter, but he'd replied there was nothing to be said about it at this stage. Hamada complained that he was himself being very seriously inconvenienced by the way these student journalists had decided to poke their noses into the affair, and the other sympathized with him. After a few words about it being just the time of year when cold beer really started to taste good, they parted.

The following day, when the Conference of Heads and Assistant Heads of Administration had just ended and Hamada was leaving the conference room, he met three of the economics academic staff who were presumably about to take part in some economics faculty meeting. One of them was wearing a white shirt with sleeves rolled up, another was smartly dressed in a plush summer jacket, while the third had on a polo shirt that was dirty and appropriately soaked in sweat. The one in the white shirt was the Professor Nomoto who'd been given such a rough going-over in *Totality*, a man quite young to be a professor, being two or three years Hamada's junior. When he saw him, Nomoto raised his hand, in which he held one of the more intellectual weekly magazines, and said,

"I've just been making the summing-up for the defense."

Hamada could only express bemusement, so he went on,

"Those people from the student paper burst in on me."

"Ah, I see."

"Taking on our mutual foe, *Totality*. So I came out fighting and gave him all I've got," said the professor cheerfully.

Hamada thanked him on his own behalf, then left with Nishi, although what he felt at that moment was not so much gratitude as a real envy of the academic staff for enjoying a freedom of expression in most matters that people like himself did not have, and even a certain repulsion for that reason. It was, in fact, just as Nishi had muttered to him as they were walking away: "Nomoto and his kind have a really easy time of it."

The same day he had to go to Horikawa's chestnut-and-green room to receive his stamp of approval. Perhaps because he was worn out by the heat, Horikawa's hair looked rather grubby, the color of nicotine-stained teeth. As usual, he produced his ivory seal from its deerskin case, stamped the document, then called Hamada back as he was about to leave, although he didn't offer him a chair this time.

"It seems Inuzuka has been digging about in your past."

"Yes, sir."

"Extremely unfortunate at this point in time."

"Yes."

"There's nothing in particular to worry about . . . although one can never be too much on one's guard. Best to bear yourself with circumspection. It's always wise to avoid any unnecessary provocation."

Hamada announced that he'd refused to be interviewed by the student paper. Horikawa closed his eyes halfway through Hamada's account of the incident, only nodding occasionally as he listened. It was impossible to gather anything from the expression on his face, like trying to read a book written in an unknown foreign language. Then he opened his eyes abruptly, and asked in a very gentle voice,

"Is your wife well?"

"Yes, thank you, sir."

"Good. That's good."

This inquiry after Yoko's health seemed like a euphemistic way of dismissing him, and after bowing low to the executive director, beneath the various portraits of former presidents and governors, he left the room. Horikawa's remark about avoiding any unnecessary provocation must have been referring to declining interviews with the student newspaper and things like that. After all, there was nothing else he could be referring to, since what sort of provocations could someone like him offer or avoid? But as he walked along the empty corridor, then down the stairs, squeezing against the wall so as not to disturb the cleaning woman in her work, and then along the brighter hallway on the first floor past students and teachers and delivery boys, he had the nervous feeling a number of times that somehow he'd innocently misread the whole situation, had made some preposterous misinterpretation of what Horikawa meant and of what was really going on.

Three days later the student newspaper appeared, and ten copies were distributed to the Registry Office. They were brought by Marko, who was wearing the same black blouse she'd had on before. When she caught Hamada's eye she pointed to the papers she'd just put on the messenger girl's desk, and when he nodded she walked off in a rather affected manner. Hamada stood up and went and picked up a copy, running his eyes over it as he remained standing.

OUTRAGE COMMITTED BY REACTIONARY *TOTALITY*: LIBEL OF ANTIWAR HERO. The headline was larger than he'd expected, and he didn't much like being called a hero, but the story hadn't been treated as sensationally as he'd feared it might be. The article made use of some fairly eccentric language at times, but that was normal in a student newspaper, and he felt it was all right after all and no serious damage had been done. It was written, by the standards of this paper, in a reasonably subdued tone, merely saying outsiders should not be allowed to interfere in the internal affairs of the university, and it was absurd that someone who had resisted the draft during the Pacific War should now be criticized for that reason. The fact that such arguments had become rampant nowadays was a good indication of the way present-day Japan was becoming more and more reactionary, and the atomic warhead of this reactionary assault was the rightist, parasitic mini-mass media (by "warhead" they must mean "spearhead," and "mini-mass" was a weird form of expression, thought Hamada), while our task was to fight against American imperialism side by side with the young people in the United States who refused to be conscripted in protest against the war in Vietnam.

This paper has tried on two or three occasions to obtain interviews with the man in question and with influential parties in the Staff Association, but unfortunately our requests have been turned down. It appears that, at this juncture, the Staff Association is attempting to play down the whole thing.

Hamada felt relieved at this and made his way back to his desk, but as he read the piece that followed, particularly its last sentence, he was so taken aback he stopped in his tracks. In fact, it might be truer to say he became rooted to the spot.

COMMENTS OF PROFESSOR NOMOTO OF THE ECONOMICS FACULTY,
WHO HAS ALSO BEEN ATTACKED BY *TOTALITY*

Totality consists entirely of incoherent bombast and meaningless, irresponsible statements. It is most unwise to judge a person's behavior in wartime from mere rumor without specific data, and even if the rumor turned out to be correct, and the man in question genuinely had been a draft resister, one need hardly point out that the former Japanese army no longer exists, and that there is no kind of legal basis upon which he could be attacked. His position is the same as those people who were repatriated after being taken prisoner by the American army. In the Japanese army, those who had suffered the "disgrace" of being made prisoner were forced to commit suicide, and presumably this magazine is trying to argue that, although such people can no longer be condemned in strictly legal terms, there is such a thing as the mood of the people, which does not forgive them. However, so long as the Japanese people continue to support the Peace Constitution, then one may say that such an argument must fail to hold water. Presumably I also shouldn't need to add that outsiders should not be allowed to meddle in our internal affairs, and that this kind of unwarranted interference must absolutely be stopped. Finally, I feel obliged to point out, in order to avoid any misunderstanding, that I myself was called up during the Pacific War in what was referred to as Student Mobilization, and I was sent to the front line.

Hamada felt as if he had been struck in the face. Rereading that final sentence, he walked back to his desk and sat down. That postscript by Professor Nomoto, written to save his own skin, made complete nonsense of all the previous "summing-up for the defense." Any reader would obviously start thinking about the reason he had felt "obliged" to mention the fact of his own "Student Mobilization," and the conclusion he would inevitably come to was that Professor Nomoto didn't want to be thought a coward; which must mean consequently that "the man in question," i.e., Hamada, was one. Thus the correct evaluation of the draft resister was that he had acted in a cowardly way.

Hamada ceased looking at the newspaper, folded it up, and put it to one side, and while going through the motions of reading a document on his desk recalled his impression of Nomoto when he'd met him in the conference room three days before, bright and cheerful, that carefree way of speaking, his arms with the sleeves rolled up and the expanse of thick hair from just below his elbows onto the backs of his hands, and the way he'd gently waved a magazine in his hand in place of a fan. And a man like that had betrayed him like this, and probably wasn't himself at all conscious that he'd done so. The telephone rang, a heavy, oppressive sound. The messenger girl came around collecting orders for lunch. An assistant from some department office came to get some rough paper and colored chalk. And Hamada picked up the student paper again and reread the comments of the professor, guessing from the style that these were not remarks taken down in any interview but had been written down by the professor and then handed over to the students. Why should he have gone to all that trouble? Because he was worried that his final words, his summing-up, not for the defense but in self-defense, might be overlooked if he didn't get it down in black and white himself. He'd had to make absolutely certain that statement was there. Hamada took out his handkerchief and wiped the back of his neck, aware of himself trembling as the temperature on this summer morning gradually began to soar. They were now living in an age when even someone like Professor Nomoto had decided, and correctly decided, that he needed to protect himself in that way if he was to survive.

There was a telephone call from both the executive directors, Horikawa and Kobayakawa, to the chief clerk, apparently to do with the arrangements for some coming meeting of the board of trustees. He left his desk in a great hurry, picking up a copy of the student newspaper from the table by the door as he went. He would probably read it right away. After he'd read it he'd talk to the two directors about it. Then Nishi got up, looking at his watch and saying he had to see the professor in charge of one of the research laboratories, stood in front of that table for a while gazing down at the student paper without actually picking it up, then left hurriedly. No doubt the first thing he'd talk about with that professor would be the question of the draft resister. Hamada began to wonder what the students running that paper really thought they were up to. Presumably they didn't grasp the fact that these references they'd made to him would do him no good at all. If they had grasped it, perhaps they'd been too happily occupied with the professional look those COMMENTS OF PROFESSOR NOMOTO would give their paper to be actually bothered about what might happen to him. Or maybe, despite all their talk about opposition to American imperialism and the preservation of peace, deep down in the dark recesses of their unconscious they were intoxicated by the thrills offered by war films and documentary books about war, swayed by cheap concepts of "courage" and "honor" they'd picked up from such sources. The overall atmosphere of the age controlled them, even them, in the true depths of their beings. In the sultry heat of the end of June, Hamada foretold that he was going to find things getting worse and worse for him from now on.

It became known all around campus that the "certain person" was Hamada. He became irritatedly aware of the occasional male student on the bus staring at him, whether out of contempt or mere curiosity he did not know, of a girl student chatting away with others on a bench by the flowerbeds who pointed him out to her companions as he walked by. He noticed how many people among the staff, particularly those who'd only been appointed this year or last, would look straight at him, and look ostentatiously away when their eyes met. He imagined they'd asked questions about him of the older employees and been given rumors rather than anything approaching the truth in reply. The only person who actually asked him to his face about his experiences as a draft resister was the old professor of English who'd been taken on here after retiring from a public university four or five years ago, Professor Sakurai.

This was one afternoon two days after that article had appeared in the student paper, when he was walking past the professor's small private office. The door had been left wide open, and the sharp-eyed Sakurai immediately spotted him and called out,

"Ah, Hamada. Do you have a few minutes to spare? I'll make you some coffee."

"That would be very nice indeed, sir."

"I can't read at home, so I come here. And here I just seem to drop off to sleep."

He put his book face down and got up from the reclining sofa, offering Hamada a chair and happily producing a coffee filter, two cups, and a can of coffee from the deep bottom drawer of his desk, and set out to get some water.

"I can do that, sir."

"That's quite all right. We old people have to get some exercise."

"I hope it's not too much trouble."

"You were supposed to protest that I am still young," said the professor, smiling, and left the room with a tiny kettle in his hand.

The blend of coffee the professor offered him was basically Mocca and Santos, and the bitter taste was just right for summer. He was delighted when Hamada praised his coffee in so informed a way, and then said,

"I was talking about you to old Oda yesterday," he said, referring to a professor of English who was head of the Faculty of Foreign Languages. "Apparently you behaved in a quite remarkable way."

"Well . . ."

"Quite remarkable."

"It wasn't all that . . ."

"How did you manage to live? Did you take a lot of money with you?"

"The money soon ran out. I did a variety of things. Quite a number."

"I suppose you must have," said the professor, nodding in apparent satisfaction with Hamada's reply, and went on to the subject of how more than forty years ago he'd fasted before the army medical exam in order to make himself look too weedy to be called up.

"I was naturally fairly thin at the time, so it did not require all that much of an effort."

Hamada felt relieved as he left the professor's office that he hadn't inquired very deeply into the matter.

It was now, for all practical purposes, the summer vacation, and there was almost nobody around. In a corner of the corridor someone had left a large stepladder, presumably because the walls were going to be repainted (had a memo been sent about that?), but there was nobody working in its vicinity. Far off somebody was whistling "When the Saints Go Marching In." In the silence he reflected that, no matter how well disposed toward him people like Sakurai might be, he should never assume he was safe because of that, and he must know what the executive director, Dr. Horikawa, thought about the whole question.

In fact, his anxieties on this score were soon ended, or at least made less than they had been, for just as he was about to enter the Registry Office he noticed Horikawa walking toward him with the other executive director, Kobayakawa. He stood and waited for them, then bowed in turn to both. Horikawa addressed him in what seemed to be enormous good humor:

"Well, Hamada, are you going somewhere for the summer?"

"Yes, sir. I've made reservations at the university hostel in Ajiro."

"And no doubt you'll be taking your wife with you?"

"Of course, sir. I don't have anyone else to take."

All three laughed. Hamada was particularly relieved to notice how cheerfully Kobayakawa smiled at him, since he'd been rather impatiently twiddling his Panama hat in his hands. He saw them off to the entrance hall and then into the Bentley, bowing again as they drove off.

This was the first time he'd been to the hostel at Ajiro, although he had been to the area itself once before. He was thinking about it as he left the station: it would have been at the end of 1941, after Inaba's funeral, that he'd come south to the Izu peninsula, spending some time on the west side before moving around to the east coast, so he must have actually stayed in Ajiro sometime early in 1942. Yes, he remembered quite well, remembered how clumsy he'd still been at sand painting while in Niigata, and that he hadn't had a clue how to handle the "mark," either at a "market" or at a "pitch" near a school, being in a continual state about everything. Then he'd come south, and at Numazu he'd shared a room with an obvious confidence trickster, a really ugly customer with tattoos all over his body, marking him as having criminal connections of some kind, and this charlatan had insisted he must have a family name, he'd never get by without one, saying he'd introduce him to a certain gentleman who would be of real service to him, and the awful time he'd had declining the offer. He remembered the scene so well he could recall they were already using blackout precautions, so it must have been 1942. Yet he puzzled over why he should have had the nerve to stay in a place as close to Tokyo as this. Had he just not been afraid then? The middle-aged man was aware that he was now himself gradually approaching old age as he indulged his feelings of bewilderment at the unintelligible temerity of the young man he'd once been.

As they crossed the bridge that led to where all the spa hotels were clustered together, Yoko asked,

"Is there anything the matter?"

"No. Nothing. I was just thinking how changed it all is."

"It's the first time I've been here, so I wouldn't know."

"It used to be more of a fishing village than a hot spring resort before."

In fact, that was an exaggeration, although it had not been a resort then but more a place where people came to take the waters for health reasons, not just to enjoy themselves. He himself hadn't come for health reasons, although he'd been ill enough. A cheap lodging house stinking of fish. Staying in the famous spa of Ito, with tonsilitis and a fever, lying in bed for four days; and when he got better and was on his way back to Atami it rained all the time. A wretched journey. A wretched, restless, anxious journey. Bamboo grass for my pillow. That new year this whole area was going wild with the feeling that the war had been won. He remembered a blind masseur and a bath attendant making bets about how soon Singapore would fall. But it did seem that he hadn't been conscious of any danger he might meet someone he knew in Ito. Or had the idea crossed his mind, and he'd simply decided not to take it seriously? Youth.

The hostel was on the outskirts of the town. In the past it would have been a country villa in quiet surroundings, but now it had a spa hotel on one side and a pinball arcade on the other. On the way he'd been looking for the place he'd stayed in 1942, but he could find nowhere that even faintly resembled it, although he felt it must have been somewhere in the area where there was now a striptease joint.

The man in charge at the university had said it would probably be full, but perhaps because some people had canceled their reservations there were only two other guests, a P.E. instructor from one of the high schools with his friend. Mr. and Mrs. Hamada were shown upstairs to a pleasantly cool room that had apparently been the study of the distinguished scholar to whom the place had formerly belonged. Hanging in the alcove was a large scroll signed by this professor emeritus, a five-line poem written in the complex script common in the eighth century, and with such aggressively fluent strokes of the brush that Hamada could only manage to work out the last line. The fish served for dinner that evening was obviously very fresh, but an excessive amount of salt had been used, giving everything the same taste, and the thought that he'd have to put up with the same thing for four days was profoundly depressing.

"We'd be better off doing our own cooking," said Yoko petulantly.

"It should be all right if we just order the fish raw or deep-fried," replied Hamada in an attempt to placate her.

They spent the next day fishing and swimming. Yoko's attempts at swimming were a slightly superior version of the dog paddle. She went on complaining about the amount of salt in the food, but that didn't stop her polishing off each dish that appeared before her. Each night she demanded his male services and, although he was anxious they might be disturbing the two people in the room beneath them, he obliged. On the second night she was particularly athletic and pleaded with him to do it again. He asked her to give him an hour to recover, but during that interval he fell asleep. The next morning they went for a fairly long walk in the hills, and Hamada was so worn out he spent the afternoon alternately sleeping and reading a magazine. Late in the afternoon Yoko said she was just going for a walk nearby, and went out wearing a *yukata*. She had on a particularly smart sash around this summer kimono, a rather expensive-looking one she must have picked up cheap at a sale, and the whole outfit suited her slight figure and white skin, making her look attractively erotic in an old-fashioned way. Hamada himself merely dropped off again, hearing the rattle from the pinball arcade from time to time, sounding in his drowsy state like a passing shower of rain.

The sound of footsteps coming upstairs woke him. He looked up to see Yoko standing in the entrance to the room, looking sad and very much alone. Hamada spoke cheerfully to her.

"I seem to have had a really good sleep. How about having a bath?"

"All right. Let's do just that. Let's go," she said playfully and led the way out of the room, cheerfully humming a TV commercial that gave a highly optimistic account of how one could enjoy the pleasures of the hot spring in the seclusion of one's own home.

First Yoko and then Hamada took off their *yukata* in the dark, confined space of the changing room, and as he was about to open the door into the bathroom he noticed in the gloom under the shelf on which the clothes baskets were kept something gold and glittering. The naked man strained his eyes, picked up the object and scrutinized it, then broke into a disappointed smile. He'd thought this was going to be an object of some value, and instead it was just a small decoration made of folded paper used in the Weaver Festival.* The top layer was of gold paper, the second of silver, followed by five layers each of red, yellow, a deeper red, then green; and the ink of whatever had been drawn on the back had blurred and spread all over like black sweat. It was just a cheap, vulgar paper ornament. The thick band that held the bundle together had the obvious drawing of the maiden and the weaver on it, shown in a bright, bluish night sky.

His wife called out to him in a sweet, cloying, inviting voice, and he put the ornament (Tiger Mark Weaver Paper) up on the shelf and opened the door.

The bath itself was very small, and it felt cramped with the two of them in it. The space outside the bath for washing was limited too. So he sat on the edge of the bath with his legs dangling in the hot water, and said,

"I found a paper ornament on the floor in the changing room. One of those for the star festival."

Then, watching the expression on her face, he continued,

"Did you buy it?"

"Yes," she said, washing the water over her neck and shoulders. "I just felt I wanted one."

---

*Tanabata, a festival held on the seventh day of the seventh month, when two enamored stars, Kengyu (Altair or Cowherd star) and Shokujo (Vega or Weaver star) meet on that one night each year, unless it rains.

"Just like a child. How much was it?"

"Ten or twenty yen, perhaps."

"About that, I suppose."

"By the way," she said, in her softest, most persuasive tones, "what's going to happen about the promise you made last night?"

"What promise?"

"You've forgotten? Well, I like that!"

"Ah, I remember. Would tonight suit you? Or perhaps because tonight is only a part of today, you'd prefer me to pay off yesterday's debt now?"

"No, you mustn't. You'll make my hair all wet."

He smiled down at her, but then the smile gradually faded from his lips.

A bright, bluish night sky. All the lights were out in all the houses, because of the blackout regulations. Tanabata; the Weaver Festival in Uwajima, July 7, 1945. It was not surprising that not many homes were celebrating the festival this year.

Akiko crept inside his mosquito net and he immediately pulled her toward him, but she said,

"Wait a minute, will you?"

"You're dressed? What time is it?"

It was light outside, with a low, dazzling sun. He raised his hand to shield himself from the rays of the sun as he asked her the time, but then, before she had time to answer, he shouted,

"An air raid warning?"

"No. Nothing like that. It's half past four, or five. I went to gather the dew off the potato leaves."

"What?"

"For the festival. It's Tanabata. Have you forgotten, Ken?" she murmured as she lay down by his side. The body of the woman who'd just been walking the fields in the dawn, particularly her thighs, gave off the perfume of potato leaves, tomato leaves. . . .

At about noon Sugiura went to the schoolteacher's next door, and got two pieces of freshly cut bamboo of the appropriate size. There was no bamboo growing on the Yuki family land. He carried the bamboo to his own room. In the afternoon Akiko went into town to buy the special colored paper used for the festival and some ordinary drawing paper, and it took her about two hours to complete her shopping expedition. The drawing paper had been simple enough, but the colored paper had been just about impossible, for there was none anywhere this year, until at last she found a tiny shop where they had some left over from last year. As she wiped the sweat off her with a towel she spoke with great pride of this achievement, until her mother said she was as proud as if she'd put out an incendiary all by herself. They spread the paper, which was nothing special but only ordinary coarse paper very plainly dyed, on the tatami. There was only one sheet each of red and yellow, and two each of dark red, purple, and orange. She hadn't been able to get gold or silver. This made all the colors look darker and gloomier than they should have, especially the red and yellow.

They both went upstairs to his room, where the two lengths of bamboo had been placed upright in a corner, and began the preparations for the star festival. Her mother was downstairs listening to the radio and looking after the shop. Since the air raids had started, the shop had ceased to take in anything, and although postcards had been sent out to people who still had pawned goods there saying no responsibility could be taken for them and would they redeem them immediately, nobody came.

Akiko took the inkstone, which she must have washed because it was remarkably clean, quite unlike the one he associated with this shop, and very carefully poured water onto it. Then once she'd scrupulously scraped it to prepare the ink, she took two pieces of red paper as poem cards, placing them before Sugiura.

"I'm to write it again this year, am I? Even though you know how bad I am."

"You're better than me, anyway."

"How does it go?"

"Have you forgotten?"

"Yes. I can't remember."

She wrote the traditional poem for the Weaver Festival in pencil on the white margin of the newspaper:

Over heaven's river
Passes the lovers' boat, its oar
Of mulberry, a paper
Right for these letters sent so many
Years to you, written in water.

She then read it aloud, misreading some of the characters.

"Haven't you got that wrong?" he asked.

"No," she said. "That's the right way to read it, because that's the way Mother taught me."

He didn't argue with her. It was an obvious misreading, but the mother had learned it from the grandmother, the grandmother from the great-grandmother, the great-grandmother from the great-great-grandmother, and so on for hundreds of years had this poem from the Kokinshu or wherever—he didn't know where—been handed down over the generations, and the misreading had become an unshakable tradition. He remembered how last year he'd wondered aloud who'd written the poem, and Akiko had promptly replied it was anonymous; and when he'd asked her if that was true she'd said she didn't know, and how could she be expected to know something like that anyway? Her mother didn't know either. Nor, probably, did her grandmother, nor her great-grandmother, nor all the rest of them over the centuries. Just handed down. Who would Akiko hand it down to?

"You said the same thing last year, didn't you, Ken? That it shouldn't be read that way."

"Um."

"You never give up, do you?"

Sugiura didn't reply to that, but wrote the poem out on the gaudy red paper. On one he had to make the last few letters small to get them all in. On the other the distribution was right, but this time all the letters looked oddly cramped.

"Hopeless, just as I said. What an awful mess."

"It's very good, very nicely done," Akiko said, using the same obvious piece of flattery she'd used last year to console him.

"Shall I draw the melons and things as well?"

"Yes, please."

"Last year I thought it was a bit funny, but didn't say anything," he said, although he meant he felt it was bucolic rather than just strange. "I mean, while these two stars are having their love affair, they're hardly likely to be eating watermelon at the same time."

"If it's not done in the conventional way Mother will be unhappy."

So, just as last year, Sugiura got out his sand painting materials and drew the seasonal watermelon, cucumber, eggplant, tomato, musk melon, two each on a sheet of drawing paper, then ripped it into two pieces. He still had some colored sand left. He'd had no contact with his connection, Ryukichi Sugawara, for a long time now, and it seemed more than likely that place of his in Shinjuku had been burned to the ground or destroyed in some way. Perhaps he was dead; and he'd never met him once, only knew him by his scrawled handwriting, a man to whom he, in fact, owed his life. Tokyo was really bad now. There was that sick joke about if you walked in Tokyo and came across what you thought was a discarded shoe, there was bound to be a foot inside it. The house in Aoyama would have been hit. Even in a place like Uwajima they'd had three (was it four?) air raids, and although there'd not been much damage to speak of so far, still there had been some. How were his family getting on? Of course, it was a waste of time thinking about it, really. Were they all dead? Or was, say, Shinji alone still alive? Or perhaps just his mother, quite unharmed? Things like that did happen. Or were they all squatting in the air raid shelter, wretchedly hungry, picking the lice off one another? Like monkeys.

When dinner had been over a little while, Akiko's mother said they should start and, just as last year, they opened the windows of his room wide, and on both sides tied the green bamboo. Then they carried various things up to his room, which was western style and yet ironically much better suited to the rituals of the festival than Akiko's pure Japanese-style room with its ancient latticed windows. It was a bright, clear night, the sky full of stars. Because of the blackout the room had to be kept completely dark, and the stars seemed much more numerous this year. There were no lights to be seen in any of the houses. Sometimes in the distance a small red light appeared, probably the cigarette of a man taking part. Laughter could be heard coming from somewhere, and a radio where someone was singing "Until the Day of Victory." A table had been placed by the window, and on this were watermelons and eggplants, as well as two empty bowls, normally used for food, which Akiko filled with water from the kettle. This was to reflect the stars, and as he looked at the two small expanses of water, he got the impression both that they did and that they did not.

When the breeze blew, the leaves of the bamboo swayed, and the paper ornaments, the poem papers, and the paper fruit, all hung by string, moved slightly as well. Amid that rustling sound he thought he could hear that of sand falling off the paintings he had made. As they looked at the black shapes of the bamboo leaves and the pieces of paper outlined against the brightness of the sky, and listened to the slight sounds they made, the three people ate watermelon. A mosquito coil was burning under the table, but occasionally the hum of a mosquito could be heard. Perhaps due to the smell of the watermelon or the leaves of bamboo, he vividly recalled the odor of Akiko's body that morning. Akiko's mother said it would be nice if the air raid siren didn't sound that night. Sugiura switched on the radio kept in his room and listened to it with the volume turned down. Akiko placed a cloth over it so that the light from the dial wouldn't show outside. A radio drama was interrupted, and the announcer spoke in a lugubrious voice. It seemed that Sendai and Utsunomiya were being hit that night. Akiko's mother said it was lucky it was up north. The radio drama began again. Akiko changed the water in the bowls at her mother's instruction. Sugiura wanted to ask if this meant that clean water in the river of heaven along which the lovers voyaged made it easier for them to meet each other, but he restrained his curiosity. He'd asked the same question last year and been told it was just something you had to do because it was always done. It was the custom.

After she'd eaten her slice of melon, Akiko's mother said she was going to sleep and went downstairs. Sugiura also stopped eating his melon, and began fondling Akiko's breasts through her dress. When the nipples went hard, he unfastened the snap at her back. The pale white face approached his, and she breathed heavily as she sought his lips. The soft, warm tongue of the woman entered the man's mouth like a gentle, living creature. Their mouths drew apart, wetting each other's chins, and the man's mouth went to the woman's breast. Her body began to dissolve, and he moved his hand from the other breast down toward her belly. She murmured that she didn't like the window left open, but he ignored her.

It was over. The two sweat-soaked bodies lay side by side on the tatami, their heads bending backward to look up at the stars. They lay there in silence, and then suddenly Akiko sat up and went on her knees over to the table to change the water in the bowls. Sugiura's eyes followed every movement of her white limbs in the dark, until she came back again to lie at his side. Finally Akiko said,

"What are you going to do when the war's over?"

"It never will be over. It'll go on and on."

"Forever?"

"Oh, I suppose it will have to end sometime, but our politicians are so stupid we'll both be dead before that happens."

"Don't say such awful things."

"The politicians are fools, and the military are even worse."

"You won't be here this time next year, I know. You don't do things like this in Tokyo, I suppose."

"I don't know even if I'll be alive this time next year."

"How awful to be only able to meet once a year. If I was them I'd have all the nights together at one time, one night after another."

"We were together last year. Where were you the year before?"

"Here in Uwajima, having a dreadful fight with Mother."

"About me?"

"Yes."

There was a pause, then the conversation continued.

"I was in Onomichi. The children made them at school during the handicraft lesson, little . . ."

"I wonder what became of that man?"

They both knew who "that man" was without further explanation.

"Could be alive. Could be dead. A man like that usually manages to stay alive, though, right through the heaviest bombardment."

"Hope he's dead. Don't you?"

"Yes. I hope Keiichi Asahina's dead. See how well I've remembered his name. Not that I could ever forget it. I sometimes dream about him . . . and the others. Not just sometimes. All the time. The man in the black suit with the high collar. The M.P. on horseback. The man when I got off the ferry from Korea. Just the other night when I went to your room, remember? Well, I'd just . . ."

"You're always coming to my room, for heaven's sake. If someone who didn't know was listening, they'd think you'd only come that once and I was always coming in here and forcing myself upon you. I like that."

"Someone who doesn't know is hardly likely to be listening, is he?"

"All right, then. I'd just like to know who came to my room, then said he'd forgotten something most important and went off to get it."

"And I'd like to know who said it was safe tonight and wouldn't let him go away and get it."

"You are awful."

As he laughed, Sugiura slipped his hand between her legs. The sweat had already dried on her body. The inside of the fingers and the palm of his right hand felt the smoothness of her thighs. The sky seemed to be clouding over. The stars were fading. The radio whispered that the American planes had withdrawn from Aomori.

"Just wait a little longer," said Akiko. "Let's talk a bit more. When it's been particularly good it tickles like mad unless you leave it alone for a while."

After four days in Ajiro, they went back to Tokyo. Ten days of his vacation remained, and he spent the time writing pieces for the radio magazine for children, giving the apartment a thorough clean, supervising a mock university entrance exam at a study center, and going to eat Chinese food with Yoko. August had been hot and September seemed worse at the beginning, but then it was suddenly autumn. It rained a lot in October, and it was one drizzling Sunday when his brother brought a girl who worked in the sales department of the same publishing house to see them, introducing her as his fiancée. He said the wedding would take place early in December, and that one of the company directors was acting as go-between. The girl who was about to become the wife of a deaf man merely sat at the side of her future husband, the cord of his hearing aid hanging from his ear, and smiled merrily. Hamada wanted to ask him about his perforated eardrum, but it didn't seem the right thing to do in front of his fiancée. Shinji appeared to have lost a good deal of that moodiness he'd had when they last met the year before (or perhaps the year before that?) and looked very mild now, even quite ordinary.

After the rain of October, November was a dry, bright month. It was on one of those fine mornings in November that the chief clerk phoned him from the executive directors' room, asking him to pay an immediate visit if his hands weren't too full at the moment. When he got there he was surprised to find the chief clerk was all alone, sitting awkwardly on the sofa as if quite overpowered by the large, luxurious room. Hamada sat down on a chair as indicated, finding the chief clerk's gesture quite comically out of place, and reflecting that this man at least had no hope of making it to director.

After talking briefly about the weather, the chief clerk said there was a matter he wanted to talk over with him. Hamada's immediate intuition was this was going to be bad news, and he was right.

"We were wondering if you'd mind going to Takaoka," he said, looking him straight in the face.

At first Hamada failed to take in the real meaning of the words; or rather, he did grasp the meaning directly but was hoping that somehow he must have misinterpreted them. He tried, in fact, to convince himself that what he was being asked to do was just to make a trip to the high school in Takaoka on some kind of business for a couple of days.

"The idea is that you're to be put in charge of the whole school administration," the chief clerk went on hesitantly.

"Is this the directors' idea?"

"Well, uh, yes. My job is simply to tell you."

The high school at Takaoka had become affiliated with the university some ten years ago, when Kobayakawa had recklessly undertaken to help out the school, which had gotten itself into financial difficulties. Since then, naturally enough, the school had been managed under a compromise system involving members of its former administration and people from the university who were part of the Kobayakawa faction. So far nobody who was backed by Horikawa had ever been sent there. In fact, Horikawa treated the school as a joke, saying it had a certain reputation for baseball (although its most remarkable achievement had only been to get through to the semifinals of the Toyama prefectural competition), and otherwise it was merely a poor school for dunces with no redeeming features. Hamada saw this move to Takaoka as an ignominious change for the worse, for it was a fact that people in high school administration had an inferior status to those at the university, their salaries were lower, and their chances of returning to Tokyo were just about nil. This was all perfectly clear from the way the former head of the Personnel Department, Ito, had accepted demotion to head of purchasing at the university rather than the alleged "promotion" to overall chief of Administration at Takaoka when a choice between the two had been forced upon him. As he sat stiffly upon the green chair, Hamada felt quite stupified, a feeling intensified by the inevitable contrast between the awareness he had now that he was going solidly down the ladder to that feeling he'd experienced six months ago when Masako had announced he was going up. He suddenly felt how much he was going to miss the life he'd led so far, the registry with Nishi sitting beside him, that poky little flat, even the area in front of his local station with its cheap noodle shops and pinball arcades, seeing it all as some welcoming home from which he was now to be exiled.

"It's also hoped that you will teach mathematics and science at the school," the chief clerk went on. "You did graduate from a science school, after all."

"Yes."

"The conditions are more than satisfactory. If you include what you'll receive for teaching, then your salary will be more than you are receiving now. In the case of Ito, he had a large family, and also property in Tokyo, so he felt he just couldn't leave, and that was the cause of the trouble. In your own case that would seem to offer no problems."

Hamada didn't reply, so the chief clerk continued:

"The way up's rather blocked for you, and your not being a graduate here doesn't help. It would probably be best for you to spend at least some time at Takaoka."

"Did that business with *Totality* have anything to do with this?"

"Well, I can't say. That's the sort of thing I wouldn't know," he replied in some haste and, in order to hide his confusion, he went on. "You're not being asked to give an immediate answer. Just think it over. But please do try to make sure you don't let the matter leak out anywhere. I do particularly want to stress that you be careful about that."

"You mean I'm not to discuss the matter with anybody, but keep it all to myself?"

"Certainly not. By all means discuss it with others. You'd be perfectly advised to do so. I'm merely talking about it leaking *outside*," he said, stressing the final word.

Hamada assumed he was referring to things like the student paper. The chief clerk stood up, and then Hamada did.

"The question of housing and other specific problems of that kind can be worked out by discussion, I believe," said the chief clerk as they walked back to the Registry Office together, as if he already considered that Hamada had given his assent to the idea of going to Takaoka. When the two entered the office, Nishi looked at them both suspiciously.

That day Hamada didn't go straight home. He went to Shinjuku, had something to eat, then thought he'd see a film. What they were showing at the first cinema he went to, however, was one about a man on the run from the FBI, and he left halfway through. But the second place he went had a war film, and he was able to stand less than 20 minutes of that. He was struck by how little his own tastes seemed to fit those of the present day. Next he went to a pinball arcade, and came away with a pack of Peace cigarettes for an outlay of 300 yen, then visited two bars where he'd been taken in the past, had ten double whiskies, and at the second bar found he had to part with all the money he had to pay the bill. Then a man he thought he'd seen somewhere before, although he wasn't sure if he was one of the customers or the bartender, grinned and stuffed a thousand-yen note into his pocket, telling him to take a cab home, refusing to take no for an answer and leading him outside and stopping a taxi for him. The next day, when he managed to struggle to the university despite a filthy hangover, he tried all day to recall who the grinning man was, but couldn't for the life of him; and the next day too, when he attempted to work out more rationally who it might have been, he arrived at no answer, and began to think the only thing he could do was to go back there and ask.

Three days after the talk with the chief clerk, before work had started that morning, the registry staff were drinking tea and discussing various things, such as the latest murder, how the voting would go in the Dean of Faculty elections, and baseball, when the conversation led from a discussion of why so very few baseball players managed to get jobs as managers, coaches, or commentators to one of the younger clerks talking about the problem of changing trades in his hometown. The example he gave was of a clothes shop on the main street that went bankrupt after the war, and became first a grocery, then a pinball arcade, a dentist's office, a record shop, a coffee house, and a butcher shop, but no matter how often the business was changed, the shop was a failure. This was probably because the building itself was in the ancient warehouse style, he said, and just didn't suit the taste of customers nowadays. This led Hamada into talking about Kifunemachi in Takaoka, presumably because his mind was preoccupied with the idea of having to go and live there, and most of the houses being in the same style. Yet Japan was full of towns where old warehouse-style buildings still existed, and there was no good reason why he should not have talked about more famous examples he'd seen, such as the Basho crossroads area in Sendai or Izuro Street in Kagoshima; but he talked about Takaoka instead, and Nishi watched his face with intense curiosity as he did so. Hamada assumed from the way he looked at him that Nishi must already have heard (perhaps only last night) about what was going to happen. It would soon be all around the university, perhaps even in the student newspaper.

Still, his talk about the dark brown ridge-end tiles and bricks of the houses in Kifunemachi was interrupted by the arrival of the chief clerk, who already looked quite exhausted, and everybody returned to their desks after greeting him. Since their meeting three days ago the chief clerk had obviously been doing his best to avoid exchanging looks with Hamada, and any business that needed to be transacted between them was done with the minimum of words. As he observed the chief clerk's attitude, he speculated on what would happen if he refused to go to Takaoka, and found it impossible to imagine how the university authorities would respond. He was also perplexed about whom he should select for the "discussion" of the matter the chief clerk had "advised," feeling something close to panic when he realized he could think of nobody at all. Up to now he'd always gone to Horikawa for his opinion; in fact, as soon as the chief clerk had brought up the matter, the person who'd sprung immediately to mind had been Horikawa. Yet he'd come to the conclusion on the same day that it would be mere stupidity to ask his opinion about this. After all, it had already been given Horikawa's approval, if it wasn't his idea in the first place, and what made Hamada feel particularly unhappy about the whole business was the sense that he had, in fact, been betrayed by Horikawa. He spent the whole of that morning, and the afternoon as well, when he was not working (and even sometimes when he was), thinking about who could possibly be suitable among the whole academic and clerical staff but only arriving at the semiconclusion that perhaps Ito in Purchasing might be the man, or even that Masako Aochi might have some surprisingly good news to tell him if he asked her, perhaps.

Late in the afternoon there was a phone call for him. It was from a man called Akasaka who'd been in Teaching Administration when Hamada first came to work there, and was now head of General Administration in one of the two high schools the university had in Tokyo.

"How did you get on the other night?" he said, as if he felt this was some kind of greeting, rather than the mysterious question Hamada experienced it as.

"The other night?"

"Ah, I see. You really were as drunk as you behaved," Akasaka said with a cheerful laugh, giving the name of a bar in Shinjuku.

When he understood this was the man who'd lent him the thousand yen, Hamada expressed his astonishment, his apologies, and his thanks, and then asked if there'd been anything odd or impolite about his behavior that evening.

"Nothing I'd particularly call rude. I can't say your behavior was impeccable, but it was pretty close to it most of the time," said Akasaka. "There was nothing wrong there, anyway, so you can put your mind at rest. As far as oddness goes. . . . Well, you did go on and on rather about the woes of the street trader's life, with a lot of jargon about family names and pitches. You're certainly clued up on lots of strange things."

Akasaka spoke quite casually about this, as if he simply found it amusing, but the words had the effect of silencing Hamada, since he knew exactly what he must have been talking about. It was Takaoka, a market called the Nighthawk Festival. There was another one there too, called something to do with sardines, although he'd no way of making sure of this, as he'd left his *Complete Guide* in Uwajima when he'd returned to Tokyo. Before going to Hokkaido he'd spent some time wandering around Ishikawa and Toyama prefectures, and then in Takaoka the man in charge of the markets had said he couldn't have a pitch because he didn't have a family name, and had turned him down twice. So two nights before when he was drunk, he'd gone back two decades in time and talked of something he'd been totally unable to do anything about, going on and on about a blind frustration felt more than twenty years ago. He wondered just how far he'd gone.

"Hello? Still there?" asked Akasaka.

"Yes, I'm still here."

"I thought we'd been cut off. I was wondering, are you free tonight? You could pay me back that thousand, and there's also something I want to talk to you about."

"That would be fine. Could you hold on a moment?"

Hamada placed the receiver on top of some papers, and went across to ask one of the staff he'd once done a night duty for if he wouldn't mind doing his that evening. The man agreed.

They met in a shish kebab joint, in Ikebukuro, and Hamada immediately handed over the thousand yen, then said,

"This just suits me, since there's something I'd like your advice on."

Akasaka didn't reply immediately, first ordering food and drink from the girl, then joking with her a while, and after that talking about various trivia until the girl brought the saké. He poured it into both their cups, then said,

"I suppose what you want to talk about is something I've already heard of? Your going to Takaoka?"

Hamada nodded.

Akasaka advised him to go. He'd probably be much better off throwing his weight around there than just being a nobody in the university. There were all sorts of perks too, although they weren't much to be proud of. No matter how long people like themselves stuck it out, they weren't graduates of that crummy university, so they'd never be put in charge of any office. All that ever happened was what Hamada had gone through, made to feel he was going to be promoted, then given the boot at the last moment. You keep feeling it just might happen this time, then you're packed off to a shitheap high school. They call it transfer, but they don't have much intention of calling you back. He'd see when he got his own damn marching orders.

When Akasaka got drunk his language deteriorated quickly and he used the argot of the streets, but he still very carefully refrained from touching on Hamada's record as a draft resister, a consideration on his part that made Hamada feel more uncomfortable than otherwise. Still, he ordered a whisky from the girl and decided to be brave.

"That business with *Totality* is mixed up with it."

Akasaka didn't say anything for a while, just drinking saké and eating grilled chicken, but he finally said as if he were talking to himself,

"He's got some sort of hold over Horikawa, has that thug Inuzuka. But I don't know what it is. Something to do with the rebate on the new building, maybe? Perhaps the sports ground? I was drinking with the builder, and do you know what the bastard said? He said there's no trade like working on schools, because you don't have to pay taxes. Like he thought we were all in the same racket with him. Provided me with a geisha too. Only she stank like hell."

Akasaka went on to give a very detailed account of this cheap geisha from the slum of Otsuka, and made Hamada really laugh as he roared with laughter too, waving the first two fingers of his right hand about as if he were determined to evoke once more the memory of that particular stink. But suddenly he stopped and spoke in an unbelievably melancholy voice.

"I wonder why they have things like wars? No matter how hard I think about it, I still can't work out why."

Hamada agreed with him and filled his cup. Akasaka said someone who'd done what Hamada did probably wouldn't go down all that great in America either, and when Hamada mumbled that he couldn't understand why he should suddenly get it in the neck about something that hadn't bothered anybody for twenty years, Akasaka ordered larger cups and began to analyze the situation. The whole country had gotten rich. Everybody felt they could afford all sorts of things now. So they started looking around them, feeling they'd grown equal to the West, if not actually superior. They were starting to think it might not be a bad idea to have another go at war, raising the prestige of the country a bit. Just like taking part in the Olympic Games. Crazy idea: the Atomic Olympics. Eisaku Sato,* with the Olympic torch in his hand, sending out mushroom clouds as he tottered by. And the people watching from the side of the road, why, they loved it. Nothing like the atomic torch relay for thrills. Now Hamada provided just the opposite image to the relay runners, and that's why they didn't look upon him in too friendly a way. It couldn't be a very nice feeling for him, but there was nothing he could do about it. What was wrong with Takaoka, anyway? What was so marvelous about Tokyo? Nothing. The geisha stank, for a start.

Yet, in the same breath almost, Akasaka flatly contradicted himself by sighing that it would be nice if Hamada could get into one of the Tokyo high schools, but there wasn't a post vacant in either of them, as he knew only too well. Then, wasn't it maybe a fact that Horikawa wanted to get him out of Tokyo?

Hamada replied by telling him something he'd never up to now confessed to anyone, about his writing on his c.v. that he was a draft resister, and Akasaka said it certainly looked as if old Horikawa had a lot to answer for, and suggested in a not very enthusiastic tone of voice that Hamada

---

*Japanese Prime Minister, 1964—72. Mysteriously awarded Nobel Peace Prize in 1974.

might do well to have it out with him once and for all, just to let in a bit of fresh air. After that unreal suggestion, he merely repeated that there must be something in it, there was something funny about Horikawa, and then clapped his hands and called the girl, ordering refills of saké and whisky.

"It might also, of course, be like this," he added, but then he paused and looked as if he were having second thoughts, so Hamada urged him to say what he had to say and not mind about him, and Akasaka continued:

"It may be that old granddad Horikawa hasn't done anything bad, and so Inuzuka's got as little hold over him as anyone else. Which means he's doing it all off his own bat. You see, when he first got you your job, the war just being over, it didn't mean much to him; but as the times changed he began, you know, to think he hadn't been so smart. Then he starts to notice all that racket going on in *Totality* and the student paper—particularly the student paper because it's all sort of anti-American. So he starts to think about things, does granddad, about the way the times they are a-changing, and how he hasn't been too smart having you around, and he starts reading the signs and thinking what's coming next, for he's a great one for seeing what's coming next, being the man who always thinks he knows what the future's going to hold."

Hamada didn't say anything but just went on smoking.

"Ah well, not to worry. The world never changes all that much," said Akasaka, meaning to encourage Hamada but sounding more as if he was trying to cheer himself up. He then got onto the subject of how he'd been beaten up the day he joined the navy, and countless times after that, and so onto his pet theory of how people couldn't be more wrong when they said the army might have been barbaric but the navy was a civilized organization.

"Has Inuzuka always been a right-wing fanatic?" asked Hamada.

"Probably has, although I'm not sure. He's just a nut case, anyway."

"Old granddad Horikawa certainly treats him like one. What about Nishi, then?"

"Nishi?" Akasaka pondered the question. "He's on pretty friendly terms with Inuzuka, isn't he?"

But the former sailor turned from this question, about which he lacked confidence, to one he appeared to feel required no hesitating doubts, the argument in favor of rearming the country. Those people soon got off the real issue by arguing by analogy, saying it was natural to hit back if you were hit, and only fools didn't lock their doors. But those examples were funny. For example, if you were walking along the street and some gangster thumped you, well obviously you'd've been pretty stupid to let yourself get thumped in the first place, but you'd be even stupider to thump him back. No, what anybody with their head screwed on would do would be to scram out of there quick. As for locking your door, in the old days in the countryside nobody ever did, and they didn't seem to have had any problems. Besides, the idea of locking it with a pistol was plain nonsense. Pistols weren't locks and keys, and locks and keys weren't used for killing people.

Akasaka was now full of that eloquence and lordliness that come from drink, and he paid the bill and led Hamada to another bar. They sat at the counter, and Hamada asked him what he thought would happen if he refused to go to Takaoka. Would they suggest somewhere else, or fire him? Akasaka said they'd most likely offer him something else, asking, presumably as a joke, why he didn't try it and see.

"Did you just go quietly yourself?" Hamada asked.

"No," he said, pressing his forhead with both hands. "I went down fighting for all I was worth. But the end result was the same. I was made to bow, as they say, to the inevitable. I just got pissed off with the whole business, and couldn't see the point in going on with the struggle."

Akasaka took care of the bill there too. After Hamada had left him and was standing on the platform waiting for the train, the thought crossed his mind that the reason Akasaka had been prepared to pay for everything was that he'd really enjoyed himself, had really been enjoying the company of not only a fellow in misfortune but someone who'd gotten a worse deal than himself, being kicked not just out of the university but out of Tokyo as well. Once the thought had occurred to him, of course, he was immediately ashamed of it. Or at least he tried to feel ashamed.

Unsurprisingly, Yoko had finished dinner ages before, but he had her prepare some rice, pickles, and tea, and while he was eating this told her about the proposed transfer to Takaoka, which he hadn't mentioned to her so far, and asked her what she thought of it. She was sitting by his side chewing gum.

"Well, if you've been told to go, that's all you can do, isn't it?"

"That may be so. Then again, it may not be so."

Hamada went on to give a painfully elaborated account of how personnel questions were handled in the university, of how much things were worked out by discussion and at which point everything was settled by decision of the directors, an account so detailed that finally he found he couldn't even understand it himself. What did become clear was that the system was founded on no fixed principles whatsoever, being simply a matter of making decisions as one went along, and it was, indeed, just that attitude that had made his own employment there a possibility in the first place. He put down his chopsticks, and at that moment Yoko said,

"If you worked for some company or a bank you wouldn't think anything of being transferred, surely?"

He tried to explain why being sent from the university in Tokyo to the high school in Takaoka was completely different from being transferred from a head office in Tokyo to a branch office in Osaka, but didn't seem able to make much headway. All he could do was frighten her with the idea that there wasn't a hope of getting back to Tokyo if he went. This did, at first, have a powerful upsetting effect, and she said she'd get her mother to go and see Horikawa and make him do something about it; but when he opposed the idea she decided they'd never do such an awful thing as that, and the best thing would be to go to Takaoka and, while they were there, he could go on working on people and they'd probably be back in two or three years. It was obvious she could only see it as basically the same kind of thing as the transfer of one of the staff of a business company, and he got tired of trying to explain the difference to her, as well as irritated by her constant gum chewing. All the time he'd been eating, and all the while they'd been having this discussion, she'd gone on chewing away, and he found the total lack of ordinary, decent manners and the sheer frivolity it betrayed when dealing with a matter of such importance quite unforgivable. Consequently he looked pointedly at the chewing gum wrapped in red, green, and yellow paper on the table, and again at one separate, barely visible piece right on the edge that only had on its silver wrapping. Yoko managed, however, to misunderstand even this obvious gesture. She took a piece of chewing gum and gave it to him (and all the while the gray object kept appearing out of the darkness enclosed by her red lips and white teeth, turning up unnervingly on one side of the mouth when he thought it was on the other). He took the white board out of its silver wrapping, put it in his mouth, and bit it. After the alcohol and the pickles it tasted extremely (and disgustingly) sweet, but the sweet taste soon vanished, leaving him a flavorless softness to chew on, and as he was doing so he suddenly reflected how Akiko would have responded if he'd discussed the question with her, imagining Yoko as Akiko and thinking what life would have been like if he'd married her. He felt that the pawnbroker's daughter in Uwajima would not have seen life in the same terms as the businessman's daughter in Tokyo, as a question of always giving in to the powers that be, of submitting to the long arm of the law.

Just where the river flowed into the sea there were a number of large concrete cubes that seemed to have been scattered at random in the water for no conceivable reason. The west Japan Sea coast in April. That river water must be cold, made of melted snow. He wondered where the landlord of his boarding house had set his eel traps. They must be around here somewhere, although just one or two wouldn't do much good, of course. On the opposite side of the river a white dog was running among the still sparse greenery. The one cherry tree on this side was in full bloom, but that morning's rain had meant its color had faded, and Sugiura, as he walked along the embankment, concluded that he was not managing to relax at all in the way he'd hoped, and so coming to this part of the world had been a mistake after all.

"After all" was right, because it hadn't been his idea to come here in the first place. He'd been reluctantly talked into it. At Tottori he'd shared a room with one of those peculiar traveling salesman who'd been so in evidence before the war, people who demonstrated some dubious technique well enough to deceive gullible country folk into buying the handbooks and such they sold that were supposed to enable the buyer to acquire that

Grass for My Pillow
[· 230 ·]

skill; this was, in fact, an intellectual version of what Sugiura himself was doing, although since it promised much more it was that much closer to confidence trickery. This particular man specialized in teaching memory skills, a man with remarkably bushy eyebrows who was continually moaning that the outbreak of the Greater East Asian War a year and a half ago had put an end to his business, since people had lost all interest in improving their powers of memory. Still, he hadn't been persecuted like colleagues of his who taught English skills, so he had that to be thankful for, and since it was all in the cause of prosecuting the holy war, they just had to put up with it. When Sugiura said he was going to Yonago he told him he'd never find lodging there, and he ought to go to Kaike, which was right next to it, had a hot spring, and was also much cheaper than Yonago, although there wouldn't be any of the famous local crab to eat since the season ended right about this time.

People who depended on the art of rhetoric for their living were obviously experts in the art of persuasion, and this man was no exception; but Sugiura had once before been persuaded by one of his colleagues that the right place for him would be Korea, and as that trip had turned out a disaster, he felt suspicious of allowing this man to talk him into even a much shorter one. Yet just as the skeptical "mark" would finally drift forward and buy the man's 20-sen pamphlet on *How to Increase Your Powers of Memory*, so Sugiura just seemed to do as he was told and ended up in a small boarding house on the outskirts of Kaike, and his premonition that he shouldn't go there turned out to be quite right in a very peculiar way. The boarding house was certainly cheap, the people running it were very nice, and it was a pleasant, comfortable place to be; but Kaike was now a hot spring that catered mainly to wounded, convalescent soldiers. It was true that old people still came to take the cure from the areas roundabout, but there were few boarding houses or inns for them (half of them looking after themselves in rented rooms in fishermen's houses), and if one ignored them, then nearly all the other available lodging in the town had been taken over by the state to accommodate these wounded men dressed all in white.

There were various wounded. Men with wooden arms and legs, with black bandages like masks around their eyes, or leaning with one shoulder on a crutch while the other sleeve flapped uselessly. Then there were men, both young and middle aged, who obviously had something wrong with them because the color of their faces was so dreadful, although it was impossible to work out what it might be. One general rule for all these wounded soldiers was that their complexions were either very good or very bad, with apparently no intermediate stage.

For the first few days Sugiura tried to spend as little time as possible in Kaike, since obviously he found the sight of wounded soldiers walking the streets or by the sea painful to behold; or on rainy days when he saw rows of their faces at windows staring into the world outside. But the serving girl at his boarding house told one of the soldiers he was a sand artist, and this led to his giving a performance at a concert party for them. Sugiura had not welcomed the idea, feeling a real grudge against the girl, but there was no way he could have refused. Surprisingly, he managed to sell a lot of sand artist kits afterward, which the soldiers did not buy to send to their children but to play with themselves. They had time to spare and loved making things with their hands, such as lucky charm bags out of lily yarn or cigarette cases out of the leather of surplus army boots. The sand artist was asked to perform at about half a dozen of their billets, and even when the sand-painting craze was over, he was still in demand among the wounded soldiers as a watch repairer and cleaner. This also started from his own boarding house, since he'd repaired the landlord's clock. Thus he spent more and more time with the soldiers, and he found the psychological strain increasingly hard to take, the feelings of self-reproach he suffered from becoming unbearably intense at times; then he would often escape by walking through the pine groves to this small estuary. One almost never saw the men in white here.

The past two days there'd been a market at the Katsuta Shrine in Yonago, plus the festival eve, and the weather had been exceptionally fine the day before; as his guidebook had told him, the number of people attending had been "large," so the whole game had been a winner and he'd made a lot of money. This morning it had been raining slightly, although it looked as if it would soon clear up, so he'd decided to have a rest, and he'd repaired the watch of a soldier with black bandages over his eyes, replaced the broken glass face, and then gone off to deliver it. The soldier strapped the watch on his wrist, raising it to his ear and listening happily to the sharp, staccato sound as it ticked away. Up to now Sugiura had always charged the soldiers for these watch repairs, but perhaps because he was feeling generous after having made such a large profit at the market, he said this time that his real job was sand painting and watch repairs only a hobby he enjoyed, so he didn't need any money. Whether it was what he'd said or the way he'd said it, the blind soldier was clearly annoyed. The twenty-three-year-old Sugiura had no idea how to handle the rage of a man whose most expressive facial organs were hidden behind a mask, and none of the other soldiers in the room seemed prepared to intervene, perhaps because they felt little sympathy toward a man who hadn't been called up, and they all said nothing. This silence upset him, with the result he was clumsy in explaining why he didn't need the money, letting slip expressions of sympathy with the other (words like "feeling sorry"), which only made him more incensed, and he poured abuse upon Sugiura, abusing him, his beard (which he must have been told about by the other soldiers), and even his incompetence at watch repairs. So all he could do was run away with his tail between his legs (and with no money, either), and he didn't feel like returning to his boarding house, so he walked through the sparse trees of the pine groves, looking at the sea to his left with the rain now over, and came to this place where the river flowed into it.

After all, thought Sugiura, you really couldn't trust the words of those confidence tricksters. It was just as old Inaba had said. It was when they were standing on that beach looking across the sea to the island of Sado. He couldn't quite remember the name of that beach—ah, yes, it was Oriigahama. Inaba had told him a story about an experience he'd had when he was just starting up in the game and was still quite young. He'd met this very persuasive man in Kobe. His trade was telling people what their names meant—he pretended he could tell their future from it, you see. Sort of a fortune-teller, and he'd said there were all these gold bars that were on some ship that had sunk in the battle of Urusan Bay, all still there, he said. And it was the famed treasure of Kato Kiyomasa, of all people. I mean, Sugi, Kato died three hundred years ago and more, and that battle was part of the war with the Russians. I ask you . . .

As he was vividly remembering the old man, he noticed a young girl sitting on one of the concrete blocks. She was looking over her shoulder at him, and she bowed hastily when she realized he was looking back. He wondered who she was, for he could not recall her face, though it was distinctive enough, with very positive features, and yet softly white like plum blossom. She had on a gray dress with a wide, deep-red collar and lapels. She was certainly not one of the serving maids, nor a nurse. When he approached and asked who she was, she gave a little cry and blushed.

"I'm sorry. We haven't really met. I saw you in Yonago yesterday and just had the feeling I sort of knew you."

Sugiura smiled, and this seemed to make her feel even more embarrassed, but also removed all sense of distance between the two of them. Sugiura was feeling a craving for human company after that clash with the blind soldier, so he stepped over the intervening space of some eighteen inches to the concrete block where she was sitting and stood by her side, finding that the surface she was sitting on sloped surprisingly steeply and the river water was flowing past at a rather odd angle.

"Do you mind?" he asked.

She moved a little to one side and he sat down next to her. He started to talk about the festival at Katsuta Shrine, but it seemed she didn't come from Yonago. Perhaps because he was still thinking about the tale of the fortune-teller and the gold bullion, he asked her if she came from Kobe, then tried Osaka, Tokyo, and various towns, until she finally surprised him by saying she came from Uwajima in Shikoku. Presumably he was surprised because he felt a doctor's son from Tokyo should (if he'd had a little more leisure, perhaps) have been able to work out by now the difference between a city miss and a girl from the provinces. He could now tell from her appearance—the gray dress with two wide red stripes, the large gray bow, and the lavender hairband; this was not what any sophisticated young lady would wear. Still, she was young (about his own age, he thought) and beautiful (her large eyes were particularly attractive), and he was completely fascinated by her, absorbed in this conversation; so much so that he never even considered the question of whether she might be traveling with someone or just by herself.

"I come from Miyazaki, but I travel about so much I feel the whole country belongs to me; lord of all I survey."

She smiled, and charming little wrinkles appeared at the corners of her eyes. She asked him if he'd been to the island of Oki, and when he said he hadn't she said she'd been once last autumn and thought the contrast between the cheerfulness of the shrine and the melancholy of the ruins of the Imperial camp was wonderfully effective, and she'd heard it was even more striking in spring when the cherry blossoms were out, so she'd come all this way, but she was so worn out by the train journey to Yonego, and the boat didn't leave until the day after tomorrow, so she'd decided to spend a couple of days at this hot spring to recover. On hearing this explanation Sugiura decided that her interest in traditional Japanese aesthetics was probably a mere affectation on her part, since it had become fashionable again through the writings of Bruno Taut* and because of the war itself; and when he went on to talk about a variety of other shrines he'd visited, she seemed to be ignorant of all of them, only interested in this one on Oki Island.

"You can't see it, can you?" she said, looking far out to the horizon for an island shape that failed to appear.

All he could see was one sail, then two, far out at sea, riding the rough waves. You could probably see the island on a fine day, he suggested vaguely, and she nodded in agreement. She said the sea at home in Uwajima was completely different from the Japan Sea. Here it looked as if magic creatures were inhabiting it. Sugiura talked about Tokyo Bay, explaining apologetically that he'd spent his childhood in Tokyo, and the girl in the woolen dress talked enthusiastically about her experience of the city, which consisted of just one visit. She talked about Ginza and Asakusa, and getting lost in a street called Nabeya Yokocho and how a little boy from a wine shop had told her the way, and how delicious the *natto*, fermented soybean, tasted; and while she was smiling at this last recollection, he suddenly felt how much he'd like to travel with her to Oki Island. So he

---

*Bruno Taut: German architect and critic who visited Japan during the 1930s and whose highly appreciative remarks about Japanese architecture, particularly on the simplicity and economy of form in domestic buildings, brought about a revival of traditional values.

asked her if she'd like to go with him, and a slight cloud appeared on her pale, white face, which he noticed and thought it must mean she was perplexed, or at least hesitant, so he immediately revoked the idea himself.

"It's all right. I was only joking. It was just that you made the idea of going to see the cherry blossoms at Oki Shrine sound so nice. Still, I can't really afford any pleasure trips. Work has to come first with me."

He stood up. The small cloud had vanished from her face, which had become slightly flushed now, the light red of pear blossom—stained by large, faintly crimson blossoms. She said she would stay there a little longer.

Sugiura walked along the grassy bank of the river, then on the sandy shore, then through the fading light of the pine groves where a wounded soldier was being slowly taken for a walk, and decided he'd made a serious blunder. A girl like that would probably be traveling with a man, either her husband or lover or some older man whose mistress she was, and had problems that someone as ignorant of women as himself wouldn't understand. And even if she were't, a pretty young girl like that would hardly want to go anywhere with a low street trader with a filthy, long beard. When she had time to kill, an hour or thirty minutes when no one was looking, she'd be prepared to talk to someone like him, but her interest wouldn't go any farther than that. Even if he'd felt he was being encouraged a bit by her attitude, it had been ridiculous to suggest going off somewhere together. He was ashamed of himself for getting carried away like that. He ought to remember who he was: Kenji Sugiura. He wasn't a doctor's son from Tokyo. He was no engineer who'd been to technical college and joined a company. He had no parents, no brother or sister. All he had was his old grandmother in Nobeoka, who was waiting for her poor, sand artist grandson to come home.

By the time he'd gotten back to his boarding house he'd decided he had to get out of this region as soon as he could. So he stood at the front desk as the smell of grilled fish for dinner drifted in from the kitchen and told the landlord he intended to leave and he'd like to have his Transfer Permit and his entitlement of ration vouchers ready in the morning; but the landlord asked him to make those arrangements himself. He had his bath, ate his dinner, and found he had nothing to do, since there were no watches to repair and he'd done a sufficient supply of sand paintings. He investigated his *Complete Guide*, looking up the section covering Shikoku and the mainland to the north of it, and in the April column he found there was a mid-month festival at Iwakuni at the cherry blossom site near the famous bridge, and he thought his best plan would be to go straight there as a first move. Then he read a book on astronomy he'd picked up cheap in Yonego, relishing the fact that he didn't have to worry about other people and could read what he liked. Normally in front of others he only read newspapers, as obviously it would look strange if a sand artist were reading a serious, hardcover book. He could no longer read magazines, since both the flimsy popular type and the fatter serious ones were flooded with that martial spirit he found unbearable in anything more than the smallest of doses.

Yet once he'd started indulging in his secret pleasure, he soon found the book was only an elementary introduction to the subject and not all that interesting. He stuck with it for an hour, then put it down, regretting that he'd bought it, and started thinking about that blind soldier and having powerful feelings of remorse at taking no fee for mending his watch. He could have asked for at least 70 sen because he'd changed the glass as well. Considering the trouble he'd taken over it, one yen wouldn't be too much. He began to recall all the foul things the man in white with the black-bandaged eyes had said to him, becoming progressively more angry and more eager for that money as he remembered one insult after another. Then he started to wonder if the blind soldier himself might not be feeling sorry about what he'd done, remorseful about his own jaundiced state of mind. Probably he was thinking it would look bad if he didn't pay up after all the things he'd said. And as these convenient imaginings of his were growing to seem more and more likely, the girl announced by howling from halfway up the stairs that he had a visitor, a woman, and started laughing after she'd said it, so he laughed back in reply, judging, as he closed his book, that this must certainly be the maid from that soldier's billet, whom he'd asked to deliver the money for him. While debating within himself what attitude he should take when the money was offered, he went slowly downstairs, to find the girl in the gray dress standing in the entrance hall.

"If you don't mind," she said, "I'd like to ask you to go with me to Oki."

"Yes," said the flustered Sugiura in reply, bowing very courteously to her.

Perhaps because he'd been worried about getting a hangover he'd probably not had enough to drink, so Hamada slept badly that night and wondered how on earth he was going to manage the night duty he had to do the following day. The only thing he'd gained from the evening was he'd made up his mind to politely decline the transfer to Takaoka and see how the university authorities would respond. He had to admit that what Yoko said was right, and that a man who was paid a salary for his labor should do what he was told. Still, even if one put aside the questions of precedent and the real meaning of all the fuss that had been going on, there was still the point that if he allowed Horikawa to get his own way so easily it would mean, in effect, he was admitting his behavior during the war had been wrong. This was what he was thinking as he failed to get to sleep, and the idea caused him profound misery. He remembered his friend Yanagi, taken off to serve in a war that wasn't worth a cent, forced to commit suicide (there could be no doubt he had been) for nothing, a healthy, generous, intelligent person; and if he was to weaken now he wouldn't know how to look him in the face, how to appease his dead spirit.

He got up and went to the kitchen, and made himself a large whisky with water (cheap whisky and with no ice, as he couldn't be bothered), then came back with it and drank it while lying on his stomach. It tasted terrible, perhaps because it was lukewarm or hadn't been diluted enough, or probably because he just wasn't in the mood, physically or mentally, for it. He left half. In the morning Yoko would take the glass of brown water with a film of dust upon it and throw it down the sink, the shiny, stainless-steel sink. Japan had lost its empire, become the tiny country it was now, and yet this sort of wasteful, luxurious behavior had become a commonplace of life. It simply proved that the wars they'd fought, the war in China, the Pacific War, had been totally meaningless, and yet he was now having to suffer because the ghost of that old futility had reappeared. Yet as he was thinking so, he felt a hatred for a way of life in which he could so casually throw away half a glass of whisky, a remorse about the luxuries he now enjoyed, seeing it as an affront to the memory of Yanagi and of all those countless other victims whose names he did not know, like that Korean boy on the night train; and the two sets of emotions and ideas clashed with each other, making the wretched drunk more unhappy as he vainly tried to sleep.

six

At the beginning of the week following the Chief Clerk's announcement of his transfer to Takaoka, Hamada was called to the executive directors' room. Only Horikawa was there, seated as usual beneath the portraits of former presidents and governors; he smilingly offering him a seat as he spoke in a very kindly manner.

"I gather the chief clerk said something quite preposterous to you the other day."

Hamada didn't quite know how to respond to this, and Horikawa went on,

"A quite extraordinary impropriety, I must say."

As he watched the perpetual, benevolent smile on the other's lips, Hamada began to think that perhaps all this talk about a move to Takaoka had been some kind of mistake, some misunderstanding on the chief clerk's part of a rash remark somebody (Nishi, for example) had made about giving him the push to that high school.

"The man is a complete idiot," said Horikawa with a sigh. "One of the worst things about being a director of a private university is that one is obliged to use people like that. And yet most people blame anything that goes wrong on the directors."

Hamada assumed an expression halfway between a smile and a servile smirk, but remained silent. Horikawa continued, in the same pleasant, friendly, slightly vacant tone of voice:

"What was written in that man Inuzuka's magazine really has nothing at all to do with it. Nothing in something like *Totality* could have any conceivable influence on questions of staffing arrangements. Certainly not in my university, anyway. Apparently when you asked the chief clerk if your move to Takaoka had anything to do with Inuzuka's article, he said he didn't know. Let me make it absolutely clear that, as far as I am concerned, whatever you did or did not do during the war is no business of mine. I am officially ignorant of it. For all I know you may have been taken prisoner by the Chinese Eighth Army. Perhaps you were a stoker on the Akagi during the attack on Pearl Harbor. Or maybe you had tuberculosis and could not serve; or perhaps you were even a draft resister. Were I to hear something from your own lips, even, there is no way I could be certain you were not making it all up, merely boasting about something you had not actually done. All these things are merely assumptions, and it is not possible to make any decision affecting personnel arrangements on the basis of pure rumor."

Horikawa then informed him in a gentle, almost expressionless voice that he'd said all he had to say. Hamada had assumed he was going to get down to the real question at that point, and was so taken aback he stood up quite automatically; at which moment, as if by some prearranged signal, there was a knock on the door, and since Horikawa made no answer, it opened and an old man in traditional Japanese dress came in. He was followed by a young girl in formal kimono who was presumably his granddaughter. Horikawa stood up and greeted him cheerfully.

"What a great pleasure to see you, Professor. The first time since your seventy-seventh birthday celebrations, I believe."

The old man's face crinkled all over with delight and, no doubt because he was hard of hearing, replied in a voice ten times as loud as the director's:

"Wonderful to see you looking so fit and well, Horikawa."

Hamada bowed vaguely to no one in particular and took his leave, but as he was going out Horikawa glanced quickly in his direction and said,

"Always remember, Hamada, to come and see me if you have any problems. Is that understood?"

He thanked him and went out into the dark corridor, beginning to wonder what he'd thanked him for. Surely he had really told him not to come and
discuss the matter with him again but just make up his own mind. In the
same way a housewife looks both at the face and the underside of a piece of
cloth before deciding whether to buy it or not, Hamada weighed the surface
meaning and hidden implications of those words, turning them over and over
in his head as he walked back to the registry. When Horikawa had finally said
he had nothing more to say, did that mean his intentions had been accurately
transmitted by the chief clerk, except in the matter of the relevance of his
being a draft resister? If so, it meant Horikawa wanted him to go to Takaoka,
and when he claimed to be officially ignorant of what he'd done during the
war, that must mean he'd been similarly ignorant when he first employed
him. All he was doing was justifying his own behavior to people like
Kobayakawa, and the remarks about Hamada perhaps simply making it up,
even boasting about it, were probably his way of indicating he felt Hamada
himself was responsible for letting people know "from his own lips" that he'd
been a draft resister, and thus also trying to clear himself of responsibility in
Hamada's own eyes. This then meant that Horikawa was feeling the need to
justify himself and, as far as this particular question was concerned, it was a
real necessity, because the fact had been common knowledge when Hamada
had started working here (that widowed student knew all about it), and it was
perfectly clear that Horikawa must have talked, since there was nobody else
who could've. Of course, he might have been unaware of what he was doing
at the time, and that was more than likely, for in 1946 it had been a harmless
piece of gossip that no one would have thought twice about before telling it
to someone else. And now, after twenty years, a matter of indifference had
been transformed into a major scandal; the unexploded bomb dropped in an
air raid had at last been dug up on the building site where they were planning to erect a massive, new, steel-and-concrete structure.

He entered the office and sat down at his desk, looking toward the window for a moment before starting work, at the tiny expanse of sky it
revealed, and he was struck by his own stupidity. Of course, the only thing
you could do with an unexploded bomb was get rid of it. What Horikawa
had been aiming at all along when he offered him the choice of Takaoka or

resignation was that he would choose the latter! It was like playing the card game Old Maid, when only two cards were left and you inevitably hid the maid under the other card to make your opponent choose it. Horikawa had put the normal playing card called transfer to Takaoka on the top, that was all. Surely that was all it was?

He leaned his face on his hand and tried to think the question out clearly. There had been only one aim, and it had always been the same. The unexploded bomb had to be gotten rid of. He started to ask himself what he'd have done if he'd been in Horikawa's shoes and Horikawa in his, and he came to the conclusion he would have thought of the same safe and easy course of action (the safest and easiest, in fact). And not just thought about it, either, but put it into effect no matter how much good will he might feel toward him. He'd done the man a considerable favor twenty years before. He owed him no debt. He felt sorry for him, but when a person is in danger himself and has already seen the warning signs, then he puts sentiment to one side and the offending person (innocently offending as he may be) just has to go.

He noticed that other members of the staff (Nishi, Murakami, the messenger girl) were looking at him, so he stopped propping his head on his hand and also stopped smiling to himself. Instead he went through the motions of looking at some document, but all the time he was thinking how much he hated Horikawa. Here was a man who'd decided, just like that, to turn one of his own men out into the cold, one of his underlings for whom he'd even gone so far as to arrange his marriage. What worse betrayal could there be than that? But these comfortable feelings of hatred did not last very long, for he began to wonder what right he had to feel them, even if he had any right at all. Hadn't he already come to the conclusion that in theory he approved of Horikawa's action? Hadn't he decided he would have done the same thing in his place? The old man was obliged to do it in order to survive. The trouble was that Hamada didn't know what he himself should do in order to survive. But it was no good trying to think about it now, and in this place. He'd have to wait until he calmed down a little somewhere else, when work was over, at home; then he could consider the nature of Horikawa's betrayal. As he sat there, the word "betrayal" began to echo in his mind.

The twenty-year-old Hamada called out to the landlady, asking if Sakai was at home.

"My goodness, how smart you look. That suit looks wonderful on you," she replied, quite irrelevantly, to his question.

He was standing awkwardly in the tiny, unkempt garden in front of the veranda. There was a flower bed marked out by beer bottles planted upside down, but no flowers in bloom. The landlady had placed a cushion on the wooden floor of the sunlit veranda, and had been reading the newspaper. The page she'd stopped reading had a huge headline, GERMAN ARMY OCCU-PIES DENMARK AND NORWAY. It was April 1940; a Sunday. Hamada had graduated from technical college in March, and had entered a small radio company immediately after his finals were over, so small it could not even be considered second rate, only third. His closest friend in the same year in college, Sakai, had gotten a job in one of the big companies.

Hamada noticed that breakfast for two was set out on the living room table, despite the fact it was already eleven o'clock.

"Is the idle man still asleep?" he asked.

"No. He's up. Of course, he might have gone back to bed again. He got up at eight o'clock. I was thinking of sleeping in this morning, but down he comes and has his breakfast, a bottle of milk, a slice of bread and butter, and an apple. I'm sure he'll make himself ill if he carries on like that. What he wants is some good, hot miso soup in the morning."

"Has he started having western-style breakfast, then?"

"Not just breakfast. It's even worse at dinner. All he has is just one tiny bottle of milk. I know it's none of my business, Mr. Hamada, but I do believe all he has for lunch too is the same little bottle of milk and a bit of fruit."

Hamada knew perfectly well the reason behind this, but he had to keep quiet and pretend he didn't. So he said in as cheerful and facetious a tone as he could manage,

"I expect he's lost a fortune playing mah jong at work. What a blot on the sporting reputation of our college!"

But she wasn't prepared to swallow that kind of foolishness; and it also seemed Sakai himself had not been very clever in making up a reason.

"Please, Mr. Hamada, you tell him. If he goes on like this he'll just end up killing himself by malnutrition. How's a great big man like that going to live on three little bottles of milk a day? He says he can't stand the rice now they're mixing imported with it, but there's nothing to stop him having raw eggs and miso soup and kelp and bread; and plenty of it. The fact is, Mr. Hamada," she added, lowering her voice at this point, "it's the army physical he's thinking about, I'm sure."

"The army physical?" said Hamada, trying to sound as mystified and perplexed as possible.

"He wants to get skinny so they'll make him grade C. I've been looking after student gentlemen for ten years and more, and I soon know what they're up to. But I don't think it'll do any good in Mr. Sakai's case. He's just too well built. It's all right for people who're already thin by nature, because they only have to cut down a little. But just look at those great shoes of his, like two aircraft carriers side by side, I do declare."

Hamada realized he didn't need to be overanxious about this woman, and felt a little more relaxed. She went on:

"It doesn't matter how bad a war is, there's always one out of ten who's not going to die. There's always a chance, particularly when you think it's only a lot of Chinks firing at you. But if he goes on the way he's doing, then he's going to be one of those nine who're going to die. I understand anyone not wanting to be taken for a soldier. My late husband was always saying he didn't want to go, but they took him and he died in Manchuria. You just tell him to eat properly; and don't just grin at me like that, either."

Since Hamada was puzzled about how to reply to all this, it was quite possible an embarrassed smile had come over his face at the time, but he decided to ignore that last remark and said he'd go and wake Sakai up. There was no need to, however, for he found him lying on his bedding upstairs fully dressed, smoking, and reading the newspaper. As a very long person, he had an especially long mattress to lie on. His face brimmed over with delight as he turned his head and beheld the friend he hadn't seen for some time. He had very childish features, but his body was so large they never seemed to give people that impression.

"Do you think France really has had it?"

"Looks like it," said Hamada as he sat down cross-legged.

"No Joan of Arc to save them," said Sakai, getting up and putting his bedding away in the cupboard. He didn't look the least bit thinner. Once the bedding had been removed, the bottle of milk that had been by the pillow and a banana peel casually discarded on the tatami became particularly noticeable.

"Have you had your lunch already?"

"Yes, at ten o'clock. Or perhaps it was nine."

Hamada decided it would be painful to pursue the topic of food, so he nodded in the direction of a folded *go* board on the table in the corner.

"Feel like a game?"

Normally Hamada didn't stand much of a chance against Sakai, but Sakai was playing extremely badly and soon conceded the game. As he was gathering the white stones, he said,

"I feel horribly listless these days."

"Your landlady's worried about you. She says you'll make yourself seriously ill."

"Maybe. Still, I can't give up now. Two months till the physical, and I've just got to stick it out. It's a great source of pleasure, thinking what I'm going to eat when it's over and I've been happily graded C. I shall certainly give three rousing cheers for the old Emperor that day."

They left the subject of food and talked about their jobs, with great passion and almost laughing themselves sick, until they decided to go to Shibuya and see a film. The two young men in their new, dark blue suits walked along Dogenzaka with its huge slogans urging people to WASTE NO RICE and CELEBRATE THE GODS IN EVERY HOME, still talking about what went on in their companies, when Hamada suddenly noticed his friend wasn't around anymore. He turned back and saw his huge figure standing still about half a dozen yards away, looking somehow feeble and unsteady on his feet, as if he'd just seen a ghost. He'd stopped to look at a wayside stall. Hamada wondered what could be so fascinating to him, but just before he was about to call out he saw what his friend was staring at. Sakai was gazing in ecstasy at a stall where the man was cooking large bean-jam buns, at the clouds of steam arising from their flabby, white forms into the air; although when he noticed Hamada's eyes upon him, he grinned sheepishly and started walking again.

They went into a theater where a German film was being shown. It was about the Boer War, done with a typically labored German pertinacity, although Hamada had told himself it would probably be pretty heavy stuff before he went in. Most of it was about some Boer settlers who'd been made prisoners by the British army, and the way they suffered from starvation and grew more and more emaciated, this being given particularly weighted emphasis in one scene where a British officer threw a large lump of meat he had on his plate to a very large Great Dane. The dog gobbled it up in no time and licked its chops with exaggerated pleasure. Hamada was just speculating how long they must have starved the dog to get it to eat as ravenously as that (two days? three days? surely not a week?) when his knee was nudged violently.

"What's the matter?" he asked.

"Let's get out of here."

"Is something wrong?"

"No. Just let's get out," hissed Sakai.

In the bright daylight Sakai turned to him, flushed, and said,

"Hamada. I'm going to eat. I can't put up with it any longer."

"Right. I'll join you."

They found a small restaurant quite near the theater. Before they went in, Hamada said it didn't look like much, and they'd be better off walking a bit more and finding something slightly superior, but the idea only seemed to enrage Sakai, as if he felt Hamada was being deliberately awkward, and he stamped in by himself. There was no way of stopping him, so Hamada went in as well. He ordered a steak, while Sakai demanded a steak, macaroni gratin, and a large pork cutlet. The waitress asked if they'd prefer bread or rice, and when Hamada said he wanted neither, Sakai asked for both.

When Hamada had finished his steak, Sakai was still only halfway through his because he'd been talking about a variety of things: about the way it had been cooked, wondering how small it was in comparison with the chunk of meat that Great Dane had eaten, and about how in the West when someone got a fish bone stuck in their throat they always swallowed whole a potato about the size of the one he had on his plate. Then he stared at Hamada's plate and said,

"You shouldn't wolf it down like that. You should do it more slowly, relishing every mouthful. Otherwise you won't be able to eat very much."

"I don't mind if I don't eat very much."

Sakai indicated his macaroni gratin and said he could have it if he liked.

"That's all right. I'm full up."

"Just like I said, you see."

Hamada observed Sakai eating as he drank his coffee, a momentous sight that rewarded observation. He put away the macaroni gratin, the bread, the pork cutlet, and the rice, yet all the while maintained a cheerful flow of conversation, principally about food. Then he drank some water and called the waitress, scrutinized the menu as if he were confronted by some famous work of art, and finally ordered consomme, butter-fried halibut, and vegetable salad, when they arrived devouring them at a good, even pace, remarking from time to time how delicious they were, and completing the performance with a deep sigh of satisfaction.

"Now that I feel myself again I can get down to some serious eating."

He had some potage, happily talking of the various merits of consomme and potage, both of which, he had to admit, had their good points. The crab croquette that followed was unfortunately made of canned crab, but there was still a good deal to be said for it, and he made a small burp as if to stress the fact. The next was young chicken deep fried, and Sakai ate with such blatant delight Hamada began to feel his own appetite returning, although he knew perfectly well he would only make himself seriously ill if he joined in now.

Sakai's face had become fairly red, looking as if he were actually intoxicated, and his overall expression was peculiarly languid, but that didn't stop him from raising his hand and asking for the menu again.

"Don't you have steak tartare here?"

"No, sir, I'm afraid we don't."

"Can't be helped, I suppose. In that case I think I'll have the ordinary steak again. It was well done the first time, so this time I'll have it rare."

The waitress was finding it difficult not to giggle as she went away, particularly when Sakai called her back and said he'd have both rice and bread with it again.

Finally he reached the coffee stage, still continuing with the talk about various aspects of food. He began an enthusiastic account of some of the local dishes in his home province of Yamagata, all exotic preparations of bean curd and noodles. He then switched the subject to the restaurants in Tokyo that served the finest steaks, speaking as if he was a considerable authority on the subject and apparently quite oblivious of the fact that he'd eaten with obvious relish the third-rate cuisine a place like this dished up. Hamada joined in at this point, evaluating the merits and demerits of the restaurants he and Sakai (and the dead Yanagi) had been to together. They spent about an hour over their coffee and conversation, when Sakai suggested they might go off and try a little sushi somewhere, and then suddenly became excited because he'd realized he probably didn't have enough money to pay for all this. Hamada asked the waitress how much it was, and the two of them emptied their wallets and pockets, but it still wasn't anything like enough. So Hamada phoned home to Aoyama and explained the situation to his sister Mitsu, saying he'd like Shinji to bring him the money. She laughed and said Shinji wasn't in, but she'd bring it herself.

"But you're not to go on stuffing yourselves while you're waiting for me. Well, I suppose you can a little."

"From that point of view, the sooner you come the better," said Hamada, putting down the phone and walking back to Sakai, who had both hands raised in supplication.

After thirty or forty minutes, Mitsu turned up wearing a checkered suit and paid the remaining debt. The three of them went on to a sushi restaurant, although they ate very little, then back to the house at Aoyama, where Sakai had dinner with the family. Mitsu teased Sakai a great deal about the kind of girl he would marry, while the mother quite seriously debated how tall such a girl would have to be, and Shinji gazed on respectfully as Sakai stowed away still more and more food.

After dinner, the two men went up to Hamada's room and lay on the floor listening to a record of Mozart's Clarinet Quintet, and then talking.

"Still, I must confess I find it a bit hard to work you out," said Sakai as he smoked a cigarette and let forth a large smoke ring. "I can't think why you had to join a deadbeat company like that."

"Well, it's not a big company, but the work's pretty interesting, and you're free to do much as you like. Of course, I still don't know all that much about it, but I reckon you're better off as the head of an ass than the tail of a horse. Little fish prefer small ponds, I suppose."

"You may be right," agreed Sakai. "The work I'm doing's not a bit interesting. Perhaps I ought to find a small pond. Still, gathering from what you've been saying, you seem to be the tail of that ass rather than its head."

They both laughed, and Hamada was satisfied Sakai had accepted his explanation. In fact, the work he was doing was just as tedious as Sakai's, and the real reason he'd chosen that company was he'd already made up his mind he was not going to enlist, so the question of employment meant nothing to him. In two months' time, in June, he would have his army physical, and the chances were he would be classified A or, at the lowest, B1. In that case he would be called up in December at the latest, and he'd have no alternative but to run. It would be the natural result of all he had thought and felt so far. All he could do was flee from one hiding place to another, since he had chosen freedom. It was the only form of protest open to him. Having decided this, he had also decided he would have to go on living as someone who was not Shokichi Hamada, although he'd not chosen his new name yet, and he would keep himself alive by wandering around the country as a radio repairman. It would probably work out, but if it didn't, he was prepared to die in the attempt. As someone who'd determined to reject society, obviously it was pointless for him to worry about what sort of company he joined, and he'd chosen third-rate employment because by so doing he would not harm anyone else's chances; although it was also true than an indifferent company (besides offering chances of early promotion, which meant nothing in his case) gave a slightly higher starting salary than could be expected in a first-rate one, and that was important because he was desperate to save money. He meant to go off with all the money he made himself, and also the savings his parents had in his name, while as far as possible he didn't want to touch any other money belonging to his parents.

They talked about the film they'd seen that day, and the subject of the amazing way the dog had eaten led on to that of dogs' teeth, then teeth in general, and Hamada said he'd been going regularly to the dentist since the end of last year, and now didn't have one bad tooth in his head.

"I suppose I ought to go to the dentist myself," muttered Sakai almost to himself, then stood up, leaned against the pillar, and said in a quite different tone of voice, "I've made up my mind. I'm going to do the same as you. I'll stop worrying about it, and just join up if I have to. There's no point at all in just making myself ill. It should be all right, anyway. If you keep your wits about you from the start, there's no reason why you should end up like Yanagi, poor devil."

"A poor devil, all right," said Hamada, still lying on the floor.

"I'm miles smarter that he was," said Sakai, letting out a deep sigh.

"I suppose it'll work itself out," said Hamada.

"There's all sorts of ways of showing opposition to the war and the army. There's no need to go to extremes about it. There are subtler ways."

"I expect you're right."

"It's those subtler ways I'm thinking of. There's no point in getting killed, and if you're going to starve yourself to death you'd be better off getting one of Chiang Kai-shek's bullets."

The dormant Hamada made only the vaguest grunt in reply to that. He dearly wanted to tell Sakai that he planned to resist the draft, since he was the closest friend he had and they'd spent ages passionately discussing questions of war and enlistment (as had also been the case with Yanagi before he'd been called up) and arrived at virtually the same conclusions; and for about a month now he'd been debating within himself if he should tell him or not. But finally he realized he couldn't. First of all, Sakai might try to stop him. Second, he didn't want to impose the psychological burden such knowledge would mean. Third (which was much the same as the second reason), he didn't want it to look as if he were telling him to do the same. Fourth, there was always the possibility Sakai might tell someone else; not the Military Police, of course, but perhaps his parents, just because he couldn't endure keeping it to himself. That was certainly feasible, and there was surely no guarantee that it definitely would not happen. He might well be so shaken by that knowledge, feel so estranged from him by it, he could well ensure that Hamada would have to endure a similar sense of estrangement in the name of some mistaken concept of friendship. That was also possible. And yet didn't this mean that Hamada himself had no faith in their friendship? Didn't his refusal to confess, and his reasons for that refusal, constitute no less than a double betrayal of his friend Sakai? He felt perhaps it did.

"You should be all right because you weren't constantly missing corps parades the way I was. They've probably got me down as not even NCO material," said Sakai.

Hamada himself felt it odd that he should so religiously have attended parades when he was already planning to refuse the call-up. He began to wonder what he'd thought he'd been doing. Had he simply been being careful in case he changed his mind? There must have been something of that. Or had it been deliberate camouflage? That was also probably there. Or was it more of an unconscious thing, an attempt to intensify his hatred of the military so that his final rejection of it could achieve a kind of springboard effect?

"I'd be quite happy to hand over to you all my officer potential, if I could," said Hamada, pretending to be joking.

"Don't say that. You ought to take good care of it, as a blessing bestowed upon you by your country."

In the interval between the third and fourth periods there was the usual commotion in the corridor, and at the same time a phone call for Hamada from Assistant Professor Kuwano, asking him to come to the department office right away, as there was something urgent he wanted to talk to him about. Hamada said to no one in particular that he was off to the Foreign Languages Department, and while the chief clerk merely nodded and said nothing, Nishi made his customary wisecrack:

"We do seem to be in demand today, don't we?"

The office was full of young members of the foreign languages teaching staff, variously talking to each other, or just sitting alone drinking tea and ignoring the others, or drinking tea and smoking and talking all at the same time. The one leaning back in his chair with his eyes closed had presumably given three classes in a row and was worn out. The one with a small dictionary in his right hand, absorbed in reading the textbook in his left, must be doing preparation for some class he was about to give. The group of four, one of whom was holding a fat volume open at a page that the others were investigating from various angles, were probably debating some crucial textual problem. As Hamada hesitated in the doorway, one of that group looked up and rose. It was Kuwano.

"Ah, thanks very much for coming. Let's go into the dictionary room next door. It's a bit too much in here."

The room next door was, in fact, just a library, but since almost half the books that jammed the shelves were dictionaries or encyclopedias, it was justifiably called the dictionary room.

"You've certainly got a lot in here," said Hamada.

"Nearly all bought with Ministry of Education funds. The university would never fork out for those sorts of things."

Kuwano walked up to a young man seated at a desk in a fairly large alcove between the shelves, probably a lecturer although he could easily have been mistaken for a student, and whispered something to him. The young man left the room, and the two of them were now alone. Kuwano offered Hamada a seat and sat down himself, remaining silent for quite a long time. Finally Hamada asked what he wanted to see him about, and Kuwano said, much to his surprise,

"There's something I have to apologize to you about."

"What?" asked Hamada, taken aback by how serious he looked.

"It's about this business of your being sent to Takaoka. I'd like to do as much for you as I can, but I'm afraid there's nothing I can do."

After Hamada had failed to make any reply, Kuwano went on:

"I was talking to Sakurai in the English Department about it during the lunch break today. Sakurai said he thinks it's an absolute waste to send you to Takaoka. The old man seems to think very highly of you. So we went off to visit Oda and see if we could make him do something about it. He's been here so long he's almost overgrown with moss, and he's very well known about the place and knows how to talk, as well. Sakurai's pretty hopeless in that respect. I'd be a better spokesman than him. After all, I've been here ten years, twice as long as he has."

"Have you been here that long?" said Hamada, choosing a harmless point at which to make an innocuous interjection.

"The point is, however," Kuwano went on, "Oda really told me off about it. Well, I suppose he had to pick on me, since he could hardly have had a go at Sakurai, so he just let me have it as a representative of something he doesn't approve of, and Sakurai kept quiet all the time, anyway. I did all the talking, and that was probably a mistake. It was disastrous for me, at least. What Oda said was this. He said he sympathized with my not wanting to see you sent to Takaoka. He said himself he thought it was a waste of a good man. You certainly seem to be popular with the old men around here, and I, of course, was very pleased to hear him say that. The trouble was what came next. He said academic staff should not interfere in matters of clerical staffing. It was impermissible. No matter how much one might consider it in the best interests of the university as a whole, the net result could only be interference in matters affecting the employment and promotion of academic staff. Was I suggesting, he said, that the directors should also be allowed to interfere in our business, since that was what our poking our noses into their business would imply? Wouldn't I mind if that happened? Of course, he went on, he wasn't talking about any blatant meddling in faculty affairs, for the directors would never make any open suggestions about any matters brought up at faculty meetings. But it could take other forms. The questions of taking on new staff and of the promotion of present staff always involved matters of salary payments, and before a head of department could submit any such formal application to the main faculty meeting, it had first of all to be approved by the executive directors. It was at that level where directorial intervention in our affairs could take place."

Hamada nodded in agreement, and Kuwano went on:

"All personnel questions in the Faculty of Foreign Languages depend on Oda's skill in handling the directors—or skill in letting himself be handled by them might be more accurate. Still, it all depends on that. Now, how these things get worked out I don't know—maybe it's a question of publications or maybe it isn't—but in some departments there seem to be an awful lot of full-time staff who just don't get promoted all that quickly. I believe there are two people who've remained lecturers for more than five years, whereas in foreign languages nearly everybody moves up to assistant professor after two, sometimes three, years. It all depends on the diplomacy of the department chairman, and I suppose Oda's worried he might get put in a position where he could no longer make use of his diplomatic skills. Anyway, what Oda said made perfectly good sense, and since Sakurai said nothing all I could do was take back what I'd said. . . ."

"That's perfectly all right, Professor," said Hamada to a man who was at least two or three years younger than himself, perhaps more.

"I'm sorry, deeply sorry. That's all I can say," said Kuwano, and went on to say it again. "I do know Oda is in a real fix at the moment with questions of promotions that ought to take place next April. We've got three lecturers who have to be made assistant professors. One of them is quite brilliant, so there's no problem about him. It's the other two who are the trouble; they're both hopeless, in fact, but since all three graduated in the same year it's going to look bad if they don't all make it together. One of them specializes in Maurice Scève, an ancient poet, and he's even been working on him in France, but he's a complete idiot; and the other is a Constant scholar—Constant wrote a massive romance called *Adolphe*—who has failed to complete a scrupulously meticulous thesis on him of quite monumental awfulness."

Kuwano went on to give an even-handed account of the two theses, bestowing insults equally upon them both, and then his own brisk, energetic interpretation of the meaning of the two French writers' work, before suddenly seeming to recall where he was and saying, in a very emotional tone of voice,

"I most fervently beg your forgiveness."

"Please don't be absurd."

"I felt I had to do everything I could, for the sake of the *amitié* between us, but my position being what it is there was nothing I could do. I really feel very bad about all this, and I can only apologize."

"You mustn't worry yourself about it, Professor. I haven't yet decided what I'm going to do, but I'm sure something can be worked out."

"I'm sure something can," echoed Kuwano, immediately looking very cheerful. "When I graduated I just couldn't find any work at all, and yet I've managed to rub along like this so far."

"That's right," said Hamada.

Up to this point Kuwano had been behaving quite nobly, or at least he hadn't done or said anything actually contemptible. What he went on to say, however, quite suddenly after pondering the matter heavily for a while, with eyes glittering, was in a different category, and it took Hamada completely aback.

"How about getting the students to act, the student union and the paper? Popular Front kind of stuff . . . ?"

Hamada gaped at Kuwano's face in astonishment for a moment, then went on to explain how things of that kind would only mean trouble for him, and there was no chance of their being successful, anyway. Kuwano accepted this, giving up the idea quite cheerfully, then bowed his head as he said once more how sorry he was, and Hamada left the room, disconcerted again by the peculiar mixture of goodness and simple-mindedness the assistant professor always seemed to display.

There was a small area in the hallway just beyond the department office where two sofas had been placed to form a kind of lobby, and on one of them Masako Aochi was seated, looking in his direction. He waved his hand at her. She was not wearing kimono but making one of her rare appearances in western-style clothes, a mustard-yellow dress that didn't suit her and that she was wearing uncouthly. Hamada sat down beside her, and she said,

"I followed you here, but I didn't get the chance to stop you."

"I didn't know."

She looked around her to make sure nobody was about and nobody passing by.

"We can talk here. I have some news for you."

"About me?"

"Yes. The student newspaper isn't going to touch your story again. The editorial policy has been changed."

"At Horikawa's command?"

"Yes. But not directly to the editor."

"Who to, then?"

"One of the graduates."

Masako explained there was a graduate working on one of the big dailies who acted as a kind of advisor to the student newspaper staff; also that each month the university editorial section where she worked paid him quite a large retainer.

"So Horikawa doesn't exercise any direct censorship on the paper, but gets it done from afar by . . . what do you call it?"

"Remote control?"

"That's it."

For a moment Hamada felt that perhaps the article that had appeared originally in that paper might have been triggered by Horikawa in the first place, but he decided the old man could hardly have the leisure to have gone that far. Still, perhaps it was the newspaper article, particularly those comments by Professor Nomoto, that had first made it painfully clear to the director that the times were changing and acted as a warning signal, giving him a premonition of a real danger about to threaten him.

Five or six language teachers came out of the office to go teach classes. One held a textbook and three pieces of chalk (white, yellow, and red) in his hand, another had only a textbook, another had nothing, and they all passed by where Hamada and Masako were sitting. The German teacher with no textbook glanced surreptitiously in their direction.

"Every ten years or so a language instructor goes through a period of acute lassitude, quoth old Oda from his own vast experience. In my own case I seem to have been going through it ever since I started in this business, and it's still going on . . ."

The voices passed away as they turned the corner and went down the stairs, and then Hamada spoke.

"Thank you for taking the trouble to tell me."

"Look after yourself."

Hamada smoked a cigarette, then went back to the registry, thinking on the way about her: about her western clothes not suiting her, about the fact that she must have gotten her information from Professor Uno of the Japanese Department who was, in effect, her husband (although they didn't seem to be actually living together); and also thinking that her final words had sounded like a farewell, a definitive, last farewell.

When he got home that evening there was an express letter from Shinji waiting for him. It said that his fiancée's parents had decided they'd like to meet his brother before the wedding. This didn't mean there'd been some sort of last-minute hitch, so he needn't worry on that score. He apologized for the suddenness of this proposal, but could he bring Yoko with him the following evening to the place and at the time written below? If either were unsuitable, would he please ring his fiancée at work in the morning.

As he changed into Japanese dress, Hamada told Yoko what was in the letter.

"That's fine by me. What about you?"

"I'm free tomorrow evening."

"Still, I wonder what I should wear?"

"I'm wondering if Shinji intends to foot the whole bill himself."

After his bath (which made him feel particularly good since he washed his hair at the same time) and dinner (the canned asparagus tasted nice) they watched TV. But while he was sitting at his wife's side watching it, he remembered he had two small articles he had to get written by the next day. They were only elementary replies to children's queries, and he felt he could write them quite easily here just as he was. During a commercial break he went off to get a pen and paper, but he kept watching the program until it had finished. Yoko picked up the newspaper to find out if there was anything she wanted to see next, so Hamada sent her off to the kitchen to make some tea and switched off the set. While they were drinking tea he asked her a question he'd been thinking about on his journey home from the university, both on the bus and on the train.

"Yoko, would you mind very much if we became poor?"

".....?"

"Where would you prefer to live, then, in Tokyo or Takaoka?"

"Of course, I'd prefer Tokyo, but . . ." she murmured, and then suddenly an expression of deep anxiety came over her face, and she asked very quickly,

"You're surely not thinking of resigning from the university?"

The shrill harshness of her voice had a bad effect on his nerves, and he lost the calm of mind that would have allowed him to explain the situation in detail to her; he merely said in frigid tones,

"I don't want to resign, and I'll try not to. Still, what it may finally come down to is that I just have to. If that happens, naturally I'll find another job. All it means is that we may have to put up with a reduction in income; only for a short period of time, of course, although . . ."

This plain account of the situation seemed really to upset her, and for almost half an hour she launched into an attack upon him, refusing to allow him to interrupt, saying she certainly had no intention of being a wife of one of the unemployed, and he should do as he was told and go to Takaoka, and he could agitate while he was there to get back to Tokyo, and what was wrong with that? The trouble with him was he was all meek and mild most of the time, and then all of a sudden he made up for it by behaving with complete selfishness, refusing to listen to a word anyone else said, just like some spoiled child. He didn't want to go to Takaoka, so he was going to quit his job. He didn't want to join the army, so he'd refused to be conscripted and run away. Always running away. And he was the son of a doctor, yet he wouldn't go to medical school. It was all the same, always wanting to get his own way when he couldn't, like some silly, spoiled child.

He would have liked to shout some abuse back at her, but he couldn't think of the right words to say. So all he could do was glare at her in silence, and she said no more but got up and went to have a bath. She made a great clatter opening the door of the bathroom, as well as when she took the cover off and when she banged the bowl on the tiled floor, and all these annoying sounds spelled out just how annoyed she was. Why had she suddenly gotten so worked up? Probably the anxiety she'd been feeling for the past week had been building up and suddenly exploded. His failure to explain things properly to her wouldn't have helped, either. No doubt it had also something to do with that particular set of values, unconscious perhaps, that her mother, as the wife of a company man, would have instilled in her. Unemployment is the final sin. It was like his own mother being imbued completely with the ideas of dishonor that belonged to the wife of a medical officer in the army. So he tried to sympathize with his

wife's dread of unemployment as he took up his pen, but the simple things
he wanted to write refused to materialize as the words would not come. All
that sounded over and over in his mind were those words of hers: "always
wanting to get his own way . . . like a spoiled child."

Yoko got out of the bath, and he heard her putting down the bedding
and then rubbing cream onto her face. These sounds were no different
from normal. She'd managed to calm down in the bath. She came in wearing a negligée, and the scent of perfume filled the room. An invitation, no
doubt.

"Don't you think you ought to give that a rest now?" she said, looking
as if she felt she had perhaps been in the wrong.

"No, I can't. I've got to get this written."

"Have you?" she said, and the expression on her face hardened again. "I
don't think I'll go tomorrow, after all."

"Why not?"

"I haven't got a thing to wear."

"Okay, then. Just as you like."

She went off to the bedroom, and he knew if he went after her he could
make everything all right; but the whole idea seemed so stupid he decided
he just wasn't going to. Was she starting that again, he wondered, the two
fingers kneading and threading, lightly beating out the rhythm, slow at first
and then suddenly quickening? He pricked up his ears to catch the sound of
her voice, but she hadn't started yet, not yet, that at least was clear, and he
recalled the pink spots on those jellyfish in the Inland Sea, the swarm of jellyfish with pink spots swaying in the water, moving up and down with the
waves. While he'd been watching them Akiko had been at his side, grown
terribly thin. She'd laughed at the way he'd been so startled and fascinated
with them. He thought of the different seas they'd seen together, the blue
Inland Sea, the quite different blue of the Japan Sea from the coast at Kaige,
and then . . . and then the blackness of Tokyo Bay at night. What would life
have been like if he'd married Akiko?

The cherry blossoms at Oki Shrine truly were beautiful. It seemed the
whole setting—the wide spaces of the shrine and the fine sense of release

they gave; the good, clean lines of the shrine buildings; and the greenery of the low hills, which the deep copper roof of the main hall bore on its shoulders—all this had been created only to intensify the whiteness of the flowering cherry.

"It's a wonderful shrine," Sugiura said. "I've been to a lot of them in my line of work, all over the country, but this is the one I like best of all. There's something about it, sort of . . ." He sought words that would sound appropriate for a street trader, but nothing would come, so he merely ended up with, "somehow ornate and melancholy at the same moment."

"It's a shrine that was just made for cherry blossoms," she said.

"They're really nice; just like you told me."

"Well, this is the first time I've seen them too, you know. When I came before the man at the inn told me, that's all. You know that one with the goggle eyes. In that inn."

"Ah, the one next door to ours?"

"I feel quite bad about not staying there this time."

"Well, it was dark when we got here. You just couldn't tell."

"They've got nobody staying there at all now, have they?"

"No, but we're the only ones staying at our place, after all. I suppose people only come during the cuttlefish season."

He was relieved to see she didn't find it all that odd he shouldn't speak entirely like a street trader. They laid out a cloth under a cherry tree and sat down with their backs leaning against each other as they ate the balls of rice. They were imitating the villagers who were there, sitting on straw matting, eating from lunchboxes, drinking saké, and singing. Since there were only three small groups of them and the shrine grounds were very spacious, they didn't spoil the view in any way.

"I wish we'd brought some saké with us," said Akiko, in a slightly mischievous voice.

"I don't, because I don't drink."

"Don't you really?"

"Really."

Akiko called him quite easily by his name now, rather than the more formal address she'd first used. They'd arrived at the main island the day before, at the small port of Hishiura, and put up at an inn there. Sugiura told the landlady they wanted separate rooms. She gave them both a queer look, but Akiko didn't say anything. On the long trip from Sakaiminato on the mainland, which they left early in the morning, until the boat arrived at Hishiura in the very late afternoon, he'd found himself experiencing more and more pleasure in talking to this pretty young girl, who had a mind of her own—perhaps almost too much—and was rather nihilistic in outlook but certainly no fool, and he did not want to undergo the shame of the girl herself instructing the landlady to give them rooms apart, so he'd been thinking he'd best do it immediately himself. When asked if they wanted saké with their evening meal he also declined right away, although Akiko looked as if she were about to say something, but didn't. They took the meal together in his room, and went on talking there until past midnight. He talked about the places he'd visited in his travels, while she seemed to be wanting to ask him about Tokyo all the time, and when she finally did he wanted to ask her about Uwajima. This conversation at continual cross-purposes gave them both considerable pleasure, however. Finally he learned that the girl seemed to have run away from home to escape from an arranged marriage she was going to refuse, and that was why she'd come as far north as this. They had sat side by side ever since dinner was over, quite naturally as the young man felt; and yet during all that time nothing had happened between them.

That morning both of them had woken up late because they were tired out from the previous day. He hadn't slept as late as that since he'd been a student; for almost three years, in fact. So late had he slept that for a while he experienced the illusion he'd become Shokichi Hamada again, and the brightness of the morning and the quiet of the inn where there seemed to be nobody around at all encouraged the idea. He went downstairs to the wash place whistling the opening bars of Mozart's Clarinet Quintet, but when he saw his bearded face in the mottled, peeling frame of the mirror he was astonished at the sight . . . and stopped whistling. A sudden wave of fear overcame him, but he felt reassured again when he noticed the inn was as quiet and deserted as before, and he became Kenji Sugiura once more. Finally Akiko got up and washed her face, and then the landlady came back and smiled mysteriously at them. When they'd finished breakfast they left their luggage at the inn and walked along the road from Hishiura to Ama, a distance of some five miles. The cherry trees at Oki Shrine would have been worth walking five hundred miles to see.

When they had sated themselves on the cherry blossoms, they went back to Hishiura, drank two small bottles of milk each, and decided they'd go to see Saburo Rock. It meant an uphill climb of well over two miles, but although they'd been walking all morning they didn't mind.

"Are you all right? Are you sure you're not tired?" he asked

"I'm fine. But I'll certainly sleep well tonight," she said as she turned and looked at him, which seemed to imply, perhaps, she hadn't slept all that well the night before.

The graveled road came to an end. What remained was only a steep path uphill through a herd of some fifty or sixty head of cattle who were grazing on the grass and lowing at each other in an idiotic way. When they realized this was the only way ahead, they looked at each other. It certainly wasn't a very pleasant prospect, but once they'd climbed the hill they'd have the view of the sea and the rocky shore, and it seemed a pity to go back after coming this far.

"What shall we do?" asked the young man, although the expression on his face made it quite clear he wanted to go on.

"I'm not frightened," she said, with the sweat standing out on her skin.

"They only get excited if you show them a red rag," he said cheerfully.

Certainly the black, black and white, and brown cows were very quiet. The two young people tried to keep as far away from them as possible, however, and when they blocked the path they would take a detour, either through the lush grass and bushes on the gentler sloping parts or up and down the steep bank. In fact, the view from Saburo Rock was nothing much to speak of, but because of all the trouble it had taken to get there they felt supremely happy as they sat on a flat piece of ground that provided a reasonably good prospect of the sea, and ate the large oranges they'd brought with them. They rested there a long time, he lying on his back, she sitting with her legs outstretched. They said little to each other, looking down at the shoreline immediately below them and at the sea farther out. Neither of them suggested they should go down onto the beach, while the sea, so far away below them as it seemed, sounded like some small girl of twelve or thirteen who talks continuously of childish things.

"Shouldn't we start thinking of going back?" he asked.

"Yes. Let's go back."

They stood up and went down to where the cows were, although a lot of them had moved slowly down into the valley, and there were only a few left now on the slope. The two people had gotten used to them and felt no nervousness now, being nothing like so cautious, although still not going right close to them as they went by. Then in one place there were two brown cows blocking the narrow path, so they made a detour, climbing up the bank then down again, but just as they were rejoining the path, an enormous black and white brindled cow suddenly appeared out of a bush, where it had probably been sleeping.

Akiko gave a long scream and started shaking with fright, covering her face with both hands. Probably in response to this cry, the cow let out a loud bellow and suddenly started moving nimbly in their direction. Sugiura pushed Akiko immediately down beneath a bush and hid under it himself as well; but in apparent unconcern at the commotion it had aroused in these two, the cow merely wandered casually by, and the young man who was fiercely holding his breath watched its muddy hindquarters pass away into the distance.

"Look at that, then. It's just moved off," he said, and the girl opened her tightly shut eyes and asked if it was really all right now, and was it really safe, while he lay down at her side and assured her there was nothing more to worry about.

Since she now felt safe, she fabricated an exaggerated expression of fear on her face, placing her relaxed hands on her liberated breast, and howling out loud how scared she'd been. He reached out his right hand and placed it over her mouth to make her be quiet, but she merely licked the back of two of his fingers, and asked him if it tickled; then licked them again.

"What does it taste like?" he asked.

"All salty."

The woman's pale face was close to his. The two faces approached each other, and the two mouths met, while the man's left arm became a pillow for her head. After a long kiss with the lips only, the woman's tongue hesitantly entered his mouth. His palm sought her breast through the covering of her dress, his fingers wandering between the region under the arm and the nipple, but the bows at the end of the two red ribbons got in his way, and his unpracticed fingers felt clumsily for the snap fastener at the side of her dress and finally found it. The series of light metallic sounds as it gradually slipped open aroused him more and more with each slight click it made. As his hand felt the softness of her breast and the hard point of the nipple, she said something that was not the language of words. Her mouth sought his again, and the man who was still a virgin moved his hand past the thickness of her dress and underwear from the breast to the stomach, then to the thighs and, after a moment of hesitation, evading the bright light of the spring sun, it entered the darkness covered by the gray woolen cloth, and his fingers were warm and damp.

The male virgin covered the woman, and the woman groaned and waited. The man tried to proceed but was unable to. He could not understand why, became flustered, tried again, but still it did not work; and yet he was ashamed to look at those secret places and forbade himself to do so.

"It's a little higher up," the woman said.

So the virgin man followed the directions of the woman who was not a virgin, and all went well. The woman spoke again as she had spoken before, in the language that was not words, but more passionately this time. A cow lowed from surprisingly close by, and then another. Watched over by cattle, under the blue April sky, they also became as they were, the bull covering the cow.

When it was over Akiko laid her face to his breast, keeping it there a long time, at last raising it, facing him, but with her hands covering it. Her face was flushed with what remained of her passion, and also with shame, and the man enjoyed the sight of those parts of her face that were uncovered, the edges of her cheeks, her ears. It was very quiet. The lowing of the cows could be heard only faintly, far off now. She gradually lowered her hands to reveal her large, mischievously flirtatious eyes, and she smiled at him, causing tiny wrinkles to appear in the corners of them. But what she then asked truly was something he had not expected.

"Please tell me. Are you right or left?"

He was completely bewildered, and when she made it clear she was talking about politics, he was even more astounded. While he was failing to find an answer she looked unwaveringly at his face, watching his expression. He wondered what she was thinking about. Had she decided he was some kind of left-wing extremist? He laughed.

"Don't be crazy," he said. "I've got no interest in politics at all. I'm just a sand artist doing his job."

Then he added as an afterthought,

"I suppose you think I'm always visiting shrines because I'm relatively adept at ringing the prayer bell?"

She had withdrawn her hands completely from her face but remained lying down, her eyes upturned slightly as she looked at him and said,

"I don't know; you sort of seem somehow leftist to me."

In 1943 to be called a leftist meant you were being considered either a layabout who looked upon the whole age with frigid, indifferent eyes or an activist who'd gone underground. This meant he could have been either terrified at the thought she'd been dangerously near the mark or amused and cheered by the absurdity of her misunderstanding. He chose the latter.

She shielded her eyes with her hand.

"Is the light too bright for you?"

"No. I'm just having a close look at your face."

"Left or right; you can tell by the face, can you?"

"No, I can't," Akiko murmured, and began to fondle his beard. As he felt the skin of his cheeks being lightly pulled, he said,

"You're hardly likely to. I'm just a sand artist, that's all."

"When did you start to grow it?"

"Not quite sure. Three, maybe four years ago. I do sometimes trim it, though. It's the sort of thing kids like."

"Well, I like it too. It's great fun. Just like a brush. And it feels lovely and prickly when you rub your hand on it like this."

"You have weird tastes. Most girls hate beards, don't they?"

"Perverted tastes, perhaps?"

They both laughed. Akiko played with his beard, stroking it and twisting it between her fingers, and said,

"I'd love to snip it all off with scissors."

"You can't do that. It's a tool of my trade."

"I want to see what your face really looks like."

"I've forgotten myself."

"I suppose you must have. Without your beard you might look the same age as me, perhaps. Still . . ." She broke off.

"Still what?" he said, trying to hide the fact that he'd been severely shaken by her thinking they might be the same age.

"Are you really only a sand artist?"

"You still don't believe me."

"I'm sorry. I shouldn't, I suppose, but it seems funny when a sand artist goes around whistling Beethoven."

He felt at least relieved she hadn't known it was Mozart.

"Whistling? When?"

"This morning. When I'd just woken up and was still in bed."

"That was Beethoven, was it? Must have been something I heard somewhere in passing, I suppose, and it just stuck."

"Yes, that sort of thing does happen."

He calmed down again, but the woman wasn't prepared to give up yet.

"Then when you were looking at Oki Shrine you said it looked somehow ornate and melancholy at the same moment."

He realized he shouldn't have said that, but all he could do now was go on maintaining his ignorance, and as he was getting ready to do so she again said something very strange.

"Just what you'd expect some rightist to say."

That there was a definite connection between traditional Japanese aesthetics, with its emphasis on such contrasts as that and its belief in the moment of contradictory insight, and right-wing ideology; and that such ideology also saw considerable meaning in the fact that the Cloistered Emperor Gotoba, one of the basic determiners of the Japanese aesthetic tradition, was an object of worship at Oki Shrine, were matters that a doctor's son who'd graduated from technical college would obviously know nothing about. Thus he cheerfully interpreted her remark as a mere display of ignorance on the part of a country girl, and simply laughed at her, assuming his laughter was an adequate retort. His other response was to press his palm and fingers against her breast, for his scorn for the country girl's ignorance had stimulated his lust, and his member was hard. The slow clicking open of the snaps and the warm, damp touch upon his fingers further aroused him; and the woman's fingers received his firmness.

When it was over the two lay side by side, and then the woman leaned over him and kissed his mouth, breathing heavily in ecstasy as she said,

"You're so sweet, so nice to me. I love you."

"I love you too."

"Won't you take me with you, for a while?"

"Can you do that? I mean . . ."

"I've got quite a lot of money. Well, it's not a lot, but at least enough to pay my own way."

She had obviously misread his pause as meaning that.

"All right, then," he said, thinking how nice it would be to go with this girl to Iwakuni, and that they'd be able to manage about money somehow; and then he drowsed off for a while.

When he awoke she was also sleeping, but she woke up as if she had immediately felt his eyes upon her, and smiled at him.

They decided to go back, walking down the hill and then along the gravel road, passing nobody, so they held hands. He started whistling the Mozart Clarinet Quintet again, wondering what had happened to his record of Reginald Kell playing it and deciding Shinji would probably be listening to it occasionally, and looked at her face.

"Yes, that's it," she said.

"I wonder where I heard it. Just can't remember," he said, feeling quite confident it would no longer arouse her suspicion, but she suddenly stopped and looked up at him.

"Tell me what it is," she said.

"What? This tune? I've already said I don't know where I heard . . ."

"No. I mean your real name."

"My real name is Kenji Sugiura," he replied, but also felt his reply had been a little late in coming.

"I don't know," she said. "But somehow I just feel it's not."

She started walking again.

"Why?" he said. "You have some funny ideas, don't you? Surely one name's enough for anybody?"

"Shall I tell you why?" Akiko said with a mischievous smile.

"Why what?" he asked, yet afraid somehow she was going to say his real name was Shokichi Hamada.

"Tell you why I think your real name's different. Would you like to know?"

"Yes. Tell me why. It should be very interesting, seeing that's the name in my ration book and written in black and white in the official register back home," he said, deciding he might as well push the deception as far as possible. "I'd be most interested to hear that."

But Akiko showed no interest in his ration book or the official register back home, which in itself he found disturbing, but said,

"When we got back to the inn from the shrine I went off to buy some milk, didn't I?"

He nodded.

"When I came back with the four bottles of milk you were just sort of standing around in front of the inn with your back to me, and I called out 'Ken' in a loud voice, three or four times, but you didn't turn around. I thought it was funny, and decided no one had ever called you 'Ken' in your whole life."

"You're quite right. The name's Kenji. That's what my grandmother has always called me, 'Kenji, Kenji, Kenji,' like some pheasant squealing away."

"But I thought they always cut the names short in Tokyo? I don't know about adults, but surely children?" she said, and then called out in a loud voice: " 'Come out to play, Ken!' I can just hear the other kids doing that."

"It all depends on the person," he replied. "There's lots of different ways."

But as he said so, suddenly a childhood recollection came back. They were all standing in front of the stone gate, asking Sho if he was coming out to play, in their singsong voices. Then they went off to the temple to catch cicadas and dragonflies, or they played baseball on a vacant lot, but the house that was right in the place the outfield stands would have been had a grumpy old man living in it who was always there (heaven knows what sort of work he did, if any), and whenever somebody hit a home run the game was over, for he'd come rushing out as once again one of his windows got broken. When did the old man move from there? Yes, it wasn't until he was at junior high school, in his first year there, probably. Or the old man might just have died. Still, by the time he was in junior high there were no more singsong voices at the gate asking if he was coming out to play.

"It's such a long time ago, I can't really remember what the other kids called me," he replied.

"He can't really remember at all, yet he certainly seems to remember all sorts of other things," she said, leaning her head playfully to one side.

"Ah, trying to get at me, are you?" he said with a nonchalant smile. "Well, the fact is I did remember a bit of my childhood just now, and quite clearly."

"I was thinking about mine as well. But I was in Uwajima all the time, so there's not much to remember. Not like you, first in Tokyo, then going to live in the country . . ."

But she stopped at that point and asked him if it was really true.

"Of course it's true. What would be the point of lying about something like that?"

"It's just I feel you've always lived in Tokyo."

"Because I'm so urbane," he said with a smile.

"Well, it's not so much Tokyo as you seem so intellectual. At least when you're just talking to me. It's different when there's someone else around, as if you're trying not to talk that way. And when you're talking like an intellectual, it's as if—well, it's hard to say, but it's like the real you, as if it's much more natural for you."

Sugiura was astonished at how observant she'd been, but he only said,

"An intellectual, eh? You're only falling for an act I'm putting on to please you. It's just that I'm, as the intellectuals would say, intoxicated with you, and I want to appear better than I am."

At this point Akiko asked him very seriously if he thought she went on about things too much and he was starting to dislike her, but he shook his head, and the cheerfulness came back into her face.

"Well, I'm glad you're intoxicated with me. So you'll take me with you, won't you, at least for a while?"

He nodded, and she went on:

"It's because I like you so much, I really do. And when this has happened between me and a man I want to get to know more about him."

Sugiura went on walking, and so did Akiko. The gravel made a brittle sound beneath their feet. Her hand was still held in his, moist with sweat. But that was also because she was holding his hand so tight, refusing to let go. Suppose he was to break free from that hand and run away? But that would only look even more suspicious, almost fatally so. Now he had aroused so deep a suspicion there were only two methods by which he could ensure its disappearance, and both were so drastic the thought made him tremble. Either he could kill her or he could tell her everything. There was no other way.

The next morning, when she was seeing her husband off, Yoko said she probably would go with him that evening. Hamada said he'd prefer that, as he wouldn't have to ring up and change the arrangements. Then on the train and the bus he thought about what he'd said to his wife last night about finding another job, and wondered gloomily what kind of work he could possibly get. Should he ask Horikawa to find something for him? No. After all, the best he could hope for from granddad would be a conventional letter of recommendation, and he didn't feel like going on his knees to him again anyway. What about Takahashi, his sister's husband? Well, when his brother-in-law had returned from Manchuria, it had taken him a lot of time and effort just to get hired by the company he was working for now, and then all these years to get promoted to section head, and he had no influence there at all, just managed the ping-pong team and showed a passionate interest in the roses in his garden at home. Then what about the man who'd first gotten him this job at the university, his father's friend, Shinjo? He'd died in a plane crash, either last year or the year before that.

How about asking Sakai? If possible, he didn't want to do that, because he felt he'd betrayed him, running away without telling him anything, without saying a word. Of course it was something he couldn't have helped. Still, Sakai had been called up and sweated it out as a soldier, and it was quite impossible that he'd accepted at any time what Hamada had done. Even if he'd accepted it in his head, emotionally he could never have done so. Then hadn't he offered him a job ten years ago (at a time too when his company still hadn't acquired anything like the kind of status it had now), and hadn't Hamada just flatly turned him down? Why had he done that? Because the university job had seemed much safer. Because he'd felt he was serving society in some way and wanted to go on doing so. Then there was a repugnance at working in a place where a close friend was the vice president. Finally there was the fear that he'd be so far behind everyone else in technical knowledge, behind those people who'd been working there for years, he'd find it impossible to compete or even keep up with them. That had, in fact, been the main reason. And now, after what had happened then, how could he possibly pluck up the courage to approach Sakai again? No, there must be some other way.

But he could think of nothing, all that occurred to him being only reflections on his stupidity in going on working in a university like this for twenty years and it never crossing his mind that, given the nature of the place, something like this was bound to happen someday. Obviously he must be of a very happy-go-lucky disposition to have been so idiotic, and it also now seemed that his having been able to do what he'd done all those years ago had nothing to do with the rash, headstrong impulses of youth but was a revelation of the character he still had. At which conclusive point the crowded bus arrived in front of the university.

Hamada remained stuck at his desk during the lunch break, writing those two brief articles. Ultimately he hadn't been able to write a word the night before. As he was passing by, Nishi observed what he was doing and said,

"Hello. Become a writer, have we?"

Hamada was not amused and did not reply.

Just before the lunch break ended there was a phone call from the editor of the magazine, and when Hamada said he'd send the articles by express mail the man said he'd come over and collect them himself right away. In fact, the thirty-year-old editor did not turn up until after three, and the two of them went off to a coffee shop just in front of the university. While they were talking about this and that, Hamada remembered those words of Nishi's and asked the editor, as a kind of joke, if his company would be prepared to take on someone like himself, and if he'd say a word to the president about it. The man replied quite seriously that he'd have to work a sight harder than he did now and anyway, he wasn't cut out for editorial work as far as he could see, and nor was anyone else for that matter, going by the awful treatment he himself received there. As Hamada listened to the string of complaints the man put together one after the other, he changed his mind and decided the best thing he could do, after all, would be to see Sakai.

After he'd said good-bye to the editor, he used the phone at a tobacconist's to call Sakai's company. The operator answered immediately, smoothly announcing the company name.

"Hello," said Hamada, keeping his eye on a small child who'd come to buy some chewing gum, for no one had yet appeared from the back of the shop, although the child had already shouted out a number of times. "Hello. Could I speak to Mr. Sakai, please? Mr. Sakai, the vice president."

"As of the first of November, Mr. Sakai has become president, and therefore I shall put you through to the president's office. May I have your name, please?"

"Hamada. Shokichi Hamada."

An old man came out from the back of the shop and took the boy's ten *yen*. Hamada was put through to the president's office. Mr. Sakai was not in. Hamada explained to his secretary that he was an old friend of Mr. Sakai's since their school days together, and wished most urgently to see him. This secretary was even smoother than the operator and also more awesomely businesslike into the bargain, swiftly replying there would be fifteen minutes available at noon on the next day. Hamada promised to be at the company at the stated time.

When he got back to the Registry Office, it appeared the chief clerk had been asking for him. There was a section in the document Hamada had prepared that morning that he did not quite follow. Hamada explained and the chief clerk accepted his explanation, but went on to add in a small voice that he would be obliged in future if he would not leave his post without permission. Hamada lowered his head in response to this blatant rebuke.

He arrived at the restaurant that evening well before the appointed time, to find his brother already there, waiting on a sofa in the lobby. He was just sitting there idly, apparently oblivious to the sound of his brother's footsteps approaching him. Hamada called out and slapped him on the shoulder, and his brother looked up with an expression of almost doglike devotion on his face, indicating with his eyes that he should sit beside him. Hamada did so, making the small table in front of them wobble noisily in the process.

"She's had to go home to get her mother. The father won't be coming because the president of his company died this morning," Shinji explained in slightly too loud a voice.

"I've arranged to meet Yoko here," said Hamada, also straining his voice.

His brother leaned forward and, after waving his hand as an indication he hadn't heard, put the hearing aid in his ear. There was now no trace left at all of the jazz musician, although at the time it had been an impression he'd tried very hard to give. Here was simply an honest face, a thin, black line dangling down the side of it the one distinguishing feature.

Shinji next produced a memo pad and a pencil from the inside pocket of his jacket and put them on the table. His brother did not touch them, however, merely repeating what he'd just said. Shinji nodded.

At that point there was a phone call for Hamada from Yoko. She'd been delayed at the hairdresser, but she'd get there as fast as she could, although she thought she might be a little late. Before this conversation had ended, the girl at reception shouted out another call for Hamada. He wondered who on earth this might be, and dashed to that phone. It was Shinji's fiancée, who'd really been calling him, and its content was the same as Yoko's, namely that they were going to be slightly late. Thus the two brothers were able to have a lengthy talk together, the first for a considerable time. Hamada felt that if he let this opportunity slip he'd never have the chance to ask Shinji about the matter again, so he said in a slightly raised voice,

"I happened to meet Mitsu in a department store."

His brother indicated he'd understood.

"Then we talked about you. Shinji, did you get beaten up because of me?"

Shinji's face became contorted and he raised his hand to his ear but soon lowered it again, pointing to the memo pad on the table. Hamada picked up the pencil and wrote.

I heard you got beaten up because of me. I'm sorry.

Don't know what you mean, Shinji wrote in reply.

Because of me you got hit by officer at school and injured eardrum.

Who told you that?

Mitsu.

How can she know? She wasn't here when it all happened. Manchuria. I did get beaten but nothing to do with you.

Is that true?

Why should I lie?

Then what was she talking about?

Must have got me mixed up with someone else.

Who?

Somebody we don't know, I expect. Nothing for you to worry about.

But why would she do that?

Just likes shooting off mouth. In old days used to get things right, though. At wedding knocked spots off President Board of Information.

O.K., O.K. Enough. Am with you. To change subject, am going to resign. Can't stand place anymore. Any ideas about jobs?

Don't do it. Stay where you are if can. Shouldn't be saying this but think you mustn't try to get own way all the time. Sorry if sounds big headed from me.

That Shinji should also have summed up his motives as "trying to get his own way" hurt Hamada. He thought he could probably make him change his opinion if he described things in more detail, but the idea of explaining all the whys and wherefores of it by this crude writing method was one he could not face. It would be more wearisome than trying to explain it painstakingly to Yoko. Also, since his brother seemed to be taking an identical attitude to his wife on this matter, perhaps he too saw his refusal to accept the draft as one more example of his simply wanting to get his own way. He decided to take up a different subject, and so bring this written dialogue to an end.

I'm meeting Sakai tomorrow. He's been made president.

Give him my best. Probably still eats as much.

They both laughed, abandoning the pencil and paper and talking instead, talking about Sakai's greediness and other subjects from the past that they both knew so well there was little problem in communication, and even when there was it didn't seem to matter. After these topics had been exhausted, they both watched from afar the television program the girls at reception and some of the waiters were looking at, and spoke no more.

The mother of Shinji's fiancée kept on apologizing for the absence of her husband, seeming to have no other subject that was of any interest to her. When the gathering was almost at its end, Shinji slipped out of the room, but Hamada went after him and the result of another written dialogue in the lobby was that they halved the bill. The five traveled halfway home together on the train, then went their three different ways.

Hamada made love to his wife that night, and Yoko was even more enthusiastic than normal, giving him various leads, which he followed. As he observed her behavior he reflected that eating out must provide women with some remarkable stimulation, but when it was over she said she'd been very worried her period might be just going to start. She went off to the bath, while he lay naked on his stomach and smoked a cigarette, hearing the sounds of water splashing as she washed and gargled, and then thinking again about the written dialogue he'd had with Shinji. He began wondering if Shinji might not have been lying. Surely there was something funny about the idea that his sister should have gotten him mixed up with someone else. It was certainly true she'd been in Manchuria at the time, but if Shinji had indeed talked to her about it, just as obviously it would have been after she'd come back, and they would have had ample opportunity to get together and almost certainly have talked about him. Shinji would have let slip some sort of complaint, then afterward would have remembered how much she talked and worked out what he'd say if his elder brother happened to hear something from her and asked him about it. More than ten years had passed, and now, that night, he'd finally made use of it. In a written dialogue the awkwardness of the lie wouldn't be all that apparent, although it was wrong, perhaps, to think of Shinji's consideration for his feelings as an awkward lie. He didn't imagine he'd be able to take the subject up with Mitsu again at the wedding, but if he did at any time she was bound to reply that Shinji had told him a lie, surely.

Yoko, wrapped in a bath towel, slid open the partition door a little, and said,

"You going to get in?"

"Um. Not sure."

She closed the door again.

That was what his sister was like. She was bound to say that. So it meant he could never know the truth. Of course, it would be more comforting to believe that Shinji had told the truth, but comfort was no criterion of truthfulness. If he asked Hiroko, perhaps she would tell him. He'd heard she'd opened a tiny restaurant in Odawara with the money she'd gotten from the settlement. Who'd told him that? He couldn't remember. And would she tell him the truth, anyway? She couldn't have been happy with the out-of-court settlement, and she probably had a grudge against him because she hadn't gotten enough money. Out of sheer spite she might lie and say Shinji's eardrum had been damaged by the beating that officer had given him at school. Then again . . .

He went into the bathroom but didn't get in the bath, just washing himself down instead. While he was cleaning his teeth he thought about his appointment with Sakai the next day, wondering if he still felt bitter about that betrayal so long ago. It couldn't have been a pleasant experience, anyway. He must have thought their friendship had been destroyed, certainly when he first heard that Hamada had resisted the draft and run away, although he'd never mentioned the subject, not on either of the two occasions they'd met since the war. Obviously he wouldn't be able to raise the matter tomorrow. He had serious doubts if a decent discussion of the question of his employment could be managed in a mere fifteen minutes. Of course, it was also possible that, although he might think he'd betrayed Sakai by his silence, it might be that Sakai himself was the guilty one for some other reason, some different betrayal, and perhaps thought so. In that case, would he think of blaming Sakai himself for it now?

The main hall of Yanaka Temple was in semidarkness, and the funeral service was taking a long time. The priest's voice was bad, and his reading of the sutra was extremely unpleasant to listen to. There were few people attending the service, as it was being kept in the family, presumably because they were trying to avoid any kind of public notice. In fact, the only people present were Yanagi's parents and two younger sisters, a few other relatives, and Hamada and Sakai. Sakai had been back to Yamagata for the New Year holiday, and had just gotten back to Tokyo to prepare for his finals. Those friends who'd been in the same year at college as Yanagi had all joined the army, so none of them attended. Sakai and Hamada had also been closer to him, although they were one year his junior. People living in a place in downtown Tokyo like Ueno were supposed to be very close to each other too, but none of the neighbors were attending this local funeral, and both Hamada and Sakai assumed this was because the times they were living in made this seem the right thing to do. It could also be that the Military Police had applied some sort of pressure, thought Hamada, kneeling there in student uniform, as he listening to the endless chanting. Last year, on the first of December, at the same time that Russia invaded Finland, Yanagi had joined the Third Division in Asabu (not all that far from Aoyama, where Hamada lived); and this year, 1940, on the seventh of January, he had hanged himself in an attic room in Headquarters company. His father received a telegram from the division saying, *Masahiko Yanagi dead stop your presence required immediately*, and when he turned up there in terror he was given a white wooden box wrapped in a white cloth. No reason was given for his suicide, although it was perfectly clear—so clear it didn't need saying—he'd been a victim of that fine old Japanese military custom whereby new recruits are given hell by the old soldiers, and he'd lost the will to go on living.

When the service ended the relatives disappeared immediately as if
they couldn't wait to get away, and Hamada and Sakai also took their leave
after a few words to the parents. They ran a shop that made *geta*, or clogs.
The father was being very brave about it and bearing himself upright, but
the mother broke down and wept, and the two students could think of
nothing to say to comfort them. Sakai, in fact, who was very soft-hearted
despite his constantly cynical pose, kept rubbing his knuckles in the corners of his eyes.

The two students, soon to graduate and also due within the year to join
the army like the man whose funeral they'd been attending, walked
through the cold to Ueno Station, then took the underground to Aoyama,
and went to Hamada's house and upstairs to his room. Up to that moment
all they'd talked about were quite safe subjects, such as which of Yanagi's
sisters was the better looking, the coming exams, and what they'd do after
graduating, since there was always the danger of being overheard. But
once they were in this room they could talk freely, and after the young
nurse Hiroko had come in and gotten the *kotatsu* table warmer ready for
them, and Sakai had joked, in broad north country tones, that it was so cold
in houses in Tokyo because they had heating like that and not the way it
was back home, and she'd finally gone, they looked seriously at each other.

"If he hadn't made friends with us, he probably wouldn't have died."

"You're probably right," said Hamada, putting his legs a little way
under the warm table. "He could well have become a model soldier."

"That's going a bit far. He was always bungling things. Clumsy. Moved
badly," said Sakai, half muttering to himself and then slipping his legs
right up to the waist, and even his hands, under the thick, rich cloth of the
table warmer.

Up until two years ago, when he'd first met these two, Yanagi had been a
great patriot and Emperor worshipper. As the son of a clog maker, he'd been
brought up in a rigid, old-fashioned atmosphere, and at junior high school
the idea of respect for the establishment had been efficiently drummed into
him, his history teacher, a graduate of Tokyo University, having apparently
influenced him a lot. When they'd just gotten to know each other, Yanagi had
become livid with rage when Hamada had referred to the Emperor as "the

Emp," but Sakai had very diplomatically smoothed the whole thing over and nothing particularly dreadful happened. But this still did not affect their friendship, which grew stronger all the time. The clog maker's son saw the doctor's son, who lived in one of the smart districts of town, and even the boy from the north, who was only the child of the mistress of a large brewer, as representing a different world where ideas were free; and although he certainly reacted strongly against the way they thought, he was also strongly attracted by it all. He was particularly delighted when he went to Hamada's house and listened to records or, on very special occasions, was privileged to hear Mitsu's fairly incompetent playing of the piano. Sakai used to maintain that Yanagi's pleasure in listening to music was, in fact, a very impure one, since it was because he liked Mitsu that he could endure her piano playing, whereas he himself thought Shinji's efforts much more tolerable despite his having had no formal lessons; the fact that Yanagi never bothered to listen to him merely proved his point.

The two launched their major onslaught upon Yanagi's beliefs one Saturday in June, just before the summer vacation was due to start, when they paid a farewell visit to his home. He urged them to stay and they did, sitting with the father while he drank and they ate iced tofu and crimped slices of raw carp, then having dinner of pork cutlets and rice, and then going up onto the drying platform on the roof to enjoy the cool evening air. For some reason they began to talk about the young officers' rebellion of February 26 that had taken place two years before, in 1936, of which Yanagi spoke very much in favor. Hamada decided to restrain himself over this, since he still remembered Yanagi's response to his flippant way of referring to the Emperor, but Sakai was quite merciless. He was considerate enough to keep his voice down but was still quite scathing in his denunciation of them, saying they were just a crowd of idiots who'd happened to get hold of some weapons and been itching to use them, like those samurai you read about in stories who used to try out a new sword on some chance passerby. All this talk about patriotism and what have you was a complete mistake, since they'd been only a mob of cutthroats just raring to have a go.

Naturally enough, this infuriated Yanagi. The common view held by most people at the time tended to be sympathetic toward the young officers, understanding the way they felt but saying they'd used the wrong methods, and Yanagi's response to Sakai's attack was an extreme version of that point of view, so extreme as to be way over on the right. He claimed that one had to accept what they'd tried to do, given the corrupt nature of the Japanese politicians and the necessity of restoring Direct Imperial Rule. Sakai replied, still in a very quiet voice, that it was nonsense to talk about restoring something that had never existed in the whole of Japanese history, and made an obviously scornful snigger in dismissing Yanagi's argument. Sakai's uncle had been one of the old school socialists, a man who ran his own small provincial newspaper, and he'd spent a lot of time with Sakai since he had no children of his own, so the influence of this failed Fabian (and that of the books he'd lent him) must have had a powerful effect on the way Sakai thought.

When the talk had reached this point, Hamada suggested they go back down inside the room. So far he'd been leaning over the railing and watching the local children playing with sparklers in the street while listening to the debate. It was still only June and there was nobody taking the air on the neighboring roofs, but he thought it would be dangerous to continue a discussion of this kind in so open a space, on a rooftop in downtown Tokyo a year after the war with China had started. In fact, it would have been dangerous anywhere in the country at that time. So the three of them went into a tiny room where the small alcove itself was jammed tight with shoeboxes.

As Yanagi went down the narrow, squeaking staircase, he said something to his two sisters, and they brought the fan normally used in the shop into the room, which had its window wide open but was still hot. They placed the fan in a corner, and it took a long time to get really going, its black blades spinning slowly for a while before achieving anything like vigorous speed. But this wasn't enough for Sakai, who couldn't stand the heat, and he took off not only his shirt but his undershirt as well, stripping down naked to the waist. Hamada kept his shirt on, making use of his own hand fan occasionally to cool himself. Yanagi was wearing *yukata*, and although there was nothing all that striking about his appearance, he wore it well.

Yanagi's mother brought them strawberry ices, and for a while they quietly ate, with tiny spoons, the sweet, red-stained snow. Sakai particularly

seemed to be enjoying his, but when he'd finished he went back to the same
subject, his voice once more carefully lowered. He said nobody among the
Japanese intelligentsia really believed that the Emperor did or should rule
the country, but they told people he did because it was a simple, convenient
method of getting the sons of ignorant farmers to die for them. It would be
a terrible business trying to explain the true nature of the state and society
to a lot of witless plebs, whereas the idea of His Imperial Majesty was useful since the clods could grasp it. But of course, for anyone with a scrap of
intelligence, that sort of stuff didn't make any sense at all.

Yanagi was clearly upset by what Sakai said, and the way he said it. He
didn't see Sakai's use of "plebs" and "clods" as an ironical criticism of the
way the powers that be who used the common people really despised them,
but as a direct expression of Sakai's own contempt for the lower classes. This
misunderstanding wasn't all that strange, since Yanagi, as the son of a clog
maker, certainly had some kind of complex about the intellectual atmos-
pheres of the households in which Sakai and Hamada had grown up. So he
grew very excited, saying that was the way people talked who didn't appreciate the good things about their own country, but he soon calmed down
and said he supposed that Sakai was really maintaining the theory that the
Emperor was just an organ of the state and not something over and beyond
it, asking Hamada what he thought. Hamada was not sure what to say, and
he didn't reply for a while. He was, in fact, of the same opinion as Sakai, and
felt he had given a very good account of his own only half worked-out ideas
on the subject, having thought more or less for some time now that all this
Emperor worship was a theory of the state cooked up for the ignorant
masses. He also believed Yanagi was someone he could trust wholeheart-
edly, and anything said to him would be all right. Still, in the eyes of a son
of a Tokyo doctor, Sakai's behavior was not something to be emulated. Here
he was, a guest in a house where he'd been fed and well treated, and it was
surely not just a piece of rustic ill-breeding but positively indecent to lay
into his host like that, using such insulting language. Hamada had known
for some time that Yanagi had a complex about belonging to the lower
classes; he also knew that Sakai was very obtuse about this, because Sakai
believed that, as the illegitimate child of a rural geisha, he belonged to the

same class of society as Yanagi, and didn't see that was a gross oversimplification of the question. Hamada had been struck by how early on in their relationship Sakai had told him who his mother was, making the confession as if he looked upon it as a perfectly ordinary piece of information about himself; and he at last came to suspect that the very fact he'd told him about it so soon and so casually was probably an indication that Sakai was, in reality, extremely sensitive about the dubious nature of his birth, and his openness about it was an attempt to control his own attitude.

For this reason Hamada found himself, perhaps only semiconsciously, choosing a subject that would allow him to say what he thought yet also avoid any ill-mannered treatment of his host, talking about not the Emperor but the Young Officers' Rebellion, criticizing it for its barbarity and total lack of any intelligible aim. How else could one account for dozens of them setting on one old man, pumping him full of holes with a machine gun, and then shooting him up again after he'd fallen? They'd talked about clearing the court of corrupt elements, so if they'd actually occupied the palace one could have seen what they were trying to do; but since they'd never gone anywhere near the place, it was just impossible to say what the hell they thought they were up to. These ideas, at least the first half of them, were the accepted ones in Hamada's household. His father was a liberal, and his mother very sternly disapproved of any going against one's senior officers, expressing a perfectly hysterical hatred of the people who'd done so. Yanagi, however, responded to the second part, muttering that he himself couldn't quite work out why they hadn't taken over the palace; which made Sakai say that if he really thought that he was a more devout believer in the theory of the Emperor as an organ of state than they were, which made all three of them laugh. This finally cleared the air, and the three young men went off to a local mah jong parlor, where they played together and Hamada lost hopelessly, while Yanagi seemed to be preoccupied with something, as he played with extreme caution. The surprising upshot of all this was that, in September when all three met after the summer vacation, Hamada and Sakai were slightly disconcerted to find Yanagi had become even more of an antirightist and antimilitarist than they were.

Mitsu came in carrying coffee and eclairs on a tray.

"Don't you find you're feeling a bit drowsy after all that?" she asked Sakai.

"Not in the least. I'm just in the right frame of mind to get down to some solid homework."

They then talked about methods of evading conscription. The idea of cutting off your right index finger so you couldn't pull a trigger had the disadvantage of maiming you for life, and the authorities had also gotten around this trick recently by sticking you into some branch of the service other than the infantry. One method was to wet your bed every night in the barracks, but the M.P.s would soon be on to you if you didn't continue the practice after you were sent home. The traditional device was to drink soy sauce just before the physical, as it gave you a high temperature, but there was a considerable danger you might do yourself real harm that way. Pretending you were insane was another possibility, but it would be difficult to learn how to fake the proper symptoms, and you'd be finished if you did happen to come up against a real psychiatrist among the medical officers.

They both sighed at this point, and as if stimulated by that desperate sigh, Sakai said,

"The real trouble, you see, is just the existence of the state itself."

Hamada was deeply impressed by words that had only been said quite casually. So far he had thought enough about the nature of the war Japan was now pursuing and the nature of the Japanese army, being quite convinced that what was euphemistically referred to as "The China Incident" was merely the prosecution of open war under a false name, and that the Japanese army was a totally corrupt and terrifying institution. For this reason he'd decided he could not ally himself with that institution, preferring to sacrifice his liberty as a citizen for the sake of his freedom as a human being, and thus arrived at the conclusion that actual resistance of the draft was the only course of action open to him. But mysteriously, he had never thought beyond that concerning the questions of war and the military in general, and when he heard those throwaway words of Sakai's he was affected in three contradictory ways. First of all he felt there was no point in thinking about such abstractions because they had no direct relevance to the reality that actually faced him; then he experienced the opposite feeling that they were questions of major importance and that merely thinking in terms of the Japanese army fighting a specific war against the Chinese meant one was simply evading the real issues; and then finally he thought that even if the real issues were still not directly related to what he had to do, they were of profound interest all the same. Perhaps because the coffee had stimulated his head enough for it to shake off the drowsiness usually caused by sitting in the warmth of a *kotatsu*, he found his mind had suddenly become very lucid.

"Go on with that, will you?" he said. "Why's the state itself the real trouble?"

"Because, as I see it, the state has no objective other than that of making war."

"Surely it's not that simple. What about a permanently neutral state like Switzerland, or Japan during the Tokugawa period?"

"Those are exceptions, the very few exceptions, which is why people notice them. The *true*" (he heavily stressed the word) "aim of the state, the principle on which it is based, is the making of war."

"But it has other aims, doesn't it? The prosperity of the people, cultural advancement?"

"Those are merely aims it pretends to have, or they're just temporary ones. Its real aim . . ."

"I'm not sure," said Hamada, implying by his tone of voice that he rejected the idea.

"Look, they say the Spartans expressed their love of country in terms of war, and the Athenians did it in cultural terms. But that's all wrong. The aim of both city states was conquest, and it was just some sort of fluke the Athenians produced that culture when what their state was really all about was war. The state's got nothing to do with culture. Or at least that's what it looks like to me. The only states in existence are ones that wage war."

"Pretty gloomy way of thinking," said Hamada, trying to poke fun at him.

"A cheerful way of thinking will still arrive at the same answer, because it just happens to be a fact. The things you talk about like the prosperity of

the people and cultural advances may exist, but they're just by-products;
by-products of a factory that's churning out war. I just can't see it in any
other way."

"So culture is like coal tar, and the basic product is the gas called war?"

"That's it. The state seen as a national gas company," Sakai said, and
smiled. "As proof of the fact, think how very few states have been concerned
with the prosperity of the people up to now. Most of them have never given
a damn about it, and yet any state you can think of in any period of human
history has always been involved in war. Every single one of them . . . with
a very few exceptions that have all been special cases."

"How would you define the happiness of the people?" said Hamada in
a facetious tone, since he was finding it impossible to refute what was being
said. But Sakai considered the question perfectly seriously.

"That's difficult, since there are obviously some people who experience
happiness in the act of war. But when you talk about prosperity and happiness you aren't thinking in such terms, I presume?"

"Of course I'm not. I'm just being a bit facetious, that's all."

Sakai stopped looking so deadly solemn but still went on seriously
enough:

"Just think about Japan since the Meiji Restoration. All we've had is
war. All in less than a hundred years," he said, slowly listing them, "the
Sino-Japanese War, the Russo-Japanese War, the Great War, the
Manchurian Incident . . ."

"But isn't that history itself only a special case? I admit it's quite natural the first history we should think about is our own recent one, but . . ."

"You may be right. It could be that. But look at other countries. Aren't
they all the same? Germany, England . . ."

Hamada didn't reply this time. He remained silent, thinking about
those festoons of the flags of all nations you saw at school sports days and
in large restaurants in department stores, that string of vulgar colors of all
kinds, reds, greens, blues, yellows, swaying in the air. Was the real intention of such displays, both for the child watching with apparently innocent
wonder the lurid bursts of brilliance in the sky and for the middle-aged
woman eating her solid, boring lunch beneath it, an announcement that

there were all these countries in the world and we would have the pleasure in the near future of fighting the whole lot of them, much like those strings of photographs of film actresses in magazines that serve only to stimulate masculine lust?

"Still, if what you say is true," said Hamada, "what's the reason the state should aim only at making war?"

"Well, I hope this won't sound too left-wing," he began.

"I'm perfectly aware you're at least pink, if not actually red."

"Agreed," Sakai said complacently. "The reason is that war is the most wasteful of all human activities. Capitalism demands waste, or, if you like, expenditure, in order to achieve profits; the more waste the bigger the profits. And the state is in the hands of the capitalists."

"What about Soviet Russia?"

Sakai couldn't answer that one, and shut his mouth tight in what looked like petulance.

"No, I'm not trying to be funny. It's an example that's bound to come to mind, seeing they've just invaded Finland."

"Still, that's a . . ."

"Well, what do you consider the aim of the Soviet state? Or, to put it another way, is the Soviet Union a 'state' in your sense of the word?"

"It is a state in my sense, and not one too. It's in a period of transition at the present time, so it's very hard to define what it actually is at this moment."

Sakai himself looked embarrassed by this evasion, and lit a cigarette.

"Wait a minute. I'll get you an ashtray," Hamada said, and left the room.

His father had gotten back from visiting a patient and was in the sitting room talking with Mitsu and Hiroko, who were waiting on him as he had his evening drink. The doctor's wife had gone to the theater and didn't seem to be back yet. In the parlor Shinji was lying on the sofa reading an intellectual paperback. Hamada got an ashtray from that room and went back upstairs, feeling that somehow at last he'd managed to understand something, that he had his own answer. He reached the head of the stairs, slid open the door, and said to his friend,

"Look, Sakai, how about putting it this way."

Sakai was smoking with his hand cupped under his cigarette as if to demonstrate that nothing disastrous would happen even if the ash did fall, and he looked quickly around at Hamada.

"What I don't like about your idea that the aim of the state is war is that, well, it's just too dreadful to be believed. But if you think about it a bit differently . . ."

He put the ashtray down on the table, and went on:

"Maybe it's not all that different, in fact, but suppose it's just that the state doesn't have any aim at all. Just as bad, perhaps."

"Not just as bad; it's worse. It's more terrifying that what I said."

"I'm not all that sure how to go on, but, say, something like this. Since basically it doesn't have any aim, it's difficult for people to support it, because there's nothing there you can give yourself to. So it develops all sorts of tensions within itself; things like party strife, class warfare happen easily. So you need some kind of outside tension, some external pressure, to hold it all together. It's the only way . . ."

"So you're saying the state doesn't create a national unity in order to handle a war situation or the possibility of one, but wars are started to create the national unity itself; or at least the threat of war is used to do the same thing?"

"Does that make sense? I'm not all that sure myself."

"It makes sense. At least that must be one aspect of it. It's impossible to be completely confident of what you're saying when talking about questions as massive as these."

"Still, whatever way you put it, finally it comes down to what you first said. It's the state itself that's bad. It's not capitalism, it's not politics, it's just the state, that spectral power that is going to turn us into soldiers."

"Die from an enemy bullet, or stay at home and get it so bad you have to commit suicide."

Hamada felt a sudden bitterness inside him at the thought that he would be safe because he wasn't going into the army, whereas Sakai would be called up; and he experienced a profound grief at the thought that this man now lying before him would certainly die, either by his own hand in some

poky attic room or shot down on the Chinese mainland. So sorry did he feel
for him that he was desperate to say some words of comfort.

"There's not all that much for us to worry about, though. So long as we
don't start anything with the Americans."

"Yes. If we fight America then we've all had it," Sakai replied. "The
resources of both countries are totally different."

They began wondering why it was Japanese people seemed quite incapable of understanding that Japan could not do anything but lose if it were
to fight a war with the combined strengths of the United States and Great
Britain. You only had to compare something like a radio valve of theirs
with one of ours to see the difference. If you thought about something like
oil, then it became even more ridiculous, since Japan had none at all. Well,
they probably wouldn't mess with America, Sakai said. It just wasn't
conceivable they would try anything like that. Hamada said he thought
so too, since they were having enough trouble with the Chinese as it was.
Still . . . Sakai said that was what the Americans probably had their eye on,
and even if Japan didn't want a war, perhaps they did. America was a state
like any other country. Whether the state had an aim or didn't have one, it
still was basically directed toward war.

Those last words frightened Hamada, and he nervously said,

"The state's not so much a specter as one of those overblown monsters
like King Kong. And the ordinary people are like those New York citizens
swarming at the base of the Empire State Building while King Kong's on
top of it. If King Kong smashes the whole thing down on top of them
they've had it, and even if he doesn't there's always the chance of being
trampled to death while they're watching him."

"And they're crazy about him really, cheering and clapping, shouting
out three cheers for the monster King Kong," said Sakai quite dispassion-
ately. "I've never been able to work out why the common people are such
absolute morons."

"But it's not the same as their everyday stupidity. When they get
caught up in war fever, despite the fact their sons and young brothers are
going to die, the way they go on with their parades and flags and lanterns
is positively bizarre, even grotesque."

Sakai responded to this with something quite cruel.

"Probably Yanagi's mom and dad would have gotten all excited if he'd been killed in action."

Hamada wasn't prepared to take up an opinion he found profoundly distasteful, but said,

"The stupidity of the ordinary people is so stupid as to be beyond belief; and the same's true of our phony politicians with all their so-called cunning."

"And it all adds up to that one, massive, gigantic stupidity called the state," Sakai concluded.

They both became silent. Sakai placed the ashtray on the floor and stretched out again. The sound of the piano being played began in the parlor, and before Hamada even thought of saying anything Sakai grinned at him and said,

"That's your sister. I can tell her playing."

As he went on smiling he said, in a voice now become profoundly melancholy,

"Why did Yanagi have to be such a fool? Whatever humiliation the army imposes on you is nothing, it doesn't mean a thing. Why couldn't he just brave it out and not give a damn about it? Then he'd have been all right."

seven

Hamada hadn't wanted to let Yoko know he was going to see Sakai today, but it struck him that morning it would be fairly pointless to go in to the university and then have all the trouble of traveling in the reverse direction from there to Sakai's company. Up to this point in time he probably wouldn't have thought a thing like that was particularly troublesome, but now that he considered himself as no longer really belonging to the university (whether he was to go to Takaoka or get some other job), he felt it would make life easier if he went on to work in the afternoon after he'd seen Sakai, rather than having to sneak out in the morning and then slip back again. So when he'd finished breakfast he just sat reading the paper and made no sign of moving, and thus aroused the attention of his wife, who told him it was time to be off.

"That's okay. I won't be going to work till this afternoon. I've got to drop in somewhere before that. I'll be leaving, say, around eleven."

The fact that she made no reply indicated she was annoyed; he pretended not to notice it and poured himself another cup of tea. She poured out a cup for herself but, unlike him, she didn't touch hers and asked,

"Why aren't you going in until this afternoon?"

"I've got business."

"What business?"

"I'm meeting Sakai. Sakai's the man who . . ."

"I know. The successful executive."

"That's right. Apparently he's been made president."

"Are you going about a job?"

"That's part of it."

Up to then Yoko had been lounging in her chair with her face half turned away from him, but now she straightened herself up, sat properly facing him, and said in a weirdly pathetic voice,

"Oh, please change your mind. I'm so worried about what will happen when you're out of work. It frightens me."

"I'm not going to be out of work."

"What's wrong with going on with the job you've got now?"

So he explained again, but she wasn't prepared to listen. She said precisely what she had before: that he should go to Takaoka, work at the school, and while he was there agitate to get sent back to Tokyo. Just how very difficult that would be was something he then tried very carefully to make clear to her but couldn't get her to understand. All she could reply was that he always behaved completely irresponsibly when it came to the point, and that she would like him to bear in mind his responsibilities as her husband, concluding with a hysterical wail that if he'd told her about this last night she could have slept longer this morning.

"All right, then. I'm going now, so you get back to bed! I suppose I'd better phone the university and tell them I won't be in this morning."

With this parting fling he got ready and left the house, phoned the university from the tobacconist's by the supermarket, and spent the time he had to kill in a coffee shop near the station. As he began drinking his coffee, he was of the opinion Yoko had gotten into that state because her period was about to begin; but after he'd glanced through four different papers he came to the conclusion he'd been ill advised to hang around the house like that, since it was bound to suggest to her what things were going to be like when her husband eventually became one of the unemployed.

It was still only a little after eleven o'clock when he arrived in front of the building where Sakai's office was located, so he went down into the basement shopping area, wandering about and watching for some time a demonstration of pastry making going on inside a little glass room, and reading a magazine at the bookstall. He presented his card at the reception desk at five minutes to twelve, and was shown into the president's office.

It was a room three times as large as the executive directors' at the university, with a ceiling twice as high, tastefully decorated in various shades of gray; and every object in it, down to the carpet, immediately suggested considerable luxury. Right in the middle of this expensive room sat one solitary man, behind a large desk with both elbows planted on top of it, his face held lowered in his hands, and fast asleep. His hair was quite gray, as if it had white sand scattered all over it, and Hamada thought at first he'd been shown into the wrong room and made as if to leave. But a woman wearing a gray suit appeared from somewhere to one side of him and said,

"It is Mr. Hamada, is it not?"

"Yes."

She approached the desk, shook the gray-haired man in a brutal fashion, and said,

"Mr. President. Mr. Hamada is here to see you."

The dozing man glanced up with a start, looking both extremely annoyed and absolutely worn out, but when he saw who it was his expression brightened immediately. It was, indeed, Sakai.

"Hello there," he said cheerfully. "Haven't seen you for ages." He pointed to a chair, but remained seated himself. "I'm very sorry my secretary chose this time, since I really would love to have a long chat with you ..."

The secretary brought Hamada some tea. He said,

"It really has been a long time, hasn't it? The last time we met in Ginza must ..."

"Yes. What do you want to see me about?"

The secretary brought in two small bottles of milk and a porcelain mug on a tray. She placed the tray on Sakai's desk and poured the white liquid into the mug. The two bottles became a semitransparent white and were taken away. Sakai began drinking the milk rather as if he were slowly masticating it. Hamada started to explain his situation of being obliged to leave his job rather than just wanting to give it up.

"The university is certainly not what you could call rightist, or even almost fascist, as some people appear to think. I must make it clear that's a misapprehension the world at large seems to share. But it is conservative, and there's a constant tendency to assume rigorous attitudes in certain things so as to keep itself above any criticism that might allow its conservatism to be made use of by extremist right-wing elements. This makes me an embarrassment . . . because of my wartime record."

It was the first time Hamada had openly mention his rejection of the draft to Sakai, but Sakai only nodded in reply; perhaps because his mouth was so full of milk it made speech on his part an impossibility, or it also might have been that his vigorous masticating of the milk had only given him the appearance of nodding. Hamada went on:

"Because of the way things are changing in the outside world, my wartime behavior has become a subject of debate recently. It's made my position there very difficult. In fact it's more than that, the general attitude being that I ought to be gotten out of the way."

Hamada gave a very detailed account of the situation, even of his failed hopes of promotion, but added that although he wanted to leave he couldn't do so without any prospects of a job elsewhere. That was why he hoped Sakai might be able to do something for him, although he'd found it hard to pluck up the nerve to ask, as he felt he hadn't behaved toward him in the past as he should have.

Sakai heard him out without saying a word and with no change of expression, except once when Hamada was talking about the proposed transfer to Takaoka and Sakai's eyebrows twitched a little; upon which Hamada hastily explained that high school administrators had much lower status, and the move was a form of exile since there was no chance of getting back to Tokyo, not even to a high school, let alone the university. This time it was perfectly clear that Sakai had nodded in response to this because, for one thing, he'd finished drinking his milk.

"Electronics or radio?" he asked.

"I'm not particular. Anywhere I can be of use. I'm just an amateur now."

The secretary brought Sakai his midday meal on a tray: noodles with deep-fried shrimp. He bit on the tail of a shrimp, and Hamada sentimentally recalled how Sakai had been in the same habit when they were students together of always eating shrimp tail first. Then he sucked in a mouthful of noodles and said,

"At the present moment what our company needs is, first of all, talent."

Sakai managed to place quotation marks around the word "talent" when he spoke it.

"Second, youth. We want technicians under the age of thirty-five. Now, you certainly qualify under the first criterion. I can personally vouch for that. When was it, now, I read that piece of yours? Only a magazine for beginners, but I could see whoever'd written it had laid his finger on something quite vital that had tended to be overlooked; I wondered who he was, and saw your name. That really pleased me, you know. But as far as the second qualification goes, well, I'm sorry, but I don't have a place for you here. It just can't be done, unfortunately. I hope you'll understand."

Sakai dipped some dozen strands of noodle in the sauce and lowered his head slightly. Hamada found himself automatically lowering his head as well. Then Sakai said unexpectedly (or at least Hamada didn't expect it),

"There's a company that's on the lookout for someone and they've asked me. I'll write you a note of introduction. Card!"

Much to Hamada's amazement, the secretary appeared out of a corner, for he hadn't realized she was still in the room, handing over a card, a fountain pen, and a seal to the president, who scribbled three lines with his fountain pen on the card, stamped his seal on it, and had the tiny woman hand the card to Hamada before he'd had time to recover from his surprise at her presence. Sakai also ordered her to get in touch with the other company and arrange an interview there for Hamada as soon as possible.

"I'll ring him myself this evening," Sakai said to Hamada. "You wouldn't object to going off somewhere in the provinces after working here a bit?"

"Of course not."

"Still, they'll make you work for your salary there, and more," he said.

Hamada nodded, the secretary telephoned, and the president ate. The secretary repeated into the telephone that it was for ten o'clock the day after tomorrow in the president's office, and Hamada wrote it down in his diary; at which point a woman around forty wearing a russet, unpatterned pongee kimono entered the room.

"I trust I see you well," she said imposingly, displaying a charming smile that did not impair in any way her great dignity.

"Hello! What a pleasant surprise," said Sakai enthusiastically, glancing at Hamada and indicating with a wave of the hand and a brief grunt of farewell that he was to go.

He left the president's room with the card in his hand. As he came out of the building into the November streets, he breathed a deep sigh of relief, and the feeling that all was well persisted as he walked along, as if a few strokes with a fountain pen had solved his problems. So strong was his sense of well-being he even fondly mocked Sakai for still behaving like some yokel from the backwoods. Just the same old Sakai, he was thinking, when he realized he had nothing to feel relieved about. It was quite meaningless, in fact, since he had no guarantee whatsoever that this firm to whom Sakai had introduced him was going to offer him employment. No matter how much Sakai might passionately recommend him this evening, the firm itself had its own needs to think about. Also, he hadn't a clue what sort of job and conditions of employment they might be prepared to offer him. As he walked among the people enjoying their lunchtime break, he felt ashamed of the way he'd been so sure about his dubious future just now. Perhaps all that sense of well-being had really indicated was a profound, if temporary, sense of relief at getting out of that splendid president's room, where he'd experienced considerable strain in talking to Sakai after all these years.

He found himself blushing, but when the tide of shame had receded it was replaced by much more disturbing feelings. When Sakai telephoned that man this evening, wasn't it possible it would be to tell him not to employ Hamada? After all, why hadn't he phoned him in his presence? The doubt grew so large it loomed in certitude, but just as suddenly it was transformed into the opposite feeling that Sakai would surely never do anything like that. In order to try to stop thinking pointlessly like this, he told himself that when a man over forty (in the old days forty meant four fifths of life had gone) tried to change his employment he must expect to have this kind of trouble. And then, enfolded in the perpendicular rays of the November sun, he suddenly muttered words to himself, remembered words: "A mere fragment of a man."

He had remembered them once before, but somehow they didn't seem quite right. Yes, he'd said them to himself just after Akiko died. But there was something uncertain. Written words, seen somewhere—where, he couldn't remember—but not quite those. Not quite those, and where, he couldn't remember. His memory had just gone to pieces recently. Four fifths. Ah, now he remembered. It was in a Chinese poem, a phrase, just two characters, "remnant" and "body," and he'd read them as meaning that but had not been quite sure. What was the first line of it?

While he was chopping firewood in the back garden Akiko came out.

"Shall we go for a little walk?"

Sugiura stored the firewood and the axe, and followed her.

"Something you want to talk about?"

"Yes."

"What about the shop?"

"Mother's looking after it. She should be all right."

Akiko's mother had been ill in bed since September with a cold that had turned into pneumonia, but a week or so ago she'd gotten up, and since two days ago she'd been able to take a bath. She still looked very worn and thin, but could probably manage the shop now with not too much trouble.

"I've got something I want to talk to you about as well," Sugiura said.

The fact was that recently they hadn't had much opportunity to talk to each other. When her mother became ill she moved downstairs at night to sleep in the same room as the patient, and although she occasionally crept upstairs late at night when she had made quite sure her mother was deeply asleep, on such occasions they didn't talk very much since they were too busy trying out new positions and angles, almost as if they were in collusion with each other to avoid the real problem of their future by this constant absorption in sexual technique.

After they'd walked through the area of houses with earth walls and lattice windows, some painted dark red and some not, they entered one of more modern houses, then one hit by air raids where the original houses had been replaced by hastily erected shacks. Sugiura talked about the price of black market rice in Matsuyama, and Akiko about this year's tangerine harvest. Since the war ended on August 15, prices had risen at a tremendous rate, and business at the Yuki pawnshop was going very well. There was still a great interest in watches, but people were more concerned with getting some enjoyment out of life by listening to the radio, and he was in constant demand for radio repairs, even having been obliged the day before to go all the way to Matsuyama to get more spare parts.

At a natural break in their conversation Akiko turned a corner, and Sugiura saw they were making not for Castle Hill but for a park called the Garden of Heavenly Forgiveness. They passed two schoolboys in puttees who were messing around pushing another one of them in a handcart. This park had originally been the garden of a mansion where the seventh Feudal Lord of Uwajima had lived in his retirement, and had formerly only been open to the public for a few days in spring and summer, to see the iris and wisteria displays, etc.; but since the year before, in order to increase food production, that land which was not a part of the formal gardens was being cultivated by schoolchildren, and one could now see the gardens at any time if one was prepared to make one's way through these fields.

They passed through the fields and around the lake, and entered a small wood. A bird sang peacefully yet vigorously above their heads. Sunlight poured in patches through the layers of branches now almost completely despoiled of their red and yellow leaves.

"I love this garden," he said. "I feel very much at peace here."

"But you've been to all sorts of gardens all over the country. Don't you find this small and boring? It's not like Korakuen in Okayama or that lovely one in Kanazawa."

"It's not like them, of course, and that's what's good about it. Nice and compact. Just what you'd expect for a wealthy *daimyo*'s retirement: beautifully laid out, all the proportions right."

In the distant fields the schoolboys were not so much working as merely playing around. The whole park was in a ragged condition, the actual garden having no attention paid to it at all, and on the lake there were bits of straw and paper floating. But this very unkempt, almost wild state had its attractions too.

"They must all be very pleased in Tokyo," Akiko said.

"Apparently even more astonished."

"I suppose they'd given you up for dead?"

"Must have. It's been five years, after all."

"It's such a pity about your mother."

"She probably died in an air raid. Father didn't say anything about how it happened. Perhaps he's losing his grip; second childhood and all that. I'm worried about him."

He'd written to his family in Tokyo on October 10. On August 15, as he gazed at the bowl he'd bought that day, he'd told himself he had to wait. He couldn't be sure what was going to happen from now on, and he'd have to stay on his guard for a while, as he felt he could still not trust Japanese society. He'd fixed the period of vigilance at two months, but his patience finally went five days before it was up. A phone call to Tokyo would have to be exceedingly long, so he wrote a letter. He could never give a brief account of himself on the phone, he knew, and he hated the thought of his mother bursting into tears at the other end of the line. Also, he didn't like to waste all that money. So on the evening of October 9 he spent an hour writing a long letter, and then went off to Akiko's mother's bedside. Akiko herself was looking after the shop and knitting. Seated there beneath a framed photograph of the Imperial Family, he showed her the name and address he'd written on the back of the envelope—Shokichi Hamada c/o the Yuki Pawnbroker's—and told her everything.

The sick woman said nothing. He thanked her for all she'd done for him, and apologized for the various lies he'd inevitably had to tell her. Akiko's mother still made no reply, her faced still turned toward the ceiling, and he was just thinking she might have fallen off to sleep when the fifty-year-old woman said something that astonished him despite the premonitions he'd already had about it. She muttered that she knew all about him because Akiko had told her, and he needn't worry. What had happened (as he gathered from what she said and from what the blushing Akiko told him later) was this.

In June 1943, just after the official announcement of the glorious mass suicide of the garrison on Attu Island, the sand artist and his wife were in a commercial hotel in Hiroshima discussing what they were going to do, and coming to the conclusion that Akiko needed different clothes and her mother would be worried about her, so she should go back to Uwajima for a few weeks and they would meet up again in Kurashiki at the end of July. The sand artist husband jokingly said that once she'd gone home she'd never leave again, but his more experienced wife (and by this time she'd found out he was also her junior in years) said passionately she most certainly would meet him at Kurashiki even if she had to run away from home again to do so. Sugiura had trusted her implicitly, and they had indeed met up again in that town with its overpowering stench of dried rushes; but while she'd been back home she'd been questioned by her mother and revealed his secret.

What had happened was that she'd been unable to endure the onslaught of her mother who, despite all the things she'd already had to put up with from her willful, wayward only daughter—perhaps, indeed, for that very reason—had drawn the line at this ridiculous idea of her wandering around the country with a sand artist about whom she knew precisely nothing. She could forgive her for making a mistake about him at first, and that couldn't be helped now, but it didn't matter how smart or handsome he might be; if she was seriously thinking of trotting about with people like sand artists for all the world as if she was actually married to someone like that, then she must be completely out of her mind.

The verbal conflict between fond mother and spoiled only child went on every night (even while they were changing the water in the bowls for the two amorous stars on July 7), until one evening Akiko told her that her lover wasn't just any old sand artist but the son of a Tokyo doctor who'd graduated from a national technical college; but her mother only said that she couldn't work out why a man like that had to mess around like some strolling confidence trickster, unless he'd already gotten some poor girl into trouble. So the argument went on again night after night, until the evening before Akiko had to leave if she were to keep her appointment in Kurashiki, when she told her mother that if she didn't let her do what she wanted she'd either run away from home or kill herself. This threat was the last straw for her mother, since the debate had been going on night (and sometimes day) for nearly a month now, with the added strain of having to keep her voice down so as not to let the neighbors know, although occasionally she had broken out in a high-pitched scream; all this accumulated exhaustion finally overwhelmed her and she burst into tears, agreeing at the same time to let her have her own way. This sight aroused an unbearable compassion in the victorious daughter's breast, and she was seized with the desire to demonstrate to her mother that her lover really had been to technical college and really was the son of a doctor, feeling this would set her mind at rest, and also that the truth itself was nothing to be ashamed of, being most elegantly romantic; and so impulsively she told her the whole dreadful story.

This did indeed put her mother's mind at rest, for she came to the conclusion she must come home earlier than she'd expected in this case, as the man was bound to get arrested some time or other. Mysteriously (or perhaps quite naturally) it never seemed to have crossed her mind to inform on her daughter's lover. It was also possible she'd comforted herself with the thought there'd at least be no gossip about relations with this man in Uwajima, where old-fashioned ideas on the subject were held. As one might expect of a widow with an only daughter, she was quite obsessed with social appearances and what the neighbors might say, and it was principally such questions she discussed upstairs with her daughter when she brought the man back with her to Uwajima. On this occasion as well Akiko threatened to commit suicide, and the mother decided she would just have to harbor the criminal in order to protect her own child, thus making an enemy of the state and society in general.

But he got most of this information later from Akiko, for at the time, the mother told him very little, probably to some extent because she was ill, although what seemed most to concern her was what was going to happen next, a question she asked him a number of times. He explained that his idea was to go first of all to Tokyo to set his parents' minds at rest and discuss all sorts of things with them, but Akiko's mother could only ask again what they were going to do next, as if she felt it was some kind of reply to what he'd just said; and she repeated it over and over again. The next morning he sent the letter off express, and a reply came back from Tokyo within the week.

Akiko sat down on the sweetly scented autumn leaves and said,

"The strange thing was that Mother didn't look the least bit surprised, although she must have been inside, I suppose. Not like me. I was absolutely amazed. I mean, the first time I heard you say you were a draft resister I just couldn't believe it."

"You thought I was making it up?" he said, as he leaned against the thick, slanting trunk of a very gnarled and ancient-looking tree.

"I suppose I must have thought you were putting me on. You were grinning all the time you told me."

"I don't think that's very likely."

This was a question they'd been over on a number of occasions, just as they had discussed several times what had happened when she'd come to his boarding house at Kaige and asked him to take her with him and he'd looked so silly when he'd made his little bow, or the way he'd behaved at Saburo Rock where he still swore he was absolutely convinced that cow was going to attack them. He still felt that he couldn't have been grinning on that occasion, and if that's what it had looked like it must have been because his face was all screwed up with tension. He tried to imagine once more that bridge near Iwakuni, recalling the background to his confession, that day in the rain.

From Oki they traveled to the mainland, first of all to Matsue where they spent three days and it rained all the time. On the first day Akiko insisted on playing *gobang* and suffered massive defeats with every game, and he taught her about street trader's slang, and they managed to pass the day like that; but by the third day she wanted to go out and asked him to take her to see Lafcadio Hearn's house. He refused and she sulked, but no matter how much she fretted and got upset, he would not give in. He was quite prepared to lose his mistress, but he swore to himself he would never do anything that might brand him as an intellectual or visit any place that had anything of that atmosphere about it. Finally he told her to take her belongings and go and look at the stinking foreigner's house before she went back to Shikoku by herself.

Akiko didn't go off in the rain, however, and the next day she seemed to have made up her mind to be a sand artist's wife. This didn't only take the form of her squatting down beside him at the roadside wearing a large straw hat and cheerfully joking with the children, for she also ceased entirely asking him, even when they were quite alone, if he was left or right or what his real name was and other things of that kind. From Matsue they went to the great shrine at Izumo, then decided not to go as far west as Shimonoseki, because the port would be swarming with M.P.s and Specials, but to Tsuwano, Yamaguchi, and Ube. Akiko attracted the children and, probably due to her frugal upbringing, she cut down his expenses on meals and other things, and restrained his habit of generously giving away pictures to children on occasion. As a natural consequence he sold more and found his work easier, although there were times he would have been happy not to have been disturbed by her chatting to the children and to have been able to get on with his painting in peace as he used to. What most troubled Sugiura, however, was the very fact that the girl he'd picked up quite by accident had completely stopped inquiring into his past affairs, for this seemed to imply she was so suspicious of him she didn't dare to ask, and thus one day it was inevitable she was going to see right through him. He knew he'd have to leave her, but he was afraid if he suggested that then the questions would immediately start all over again, about his real name, his real age, and the rest of it. But he'd made up his mind. The question now was only where. It would have to be a place where there was absolutely no danger whatsoever of their being overheard; and as he worried over this he felt bitter about ever having started on this love affair in the first place.

It was raining in Iwakuni. On the morning of their second day, when the rain had turned into a fine drizzle, the two left their inn with borrowed umbrellas and went to see the famous Bridge of the Brocade Sash.* The water of the Brocade River** was a blue-tinged gray, and the row of unique pine trees seemed to be waging an unequal struggle with death, while the wooden bridge itself, built some three hundred years

---

*Kintai bashi.
**Nishiki gawa. The bridge was washed away in a flood in 1950 and rebuilt in 1953.

ago, was doing its level best to establish some kind of harmony between its own extreme artificiality and the surrounding natural world. What was really remarkable was that there was not a soul on the bridge or any sign of anyone about to cross it, and his immediate response after the first shock of surprise was that here was a chance not to be missed since it would hardly recur. So as the two stood on the central hump, leaning on the railing and looking upstream, the man said he was going to leave her. The woman asked him if he'd grown tired of her, and elicited the reply that he hadn't. Why, then? she asked, and he gave various reasons, which she proceeded to reject one by one. For example, he claimed that the sand painting could only provide a livelihood for one, as he also had to send money off to his old grandmother in Miyazaki, whereas she replied that the paintings had been selling well and she wasn't being any financial burden on him at all. The woman pleaded with tears in her eyes to be allowed to stay with him a little longer, and her melancholy face stained by the yellow light cast by the oil paper of the Japanese umbrella had a deep emotional effect upon him, so strong that he suddenly realized he was confessing his secret to her. Whether it was because he'd calculated a knowledge of the truth about him would frighten her away for good, or on a sudden impulse to get it all out of his system and make himself feel better (like taking a laxative), or that he was finding it too hard to go on pretending just to be her lover (if love it was) and nothing else—whatever it was, something had impelled him to tell her. Then the sky suddenly grew bright, and the rain came on heavily, and the woman in the yellow light stood struck with amazement, staring fixedly at him as if she were looking right through him at another version of the same man standing right there behind this one.

In the Garden of Heavenly Forgiveness, however, Akiko picked up a red leaf that had insect holes in it, and said,

"I suppose a woman just wouldn't notice something like that in a man, because we don't have to worry about becoming soldiers ourselves."

"And you have no brothers, either."

"That's what it was too. When I think about it now it seems so strange I never noticed anything."

He sat down next to Akiko, not on the fallen leaves but on the bare ground, and looked at the ripples on the surface of the lake for a while. He heard what seemed a different bird singing somewhere behind him and looked around, seeing no bird, of course, but noticing how much the tree he'd been leaning against before, with its gray bark with large white dapples in it and the slight bend of the thick trunk, reminded him of the shape of a woman's waist.

"Still, I assume the decisive factor was that your first lover was rightist in tendency," he said with deliberate pompousness. "After that any man you fell in love with would look to you as if he must be way out there on the right."

Akiko put her hand over his mouth. As he smelled the odor of dead leaves, earth, and the woman's flesh, he reflected once more, for the umpteenth time since he'd first heard about the man on the upstairs floor of that tiny lodging house in Awajishima with only two rooms (in fact it was only a noodles shop with a spare room), on the peculiar irony of a draft resister being mistaken for some sort of fascist. This first lover of hers was a right-wing student from the same town of Uwajima who was attending some university in Tokyo, and on his return home after graduating the two of them ran away to Oki Island in a virtual elopement. Still, eventually the money ran out, and she went back to Uwajima and he went off to Tokyo again, and after a while she heard two bits of rumor about him, one that he'd caused bodily harm to someone in Tokyo and the other that he'd gone to Manchuria. Finally, when her mother proposed an arranged marriage for her, at first she accepted the idea, but then she decided to run away from home and make her way to Oki again.

She still held her hand over his mouth, but the scent of the leaves and earth had faded now, leaving only the odor of the woman's skin. He decided this was the moment to tell her about his plan. It was something he'd been thinking about since the day before, the idea of setting up a radio repair shop on the main street here in Uwajima. He was not thinking about taking her back to Tokyo, but of living with her here in this country town, growing old here together. Of course, he wouldn't be able to go on being Kenji Sugiura forever, but even if he became Shokichi Hamada on the surface, in his heart he would stay the person he was now, the person he wanted to remain, the person he wanted essentially to be. When he went back to Tokyo in the near future, his idea was simply to assure his father he was all right and then get enough capital to start his radio shop.

The schoolboys had disappeared from the distant fields. The woman removed her hand from his mouth. He was just about to tell her his plan, but she forestalled him.

"I'm going to get married."

"Wait a moment, Akiko! What do you mean?"

With his arm around her shoulders, she explained. There was a rich widower in the nearby town of Iwamatsu who wanted to marry her. Apparently he knew all about the two of them, and one of his conditions was that she make a complete break with him before she became his wife. Her mother was old now, and she thought she ought to allow her to settle down and be at peace with the world. When her mother had first suggested the match she'd refused it, but Mother said if she didn't accept she'd kill herself. That's what made her make up her mind, although it was funny that finally her own constant weapon had been used against her.

He then explained his own plan, but she didn't give it a moment's thought. She said he was just thinking of that because he felt he ought to do the right thing by her. On the night of August 15 when he'd been gazing at that china bowl, she'd understood. It was over. At the time she'd thought she'd been thinking about the war, but it wasn't so. She'd really understood then in her heart that it was over between them. It was over.

He tried to argue with her, but she didn't reply to any of it, only said she must go to Iwamatsu at the beginning of December. She said she couldn't find the right words for what she wanted to say, but she had truly been happy with him. Truly.

A man with a field service cap on his head and shod in field sneakers was coming slowly toward them. When he finally came close it was clear he was quite old. The old man said,

"I believe you are not members of the Date family, nor are you employed here. I'm afraid this is not allowed. This is private property and not a public park, and no one is allowed, without permission . . ."

Akiko stood up, and Sugiura felt drawn to his feet with her; and she greeted the man, who immediately changed his tune.

"Ah, the young miss from the Yuki pawnshop. What a pity about your father, dying as young as he did. . . ."

Akiko cleverly put in a word here and there, which sweetened the old man's temper even more, and he produced a watch from his waistcoat pocket.

"Oh, as early as this, is it? Still another thirty minutes to closing time."

But Akiko and friend did not take advantage of this leniency, allowing the old man to lead them around the lake. They praised the gardens, and the old man, who was caretaker of the place, gave a brief account of its history, concluding with an anecdote.

"Lord Date, the creator of these gardens, who lived to the ripe old age of one hundred, when asked by a retainer the secret of his longevity, replied that it was because he restrained himself with women. When asked at what age he had begun this habit, he said he had commenced to restrain himself at the age of seventy-five."

The old man smiled sadly and went away. He must have been around sixty, and Sugiura wondered at what age he'd begun to restrain himself. The two left the autumn garden and began walking leisurely in the direction of the gate. Near the gate was a notice board made of zelkova or some other light wood, and written in black on it was an account of the genesis of the gardens, including a brief history of the Date family; information about Lord Date, the creator of the gardens (although with no mention of the secret of his longevity); and a Chinese poem of Date Masamune, from which the name of the garden had been taken. The poem was of four five-syllable lines, and the solid phalanx of Chinese characters caused Sugiura or Hamada problems of interpretation, since it required skill to turn them into a grammar a Japanese could understand.

> HORSE ON YOUNG BOY PASS
> WORLD FLAT WHITE HAIRS MANY
> REMNANT BODY HEAVEN PLACE FORGIVE
> NONE JOY THIS LIKE WHAT

So he produced something like this:

> On horseback the young boy spends his time
> The world is flat, white hairs are on his head
> May heaven forgive this remnant of a man
> Whose body knows no pleasure of its own

But he wasn't at all sure he'd read it right. He hadn't been much good at reading Chinese even when he'd been at school, and the character at the end of the third line, after "place," was very difficult to read because there was a caterpillar on it, although it could only be "forgive," since that was the title of the garden. He looked closer and studied it, although the fat black, white, and yellow caterpillar still caused problems. "Place" itself was a problem. Should it be read more or less as having a specific meaning, i.e., the remnant body was the thing heaven would forgive, meaning one would be forgiven because one was a mere remnant of a man? Or was it the more abstract meaning indicating possibility, i.e., even if one was only the remnant of a man one was still theoretically eligible for heaven's forgiveness? With his knowledge of Chinese it was impossible to decide.

While he puzzled over this, suddenly he felt an insight, as if he had been presented with an image of what remained of his life, the remnants of his body, his leftover life, caught up in a sense of wonder almost, stupefaction perhaps, at the length of the journey this frame of his still had to go, like a traveler who has just set out on his journey to a distant city that can only be reached by crossing one desert after another.

> My youth I spent upon the horse's back.
> The world was only wide; my hair grew white.
> What now remains of me may heaven forgive.
> God knows the body itself no pleasure has.

"I wish I could see you with your beard once again, Ken. But there's no chance of that."

"None, I suppose," he replied as they walked away. "I'd never be able to grow it in one or two weeks."

"I thought the beard suited you much better than that moustache."

"You like beards that much, do you?"

Akiko gave a little nod, and at that moment he had the sudden suspicion that fascist student had probably had an enormous beard, and he found the idea distinctly unpleasant. To forget this pang of displeasure, he said in a deliberately cheerful voice,

"Maybe I'll grow a beard again when I'm sixty or seventy. Come and see me then. It'll be all white, I expect, although you'll be a wrinkled old lady by that time anyway."

As he stood on the platform waiting for his connection, Hamada stroked his face from the cheek down to the chin. What now remains. What remained of Akiko's body was white bones. And he was the remnant of a man. Then he noticed a smiling face immediately in front of him and he smiled feebly back, until he realized it was Professor Sakurai and made the proper bow.

"I've got no classes this afternoon, so I was thinking of going to look at some paintings."

"What a good idea."

"Just the other day I went with Kuwano to talk about you to Oda, but he just told me off. Gave me a lecture about academic staff not interfering with matters to do with clerical personnel."

Hamada lowered his head.

"I suppose that means you'll be going to . . . uh, whatever the place is called?" the professor said, looking rather anxiously at him.

"I haven't yet made up my mind, sir," Hamada replied.

"Well, you know, I also haven't . . . ," but whatever the professor said after that was drowned in the general hubbub, and all Hamada could do was watch the slow movements of his gray lips, until suddenly the sound was switched on again, it seemed, and he heard:

"So I'll be leaving you now."

He watched Professor Sakurai as he went away up the stairs, clutching a bundle of something wrapped in a dull cloth to his breast. And then his train arrived.

As he hung on to the strap, waiting for the bus to the university to leave, someone addressed him by name. It was Professor Nomoto, who was seated just in front of him. He was holding a large brown envelope on his lap, and worked himself to one side, making room for Hamada to sit down, indicating the dark blue space with his finger. Hamada thanked him and sat.

"Look, Hamada," said the young professor, putting his mouth close to his ear. "I've been hearing about you, but I'd better make it clear that I'm completely against the idea."

Hamada wasn't sure what he was completely against, so he merely looked slightly bemused.

"I don't think you should just give in like that. That would be simply accepting defeat. You've got to fight against this reactionary spirit that exists in our university. Fight and go on fighting till the end."

Hamada interrupted him at this point, saying he might give up his job but nothing was settled for certain yet, which not only seemed to surprise the economics scholar but also apparently made him lose all interest.

The bus was full now, so crowded with students in suits and sweaters and uniforms that the two could hardly see each other's faces. The bus started, and all the way to the university, and even after, they said nothing to each other.

Hamada went through the main gate, then halted to make his obeisance to the shrine. Two girls, dressed in traditional white, who were presumably involved in some kind of Shinto ritual practice going on in there, entered the shrine laughing about something with each other. As he watched them go he reflected that he wouldn't be doing this sort of thing much longer, since they probably didn't have a shrine at the high school in Takaoka. If he didn't go to Takaoka there'd be even less reason for doing it. He walked toward the school buildings and noticed Professor Nomoto standing talking to a student. Talking about revolution, probably; rebellion, resistance, peace; or maybe just discussing some party his seminar students would be giving for him. An awful lot of people seemed to have heard he was leaving. Perhaps even that student knew. He felt a mild surprise that these matters apparently got decided before anyone had offered his resignation or been given the actual boot, although he'd never been in the least surprised in the past when the same thing had happened to anybody else.

Just in front of the main entrance hall, Hasegawa, the young messenger, was putting away some chairs. They must have been taking some official photograph there, most likely the president with that visiting American scholar.

Hamada called out a few words of thanks to him, but Hasegawa said nothing, just making a rather surly nod. It was perfectly obvious that he'd already heard the rumor, anyway. The whole university was getting itself ready to drive him out, a solid phalanx gradually pressing down upon him. This impression was confirmed by what happened as soon as he entered the Registry Office, for the chief clerk signaled that he wanted a word with him, and the quiet words whispered in his ear were:

"We are in rather a hurry about the Takaoka business. What are you going to do?"

"Would you mind waiting another three days? I should be able to give you a definite answer by then."

"Another three days," said the chief clerk, ensuring his eyes and Hamada's should not meet. "I suppose that should be all right."

Hamada went to his desk and, after exchanging greetings with Nishi, tried to get down to work, but he was so preoccupied with how his interview would go on the day after tomorrow he found he could do nothing for a while. Of course, even if things did go well, it was unlikely that anything could be finalized in just one meeting; impossible, perhaps. In that case he was thinking of accepting the move to Takaoka and assuming things would be settled before he actually had to move. If things remained uncertain beyond that time, then perhaps he could arrange to go alone to Takaoka, leaving his wife behind in the apartment, or even have his appointment delayed on the excuse of having to attend his brother's wedding. The fact was that the recommendation Sakai had written ("Shokichi Hamada has been my closest friend since we were students together and I should appreciate any consideration shown him") was a pure formality, and what really mattered was the phone call he would make that evening. "This man is coming to see you, but I don't advise you to employ him. He's a bit over the hill and has a rather dubious past. Yes, that's right. I'll give you the details some other time. Just handle him in any way you think fit. Yes, that's quite all right by me. Perfectly all right." If Sakai's phone call was like that, then the whole thing was hopeless from the start. If it wasn't, however; if it was very positive indeed—well, that would still only mean the first hurdle had been safely crossed.

There was a phone call from an assistant in the Archaeology Department inquiring about furnishings. Hamada replied to it. Then one of the junior staff brought a bundle of accounting slips for him to stamp, and he went through them all carefully one by one as he did so. The chief clerk asked Nishi about something to do with social security, and Hamada mildly noted that Nishi gave him the wrong answer. He prepared three documents and had the chief clerk stamp them. He meticulously dealt with all the papers accumulated in his in-box, as if he felt that only by so doing could he kill the anxious hours between now and ten o'clock on the morning of the day after tomorrow. Thus he made one step forward, one step then another, moving slowly forward, traversing that enormous space of time, that blinding darkness that lay between him and the moment that mattered. Only forty hours, and it was absurd that so short a period of time should induce so tremendous a sense of an enormous space to be traveled; but that was how it was, short and unbelievably long; a feeling he'd experienced before, been made to feel before. Where, when was that? Yes, now he recalled that concrete passageway, not one hundred and fifty yards long. It was 1942. April.

The ferry left the pier at Pusan at eleven-thirty and was due to arrive at Shimonoseki at seven-fifteen the next morning, but they were delayed slightly and it didn't dock until just before eight. Sugiura had already shouldered his belongings, looking forward to getting out of the third-class passenger saloon with its awful fug and stench of garlic, putting on his shoes that he'd kept carefully wrapped in newspaper and setting off walking with his Korean co-passengers, feeling that he was at last back in Japan. He didn't think in terms of being "home," but he was still glad to be back, for his stay in Korea had been a complete failure and he'd grown sick to death of the place.

After spending December 1941 and January 1942 in Izu, he had taken the Eastern Sea Road, the old route west, and when he heard the news in February of the fall of Singapore he was in Okazaki. It was early in March, in a commercial hotel in Nagoya, where he was sharing a room with another traveling salesman (a con man whose specialty was techniques to improve your speed with the abacus), that he heard about what a great place Korea was, and he felt he must go. This man assured him the places where the food situation was still good were Taiwan and Korea, and in particular he sang the praises of Korea, where the leaves came out in early April and from March onward it was the dry season, really lovely weather right up to the end of May. There was also the fact that Inaba had talked so longingly about the place only six months before, so by mid-March the sand artist had made his way as far as Shimonoseki and boarded the Pusan ferry. He thought he'd do best to start off there and not go all that far north because of the cold.

But that year it rained a lot in March, even snowed, and the weather in April wasn't very springlike either, and his business went badly. Sugiura got fed up with things, and although he'd meant to stay until the end of May, when he reached Seoul he retraced his steps south, and eventually decided to go home. It hadn't struck him that food was all that abundant there, and the bedbugs and lice really got on his nerves (several, if not dozens, had been making a meal of him on the boat, even), while he found the way the Japanese mistreated the Koreans very hard to take; all in all, Sugiura's memories of Korea were not very pleasant ones. This gloom was reinforced by his having only two yen remaining in his wallet after he'd bought his ticket back to Shimonoseki.

Still, the gloom was only that experienced by a young man of twenty-two, easily dispelled by a good breath of sea air. As the third-class passengers filed out (Japanese first, with the Koreans following and Sugiura midway between them), he felt his lungs were being cleansed by the cold, sea-scented air, and the young sand artist decided things were going to be all right now. He could make a bundle in May and June, then go up to

Hokkaido again for a while during July and August. Perhaps he'd be better off staying in Shimonoseki rather than taking the train right away, finding a lodging and making some money here.

He was walking slowly along a wide, gray passageway, its roof supported by thick, round columns on both sides, gradually falling behind the Koreans. Spending the summer in Hokkaido was a very good idea. Plenty of greenery up there; very restful for the eyes. Be a change after all those bare hills in Korea. How sick he'd gotten of the sight of them day after day. Plenty of cheap milk to drink in Hokkaido. Potatoes as well. They'd make a better meal than the stuff they dished up in the commercial hotels in Korea.

Out from the shadow of one of the columns appeared a man in a brown suit over a brown sweater, who called out to him.

"Hello. You back already?"

The man was around forty. His eyes, under his large gray cap, were very sharp, and Sugiura's immediate reaction was he must be a plainclothes policeman, a detective of some sort. He stopped and said "Yes," feeling annoyed with himself that he couldn't find more to say than that.

"How did you find Korea?" the man in the gray cap asked.

"Not much of a winner," said Sugiura, pleased that the slang word had come so easily. "A bit too much of the wet and the white for my liking; if you're up on our lingo, captain, as I bet you are."

The detective made a wry smile at this, presumably because he'd understood the references to rain and snow, and a large mole at the side of his nose moved slightly. At that moment Sugiura understood the implication of the way he'd greeted him: "You back already?" The policeman must have been standing behind one of those columns when he went off to Korea, and he'd remembered his face. It wasn't all that strange, because his beard made him stand out. It was perfectly natural; but that reflection didn't help to control his rising sense of fear. He really must find the right thing to say to him. But the detective spoke next.

"You feel happier at home?"

"Do you know Korea, captain?"

"I've gotten to know more than enough about it through my contacts here every day, thank you."

The policeman set off walking, and Sugiura went along with him. Two trolleys loaded with baggage started to overtake them. A large wooden packing case fell off one of them, and both trolleys stopped while the porters of both lifted it back on again, blocking the path of the sand artist and the policeman. Ahead of them stretched the columns and the gray passageway, a hundred yards of it still, perhaps more. He'd probably have to walk all that distance with this man. He might even come with him all the way to the ticket barrier; maybe even farther than that. "You back already?" "Back already?" Had he been here every day waiting for him to come back? Just over a month ago he'd seen him leave that night, at ten o'clock, and he'd gone to the police station and been looking through the wanted photos and found him there. "You back already?" That meant he'd come back earlier than expected. He'd come back and fallen into his hands. That's what he'd meant. But of course it didn't have to mean that. It didn't. It was ridiculous. How likely was it that he'd just happen to come across his photograph that night? Pieces of pure coincidence like that didn't happen. Nobody had that kind of luck. Or perhaps they did. Suddenly his thoughts were turned upside down. After all, who'd ever heard of a draft resister avoiding arrest? Nobody had that kind of luck.

The wooden packing case was pushed on top of the others, the pile was made steady, and the two trolleys started moving again. Sugiura began to make conversation as he walked.

"You know, it's really funny, captain, the way the games the kids play over there are just like the ones we play back home. They use almost the same language in some of them too, only it sounds a bit different, being Korean . . ."

The policeman merely gave a grunt indicating his complete lack of interest, although there was no diminution of his interest in Sugiura, for he stuck with him all the way.

"I was really impressed by that," said Sugiura, arousing another similar grunt, and as he was measuring with his eyes the seventy yards still to go, the policeman started asking him questions.

"What's your game?"

"Sand artist."

There was no grunt this time, just a brisk nod and another quick question.

"Who's your connection?"

"Mr. Ryukichi Sugawara of Shinjuku in Tokyo."

"Family name?"

"I don't have one."

"You don't?" The detective raised his voice slightly.

"No. People are always telling me I'd do better with one, but I feel easier without. The guys call someone like me a 'loner.' But you know all about that, don't you, captain?"

The "loner" piece of argot seemed to have been effective, for the policeman made a much larger nod this time, and muttered:

"So you're a loner sand artist, are you?"

"That's right, captain. I like being able to go my own way, you see . . ." he said, realizing he'd gotten carried away and gone too far. He'd been stupid to say something that might be slightly suggestive of the sort of person who resists the draft, but when he glanced at the dark face of the other he noticed no alteration in that constant poker face.

"Being a sand artist, you must know a lot about children, then?"

"Yes."

"That makes sense, anyway."

The fact that the detective felt this made sense seemed to suggest some of the other things he'd said didn't. Sugiura began to be worried. But there was only thirty yards to go, now. Perhaps as few as twenty.

"Always been a sand artist?"

"No, I did repairs before. Clocks and watches, and a bit of radio work."

"Looks like you're a bit of an educated man, then?"

"Educated, captain? Nothing like that, believe you me."

"A bit of an intellectual, so you don't like having a family name. Bit of a libertarian."

"Come off it, captain. A libertarian? Are you trying to damage my reputation?"

"It makes sense."

Sugiura couldn't be at all sure what was making sense, or what sort of sense it was making. Did he mean the answers he'd given all fit together, were not contradictory? And if they did, was it a good thing? Or did it mean he'd just cooked up the sort of story he'd expected, that it all fit in with the detective's previous assumptions? Or was it that . . . ? Ten yards to go. Libertarianism and draft resistance: they made very good sense together. If he could only get away before this ten yards was over.

"Sand artist."

"Yes."

"Before I leave you, there's just one more thing I'd like to ask."

"Yes."

The policeman stopped, and so did the sand artist. The face with the mole approached him and smiled.

"I'm just doing my job, just like you, you see."

"Yes."

The trick was to put the suspect at ease, then catch him out. "Before I leave you" was the same sort of ploy. So was the smile.

"What's your name?"

Sugiura gave his name, and how it was written.

"Any other?"

The detective was looking him straight in the eyes now, brown eyes that were a color intermediate between the brown of his sweater and the brown of his suit. The whites were streaked with red lines.

"I've only got one name, captain," Sugiura replied, returning the detective's gaze and making himself go on doing so.

"Permanent domicile?"

Sugiura fluently recited the false address.

"My present address is the same, although I only go there once a year."

"Date of birth?"

Sugiura gave it, and also the sign for that year when he was asked it as well.

The detective went silent, and it seemed the whole of the surrounding world had become quiet too, as the megaphone calls of the station staff and the cries of the coolies carrying the baggage receded into the far distance. As he listened to the sound of his own breathing, Sugiura looked at the detective, at his eyes, his nose, the mole by his nose, the lips with their dried, peeling skin. Now he was going to ask why he wasn't a soldier. He'd reply to that one with the answer he had ready. Would he see through the lie? Would he fail to see through it? One chance in two. Maybe once chance in ten. The great thing was to bluff it out; lie and bluff it out.

"Thank you for your trouble," was what he said.

Sugiura gave a little grunt of disbelief, but the detective didn't seem to notice. He rubbed the mole softly with his right index finger as if it had suddenly started to itch, then turned away, turned his large back to the sand artist and walked off. But Sugiura himself didn't start walking straight away. As the world of noise came back to life he stared after the man in brown, his mouth hanging crudely open as he took three or four huge, deep breaths, although he knew perfectly well that it would be most dangerous if someone were to observe him just standing about with such a cretinous expression on his face.

The baby-faced owner of the Hare came into the registry to collect used plates and bowls.

"You're as fast as a tortoise when it comes to collecting empties, Hare," quipped Murakami, one of the junior staff.

"As fast as a hare," said the forty-year-old man who still looked like a child. "Unlike what you read in your storybooks, the hare is, in fact, much faster than the tortoise," he continued, as if there were indeed a shop called Tortoise with which he was in fierce competition.

Somebody sniggered, and a number of people grinned, while the chief clerk, presumably on his way to the toilet, stood at the door and slapped the restaurant proprietor on the shoulder, making some joke that provoked his own huge laughter, and then went out into the hallway. The Hare also left.

Hamada reflected that life was somehow like that, an idle, ambiguous race that just went on. Average life expectancy kept going up, so the race got longer. You were obliged to live to your sixties and seventies now. All sorts of things happened, all sorts of things appeared to threaten that life: retirement, the whining of your wife, getting deaf from taking the wrong medicine; but it went on, like walking a hundred and fifty yards down a concrete passageway under constant threat from police interrogation. When he'd been asked what his other name was, his blood had run cold. He'd felt this was the end, this was final, now it was all over: a feeling like falling endlessly down a well. Still, somehow you managed. The whole point about life was that somehow you always managed. Even Shinji had managed to get married. He thought of his brother's fiancée, that youthful, happy round face overflowing with health and vitality, and decided she looked all right. She was a bit more than all right, as he'd decided numerous times already, and he knew (a thought he'd had just as often, perhaps ten times as often) he had a great deal to be thankful to her for.

Then quite suddenly he felt exhausted, for no reason he could understand until it struck him he was hungry. But it was only 2:45; why should he feel hungry at this hour? Of course, he'd had no lunch today. He'd forgotten about that, and he laughed inside. But the laughter was unreal. His forgetfulness was only an indication of how much the question of employment had become one long, painful obsession, and his laughter was as meaningful as the crackling of dust accumulated on a long-playing record. It meant no lightening of the heart.

Hamada gave a hundred-yen note to the messenger girl, apologized for asking her to go on a private errand, but would she mind getting him two bottles of milk from the student canteen? She went.

The phone on Nishi's desk rang, and he picked up the receiver. After a certain amount of bandying with the person at the other end, he caught Hamada's eye and said it was his, and passed the long black object over. Hamada received the object, noting that the cord had become entangled in the papers on Nishi's desk, and as he straightened those out he spoke into the receiver.

"Hello. Hello."

It was an unknown man's voice at the other end of the line.

"Hello. Is that Mr. Hamada? Mr. Shokichi Hamada?"

"Speaking."

"Mr. Shokichi Hamada?"

"Yes. This is Hamada."

"You're quite sure? Hello . . . Mr. Shokichi Hamada? . . . Mr. Shokichi Hamada of the Registry Office?"

The man was verifying the point so meticulously he was getting on Hamada's nerves, and there was also a kind of perfunctory drawl in his voice he found particularly unpleasant. But he decided to swallow his annoyance and replied,

"Yes. There has been no mistake. I am Shokichi Hamada of the Registry Office. You have the right person."

The chief clerk came in wiping his hands on his handkerchief and went to his desk.

"I see," said the voice at the end of the line, and then, as if he were reading out a message of bereavement, in solemn, funereal tones:

"Hello. Now, what I am about to tell you may come as a great shock."

The man hesitated, and Hamada said in annoyance,

"Hello. Would you mind telling me what you want?"

"It may come as a great surprise, but I must ask you not to be surprised. Not to get too excited, that is. You don't want the people around you to know all about it."

Hamada went tense, and spoke in a much lower voice.

"Hello."

The man said he was Inspector Somebody from the Yotsuya Police Station, and the fact was . . . Was he ready? He must try not to get too upset, but keep control of himself. . . . The fact was his wife, Yoko, had been arrested for shoplifting. The man investigating the matter was one of his subordinates, but as the officer in charge it was his job to let him know.

Now it was the inspector's turn to shout "Hello, hello," since Hamada said nothing in reply.

"Hello. Have I made myself clear? Shoplifting. Sh . . . op . . . lift . . . ing. That's the charge."

"I see."

He found himself unable to question the validity of the charge. The way the man spoke was heavy with calm authority, making it undeniable that what he said was true.

"For that reason we would like the husband . . . Hello . . ."

"Yes."

"We would like you to come here. That's always the best way. Could you come over right away? I realize you must be busy, but this is very urgent."

"Yes."

"Hello," the voice bellowed from the other end.

"Yes, of course. I'll come straight over."

His throat had suddenly gone peculiarly dry, and his voice sounded to himself like a thin, high-pitched squeak.

The receiver had clicked down at the other end. He put down his own. He looked at the long, black object, which was receiving the light both of the sun from the window and of the strip lighting above, and shone a variety of colors, none of them really black.

"Is something wrong?" Nishi asked.

"Um."

"Has something happened? You've gone quite pale," Nishi insisted.

Hamada didn't reply, but walked over to the chief clerk. Out of the corner of his eye he saw Nishi raise both arms slightly, presumably a gesture of amazement, and the black cuff covers moved like the two poles of a level crossing gate. Hamada asked the chief clerk to give him leave for the rest of the day, as something urgent had just come up, and after looking up at him with a very suspicious expression on his face, he slowly nodded his agreement. Hamada left the office almost at a run, at the doorway bumping against the shoulder of the girl who'd just bought him the two bottles of milk he'd asked for. She gave a shriek and dropped one of the bottles, which broke on the floor. The white liquid spread quickly out, forming a shape like the map of an unknown continent, the damp pieces of broken glass seeming to be the mountainous regions on that map.

Hamada apologized to her as he went out. He was just about to set off running from the entrance hall to the main gate when he heard a voice coming out of the dazzling sunlight.

"Hey, Hamada, what's wrong?"

It was Assistant Professor Kuwano, who was standing there with his hands in his trouser pockets.

"It's my wife . . ." said Hamada, who stopped briefly before setting off again.

"She's been hit?" howled out Kuwano, as if it were some kind of imprecation, stamping one foot excitedly on the ground.

Because he wasn't sure what Kuwano meant and wanted to find out, he automatically took two or three paces toward him, as did Kuwano toward Hamada.

"The whole place is swarming with insane drivers these days," the owner driver said bitterly. "Here, take my car."

He took the keys out of his pocket and pressed them into Hamada's right hand.

"But I haven't got my license on me, sir."

"That doesn't matter. Damn the license. Just get going," he shouted excitedly. "It's over there."

He pointed in the direction of the small amber car parked in front of the main gate. Hamada nodded his thanks and ran off, not bothering to bow to the shrine but heading straight through the main gate and into the Renault. As he put the key in he hesitated a moment, wondering if it was wise to drive to a police station when not in possession of a license, but he told himself he cared as little about that as Kuwano; probably much less, in fact, for hadn't he defied the whole country twenty years ago, running all over the place, a criminal in everybody's eyes? And hadn't he felt a sense of brotherly kinship with that harelipped thief and murderer? And, more to the point, wasn't he the husband of a shoplifter? He turned the ignition key. It made a small, harsh sound.

When he presented his card at the desk, the policeman reading a sports paper had obviously heard about him, probably even before the phone call had been made. He pointed to a blackened wooden door and told him to go through that to Room 3. Hamada opened the door and entered a wide, dark corridor, looking for the number 3 among the small rooms on both sides. He found it and knocked on the door. A sonorous voice responded from inside, and he opened the door and entered a grubby, pale blue room. There was a large window directly in front of him, and the sunlight was flooding in. Sitting with his back to the window, at the head of a long, narrow table, was a man who was younger than he'd expected, perhaps the same age as himself or slightly older. There were wooden benches on both sides of the table. The inspector stood up, indicating with his hand that he should come on into the room. He had some document on the table before him, and in front of that an object Hamada recognized: the large red bag Yoko used for shopping. He edged his way through the narrow space between the bench and the wall, rattling the bench as he did so and wondering suspiciously where Yoko was. He looked around and saw a woman seated on a small chair next to the door. She was wearing a dress he also recognized; her face was covered with a handkerchief, and her hands covered that.

Hamada produced his card and the inspector produced his. He sat down on the end of the bench. The bench was unstable and creaked occasionally. The inspector had shaved badly that morning, patches of stubble appearing here and there. He introduced himself as a man who'd been a student in the law faculty of the university where Hamada worked but had left without taking a degree.

"In a situation of this kind it's best to handle it this way, I think. Since it's the first time the police have been involved."

Hamada thanked him, but the inspector went on in the same casual voice,

"Although it's not the first time she's done it, by any means."

"Not the first time?" repeated Hamada, and the inspector explained.

Yoko had been caught in a department store in Shinjuku stealing a five- or six-year-old child's dress, a candlestick with a red candle in it, and a U.S.A.-made metal scrubbing brush. The house detective took her into a room and investigated her, but all she would say was that she'd pay for them, and in fact she had enough money on her to do so. However, another of the staff who'd just gotten back from lunch recognized her as the woman who'd been caught lifting a purse, a pair of embroidered slippers, and a folding umbrella from this same store only two weeks before. As it was a first offense, they'd let her off after giving her a good talking to, but this time they were furious because they felt she was trying to take advantage of them, and they decided to treat her as a habitual offender and call in the police. Under investigation she'd been a bit adamant at first, but finally she'd confessed.

"Women often do things like this when they're feeling depressed by a menstrual period, but in this case it's been over for a fortnight so that can't be the reason," the inspector said, and when Hamada nodded he went on: "My own belief—purely a supposition—is that she's had this tendency for quite some while."

Hamada couldn't make the effort to nod this time. He just looked at the inspector from under his eyelids. The inspector looked completely confident in his assumption and, as if to confirm it, at that moment a peculiarly flutelike sobbing broke out behind him as Yoko burst into tears.

"Look, Yoko," he said, turning around on the bench toward her. "What about that baby dress and booties you gave to the neighbors last spring? Were they stolen as well?"

His wife's sobbing rose higher.

"Stop crying and answer. Did you steal them?"

The face covered with a handkerchief and two hands slumped forward. It meant she had nodded.

"Tell me where you stole them," Hamada shouted and then, after waiting a moment, shouted again: "Tell me!"

The voice in which she replied was very similar to the one she gave when in raptures in bed. In fact it was almost identical, halfway between a sob and a scream.

"Probably . . . Ikebukuro."

"You don't remember because you're always at it, are you? I suppose you stole that Tanabata paper in Ajiro as well?"

After another outburst of sobs she said, "Yes."

At this point the inspector interrupted Hamada's interrogation.

"I've got some other business to attend to, and I think it might be best if you went home first and then talked to her about it there. Get it all out of her, that's the only thing to do. Then, well, you'll just have to take the stolen goods back to where they came from. Say your maid did it, or something like that. If it's a lot of trouble, you can bring the things here. Have a good look right at the back of cupboards, and under the sink in the kitchen. The kitchen needs a good look if there's any removable floor-boards. They mostly put things in places like that."

"You've been most considerate," said Hamada, and lowered his head again.

"The best thing is for the husband to watch her. A really ingrained habit takes a lot of curing, though. Still, in this case, I think we can be lenient."

Hamada lowered his head once more, and the inspector pushed Yoko's shopping bag toward him, indicating with a gesture that they could go. Hamada stood up, this time edging between the bench and the table, and went up to the woman sitting by the door.

"Okay, Yoko, get up."

His wife stood up, but still with her handkerchief and hands covering her face.

"Wipe your face and put your handkerchief away," he ordered her.

Her face appeared: dirty, bloated, pale, and haggard. Her mascara had all come adrift, making her look as if she'd been given two black eyes through constant pummeling. Her lipstick had created a faint red patch on the tip of her nose. She looked hideous; it was as if he'd been given a glimpse of what she'd look like if she were suddenly to die.

Near the black wooden door at the end of the double row of small rooms there was a wash place. He made her wash her face and gave her his own handkerchief. She dried her face with it. Then husband and wife left the police station and got silently into the Renault. He said nothing about the car. She didn't ask anything, either. The car moved off.

As he drove slowly through the late-autumn streets with their large, dead yellow leaves, yellow-looking dogs, yellow caps of small children, he realized it hadn't been so bad when he was driving from the university to the police station. He'd been totally absorbed in the act of driving, which he hadn't done for some time, and there'd still remained the slightest of hopes, even if only the very slightest, that the whole thing might have been some peculiar form of misunderstanding. But now even that faint hope had gone, and he'd grown used to driving again. He had leisure to taste all the bitterness of what had happened.

The inspector had said she'd been suffering from kleptomania for some time, and Yoko hadn't disagreed. Cheap paper ornaments, baby booties. But how could you account for a dress for a child of five or six? They certainly didn't have one at home, and there was no child of that age living nearby. Was she that lonely for a child? Had it been that bad for her when she lost her baby? Was her craving for sex every night just a desire to get pregnant? But what did she want with a candlestick with a red candle in it? The American scrubbing brush could be used, of course, but even if it was imported it still couldn't be all that expensive, not even as much as a thousand yen or, at the most, two. She could have found that much money; she'd had enough money in her purse, anyway. The embroidered slippers weren't in the least functional, and he'd already bought her a folding umbrella. At this point the face of the man driving illegally while not in possession of an authorized license suddenly contorted. What about the purse of hers, the red one with the gold stripes? She'd probably stolen that too. It was very likely indeed. How much did she have hidden away at the backs of cupboards and under floorboards in the kitchen? When the inspector had mentioned that, she hadn't said a word.

As he halted at the red light at an intersection, the driver of a small truck shouted something at him. He rolled down the window. The driver told him his lights were on. Hamada thanked him and switched off the headlights. Yoko was leaning half against the door, looking at her husband. When their eyes met, she quickly looked away. The fact was she hadn't been able to deny it. She must have lots of things hidden under the removable floorboards: one of those dolls with brown hair that drank milk, shoes made in Hong Kong, cans of asparagus. . . . This caused his face to twitch again, as the column of cars surged forward and the light changed to green apparently in response to their urging. Now what had made the idea of cans of asparagus come into his mind? Was it because they'd had asparagus at their dinner with the mother of Shinji's fiancée? No, it wasn't; and he knew it wasn't. It was on the night before that, when they'd had asparagus for dinner at home, and he'd reflected that they were living in real style. That had most likely been stolen. It almost certainly had. Then hadn't he said once it was extravagant to cook with butter when margarine would do for him? And hadn't she replied it was all right because she'd picked it up cheap at a sale? He wondered if he could turn right at the next intersection. If he couldn't it must be the next one. He couldn't. In the past he'd been living off a pawnbroker's daughter, and now it was off a shoplifter. Turn right here. Just follow the car with the white license plate. At least it couldn't be a one-way street. Mustn't get too close, though. Old people shouldn't be allowed to wander down narrow streets like this. Nor should children, for that matter. She'd been a kleptomaniac for some time. Since when? Since she was a girl? If that was so, then the miscarriage had nothing to do with it. Now this was much easier, a nice wide road. Must be halfway by now. No, not yet. Just getting outside the old city limits.

But almost as soon as he'd gotten outside the city, as if it had been waiting for the car to reach the suburbs, a sudden startling insight overwhelmed him, a suspicion that seemed to well up violently inside. If she'd had the habit since she was a girl, then wasn't it more than likely her desperate parents (desperate because every match they arranged for her was broken off, or even because there'd never been any despite the fact she was so nice looking) had approached Horikawa and asked him to find someone for her? He tried a number of times to discard this idea, telling himself there was no reason to be that distrustful of people, but he kept finding there was, and the argument made sense. Here was this girl, young, pretty, so young and pretty he'd thought she couldn't be a virgin, although he hadn't much minded and she turned out to be a virgin anyway. It's true her family wasn't all that rich, but the father had a job in a first-class company (perhaps not quite first-class, but still), so why should they want their daughter to marry someone like him? And Horikawa must have been completely taken in by them too. He tried conjuring up how ordinary and straightforward Yoko's parents looked, and this made him feel even more suspicious. How pleased they'd looked! As pleased as Punch, as if they'd at last disposed of a really troublesome burden. They must have been having problems with their kleptomaniac daughter for years!

Another suspicion followed that one. Might it not be that Horikawa had known all about Yoko's unfortunate tendency? Wasn't that why, every time they met, he invariably asked if his wife was well? Of course, that in itself proved nothing, but he certainly seemed to be on very close terms with the family. There was a genuine possibility he'd known about it, that was for sure. After all, wouldn't he think it strange there'd been no proposals made for such a pretty girl? He'd known, all right. He'd known everything. And the old fox had decided a girl with itchy fingers would be a good match for a draft resister. . . . No, that was pure assumption. He must reject that. So he tried to remember all he could of Horikawa's language and behavior at the formal introduction of the couple and at the wedding reception, finding not one thing to support any such assumption; but the suspicion itself had taken firm root within him. And if Horikawa had known about Yoko's secret in the same way he'd known about his, wasn't it possible he'd also told people about it as well? This idea came only slowly, but come it did, rejected at first as impossible, but then producing another: the idea that other people in the university must also know about it. Who? Kobayakawa? Nishi? Masako Aochi? Professor Oda? Inuzuka?

A wall of faces arose before him, and they all began to jeer. He could hear Nishi's unique, bellowing voice among them. Their cheeks crinkled. Their eyes narrowed. They lowered their eyes. Now they were trying not to laugh, but their lips trembled and they had to. And with that soft wall of faces before him, enduring the mockery, contempt, and scornful pity expressed on each one of them, he drove on. Not much farther to go. The wall vanished. He drove his borrowed car through the November afternoon, although there was no trace of the season on this wide, long, straight road. As he drove he made an effort to diagnose himself. Perhaps there was something wrong with him that he should be in this constant state of suspicion. The things that had happened to him recently had gotten him into the habit of mistrusting everything. His mind had become warped. Perhaps it was some kind of mild nervous breakdown. Perhaps even a serious one. He glanced at the passenger seat. Yoko was sitting absolutely still, her head lowered.

He turned left onto the road leading to their apartment block. Terrible the way someone could park as close to a bend as that. Only about five yards away. Watch out for that delivery boy on a bike. Some children playing with a ball. People shouldn't park like that; they should get farther to the side. That's why the telegraph poles get all worn down, cars always knocking against them. Turn right here. Turn the car around before park-

ing it. Three-point turn. Right. Should be okay. Perhaps forward a bit
more. Now in a bit to the left. That's it. Haven't lost the old touch.

He released his hands from the wheel and wiped the perspiration off on
his trouser knees. He eased his shoulders backward a little with the small
of his back still against the seat. His hips didn't seem to have felt any strain
at the moment, but they'd probably be hurting by tomorrow morning.

"Well, here . . ." he started to stay, but when he looked to his side he
noticed with astonishment that Yoko was fast asleep, her two hands folded
neatly on her lap, her face lowered, her measured breath coming very quietly.

Her face was no longer swollen and ugly but had a childish innocence
about it, as well as a slight weariness. A young face, still with the traces of
girlhood; the neck just a trifle too long, the lips slightly open, the long eye-
lashes of which she was so proud since she was always saying she didn't
need false ones. He leaned one elbow on the wheel, his body half turned
toward her, and gazed in amazement at that face.

As his surprise began to fade, it was transformed into a feeling of envy,
building up drop by drop in his heart until it was a flood of emotion. He
wondered what he was envious of, but decided not to try to work this out
rationally, simply waiting for the emotion to reveal itself. He watched the
sleeping woman's face and waited.

Then suddenly the answer came, but it was just like answering an
awaited phone call and discovering it was a wrong number, feeling all the
dull, irritated sense of letdown that induces. How could he have been envious of anything as stupid as that? He'd been envying her her freedom, her
woman's freedom, indulging the childish feeling that women are well off
because they have an easy life. He'd been fascinated by the sense of freedom he thought he could see in the drowsing woman's face; or more probably it was just a straightforward response to the fact that her face asleep
looked peculiarly pretty and young.

Yet this rejection of the emotion only seemed to make it stronger. The
idea of freedom so hastily denied began to flow through the whole of his
being, a slow movement upward of the simple reflection that for so long
now he'd been enslaved by something, something not yet clear to him; as

if some floorboard over the deeper regions of his mind had been removed, carefully, nervously, and now he could find what had lain there concealed so long, as the light of the sun shone dazzlingly into that region of darkness, disclosing at last the sad, small jewel of freedom. Why had he never made use of it when it had been there all the while? Why, for example, couldn't he become, say, a TV repairman? Why did he think it was wrong? What was wrong with it? What was wrong with being free like that? Why, indeed, had he never even thought of doing something like that? After all, was it really all that long ago that he'd been sitting by the wayside, surrounded by the cheerful voices of children, with the sweat gradually accumulating in his beard? Yes, it was long. It was twenty years ago. More than twenty years ago.

He had a vision of what life could be, imagining it to the rhythm of his wife's quiet breath. He would be a mechanic, a repairman. He would only wear a collar and tie three or four times a year. And that would be all right. If it came to that, then it would be all right. It would be more than all right. It would be good. It would be more than good, for he'd always liked tinkering with machines. He must never forget that he'd broken the most powerful of all the commandments our society imposes, stronger than the commandment not to steal, stronger even than the commandment not to kill. He was a man who had gone against the stream. He had offended, and he had to be plucked out. He had gone against the state, against society, against the establishment, all there was to go against; and a man who has once rebelled in that way has to go on doing so until the very end. There is no other path for him. There is no way back. All he can do, forever and ever, is continue on his perilous voyage, continue his restless journey, and lie down each night with only bamboo grass for a pillow.

Yoko closed her lips, lips from which the lipstick had flaked off, and frowned, slowly raising her head as she gradually approached the moment of awakening. And at that moment he felt a mysterious uplifting of his troubled heart.

The flag of the Rising Sun hung pinned to the crossbeam. Written in black ink on the white cloth were the words, CONGRATULATIONS ON YOUR CALL

UP: SHOKICHI HAMADA. An old relative who prided himself on his calligraphy had brought it the day before. His mother was sitting immediately beneath it, and she said,

"It would have been so much nicer if we'd asked one or the other of your friends. But you insisted you didn't want anybody."

"I didn't insist. It's just as I said. Yanagi's dead and Sakai's with his division in Yamagata."

"I suppose Sakai's getting on all right."

"Well, we can suppose anything. There was a postcard from him the day before yesterday. . . . Oh, you've read it? It didn't say very much. 'I am performing my military duties to the very best of my ability.' That's probably all they're allowed to write."

"I do feel sorry for the two of you, having to become soldiers. But you were both graded A, so it couldn't be helped. When I was a little girl I was firmly convinced all soldiers had a bad smell. Father always used to say so. 'Your common soldier smells; he stinks to high heaven.' "

"Look, Mother, do you mind if I go into the kitchen and get a bite to eat? Just a nibble from the feast we're having tonight."

"Well, that is a little surprising from you, I must say. Yes, of course you can. From tomorrow you won't be able to. But don't you think you should go to the barber's first?"

"I'll have a bite to eat, then go to the barber's," Hamada said, and stood up.

He'd been talking to his mother in the sitting room, around the porcelain bowl with the small charcoal fire. She stood up as well, saying as she did so,

"I won't grill the steak till later. I shall start cooking the tempura at six. I've ordered the raw fish for six as well, so there's not really . . ."

". . . anything to nibble," he said, and went to the kitchen. "Still, this will do fine."

While his mother and the maid laughed and looked on, he ate some salted, sweetened chicken and potato, thinking of it not so much as part of his send-off party this evening but as breakfast for the next morning. Tomorrow morning at ten o'clock he was due to enter the barracks of the

Third Division at Akasaka, and this evening there was to be a farewell party for just the family. His mother had been determined to make it something of an occasion by inviting relatives and friends and people from his firm, but he'd stopped her. He no longer had any contact with the people he'd known at school, his relationships at work were quite perfunctory, and his two close friends were not available.

He went upstairs to his room and changed out of his splash-patterned kimono into trousers and sweater, strapping on his watch. Yesterday he'd given his own, a Waltham pocket watch he'd fixed a strap on, to Shinji in exchange for his brother's Japanese one, saying it would be a waste to take something as valuable as that into the army. He felt his breast to make sure he had his wallet, savings passbook, and seal in his shirt pocket, then looked around the room. He'd forgotten nothing. His desk and drawers had been left quite tidy. He wondered if they would understand that the neat order in which he'd left everything was meant to serve instead of a farewell note. He looked at his desk, at the electric gramophone he'd made himself, at his bookshelves and record cabinet. Then he sat down in his chair for a moment, but immediately got up again. He couldn't hang around here. He had to get to the bank before it closed, otherwise the whole thing would be disastrous.

He went once more to the kitchen. His mother, the nurse Hiroko, and the maid were there, talking about what a nuisance it was you could no longer buy bleached cotton.

"Oh, you could have gone to the barber's in your kimono," said his mother. "And why you should have decided to change into the shabbiest of your ordinary clothes I can't think."

"Is Father visiting?"

"Yes. The doctor has gone to Ginza," Hiroko answered.

The owner of a large eel restaurant in Ginza was one of his father's most important patients, the wife in particular being a constant devotee of hormone and vitamin injections.

"Where's Shinji?"

"He said he was going to a friend's house on his way back from school to do some study together. It's still early, so he's probably not left school yet. But he said he'd certainly be back by six."

"Right, I'll be off, then," he said, absent-mindedly adding "Good-bye," but nobody seemed to notice anything strange.

"Off you go then," said his mother. "And take care."

Hiroko and the maid also made similar remarks as he left, implying he would be back shortly.

He left the house and went through the gate. The small pine by the gate was glittering as ever with rosin. Good-bye. Good-bye. After a short distance he arrived at the barber shop he was supposed to be going to, but he walked straight by. He walked to the tram stop, and took the tram to the bank. At the bank he took his savings passbook out of his shirt pocket and withdrew all he had except one yen. He'd decided not to take out everything because there was always the possibility they might think it funny and phone his home. But the girl at the counter wearing a net to protect the permanent waves of her hair didn't seem to find it in the least suspicious. He left the bank and took the underground to Ueno, where he entered a crowded barber shop and had his hair square cropped. His new appearance in the mirror looked peculiarly disgruntled, as if he'd just eaten something that disagreed with him. Then he went to the luggage check office at the station and presented a receipt, and the clerk produced a large, secondhand suitcase from somewhere deep inside. He paid the money and received the suitcase he had deposited a week before. The cropped-headed young man, carrying his suitcase, chose a cheap boarding house in front of the station, saying he was tired out and wanted a room for an hour to lie down. He was shown to a room where the cracked window had been mended with sticking plaster. He told the maid who put down the bedding to be sure to wake him in an hour.

When one hour later the maid called out and then slid open the door of his room, the young man she saw was no longer wearing a sweater but a jacket, and he'd changed his striped trousers for brown corduroys. He paid the bill, put on a new but very cheap cap, and left the lodging house with two suitcases. He went to another, this time privately run, luggage check counter, and deposited the large suitcase again. The owner, who wore a grubby bandana tied around his forehead, asked him cheerfully if he was going to collect it the same day.

"I don't think I'll be able to," he said.

"In that case we'd better dump it over there."

He received a ticket and put it in his pocket, and set off carrying the smaller, more old-fashioned suitcase, glancing at the brown suitcase that had been put in a far corner, as if he were saying good-bye to all that remained of Shokichi Hamada, for all that remained was inside it. He was, in fact, no longer Shokichi Hamada. The trousers and shirt he'd bought at an old clothes shop had "Sugi" in red thread inside them, simulating a laundry mark. The two shirts of his own that he'd brought with him, the two most worn of all he possessed, now had the sewn mark of "Hama" replaced by the "Sugi" he'd put in himself. The lining of his cap had the name "Kenji Sugiura" in white tape sewn into it, and the wretched suitcase he'd bought at a junk shop had a piece of paper with that name on it slipped into the name slot. He'd been careful to use a piece of ordinary thick white paper, not the reverse side of the name card of some friend. He was Kenji Sugiura. Everything related to Shokichi Hamada, his savings passbook, his seal, his sweater, his trousers, everything, had been thrown into that discarded suitcase. Of all the objects inside the black suitcase he now carried, only the radio repair tools had belonged to Shokichi Hamada, but his name had been carefully removed from every one of them. He was now Kenji Sugiura.

Sugiura stopped a cab and told the driver to go to Tokyo Station. The driver hummed the hit song of 1940, the patriotic rubbish celebrating two thousand six hundred years of the Imperial Succession, as he drove. He also saw, in his back mirror, his becapped passenger scatter a handful of tiny pieces of paper out of the window as they passed the main bridge into the Imperial Palace grounds. It was his luggage ticket. It might have been a good idea to deal with the call-up papers in the same way. That was the right place to return them, thought Sugiura. But there was no need, for he was not Hamada, who did not exist. He was no longer one of the good, obedient people who accepted the call, fought, and died. All of them had a common fate to which they would submit. It was the commonness of their fate that made it tolerable for them, even, at times, a cause of celebration. But it was not mine, he recollected. My fate was solitary, was mine alone; and it was no longer a question of choice, for I had chosen, had chosen freedom, the freedom of the rebel, of the traitor, of the man who says no and goes on saying it.

It was faint twilight when the taxi pulled up at Tokyo Station. He produced his ticket to Miyazaki from his wallet and passed the ticket barrier. Good-bye. Good-bye. He joined on the end of the double file of a long line, becoming one of the wretched common people who waited as he did. Good-bye. Good-bye. The line began to move forward. The porters cried out. Then everybody started running, and he ran with them, carrying his suitcase. Good-bye. But the twenty-year-old man, the young man, still did not really know to what he was saying good-bye, nor how decisive this statement of farewell was to be.

postscript: sugiura's travels

Since the most striking feature of this novel is the disorganized chronology of the five wartime years, it must be considered a major part of the meaning of this work. Any attempt to clarify it could be seen as irrelevant or even pernicious by a Japanese reader who has the general historical and geographical knowledge to gradually work things out for himself as the novel proceeds. But to a foreign reader, most of the place names probably mean either nothing or very little; consequently, an attempt to rationalize the chronology of those years has been made here. A map of Japan will make the following information clearer (the kind a standard atlas provides will be adequate, although the more detailed, obviously, the better).

Essential points of orientation are the four main islands of Hokkaido, Honshu, Shikoku, and Kyushu, and the positions (starting from Hokkaido in the north and moving gradually south and west to Kyushu) of Sapporo, Akita, Sendai, Niigata, Tokyo, Nagoya, Osaka, Kobe, Okayama, Hiroshima, Shimonoseki, Miyazaki, and Kagoshima. From these, indications (not precise but sufficient) can be given of the places Sugiura visits and the order in which he visits them.

In October 1940 Sugiura leaves Tokyo by train for MIYAZAKI in the southeast of Kyushu, and after a short stay moves 50 miles north (still on the same east coast of Kyushu) to NOBEOKA, where he remains until April 1941.

He then goes to the far northwest of Honshu, to YOKOTE (about 40 miles southeast of Akita), after brief stays in MASUDA and ASAMAI in the same area. He stays three months in Yokote learning the clock repairer's trade, then goes south along the Japan Sea coast to FUKUI, then KANAZAWA (in the Hokuriku region, 100 miles due north of Nagoya). In the autumn of 1941 he retraces his steps as far as NIIGATA, where he becomes a sand artist.

Toward the end of 1941 he goes to the IZU peninsula (about 60 miles southwest of Tokyo) to ATAMI. Then in 1942 he moves to nearby AJIRO, west to NUMAZU (80 miles from Tokyo), OKAZAKI (25 miles east of Nagoya), NAGOYA, and then finally to SHIMONOSEKI, where he takes the boat to Korea. He spends March and April there. He returns to Shimonoseki, is then in TAKAOKA (200 miles northwest of Tokyo, where Hamada's university has a high school), and after some time in this region (ISHIKAWA and TOYAMA prefectures) makes his way to Hokkaido, where he spends the summer in HAKODATE (100 miles south of Sapporo), SAPPORO, and ASAHIKAWA (70 miles northeast of Sapporo).

In December 1942 he is in WAKAYAMA (30 miles southeast of Osaka) on the west coast of the Kii peninsula, and in the spring of 1943 in KAIKE near YONAGO (on the Japan Sea coast 70 miles due north of Okayama and 40 miles due south of the Oki Islands). Here he meets Akiko; he travels with her to OKI, then back to the mainland and west along the Japan Sea coast to MATSUE and IZUMO, then YAMAGUCHI (20 miles east of Shimonoseki), UBE (10 miles east of Shimonoseki), and east again to IWAKUNI (30 miles southwest of Hiroshima). He reaches HIROSHIMA in June, where Akiko leaves him, ONOMICHI (50 miles east of Hiroshima), KURASHIKI (10 miles west of Okayama, where Akiko rejoins him in July) and OKAYAMA, AKO, HIMEJI, and AKASHI (these last three on the road between Okayama and Kobe). He then crosses over to Shikoku via the island of AWAJI (AWAJISHIMA, in the Inland Sea just south of Kobe) to UWAJIMA on the west coast of Shikoku in October 1943.

He leaves alone in November 1943, traveling via AWAJISHIMA and KUMANO (on the east coast of the Kii peninsula, 100 miles southwest of Nagoya) to ISE (on the same coast, 40 miles southwest of Nagoya), then farther east to KOFU (75 miles due west of Tokyo) and finally MATSUMOTO (150 miles west-northwest of Tokyo), from where he returns in haste to UWAJIMA in Shikoku in April 1944. He remains there until October 1945.

OTHER WORKS IN THE COLUMBIA
ASIAN STUDIES SERIES

MODERN ASIAN LITERATURE

Modern Japanese Drama: An Anthology, ed. and tr. Ted. Takaya. Also in paperback
  ed. 1979
Mask and Sword: Two Plays for the Contemporary Japanese Theater, by Yamazaki
  Masakazu, tr. J. Thomas Rimer 1980
Yokomitsu Riichi, Modernist, Dennis Keene 1980
Nepali Visions, Nepali Dreams: The Poetry of Laxmiprasad Devkota, tr. David
  Rubin 1980
Literature of the Hundred Flowers, vol. 1: *Criticism and Polemics,* ed. Hualing
  Nieh 1981
Literature of the Hundred Flowers, vol. 2: *Poetry and Fiction,* ed. Hualing Nieh
  1981
Modern Chinese Stories and Novellas, 1919 1949, ed. Joseph S. M. Lau, C. T. Hsia,
  and Leo Ou-fan Lee. Also in paperback ed. 1984
A View by the Sea, by Yasuoka Shōtarō, tr. Kären Wigen Lewis 1984
Other Worlds: Arishima Takeo and the Bounds of Modern Japanese Fiction, by
  Paul Anderer 1984
Selected Poems of Sŏ Chŏngju, tr. with introduction by David R. McCann 1989
The Sting of Life: Four Contemporary Japanese Novelists, by Van C. Gessel 1989
Stories of Osaka Life, by Oda Sakunosuke, tr. Burton Watson 1990
The Bodhisattva, or Samantabhadra, by Ishikawa Jun, tr. with introduction by
  William Jefferson Tyler 1990
The Travels of Lao Ts'an, by Liu T'ieh-yün, tr. Harold Shadick. Morningside ed.
  1990
Three Plays by Kōbō Abe, tr. with introduction by Donald Keene 1993
The Columbia Anthology of Modern Chinese Literature, ed. Joseph S. M. Lau and
  Howard Goldblatt 1995
Modern Japanese Tanka, ed. and tr. by Makoto Ueda 1996
Masaoka Shiki: Selected Poems, ed. and tr. by Burton Watson 1997
*Writing Women in Modern China: An Anthology of Women's Literature from the
  Early Twentieth Century,* ed. and tr. by Amy D. Dooling and Kristina M. Torge-
  son 1998
American Stories, by Nagai Kafū, tr. Mitsuko Iriye 2000
The Paper Door and Other Stories, by Shiga Naoya, tr. Lane Dunlop 2001
Grass for My Pillow, by Saiichi Maruya, tr. Dennis Keene 2002

TRANSLATIONS FROM THE ASIAN CLASSICS

Major Plays of Chikamatsu, tr. Donald Keene 1961

Four Major Plays of Chikamatsu, tr. Donald Keene. Paperback ed. only. 1961; rev.
    ed. 1997

*Records of the Grand Historian of China, translated from the Shih chi of Ssu-ma
    Ch'ien,* tr. Burton Watson, 2 vols. 1961

*Instructions for Practical Living and Other Neo-Confucian Writings by Wang
    Yang-ming,* tr. Wing-tsit Chan 1963

Hsün Tzu: Basic Writings, tr. Burton Watson, paperback ed. only. 1963; rev. ed. 1996

Chuang Tzu: Basic Writings, tr. Burton Watson, paperback ed. only. 1964; rev. ed.
    1996

The Mahābhārata, tr. Chakravarthi V. Narasimhan. Also in paperback ed. 1965; rev.
    ed. 1997

The Manyōshū, Nippon Gakujutsu Shinkōkai edition 1965

Su Tung-p'o: Selections from a Sung Dynasty Poet, tr. Burton Watson. Also in
    paperback ed. 1965

Bhartrihari: Poems, tr. Barbara Stoler Miller. Also in paperback ed. 1967

Basic Writings of Mo Tzu, Hsün Tzu, and Han Fei Tzu, tr. Burton Watson. Also in
    separate paperback eds. 1967

The Awakening of Faith, Attributed to Aśvaghosha, tr. Yoshito S. Hakeda. Also in
    paperback ed. 1967

Reflections on Things at Hand: The Neo-Confucian Anthology, comp. Chu Hsi and
    Lü Tsu-ch'ien, tr. Wing-tsit Chan 1967

The Platform Sutra of the Sixth Patriarch, tr. Philip B. Yampolsky. Also in paper-
    back ed. 1967

Essays in Idleness: The Tsurezuregusa of Kenkō, tr. Donald Keene. Also in paper-
    back ed. 1967

The Pillow Book of Sei Shōnagon, tr. Ivan Morris, 2 vols. 1967

Two Plays of Ancient India: The Little Clay Cart and the Minister's Seal, tr. J. A. B.
    van Buitenen 1968

The Complete Works of Chuang Tzu, tr. Burton Watson 1968

The Romance of the Western Chamber (Hsi Hsiang chi), tr. S. I. Hsiung. Also in
    paperback ed. 1968

The Manyōshū, Nippon Gakujutsu Shinkōkai edition. Paperback ed. only. 1969

Records of the Historian: Chapters from the Shih chi of Ssu-ma Ch'ien, tr. Burton
    Watson. Paperback ed. only. 1969

Cold Mountain: 100 Poems by the T'ang Poet Han-shan, tr. Burton Watson. Also
    in paperback ed. 1970

Twenty Plays of the Nō Theatre, ed. Donald Keene. Also in paperback ed. 1970

The Shorter Columbia Anthology of Traditional Chinese Literature, ed. Victor H. Mair 2000

Mistress and Maid (Jiaohongji) by Meng Chengshun, tr. Cyril Birch 2001

Chikamatsu: Five Late Plays, tr. and ed. C. Andrew Gerstle

The Essential Lotus: Selections from the Lotus Sutra, tr. Burton Watson 2002

Early Modern Japanese Literature: An Anthology, 1600–1900, ed. Haruo Shirane 2002

STUDIES IN ASIAN CULTURE

The Ōnin War: History of Its Origins and Background, with a Selective Translation of the Chronicle of Ōnin, by H. Paul Varley 1967

Chinese Government in Ming Times: Seven Studies, ed. Charles O. Hucker 1969

The Actors' Analects (Yakusha Rongo), ed. and tr. by Charles J. Dunn and Bungō Torigoe 1969

Self and Society in Ming Thought, by Wm. Theodore de Bary and the Conference on Ming Thought. Also in paperback ed. 1970

A History of Islamic Philosophy, by Majid Fakhry, 2d ed. 1983

Phantasies of a Love Thief: The Caurapañcāśikā Attributed to Bilhaṇa, by Barbara Stoler Miller 1971

Iqbal: Poet-Philosopher of Pakistan, ed. Hafeez Malik 1971

The Golden Tradition: An Anthology of Urdu Poetry, ed. and tr. Ahmed Ali. Also in paperback ed. 1973

Conquerors and Confucians: Aspects of Political Change in Late Yüan China, by John W. Dardess 1973

The Unfolding of Neo-Confucianism, by Wm. Theodore de Bary and the Conference on Seventeenth-Century Chinese Thought. Also in paperback ed. 1975

To Acquire Wisdom: The Way of Wang Yang-ming, by Julia Ching 1976

Gods, Priests, and Warriors: The Bhṛgus of the Mahābhārata, by Robert P. Goldman 1977

Mei Yao-ch'en and the Development of Early Sung Poetry, by Jonathan Chaves 1976

The Legend of Semimaru, Blind Musician of Japan, by Susan Matisoff 1977

Sir Sayyid Ahmad Khan and Muslim Modernization in India and Pakistan, by Hafeez Malik 1980

The Khilafat Movement: Religious Symbolism and Political Mobilization in India, by Gail Minault 1982

The World of K'ung Shang-jen: A Man of Letters in Early Ch'ing China, by Richard Strassberg 1983

The Lotus Boat: The Origins of Chinese Tz'u Poetry in T'ang Popular Culture, by Marsha L. Wagner 1984

Expressions of Self in Chinese Literature, ed. Robert E. Hegel and Richard C. Hessney 1985

Songs for the Bride: Women's Voices and Wedding Rites of Rural India, by W. G. Archer; eds. Barbara Stoler Miller and Mildred Archer 1986

The Confucian Kingship in Korea: Yŏngjo and the Politics of Sagacity, by JaHyun Kim Haboush 1988

COMPANIONS TO ASIAN STUDIES

Approaches to the Oriental Classics, ed. Wm. Theodore de Bary 1959

Early Chinese Literature, by Burton Watson. Also in paperback ed. 1962

Approaches to Asian Civilizations, eds. Wm. Theodore de Bary and Ainslie T. Embree 1964

The Classic Chinese Novel: A Critical Introduction, by C. T. Hsia. Also in paperback ed. 1968

Chinese Lyricism: Shih Poetry from the Second to the Twelfth Century, tr. Burton Watson. Also in paperback ed. 1971

A Syllabus of Indian Civilization, by Leonard A. Gordon and Barbara Stoler Miller 1971

Twentieth-Century Chinese Stories, ed. C. T. Hsia and Joseph S. M. Lau. Also in paperback ed. 1971

A Syllabus of Chinese Civilization, by J. Mason Gentzler, 2d ed. 1972

A Syllabus of Japanese Civilization, by H. Paul Varley, 2d ed. 1972

An Introduction to Chinese Civilization, ed. John Meskill, with the assistance of J. Mason Gentzler 1973

An Introduction to Japanese Civilization, ed. Arthur E. Tiedemann 1974

Ukifune: Love in the Tale of Genji, ed. Andrew Pekarik 1982

The Pleasures of Japanese Literature, by Donald Keene 1988

A Guide to Oriental Classics, eds. Wm. Theodore de Bary and Ainslie T. Embree; 3d edition ed. Amy Vladeck Heinrich, 2 vols. 1989

INTRODUCTION TO ASIAN CIVILIZATIONS
Wm. Theodore de Bary, General Editor

Sources of Japanese Tradition, 1958; paperback ed., 2 vols., 1964. 2d ed., vol. 1, 2001, compiled by Wm. Theodore de Bary, Donald Keene, George Tanabe, and Paul Varley

Sources of Indian Tradition, 1958; paperback ed., 2 vols., 1964. 2d ed., 2 vols., 1988

Sources of Chinese Tradition, 1960, paperback ed., 2 vols., 1964. 2d ed., vol. 1, 1999, compiled by Wm. Theodore de Bary and Irene Bloom; vol. 2, 2000, compiled by Wm. Theodore de Bary and Richard Lufrano

Sources of Korean Tradition, 1997; 2 vols., vol. 1, 1997, compiled by Peter H. Lee and Wm. Theodore de Bary; vol. 2, 2001, compiled by Yǒngho Ch'oe, Peter H. Lee, and Wm. Theodore de Bary

NEO-CONFUCIAN STUDIES

Instructions for Practical Living and Other Neo-Confucian Writings by Wang Yang-ming, tr. Wing-tsit Chan 1963

Reflections on Things at Hand: The Neo-Confucian Anthology, comp. Chu Hsi and Lü Tsu-ch'ien, tr. Wing-tsit Chan 1967

Self and Society in Ming Thought, by Wm. Theodore de Bary and the Conference on Ming Thought. Also in paperback ed. 1970

The Unfolding of Neo-Confucianism, by Wm. Theodore de Bary and the Conference on Seventeenth-Century Chinese Thought. Also in paperback ed. 1975

Principle and Practicality: Essays in Neo-Confucianism and Practical Learning, eds. Wm. Theodore de Bary and Irene Bloom. Also in paperback ed. 1979

The Syncretic Religion of Lin Chao-en, by Judith A. Berling 1980

The Renewal of Buddhism in China: Chu-hung and the Late Ming Synthesis, by Chün-fang Yü 1981

Neo-Confucian Orthodoxy and the Learning of the Mind-and-Heart, by Wm. Theodore de Bary 1981

Yüan Thought: Chinese Thought and Religion Under the Mongols, eds. Hok-lam Chan and Wm. Theodore de Bary 1982

The Liberal Tradition in China, by Wm. Theodore de Bary 1983

The Development and Decline of Chinese Cosmology, by John B. Henderson 1984

The Rise of Neo-Confucianism in Korea, by Wm. Theodore de Bary and JaHyun Kim Haboush 1985

Chiao Hung and the Restructuring of Neo-Confucianism in Late Ming, by Edward T. Ch'ien 1985

Neo-Confucian Terms Explained: Pei-hsi tzu-i, by Ch'en Ch'un, ed. and trans. Wing-tsit Chan 1986

Knowledge Painfully Acquired: K'un-chih chi, by Lo Ch'in-shun, ed. and trans. Irene Bloom 1987

To Become a Sage: The Ten Diagrams on Sage Learning, by Yi T'oegye, ed. and trans. Michael C. Kalton 1988

The Message of the Mind in Neo-Confucian Thought, by Wm. Theodore de Bary 1989